LIMBO

C.G. BLAINE

ISBN-13: 978-1-950847-20-4

For anyone who needs to hear it:
Do not let them make you miserable.

Five Years Ago

Small moments easily reshape our lives. They carry the potential to send us in a completely different direction without us ever being aware of the other possibilities. But sometimes, we can identify such occurrences as they happen. Maybe even sense them beforehand. If we're lucky, we can make a conscious choice about which path we want to travel.

My fears lie in the moments on the other side of that coin. The ones where we know a certain event will change everything for the worse, and we can't do shit about it. Even when a part of us deep inside screams out a warning, we're forced to just sit by, watching it all unfold around us.

Helpless against it.

As soon as the T-shirt lands in the suitcase, I snatch it up and toss it back on the bed. Pete shakes his head, placing the next one in without missing a beat. I pick that one out, too, and fling it across the room. I can keep it up all night, week, summer. Whatever it takes, as long as he stays.

His eyes never leave the pile of clothes, but when I reach for the shirt in his hand, he grabs me around the waist and throws me onto the suitcase.

"There," Pete says, smashing the lid down on top of me. "Done packing."

I flip it open and pull him down with me. "If we break the suitcase, you can't go."

"No." He presses his forehead against mine. "I'll still have to go. I'll just show up with garbage bags."

His amber eyes gaze at me with the same soft look he's given me since we were four. The look I will suffer without for almost an entire summer when the eyes and their owner go away, taking with them one of the few decent parts of my shitty life.

And I can't stop it from happening.

"You know I'd stay if I could, Cal."

He rolls us out of the suitcase, and now I stare down at him. I study him, worried two months away will cause me to forget the details I've spent almost ten years memorizing. A faded scar across his jaw from his accident when we were ten. Sandy hair that lightens drastically in the sun. The way one side of his mouth always turns up a little more than the other—especially when he's up to something.

A throat clears as the door creaks open. "Door open, Peter."

"Yes, ma'am," he says, neither of us moving.

"You leaving soon, dear?" his grandmother asks. "It's after ten."

I wink before I climb off him and the bed. "Yes, Mrs. Davies. I was just on my way out."

"Bye." Pete grins, the right side a little higher. "I'll see you in a few months."

"Bye, Pete," I say. "Enjoy your summer."

His grandmother accompanies me downstairs and through the living room where his grandfather waves a goodbye. Luckily, I make it out of the house without either of them asking how I plan on getting home. A few days ago, I told them I would walk the five miles to town, and they insisted on giving me a ride. But tonight, I'm free to sneak around the old farmhouse to the large oak tree outside of Pete's bedroom.

He nailed in a small board on the backside a few months ago to provide an extra handhold and make my climb easier. After wiggling out on the limb, I hop off onto the slanted roof and balance the last few steps to the window. When I crawl in, he's waiting on the bed, the closed door the only evidence he's even moved since I left.

"Took you long enough." He stretches out, arms behind his head.

I wrinkle my nose at him and grab his phone from the nightstand. My first call goes to my cousin, Trey, reminding him to pick me up in the morning. The last time he forgot, and I actually ended up hiking the entire five miles. He also serves as cover for me if my parents call. Not that they've ever cared enough about my well-being to check on me.

The second call goes to them—as well as a third and fourth when neither answer.

On the fifth try, Graham finally barks a, "What?" into the phone while Lara's dramatic sobs play in the background.

So, they're *still* fighting. On hour five at least. I consider climbing back out the window, down the tree, and knocking on the front door for a ride home to check on my little brother and baby sister, but Pete smiles and makes up my mind for me. No chance I'll miss spending one last night with him.

"I'm staying at Trey's," I say.

The call ends without a response.

I shove the not-even-remotely packed suitcase to the floor along with the pile of no-longer-folded clothes and crawl into the bed. Pete's arms close around me. He holds me tight against him, and I bury my nose in his shirt, breathing him in while I can. A life lacking in security makes me cling to anything dependable, and the feeling that everything will change when he goes away nags at me more than before. Call it foresight, intuition, or whatever, but some part of me knows nothing will be the same when he comes back.

Especially not me.

170 Days Until 19

Now...

Every now and then, my step swerves to the right when a tug on my arm jerks me over. Even if I brace myself, it manages to veer me off course. There's probably a metaphor for life in there somewhere, but I'm tired and not in the mood to sort it out.

The dangers associated with linked-arm walking go underreported, and the risks appear to increase when one participant bounces around shivering.

"You're going to give me whiplash," I say, prying my arm loose from Felicia's.

"But we need each other's body heat to survive, Callie."

"I also need an intact spinal column."

"I suppose that's true." She laughs, inching her scarf higher to cover her mouth.

Given the speed at which her teeth chatter, she probably regrets joining me on my morning journey for a decent cup of coffee. Most days, I choke down our suitemate Jess's hopeless attempts at mastering the coffeemaker, but Mondays require something stronger and more tolerable. But even without the need for caffeine, I love walking the old part of Easton's campus on cold mornings. The colder, the better. Instead of weaving in and out of zombie students on their way to an early class, we enjoy abandoned sidewalks, a quiet calm taking over our surroundings.

"Two minutes. Pick it up, dude," a guy shouts.

Or not.

Felicia and I both scan for him. The low foot traffic should make him easy to find, but his voice bounces between the brick buildings. The few other people in the area also glance around, but none of them appear to track him down either.

I'm still looking when an elbow jab from Felicia brings my attention back ahead of us. A guy dashes out from behind a building, wearing nothing but a gray towel around his waist. Not what I expected to encounter when I left the dorms. He secures the towel, stopping to talk to a girl. An interesting time to flirt, considering the below-freezing temperatures, but hey, to each their own.

Felicia's steps slow as we watch them. "Is it a frat stunt?"

"This early?"

"There has to be a good reason."

A reason sure, but I doubt a good one.

When he sprints off from her, he heads straight toward us. As fast as he approaches, I think he's about to plow right into us, but at the last second, he jerks to a stop in front of me.

"Can I kiss you?" he asks, frantic green eyes searching mine.

He can't be serious. But he must be because, when I don't answer, he redirects the same question to Felicia. She looks to me for guidance, and I shrug. She drones on about wanting a guy, and Towel Boy surfaces, dark hair a disheveled mess and abs for days. If she wants to kiss him, I won't stand in her way.

She misses her chance, though, when the phantom man yells, "A minute-thirty."

Towel Boy looks torn before he runs off and shouts back, "Not helpful, Rusty."

I track his gaze up the side of a building. On the roof above us I find mystery voice Rusty, staring down at us, wearing a black leather jacket, a red bandana, and dark jeans with a giant rip at the knee.

His laughter floats down as he waves a fingerless glove at us. "Good morning, ladies."

The redhead to my right arches a brow, and her mouth lifts into her *my one true love* smile. Between her, Axl Rose, and Towel Boy, it's all growing far too outrageous to experience uncaffeinated. I grab Felicia's arm and drag her down the sidewalk before she further engages.

"One minute ten seconds," Rusty shouts.

"One of us should have kissed him." Felicia glances back. "A sexy guy in a towel this close to Valentine's Day? A gift from Aphrodite herself."

I peek over my shoulder as well. Another girl looks ready to slap Towel Boy, but she storms off without resorting to violence. His shoulders seem to heave in a sigh, and he rubs his forehead, letting his head fall back. Only it jerks up after a second, and our eyes meet.

Oh no.

Recovering from his initial rejection in record-breaking time, he sprints back over until he's blocking our path.

"Ladies, I apologize for earlier." He sounds much calmer, a confidence about him this time. "I understand the oddity of my behavior and will gladly explain—"

"Forty seconds."

He flips off his friend before continuing, "My name is Jordan. I love dogs, tolerate cats. I have a weird affinity for late eighties slash early nineties music. Is this getting me anywhere?"

"Thirty." Rusty's voice echoes. "You're screwed, man."

"Shit, uh…" Visibly shivering by this point, he scrubs his hands together.

Damn it if he hasn't won my sympathy.

"What happens if time runs out?" I finally ask.

"What?" His eyes lock on mine again, surprised by my sudden interest.

"When his countdown ends, what happens?"

"I lose the towel and am down to a G-string." He flashes a smile through chattering teeth, and I shake my head, reluctantly amused.

At least he's wearing something under the towel. A few years ago, I streaked down Main Street on New Year's Eve. Talk about a poor life choice. Within a few minutes, my fingers and toes stiffened and burned anytime I tried to move them. They turned a shade of red similar to his hands and feet.

"Fifteen … fourteen…" The countdown clock in human form continues above us.

I expect Felicia to make her move. Another chance for a love connection dangles in front of her, yet she seems less than keen on taking it. She looks at me and then gazes down at her suddenly interesting boots, her already-pink-from-the-cold cheeks blazing brighter behind her freckles.

By now, Jordan's shivering almost violently, his eyes imploring me to save him. My eyes roll in response. What the hell, right? He's already divulged more information about himself than some guys I've slept with.

I let out a quick sigh. "I have a strict policy against weirdness before coffee, but kissing you wins out over seeing you in a thong."

He stares at me for a second, and then his mouth perks up on one side.

"Five … four…"

Yeah, we get it, Rusty.

Jordan still looks doubtful I'll go through with it until I step forward, closing the distance between us. It must be enough to convince him, and he dips his head, making up for a considerable height difference and bringing his mouth to mine. Some people experience fireworks when they first kiss … we get cursing from a rooftop. His lips create an icy sensation, almost burning where they brush mine. I expect the kiss to be quick, but then his hand sneaks around to my back. He presses me closer until my chest bumps into his. A little handsy for a stranger-danger kiss, but my sensible side clearly slacks on the job because I let him hold me against him. I even lean in for more until a freezing hand slips beneath my scarf. The shock against my warm skin breaks me away from him, a concern for his well-being taking over.

"Here," I say, unwinding my scarf. I slide off my hat and hold them out for him. "Keep them. I don't want you to die of hypothermia."

Without hesitation, he puts on the fluffy purple scarf and bright pink stocking cap. I suppress a smile, almost feeling guilty for how ridiculous he looks. He doesn't seem to mind, though, a cocky grin appearing. It's an expression I recognize all too well, easily worn by one of *those* guys—too confident for their own good. Any worry over wounding his precious ego vanishes then, and with no interest in any awkward post-kiss conversation, I step around him.

Felicia catches up within a few steps. "Callie. Oh. My. God."

I shrug, attempting to downplay the situation. Kissing a random guy on the sidewalk is a one-time deal. The sooner she forgets about it, the better.

We walk a little ways before I check over my shoulder. Jordan's rushing in the opposite direction, and I wait for him to disappear into a building to rummage through my bag. Courtesy of his unwavering confidence, I feel guilt-free while grabbing a plain black scarf and matching hat.

Sorry, Towel Boy.

Felicia's jaw drops. "You knew you had those the whole time?"

I shrug, putting them on. "I always keep a spare in my bag in case of an emergency."

Our smiles spread slowly before we burst out laughing. Then we relink arms, dangers be damned, and leave our excitement for the day behind us.

The busiest time at Java Quest usually starts later, but with the cold front, everyone wants coffee. Felicia offers to wade through the bodies at the counter, so I secure us the last high-top table in the back. I tuck my hat and scarf in my bag and toss my coat over the chair next to me.

After a few minutes, she comes up behind me. "Black with an extra shot of espresso."

I grab the cup from her hand, not willing to chance anything else happening before a sip. "Oh my God. It's so much better than the black sludge."

Felicia lays her coat over the back of her chair across from me. "We should do this every morning."

Right, because not once in the past five months of sharing a dorm suite have I given off the impression of being a morning person. She, however, can roll out of bed at the crack of dawn and perform a musical number, surrounded by birds and singing mice.

"Maybe once a week," I tell her. "If you're lucky. And I'll need a cup of coffee before we leave."

She laughs, but it cuts off, her hazel eyes bulging at something behind me. "No way," she whispers.

I don't have time to ask before someone slides into the chair between us, his green eyes meeting mine.

"The wildest thing happened to me this morning, let me tell you."

No fucking way more accurately sums up Towel Boy—now fully clothed—sipping his coffee, all nonchalant, next to me. He knows how to make an entrance; I'll give him that. I look away from him as I fight off a smile. This guy does not need any encouragement.

"So, as I was saying…" Jordan shifts his attention to Felicia. "My temper got the best of me over the weekend, and I broke something that wasn't mine. Even though I replaced the drum, my buddy chose to punish me. Which is how I ended up running around campus, wearing a towel, trying to find someone to kiss me in under five minutes."

His eyes dart to the side for mine, checking for a reaction. One I have no intention of giving him.

Luckily, Felicia's bubbly personality requires her to respond, and she giggles. "See, Callie? I told you there was a good reason."

I disagree a temper tantrum counts as a *good* reason, but it's a reason nonetheless.

His gaze slides back to Felicia. "Officially, I'm Jordan Waters. And you are?"

"Felicia. Felicia Gibson." She glances over to me. "This is Callie Henders."

The second my name leaves her mouth, he's back to me, drawing my hat and scarf from his pocket. "I believe these belong to you."

"Thank you," I say. My hand brushes his when I take them. The warm skin is quite the contrast from the last time. I shove them in my coat, his eyes waiting when I look back.

"Thank you for not letting me die of hypothermia," he replies.

I give him a small smile, not swooning like Felicia on the other side of the table. Women probably don't resist him often, but I have a rule about cocky assholes. Stay away. While he hasn't proven an asshole yet, it usually follows close behind the first part.

Once he realizes he won't get anywhere with me, he pushes his chair back to leave. The feet scrape over the floor, and everyone around us stops talking, their faces twisting at the awful screech of wood dragging on linoleum. Even with the terrible sound, I can't help but smile. After the entrance, I should have known his exit would be equally dramatic.

"Ladies." He stops next to me, waiting for me to glance up at him before he continues, "I want you to know that I plan on being fully clothed for all future encounters."

As he walks off behind me, someone catcalls him. I'm about to look back when a dangerous gleam enters Felicia's eye.

"What?" I ask, her phone emerging from under the table.

"He said Waters, right?"

Let her fact-finding mission begin.

169 Days Until 19

In the hopes of drowning out the persistent redhead on the other side of the curtain, I place my head directly under the showerhead. Nope, it doesn't work.

On my way to the shower, Felicia asked if I wanted to go to a party later. But not just any party—the *best* party of the year. She then followed me into the bathrooms and launched into a full account of the festivities. Never mind the details she's listing sound exactly the same as the ones from the best party of the year we went to two weeks ago. Actually, it sounds just like every party at Easton. Which makes sense, considering the limited number of ways for drunk college students to socialize.

Red cups, kegs, a beer pong table, loud music, a few variants of strange but recognizable smells, plastic vodka bottles, an overabundance of polo shirts, and during the winter, whatever brand of black coat is on trend—that describes every one. Even a theme creates minimal distinction. Luau, toga, black light, or anything but clothes, it doesn't matter. Drunk girls cry in the bathroom or a corner. People do keg stands and play flip cup and get high. A girl hooks up with a guy, and everyone knows about it, except for the girl's guy and the guy's girl.

Really, I should be grateful she's talking about anything other than Jordan Waters. Ever since he walked out of the coffee shop yesterday, every one of her conversation topics has centered on him. All the information she learned via social media, she desperately wants to share, but each time she asks what I want to know, I answer with one word: nothing. It's driving her nuts.

"Callie, are you even listening to me?" she asks.

I shut off the water and snag my towel off the hook. "Were you estimating the expected ratio of frat boy to female undergrad?"

An over-the-top sigh answers me.

I squeeze the excess water from my hair and secure my towel before ripping back the curtain. "I'm sorry. You were saying?"

"Just tell me if you're coming." She tosses the end of her braid over her shoulder. "They're going to have live music, and I hear the band is the best."

I provide the eye roll she deserves. The best party, the best band. Everything in her life lands in the best category. "Well, I can't turn down a chance to see the *best* band."

She squeals and bounces around on the bench. My ass, already jaded at eighteen, envies the level of enthusiasm she shows over a party. But then again, her emotional responses always outweigh mine. Hell, I can count the number of times I've cried over the past six years—almost the last ten—on one hand, but it requires both hands to show how many times she smiles in any twenty-minute period.

"So," I say, running a brush through my hair, "what's the name of the *best* band?"

I need a third hand because she smiles again. "Beta Void."

"Huh. Cool band name."

She stares at me, her expression holding.

"What?"

"Nothing," she coos. "I'm just glad you're coming."

"Okay, weirdo." I throw my stuff in my shower bag and leave her sitting there to hang out in the bathroom alone.

When I walk into our dorm suite, Jess glances up from her studying. A hand runs through her honey-brown hair, pushing it back. "Cam and I are watching a movie later if you want a vote."

"Cam?" I stop in my tracks. "As in my roommate, Cam?"

The blonde goddess—who is in fact my roommate, Cam—steps out of our room on the other side of the suite. Holy shit, welcome to the apocalypse.

"Did I hear my name?" she asks.

My eyebrows shoot up, and I extend my hand. "Oh my God. Hi. I'm your roommate, Callie."

"Ha," she says, pushing past me. "Maybe your shitty jokes are why I never stay here." She climbs over Jess, sitting on the floor in front of the couch, and sprawls out on the cushions. "Sawyer's at some work thing the next few days. I'm not staying at the apartment alone with her creepy roommate."

Well, at least I rate less creepy than someone. Since we moved in, she's maybe spent one night a week in our room, the rest at her girlfriend's apartment off-campus. I never complain, thoroughly enjoying the cramped room to myself.

In the middle of the floor of my—our room, I dodge her overnight bag and discard my towel in the laundry basket. From the way it tumbles off the top of the heap, seven days will hold as my new record for not washing clothes. Not my proudest accomplishment.

Dressed in the first pair of jeans and sweater I stumbled upon, I settle in on the bed with my books to study. If I time everything right, I can knock out a few assignments and a load of laundry before we leave for the party.

The calendar from my brother, Connor, hangs on the wall next to me. Out of habit more than anything else, I scratch the tip of the pen over the day's date, crossing out the number. One line, two, then a third, pressing harder, and another.

"You never answered." Jess startles me from the doorway, and I drop the pen onto my open book.

"About what?" I ask.

"Movie tonight?"

"Sorry. Frat party with Gibson."

Words I will soon regret.

Mid-dry cycle, Felicia drags me out of the laundry room. I try to fend her off, but the chick has the grip of a gorilla and the patience of whatever can't wait another thirty damn minutes. After she strong-arms me up the stairs, I admit defeat and text Jess to save my clothes before some coed casts them aside or claims them as their own.

As Felicia drives, she returns to her new favorite topic—Jordan Waters. She's working her way toward a pillow over the face if she keeps it up. By the time we're walking up the street to the party, I think she might explode.

"Are you sure you don't want to know anything about him?" She gallops sideways to guarantee she sees my response.

For the millionth time, I shake my head.

"You are torturing me," she whines.

Same, babe.

I take a deep breath and count to five before exhaling. "No information will change my mind. Running around campus in a freaking towel? Strike one. The cockiness? Strike two. The fact that he—"

"The fact that he looks drool-worthy?"

I laugh, unable to disagree. "Not what I was going to say, but yeah, sure. Strike three."

"But you would make a perfect couple."

Now she's teetering on the edge of delusional.

"No, we wouldn't," I tell her. "Relationships are complicated, and I'm terrible at them. Plus, you're certifiable if you think he's the relationship type."

"What type is he then?"

I don't even need to think about it, having already pinned him. "The one incapable of committing to the same girl for more than one night. Two if he's bored or desperate. He relies on his confidence and smooth lines to do all the work for him. Whatever requires the least amount of effort on his part."

She bumps her shoulder into mine. "I think you're wrong."

I sigh at her unshakeable belief in people but hope no one ever makes her lose it. The world needs people like her to balance out people like me who expect everyone to let them down. Of course, that's the only thing no one ever disappoints me on.

We drop the conversation on our way up the stone path to the house. Music pounds through the walls and floods out into the street when the door opens. A stale smell of alcohol and weed mixed with bodies signals a frat party.

Felicia flashes a smile when her friend Becca meets us and squeals. She runs a finger over the new bright purple streak in Becca's black hair before she secures my hand. The three of us chain through the crowd toward the stairs. Halfway up, I let go, a flash of color catching my eye. At least twenty people below are wearing pink beanies similar to mine. No, identical.

What the hell?

At the top of the stairs, another girl wearing the exact same hat bumps into me. I catch up to Felicia and Becca in a room lit by the hallway light with a bed full of coats, and I add mine to the pile.

"What's with all the hats?" I ask.

"Don't tell her, Becs." Felicia smirks.

Becca ignores her and hands me her phone. "Beta Void posted the picture yesterday, and it blew up."

I laugh at a picture of Jordan in a very recognizable getup. Damn it. I officially feel guilty about not giving him the other hat and scarf. But just a tinge because he still looks plenty sure of himself and seems to have acquired quite the fan base.

Wait. Beta Void?

"The band playing downstairs?" I ask.

Becca nods, and I glare at Felicia. The wicked gleam returns to her eye. She set me up.

"Maybe you should be normal and use social media," she says.

I resist the urge to shove her smug ass off the bed and look back at the photo of the guy who I couldn't have picked out of a lineup two days ago. Dark hair sticks out from the bottom of the stocking cap. Enough stubble lines his strong jaw to look like he shaved the day before, even though it probably looks like that every day.

Felicia rips the phone away. "Want to stop ogling the picture and go see the real thing?"

She doesn't give me an option, pushing me out the door.

We locate the keg in the kitchen—always the first stop—before heading to the living room. In the corner on a makeshift stage, the band's playing. The distortion in their song is reminiscent of grunge. Early nineties. I half-expect them all to wear flannel shirts in true Cobain fashion, but the only coordination among them is pink hats. Except for Jordan. He stares down at his guitar with his hair styled into a precise mess.

"Lead guitar for Beta Void, obviously." Felicia talks in my ear, taking advantage of a momentary lapse in my resolve. "Twenty. Junior. Perfect GPA. Philosophy major. I'm not sure of his future plans though. No one seems to know."

My phone vibrates as Connor's picture lights up the screen. *Fuck.* A knot forms in my stomach.

"I'll be back," I tell Felicia.

She nods, and I head toward the door. I answer the call to keep it from going to voicemail but don't talk until I make it outside, away from the noise.

"Connor, everything okay?"

"Yeah, sorry," he says, sensing my unease. "Can I vent?"

I sit down on the side steps off the porch, out of the way and quiet, and switch from school to home mode. "Let's hear it, kid."

"They turned who pays for new basketball shoes into a huge fucking fight."

"Please tell me it was over the phone."

"Yeah, she called him on speakerphone so I could 'hear how he talks' to her. It started with her screaming that he never buys us anything. Then he said she just wants more money to spend on herself. He ruined her life. She wasn't worth it. He's a prick. She's a slut. A broken chair and shattered phone screen later, and I'm supposed to make the shoes I have work. No big deal, right? I can easily make my feet smaller."

Just for once, I want my fifteen-year-old brother's problems to consist of a girl not liking him or a teacher giving him a bad grade. Instead, they always involve Graham and Lara's never-ending struggle for control. The two of us and our six-year-old sister, Cate, are the most used pieces in a game to see who can out-selfish the other.

As much of a fucking nightmare as it was growing up with my parents in the same house, their divorce a few years ago managed to make everything even more destructive, but in different, unexpected ways. Not for them of course. Just us.

"Maybe it's time I drop the sports," he says. "I probably won't get a scholarship anyway. I can get a job and start saving to move out of this hellhole when I turn nineteen."

More than anything I want to tell him, *Eighteen, Connor. You can leave when the custody agreement ends at eighteen.*

Except, since I turned eighteen in July and still drive back every weekend because of our manipulative, sorry excuse of a father and piece-of-work-in-her-own-right mother, he would reply, *You know that's not true, Cal.*

And he'd be right, so why bother?

I go with the old fallback—anger and resentment. "Fuck them, Con. Where are you right now?"

"My room."

"Go to mine and look on the far-right side of the closet." I wait, listening to the creak of my closet door and clothes hangers dragging across the wooden bar. "You see the garment bags?"

"Four of them," he says.

"They're my formal dresses. Eight all together. Sell them for fifty dollars each and buy the shoes. The extra we'll use for baseball cleats this summer or Cate's swim lessons."

"But Cal, I…" His voice cracks as he trails off. "I can't."

"I won't be wearing them, and I'm certainly not letting you give up basketball."

"You already—"

"Sell the dresses, Connor. Don't you dare let them make you miserable."

He stops arguing, and a silence settles between us as he sorts through whatever he needs to in his head. I just sit here and let him because nothing in my world can hold any significance again until my little brother feels a little less alone in his.

Eventually, he sighs. "Thanks, Cal."

"Goodnight, little brother."

When I end the call, my eyes burn, but as always, the tears never come. Instead, I shiver, feeling all the hurt dive back below the surface where it lurks. I stay on the steps a little longer, letting the freezing night air numb the rest. Physical pain is easier to handle than emotional torment. I'll choose it every day of the fucking week.

Felicia's flirting with another contender for the love of her life when I go inside. Not wanting to interrupt them, I wander through the house to Becca, who is schooling a frat brother at beer pong. The game holds my attention for a few minutes before I go for a refill. On my way to the kitchen, Jordan catches my eye from the stage and nods. As smooth as the move is, he probably practices it on plenty of girls.

Everyone around me laughs and enjoys themselves, but I can't shake my call with Connor. I feel three hours away and stuck a few years in the past. A prime example of why I keep everything else separate from school.

Until my head clears, I find my coat in the pile upstairs and decide to seek refuge on the porch. The fresh air helps as I lean against the banister. I empty my beer cup and consider relaxing my two-drink rule for the night. A tempting idea after the reminder of exactly how much I hate Graham and Lara. Also not the best one due to the reminder of exactly how much I hate Graham and Lara.

A vicious circle, my life.

The music cuts off inside. I close my eyes and enjoy the calm until the bass beat resumes. I jump when the door swings open and bangs against the side of the house. A blur of a person dashes down the steps. He stops at the end of the sidewalk, hands on the back of his head, and searches up and down the street. He curses and drops his arms to his sides as he turns around.

Jordan Waters. Impossible to avoid.

Head hung, he trudges his way up the sidewalk. But then he pauses on the step, and his mouth kicks up when he sees me. "Callie Henders."

"Too many clothes on to enjoy a run?" I ask.

He strolls over. "Actually, I spotted a red coat leaving and hoped to catch it."

"No redcoats, but Paul Revere rode through a few minutes ago."

"Clever girl."

His T-shirt stretches tight over his biceps and chest as he hops up on the banister next to me. I should move away, but the spicy-woodsy scent from yesterday hits me, and he smells really fucking good. So, I stay with the warmth of his leg on my arm.

"Shouldn't you match the rest of your band with a pink hat?"

"I've experienced the real thing," he says. "A cheap replica will never do it for me now."

"I told you to keep it." I offer him the hat from my pocket. "It's the least I can do, considering the picture."

As he jumps down, he pulls it on. "I think you owe me something else, too."

Curious where he's headed, I wait.

"Which do you prefer, dogs or cats?"

The innocent question surprises me. "I'm also more of a dog person, but I like some cats."

"Music preference?"

A musician asking sounds like a trick question. "General or specific?"

"The more specific, the better," he says.

"Eighties hair bands, nineties grunge, late-nineties alt-rock." I almost leave it out but decide to own it and add, "With a guilty pleasure of anything two-thousands pop."

The way Jordan looks at me changes, his eyes smoldering. "Where have you been all my life?"

And there it is—the arrogant execution of a well-rehearsed line. I take it as my cue and plaster on a small smile, walking away from him.

"Hold on, we're not going back to this." He places himself in front of me, determined. "The polite-smile-and-not-talking thing. I've invested too much time to go back to that."

I laugh at his assertion. "Too much time? We've had maybe seven minutes of interaction."

His eyes narrow as if my statement is equally ridiculous. "Interaction, yes. But I spent time yesterday morning tracking you down at the coffee shop. I spaced out through classes both yesterday and today, trying to figure out why you wouldn't talk to me." He counts the examples on his fingers. "I scoured social media last night, trying to track you down. A complete failure, by the way. And since you walked in tonight, I've been practicing talking to you in my head."

I study him, unsure of whether to believe him. If true, he's put forth a legitimate effort, and I misjudged him. Not something that often happens when it comes to guys. Before I decide one way or the other, the door behind him opens, and who I believe to be a shirtless Rusty exits.

"Ready, Jordan?"

"Really not a good time, Rustin," he says, not taking his eyes off me.

"Yeah, we don't care. Oh…" Rusty's expression brightens when he sees me. "Hey, Callie." He says my name as if we are old friends and waves before going inside.

Surprised, I look back to Jordan. "You told your friend my name?"

"No." But he says it too fast. He rubs his forehead. "Can I borrow your scarf?"

A strange request, but I hand it over.

"We have another thirty-minute set before I'm finished for the night. Then I'm going to win you over." He backs to the door and pushes it open. "Drink. Stay. Good Callie."

"You're going to win me over?"

"Yeah, you don't want to miss it." He steps back once more into the house and winks, shutting the door.

I return to the banister and smile. He's right; I don't want to miss whatever winning me over entails. Especially after the work he's put into getting me to stay. In all fairness, though, I would have gone back inside regardless of Jordan Waters chasing me down. I kind of have no choice.

Felicia's my ride.

The band starts playing as I walk over the threshold. I immediately feel Jordan watching me. Surely, he credits himself with my reappearance, so to avoid further inflating the kid's ego, I climb the stairs without looking at him.

When I come down from dropping off my coat, all the bodies crammed into the living room increase the level of difficulty in locating Felicia. I navigate through a maze of backs and shoulder blades and fight my way out near the couch where she's perched. Well, she is until she launches herself at me. She seizes hold of my chin and points it toward the stage.

It's worth the possible bruise on my jaw to see Jordan playing his guitar, sporting the hat, scarf, and nothing else but a towel. He directs a smirk at me, and despite the overconfidence playing across his face, I smile back. How can I not at this point? His expression softens in response and develops into a real smile. Fuck if I don't feel that one everywhere at once.

A tug on my hand drags me over to the couch. I squeeze in between Felicia and Becca to watch the show. Other than a few times when he glances down at the guitar and once when he says something to the singer, Jordan's attention stays on me through the entire set. A few times, I look away just to break his gaze. Only one other person has ever stared at me so intensely. I don't want my mind to create an association between the two.

Jordan holds the last note to the song well after everyone else has stopped. By my approximation, his half hour is up. The singer nods in his direction and then checks over his shoulder. Behind the drums, Rusty laughs, his head falling back.

"Unfortunately, guys and gals and non-binary pals, our evening with you has come to an end." The singer grins, one hand on the microphone, and the room fills with groans. "I know. I know. But lucky for you, Jordan, in all his scantily clad glory, has made one final song request."

Jordan regains the crowd's favor as he plays the easily recognized notes of the eighties hair classic, "Sweet Child o' Mine." At least I know he pays attention. For the chorus, he joins the singer at the microphone—eyes always on me.

During his guitar solo, Felicia leans over. "You're the girl with the blue eyes."

I roll those blue eyes at her but smile. As it turns out, changing my mind is completely possible. It only takes a rambling confession, embarrassing outfit, and a Guns N' Roses song.

At the end of the song, the singer rips the towel off, leaving Jordan onstage in his boxers. Unfazed by the move, he gives a deep bow, throws off the strap, and sets down his guitar. He makes yet another dramatic exit, leaping off the stage and dashing through the crowd to the stairs.

"All right, folks," the singer says, "for real this time. Have a good night."

Space opens up as people disperse throughout the house. Becca's one of them, returning to the other room. The same guy from earlier regains Felicia's attention. It allows me to make my way across to the stairs without her eagle eyes noticing.

He's in the room of coats, back to the doorway and dressed. I watch his reflection in the mirror on top of the dresser as he sticks my hat and scarf into my coat pocket.

"So much for being fully clothed for all future encounters," I say.

He looks up, his gaze meeting mine in the mirror. "A senseless thing to say." He rotates around, facing me. "I meant, all future encounters in public. I guess I failed on that front as well."

On my way over to him, I run my hand along the objects on a shelf lining the edge of the room. It's been a long time since I followed a guy into a bedroom at a party. The only reason I chose to now, I can only blame on that damn smile and song.

"An interesting song choice."

"What can I say?" He steps to the right, bumping the corner of the dresser. "Inspiration struck."

I stop in front of him. Even in the limited light streaming in from the hallway, I watch his gaze lower to my mouth. My pulse picks up, breaths faster. The moments leading up to a kiss are intoxicating, all the want and anticipation.

When he pushes my hair back, he keeps his warm hand on my face. His eyes flick up for a second before he lowers his lips onto mine. They feel warm now, and so fucking good.

The hand on my cheek moves to the back of my neck. Mine slide up his chest as he deepens the kiss.

Jordan's tongue glides over mine until a creaky floorboard in the hallway sends me backing across the room. An overreaction? Maybe. But one Callie rule I won't break: no public hook-ups. No matter how tempting the idea or guy. They can destroy a reputation, and those things are damn near impossible to repair.

"Sorry." I touch my lips, the sensation of his lingering on them. "I'm unsure about this…"

A laugh from the hall has me checking the door. Given my current level of paranoia, this is definitely not happening here.

I'm about to finish my sentence and suggest we go somewhere else when Jordan smirks. "If you put your tongue in my mouth unsure, I'm dying to see where you put it when you're certain."

Shock, hurt, and anger—in that order. They cycle through me so fast that I can't even identify them until the last one latches the fuck on. I would rather he hit me in the face than suggest I am easy.

His eyes widen, his expression vanishing. "I am so sorry, Callie. Sometimes, the asshole falls out of my mouth."

I grab my coat, unable to decide which pisses me off more—him saying it or the fact that I ever gave him a chance to by following him upstairs. "I was going to say, I'm unsure about this being the best place, considering everyone's coats are in here." He touches my arm on my way past, and I spin around. "Do not touch me. I was right the first time."

My feet can't carry me downstairs and out the door fast enough. I need to get away from arrogant guys and their smiles, predictable parties, phone calls reminding me of home, everything. I reach the end of the sidewalk and jerk to a stop.

Fuck. Felicia's my ride.

I pull on my coat and slide my phone from my back pocket to call either her or a cab. The door bangs open behind me. I whirl around as Jordan flies down the porch steps. Not waiting around for him to catch up, I storm off toward the dorms. Some poor guy even jumps off the sidewalk just to get out of my way.

"Callie." Jordan trails after me. "I'm sorry. Please, just let me give you a ride."

"Get away from me."

"Or call you a cab at least."

"No." I pick up my pace to put more distance between us.

"Please, I'll wait with you."

"Oh, well, in that case, hell no." I check over my shoulder, and he's chasing me across the street. When he gets beside me, I hold up my phone. "Do I have to call the cops for you to leave me alone?"

At first, I think he stops, but as the music from the party fades out, his footsteps crunch snow behind me. Fucking great. The sound grows louder until they're almost next to me again.

I shake my head, not looking at him. "If you want me to use the pepper spray on my keychain, keep walking."

Silence.

Five Years Ago

Sun shining through the windshield heats the truck's cab. With my feet out the window, I lie across the cracked vinyl bench seat and enjoy a rare moment of silence. The material covering the ceiling of this beater sags in the middle. A pushpin would fix the problem, but as long as it runs, Trey couldn't care less about the appearance.

I almost fall asleep until footsteps on the gravel outside interrupt the peace. Trey climbs in and slams the creaky door to make sure it shuts. He nearly fell out on a sharp turn once and has developed the habit for his own safety. After a few pumps of the gas pedal, he cranks the ignition. The beast roars to life, and he throws the truck in gear, kicking up rocks as we peel out of the gas station's parking lot.

Thank God for him keeping me sane since Pete left for camp a few weeks ago. Although we would have become inseparable over the summer with or without Pete. I love being around him and not just because he is sixteen and can drive me around. My cousin understands me unlike anyone—even more than Pete or Connor. The fake smiles that fool them, I never even attempt with Trey. They would never work. In fact, he'd probably feel insulted that I tried.

A hard brake threatens to throw my ass to the floor, so I pull my legs in and sit up. The truck fishtails as we fly down the gravel street at least twenty over the speed limit. No one so much as bats an eye at us. Even if Trey weren't the sheriff's son, the chances of anyone giving a shit about us tearing through Sutterville are low. Bored kids need something to do during the summer in a town of fewer than four hundred people. Unless the activities involve arson, most people look the other way.

In a shocking turn of events, Trey respects the stop sign on Main Street. A truck with a lift kit drives in front of us. The blond with one hand on the wheel relaxes in the seat, his other hand hanging out the window. He nods, a dimple appearing in his cheek as he half-smiles.

Holy shit, he's gorgeous.

"Who the fuck is that?" Trey asks. The truck lurches forward when he hits the gas, ripping me out of a hormonal teenage daze.

"Someone moved into the Hansen house yesterday," I say.

He drives over to Jeffers Street, and sure enough, a never-before-seen car sits in the driveway. No one ever moves in—or does anything else for that matter—without everyone knowing about it within twenty-four hours. Most people have lived here their entire lives, and a new family brings out the town's nosy side. Until now, I thought of myself as an exception. But damn, I want to see that truck again.

Wish granted. It idols at the stop sign when we return to Main Street. My heart pounds as we pull up beside him, slowing down.

"Nice truck," Trey says.

"Thanks." It's a normal enough voice, but somehow, it cuts all the way through me. Low and unshakeable, like the feeling from the last night I spent with Pete.

I intend to just glance out the dirty back window of the cab, but my eyes lock on his intense gaze. It holds me there, to him. *He takes my breath away* sounds rather dramatic, but in all honesty, I'm focusing on each breath to avoid hyperventilating. His head cranes around, watching us drive away, watching me.

Trey's phone rings, bringing my attention back to the dingy cab.

"Shit," he says. "It's Dad."

I sigh. "It's fine. I should check in on Connor anyway."

He drops me off at my house and promises to come back for me later. Not soon enough though.

Two steps into the kitchen—

"Where the fuck have you been?"

Graham can't even bother to open his eyes to bitch at me from his recliner in the living room, so I pass the doorway without answering him. More often than not, I never respond, and he never notices. I open the door to Connor's room where he's feeding Cate. Precisely what a ten-year-old should be doing on his bedroom floor—spooning strawberry yogurt into a one-year-old's mouth.

"Hi," he says, not losing focus on the task at hand.

"Where's Lara?"

He shrugs. "She left after lunch."

In other words, no one other than him has paid any attention to the baby for the past few hours.

"Here." I push the dark hair out of his eyes. "Go play."

"I'm fine, Cal."

I swipe the spoon from his hand. "I didn't ask how you were, Con. I said, go play."

My command receives a lopsided grin before he snatches up his basketball and dashes out the door.

"Slow the fuck down," Graham yells at him.

I roll my eyes, picking up Cate and the yogurt container. A mess of a smile meets me as she giggles. Her brilliant blue eyes and brunette hair are a perfect match to mine. And our mother's. Anytime someone points out how much I look like Lara, I want to run to the nearest pair of scissors and start cutting. I think it's a cruel joke, how much I resemble her, considering my worst nightmare is being anything like the woman.

Once I finish feeding Cate, I give her a bath, not seeing any other way to get her clean. She then hangs out on the kitchen floor while I make supper for Connor and me. Even if Lara stumbles through the door, she won't be in any condition to care for her children.

I shout at Connor to come inside and haul Cate to the living room. I leave her on a still-asleep Graham's lap. "Watch her while I take a shower."

He sits up, annoyed. "Where's the slut?"

I walk away, not answering, not caring.

168 Days Until 19

When I'm halfway to the dorms, a car drives past. The sloppy-drunk passenger yells something incoherent out the window. I pull out my phone. *Great.* After midnight.

It finally sinks in how stupid I am to be walking alone at night. Especially since I don't actually have any pepper spray.

Before I worry much, faint footsteps resume behind me. I won't give him the satisfaction of looking back, but part of me relaxes, knowing Jordan is still following. When he catches up again, rather than run him off, I ignore him. He lets me, staying quiet, his steps in time with mine.

Several blocks later, I check for cars out of the corner of my eye and realize the guy isn't wearing a coat. Goddamn it. Why can't he ever wear weather-appropriate clothing? I yank off my gloves and hold them out in his direction. Irritated or not, I'm still not willing to let him die of hypothermia. Especially if he's playing security detail. He takes them without a word.

Like at the party, I can feel his gaze on me. Sure enough, he stares. I roll my eyes, returning my attention straight ahead where it stays for the rest of our walk.

As we reach my building, I turn up the sidewalk. For a second, he keeps going straight but veers back and follows me all the way inside to my suite door on the second floor.

This is why you never feed a stray—or clothe one in my case. They expect it to keep happening, and eventually, you feel responsible for them not freezing to death, so you let them in the house. Exactly what I do when I unlock the door and leave it open for him.

From the couch, Cam's and Jess's eyes bug out, and their mouths fall open at the sight of him entering behind me. I never bring guys to the dorm. Another rule apparently arbitrary when dealing with Jordan Waters. If I maintained any plans to sleep with him, it would bother me more, but he destroyed any chance of that happening.

I gesture back at him, not slowing down for more formal introductions. "Jess, Cam, this is Jordan."

While they gawk, I hang up my coat. Then my shadow accompanies me to my room. He stops inside the doorway, eyes scanning. They hover on my bed for a second before climbing the wall to my countdown calendar.

One hundred sixty-eight days until nineteen.

His viewing tour of my dorm room moves on to a photo on the nightstand of my siblings and me. He should easily place Cate as my sister, her face almost a replica of mine. Few similarities exist with Connor—hair color and cheekbones. The height, the jaw, the eyes—tall, square, and dark—those are from Graham's side. All shared with our cousin, Trey.

"Call a ride," I say, snagging the gloves from his hand.

"Phone's dead."

I toss him mine and leave him to it. I glance around for my clothes basket, eager to change the second my guest leaves. Not seeing it, I open the dresser drawer, but the full-length mirror in the corner distracts me. It angles enough to show Jordan behind me, focused on the screen, and in his own words, inspiration strikes. I'm a slave to my pettiness.

Slowly, I peel my sweater off still facing away from him, and his head jerks up. With his full attention engaged, I wiggle my jeans down over my hips and step out of them. He watches as I unclasp my bra and make a show of sliding the straps down my arms until it falls to the floor. I grab a tank top from the drawer and then turn around while pulling it on. It gives him plenty of time to see what he'll never get. When I look up, his heated gaze drops back to the screen. I'm confident my tits served their intended purpose when he shifts his stance and lowers the phone over his zipper.

"I'll be right back." I try not to laugh on my way past him and stop long enough to say, "Oh, and I really hope you enjoyed the show because I'm *certain* you won't receive another one."

Closing the door behind me, I leave him alone with his hard-on to contemplate his actions. It might not be the most mature form of payback but satisfying nonetheless.

The movie keeps both Jess and Cam distracted while I cross the suite in my panties. My clothes basket waits for me outside of Jess and Felicia's door, and I put on a pair of shorts. On my way back to my room, I lean over the couch to see what they're watching.

"Glad I chose to sleep in our room the night you get a sex life," Cam says, her attention never leaving the TV.

"I hoped it would scare you off."

She smiles over her shoulder.

Jess whips around and kneels on the cushions. "The first guy you ever bring here is Jordan Waters?"

"You know him?" I ask.

"I know of him, but a lot of girls *know* him." She pauses, biting her lip like there's more. "Just don't expect more than a one-night thing. He doesn't stick around or call or anything."

I pinned him from the first cocky grin. "Nothing is happening. He's just waiting for a ride."

Her eyebrow shoots up. "Nothing? I mean, come on, it's *Jordan Waters.*"

"Trust me," I say.

I'll send him on his way with no hard feelings and chalk the night up to a learning experience about why to never let a guy make me doubt myself. A lesson beat into my brain a few hundred times already, but hey, one time, it's bound to stick.

"A damn shame." She shakes her head. "Here I thought, I'd underestimated you, Henders."

Oh, she severely underestimates me, but I prefer it that way. "Watch your movie, Ramos."

She sticks her tongue out and flips around.

I return to my room to find Jordan sprawled out on my bed. "Cab will be here in ten." He hands over my phone. "Someone texted."

A picture of Connor, wearing my strapless red gown with gold trim, pops up in my messages.

> *Can't sell this one. It makes my eyes pop.*

> I laugh and send, *It's all yours, gorgeous. Go to bed.*

"Boyfriend?" Jordan asks.

I fish out the charging cable from between the bed and nightstand, my arm brushing his when I plug in my phone. "It's my little brother."

He sits up, eyebrows drawn in and eyes focused. "Do you know anyone between the ages of eighteen and twenty-two on the West Coast?"

I tip my head to the side. "That's an oddly specific question, but no, I can't think of anyone."

"What does your father do?"

I roll my eyes at the mere mention of Graham. "Factory worker."

"Are you Italian?" He shoots off questions like we've entered the rapid-fire portion of the evening.

"Not to my knowledge."

"Any ties to the Mafia?"

"No?"

"Would you honestly tell me if you had ties to the Mafia? Is that, like, a rule or something?"

"What are you talking about?" I ask, completely lost.

"Nothing." He licks his lips, studying me. "I'm incredibly sorry for what I said earlier. I meant it as a joke, but after that, I might refrain from making any jokes ever again."

"Apology accepted." I give him a small smile, the one he called *polite.* "And I'm sorry about my retaliation. It was childish."

But fun.

"Great. We're both sorry and both forgiven." He pushes off the bed. "Now, back to winning you over."

Clearly *winning you over* translates to *trying to fuck you*, and he can't think he still stands a chance. Except the way he looks at me says otherwise. I sort out my textbooks for tomorrow's classes, avoiding the gaze locked on me.

"Don't waste your time," I tell him.

He chuckles. "Oh no. We're far beyond that argument."

Rather than decipher what the hell he means, I need to shut him down. "Look," I say, abandoning my books, "between school and everything else, my life is complicated enough. I can't handle anything else right now."

"Your life's complicated," he echoes.

I nod, unwilling to dive into details with the dude.

"So, you need someone to make your life easier," he says.

"Yeah, because it's that simple." Something tells me, Jordan Waters lives the least complicated life possible and can't begin to imagine the shitshow I deal with on a regular basis. But sure, someone can just *voilà* and simplify my life.

A spark hits his eye, his grin broadening. "I accept this challenge."

And the conversation takes a hard right turn into, *Huh?*

"What challenge?" I ask.

"You need someone to make your life easier. I can help. When you end up finding me irresistible along the way, we can work something out."

How we went from the Mafia to him deciding to help make my life easier, I'm really not sure.

"Actually, I'm saying—"

"You already find me irresistible?" he says.

"No."

He shrugs, stepping closer to me. "You will."

I stare at him, annoyed yet amused by his unwavering certainty. "I'm not going to find you irresistible."

"Of course." He exaggerates a wink. "All right, beautiful, as much as I'd love to stay and chat about you falling for me, my cab should be here any minute. I'll see you tomorrow."

With Jordan now occupying the driver seat, I've lost all control over this situation. He kisses my forehead on his way past, and a single gesture has never irritated me more. He strolls his way through the common area and tosses a wave at my suitemates on the couch before disappearing out the door.

What the fuck just happened?

I only spend a short amount of time attempting to make sense of it all. He left, and I've learned my lesson. Again. Hopefully.

Guys like him have such a short attention span that I check Towel Boy off my Shit to Worry About list. Not that he ever rated high in the first place.

By the time I finish brushing my teeth, I've mostly forgotten about tonight. Too bad when I crawl into bed, not thinking about him becomes a hell of a lot harder with his scent all over my pillow. God, he smells amazing.

***

With a project due and my overachieving partner demanding we meet before class, I drag my ass out of bed far too early.

My second class doesn't start until after lunch, allowing me to forgo a shower until later. For the time being, I take a swig of mouthwash, throw on sweats and a hoodie, and fit most of my hair in a knot semi-centered on the top of my head. I bypass the mirror with purpose and sling my bag over my shoulder.

When I open my bedroom door, I jerk to a halt. Jordan Waters jumps up off the couch with a cup of coffee in his hand, and what fresh hell is this? I almost slam the door shut but don't because coffee.

"Felicia told me how you like it. I also added an extra shot." He beams, way more chipper than I can handle at such an hour.

I can't decide who to glare at first, him or the traitorous woman watching everything unfold over the back of the couch. Him. Definitely him.

"How?" I grab the coffee and take a much-needed drink.

"How did she tell me?" he asks.

I raise my eyebrows rather than answering.

"I texted and asked."

Damn it. I have no one to blame but myself for leaving him alone with my phone. Callie Henders will never do another good deed as long as she lives.

"Did you hijack my number, too?"

"No," he says, "but you'll give it to me."

His self-assurance astounds me. "I told you, I'm not worth wasting your time."

"And I said, we're beyond that. Mission Win Callie Over has already commenced."

Good Lord. Sex with me garners itself an actual title now.

"I don't have time for Mission Win Over—"

"Mission Win Callie Over. I'm thinking of having T-shirts made."

His grin appears, and I need so much more caffeine before further engaging with him.

I roll my eyes and walk away, holding up my cup. "Thanks."

What nonsense he says about giving me a ride, I'll never know because I slam the door shut behind me.

Once a girl disappears into her room across the hall, I pull my sweatshirt away from my chest and stare down the neck hole. "This is all your fault, you know?"

My tits never respond.

———

My partner and I are the last scheduled to present for the day, and the numerous group presentations ahead of us become monotonous. So, of course, I spend the time replaying the events of the past twelve hours instead of focusing on what I'll be saying about ancient Egyptian civilizations.

Great. Jordan is already disrupting my life.

On my way out of the building, I'm desperate for a shower. I pull on my coat, only half-paying attention, and almost miss him leaning against a tree with another coffee in hand.

Now he knows my class schedule. Felicia playing his accomplice is growing old very quick.

"Hey. You need a ride?" he asks, jogging over.

I breeze past him, snagging the coffee from his hand without so much as a thank-you nod. Unfortunately, not thanking him for the coffee bothers me nearly as much as him showing up in the first place. I glance back, and our eyes meet. I decide the acknowledgment counts and keep on walking.

A search for Felicia at the dorms turns up nothing. She either left early for class or is hiding from me. Neither will protect her forever.

I swap out my messenger bag for my shower bag. When I climb into the shower stall and shake out my messy bun, Jordan's woodsy scent hits me, still in my hair from the pillow. I can't help but laugh. He's impossible to avoid, even in the bathroom.

With my hair smelling like my coconut shampoo rather than Jordan, I return to my room. There's a note waiting on the door, and I rip it down before reading it.

Lunch in the fridge.
—Team Jordan

Sure enough, the mini fridge contains a sandwich from a sub shop Felicia and I frequent together. Damn that woman. She knows my lunch normally consists of a handful of dry cereal, and I won't overcome the temptation of real food.

I eat the sandwich. Devour it actually. But I've never consumed a meal with more disdain in my entire life.

A knock fifteen minutes before my next class fails to surprise me since, over the course of a day, I've gained a personal assistant, chauffeur, and chef, all wrapped up in one overly confident package. I answer and step into the hall.

"Do you need a ride to class?" Jordan asks.

"No, I don't. You really should stop wasting your time. I have a car. If I wanted to drive, I would." I back in and close the door. Then I remember the delicious sandwich I scarfed down as my first substantial meal in three days and open the door again. "Thank you for lunch."

"Anytime, beautiful."

He smiles, the sincere one, and I shut the door on him, feeling that damn smile everywhere.

———

After my study group, I climb the stairs and pause coming around the corner. Jordan's sitting in the hallway on his phone in front of my suite. Figuring he can handle one more rejection for the day, I step over his long legs and manage to shut the door before he even stands up.

A smile tugs at my lips as I turn around, but then my eyes narrow at Felicia on the couch. "Traitor."

She giggles and follows me to my room.

I unload my books, leaving out my humanities reading. "You realize, he's only doing this to screw me, right?"

She leans in the doorway. "And you realize, he's dedicated not only one night, but also an entire day to you, right? I remember someone saying he wasn't capable of such a thing."

"An anomaly, I assure you." I almost tell her it all has to do with my tits, but that means explaining my strip show, and I'd rather not share that gem. It's far, far, far from the bottom of the barrel, but I like my suitemates all thinking I'm some virginal saint. So instead, I say, "His interest won't last past today. In fact, he'll probably stumble into a pretty little coed on his way out the door."

I ignore the tiny tinge of irritation the idea brings on.

Her eyebrow arches. "He's going to prove you wrong. Wait and see."

I smile, the odds of that happening abysmal. "Wanna bet?"

"Ten bucks says he's back tomorrow morning."

She extends her hand, and I shake it.

"You're on, Gibson."

The gleam enters her eyes, and she bounds out the door. I shut it behind her and drop onto my bed, opening my textbook. I'm only through a page when someone knocks. Since Jess nor Felicia understand the concept of privacy and regularly barge their way in, I assume Felicia has let in her new best friend.

My attention returns to the page but not for long. I look up again at the next knock just in time to see a piece of paper appear under the door.

I toss my book aside and go scoop it up from the floor. I flatten the paper out to read Jordan's note.

Need anything? Water? Snack? Company? - J

I hate to admit it, but the guy continues to prove his own unique blend of exasperating and amusing.

I grab a pen from the desk next to me and write back, *No*, before returning it.

The paper crinkles on the other side of the door.

"But thank you," I add quietly. I blame it on the fact I've been drilling into Cate that *manners matter* the last few months. Obviously nothing to do with the guy himself.

"All right, beautiful," Jordan says, his voice soft. The corner of the paper slides back under the crack. "If you change your mind, let me know. I'll see you tomorrow."

I grab the note and go back to my bed, highly doubting it. The straight dude obsession with breasts confounds me, but even so, I can't imagine him enduring another day of rejection just for a chance to see mine again.

It's not until I've finished my reading and run through my nightly routine that I crawl into bed and look at the note.

Save as Jordan the Irresistible. Then his phone number.

I smile, sinking into my pillow that still smells like him, and for the second night in a row, I try like hell not to think about Jordan Waters. The more time I spend around him, the more I believe he planned it that way all along.

167 Days Until 19

Seven more minutes until I am ten dollars richer. The money, however, interests me far less than delivering a smug *I told you so* to Felicia.

Cam packs her bag to return to her girlfriend's apartment while I tie my sneakers. It's back to living like a single, except maybe a day or so a week. She drops the bag by the door on her way out to the common area and closes it behind her.

I recheck the time. Five minutes. Of course, if Jordan doesn't show up, I need to survive without coffee until after class. A crap scenario, given my less than charming mood, but better than chancing Jess's latest experiments with flavored blends.

My heart lurches when the door flings open.

Felicia pops her head in, beaming. "Jordan's here." Then she's the one mouthing the coveted, *I told you so.*

I flip her off before she disappears, and he takes her place. He knocks on the doorframe and rests a shoulder against it.

"Back for more ego-shrinking?" I say on my way over to him.

He hands me the cup I seek. "Hopefully you do a better job today. Yesterday wasn't that impressive."

I smile at his challenge but then switch on my game face. He watches me watch him, my finger tapping the cup. Maybe it's time I work the system a little. Use my stable boy to my advantage.

"You owe Felicia ten dollars."

"*You* owe Felicia ten dollars," he counters. "You should never bet against me."

Unsurprised she told him about our wager, Team Jordan and all, I alter my tactic and turn around. "Fine." I bend over further than necessary to pick up my bag, giving him a perfect view of my ass. When I straighten up, I stare him down. "I'll find time between classes and studying to get her money. You're doing a superb job of making my life *less* complicated."

He holds my stare, but I won't back down first. Jordan Waters might be stubborn, but he's never gone toe-to-toe with me. His arm moves, and once he looks down, I glance to see the wallet in his hand. Almost too easy.

When his eyes come back to mine, I try to take the ten he pulled out, but he rips it away and holds it over his shoulder where I can't reach.

His lips turn up into a smirk. "Do you need a ride to class?"

"No." My voice stays low, our gaze locked. "I also don't need a ride after class. Thank you for the coffee and settling my bet, but you shouldn't waste your time."

I lean closer until his breath hits my face, coffee and mint. Once I can reach, my focus shifts to his hand, and I swipe for the cash again. A miscalculation on my part. The second I look away from his face, he drops his lips onto my forehead.

"See you after class, beautiful," he says, walking away.

I'm both surprised and irritated at how easily he turned my distraction around on me. Before leaving, he stops in the common area to talk to Cam. *Just great.* Felicia has already sworn her loyalty, Jess hopes to one day join his harem, and now he's set his sights on my sweet Cam. At his current rate, he'll recruit everyone in my life to help him sleep with me by the end of the day.

Determined to gain the upper hand, I text Felicia.

> *What's the name of that soup I like from the deli?*

I'm tucking my phone away as Jordan leaves, and Cam cranes her neck around from the couch.

"You're going to fuck him," she says.

"Take that back, Cameron."

She shakes her head. I tear through the room and dive over the couch at her.

After class, I see Jordan waiting for me through the glass doors. In the spirit of upping my game, I head in the opposite direction toward the exit at the other end of the hall. Let's see how well his ego tolerates a disappearing act.

I walk out into the courtyard with a closed-for-winter fountain and concrete benches set next to bare flower boxes. A depressing sight compared to the first time I saw it, humming with students and vibrant colors everywhere. Proof nothing stays bright and shiny forever.

As I follow the sidewalk, I keep to the side, out of sight of the front of the building. All for nothing when Jordan calls my name. He rushes around the building to catch up with me. Rather than make it easy on him, I speed down the sidewalk, pretending not to see him. Again, pointless. Heads start to turn in his direction, and when I glance back, he's full-on sprinting toward me.

"I brought coffee," he shouts.

I stop, well aware that coffee will cause my downfall in life. While everyone around us stares at him barreling toward me, I turn around and wait. Once he catches up, he doubles over, hand on his knee, panting. Unless he sold his soul for the abs and V hiding under his shirt, I doubt forty seconds of physical activity has him half as bad off as he wants me to believe.

Not receiving the pity he desires, he straightens up. The twinkle hits his eye as he lifts the cup to his lips and proceeds to chug my coffee. It catches me off guard, his dramatics somehow both annoying and charming, and my lips turn up.

"Here." He thrusts the half-empty cup into my hand. "Do you need a ride?"

"No." I back away from him. "Thanks for the coffee … kinda."

"See you later, beautiful."

"We'll see." I spin around and glance over my shoulder. "I might get better at hiding from you."

By the time I get to the dorms, I've developed a game plan for the afternoon. I'm studying in the middle of a circle of books on the floor of my room when I hear a knock.

Expecting Jordan, I swing open the suite door and scowl at … a sack on the floor. It has a recognizable logo from the deli downtown. I check inside and find the soup I texted Felicia about earlier. I poke my head into the hallway, spotting Jordan walking away.

"Thank you, but you should stop wasting your time," I call after him.

He rounds the corner, never looking back.

After eating what tastes like victory, I gather up my books a few hours early. For my afternoon class, Jordan can knock all he wants. I won't be here.

Take two of my disappearing act leads me to the library in the middle of campus. Less than convenient, given the location of my next lecture, but effective for evasion. With a novel for Lit, I sink into an overstuffed leather chair, settling in for the duration.

Or so I think.

A few chapters in, a throat clears across from me, and the spark of him watching me hits my chest. My eyes widen, slowly traveling from the pages to Jordan freaking Waters sitting on the arm of the chair facing me.

"A safe house is a much better choice when going underground." A smirk accompanies his unsolicited advice.

"Are you…" I trail off, not wanting to outright accuse him of following me, but I never told anyone about going to the library.

"Following you?" He takes care of the accusation for me. "Absolutely not. I only show up where I already know you'll be. There's a difference." I tip my head to the side, questioning whether a differentiation truly exists, so he holds up his laptop. "I have a paper due tomorrow."

Once again confident that he fits the description of horny college guy, the tension leaves my shoulders. "Oh."

"Do you need a ride to class?" he asks.

My gaze drops to the book. "No."

"You would make all this a lot easier if you would just—"

"Spread my legs for you?" I supply the honest end to his sentence, looking up.

That damn smile appears. "Not what I was going to say, but we can do it your way. I'm only trying to make your life easier. You should consider leaning in."

I suppress the hell out of a smile and force an eye roll. I return my attention to my novel, and Jordan lets out an exaggerated sigh. Once his shadow stops darkening the page, I glance up and watch him walk out of the library.

It's just a facial expression, Henders. One attached to an arrogant guy at that.

Thursday night means movie night for those of us who regularly sleep in our suite. But when I step out of my room, only Felicia is waiting on the couch.

"Jess?" I ask, claiming my spot at one end of the couch.

"She's on Vee patrol." Felicia hands me the remote.

"The same guy?"

She nods.

Jess's sister, Vanessa, loves herself a project, but—shocker— they never work out for her.

Last semester, she chased no less than five guys, each telling her from the start that they wanted nothing serious. Of course, she agreed and then fell head over heels for them anyway, convinced she could change their minds. Typically, she recovers and moves on within a few weeks, but she still can't let go of one from over winter break. Although, from the sounds of it, he's dropped off the face of the Earth to avoid her. Jess volunteered to serve as her sponsor, keeping her distracted so that she won't attempt to track him down.

I scroll through the movie options Felicia added to a list on the streaming app and shake my head. "No to every one, Gibson."

Her obsession with documentaries and artsy flicks will create a rift in our suite if we let it. Since I picked last time, the choice of the night belongs to Jess, so I channel her and select a romantic comedy from her profile.

"Compromise?"

Sappy Felicia enthusiastically nods, and all snuggled up in a blanket, I queue it up. Within the first fifteen minutes, someone taps on the door. Someone almost always being Jordan Waters.

"No." I push pause on the remote as Felicia jumps up. "Don't answer it."

She ignores me, answering with a cheesy grin. "Hey, come on in, *Jordan*."

He follows her in, and I roll my eyes, pushing play on the movie again.

"I was driving by and thought—"

My finger presses the volume button until the movie drowns him out. I cup a hand to my ear, signaling I can't hear him.

He tries again, so I hold the button and mouth, *What?*

His eyes close for a second, a chink in his self-confidence armor. Recovering as quick as ever, he smirks on his way over. He leans down, his face a few inches from mine when he starts talking. I can't hear him over the TV and study his lips, hoping to discover that I'm a lip-reading expert.

Oh … little … no…

Probably none of those words. Damn it. Intrigue wins out, and I hit pause on the remote.

"All the king's horses and all the king's men couldn't put Humpty together again."

A fucking nursery rhyme.

I smile—frustrated, amused, and bested. He smiles back, the real one he gives more often. For a moment, I almost forget he's using a fake challenge to try to screw me. For a moment. And almost. My expression fades, returning to its natural state—unimpressed.

He stays close with his intense green eyes on me. "Do you need anything?"

I shake my head, distracted by his gaze lowering to my mouth.

Another moment. Another almost.

He straightens up fast. "All right, beautiful, I'll see you tomorrow."

My brain functions better with him farther away and snaps into challenge mode. "Come prepared. Felicia and I bet double or nothing."

We never made such a bet, so Felicia glances over. I shoot her a look, warning her not to say anything.

With a sigh, Jordan pulls out his wallet. "Here. Take my money now."

She plucks the twenty from his hand and drops back onto the couch. I have to press my lips together to keep from laughing at how easy he makes taking his money. It looks like he's leaving when, suddenly, he leans down and plants a damn kiss on my forehead. I roll my eyes, and not to be outdone, he makes a face while dramatically rolling his back. I smile as he walks away.

The door shuts behind him, and I stretch out on the couch. "After the movie, you're buying me ice cream with your winnings."

She giggles, pulling my feet into her lap. "Maybe a new car if he keeps this up."

"I hope he gives up before then." I resume the movie, and we both jump as the sound roars back, still at max volume. I scramble for the button, laughing. "We're blaming that on Towel Boy, right?"

"Right," she says. "Also on you for flirting back."

I kick at her even though she's right. Whether I like it or not, he gets under my skin more than anyone has in a long time. But in less than twenty-four hours, most of the state will separate us. An entire weekend without contact should help him lose interest. Once I return, everything can return to normal—predictable. Exactly the way I want it.

166 Days Until 19

I hate Fridays.

The reason varies depending on the week. This particular one I despise because I look like a goddamn twelve-year-old. No makeup, hair back in a braid, breasts lost in the sea of fabric provided by a T-shirt a few sizes too big, and the illusion of no ass, thanks to baggy jeans. Hell, if I could spontaneously summon zits to further decrease my appeal to the opposite sex, I would.

I zip up my bag full of similar outfits for the next few days and load my messenger bag for my morning class. A knock sends me spinning. Jordan is standing in my doorway earlier than I'd anticipated. My first class doesn't start for an hour and a half.

Despite my appearance, his gaze rakes down my body and back up. So much for lowering my chances of inciting male attention. Flattering yet disheartening at the same time.

"Hello, handsome," I say, relieving him of the cup in his hand.

"You're talking to the coffee?"

I nod and notice the bag in his other hand. "Is that a bacon ciabatta?"

He hands me the sack, and sure enough, the delicious breakfast sandwich I casually mentioned to Felicia last night is waiting inside. I take a bite and moan. So freaking amazing.

He clears his throat. "Do you need a ride this morning?" he asks, his voice gravelly.

My focus shifts back to him as I sit on the bed. "No, Jordan. I also don't need a ride after class or later. Thank you for the sandwich and the coffee, but you shouldn't waste your time."

"So I've heard." He leans down to kiss my forehead. "See you after class, beautiful."

My lips twitch at his blatant disregard for my speech. At this point, I wonder why I even bother. Probably because it's our game, and I'm not hating playing.

As usual, when I want time to slow down—or even better, stop—it does the opposite, and far too soon, I'm walking to class. In another blink, we dismiss, the professor seeming more eager than the students to get a start on her weekend. I, however, drag my feet, walking out of the building like a pouty Cate being forced to anywhere.

My coffee jogs toward me, bringing Jordan along with it. "You need a ride?"

"No, but thank you."

"I'm concerned *yes* doesn't exist in your vocabulary." He hands me his offering. "A fantastic word. Useful in a number of situations."

I shrug, stepping around him. "Another failing of the public education system, I guess."

He catches up and walks backward in front of me. "Well, if you ever need a tutor to help expand your verbal skills, just let me know. My lexicon's *huuuge*."

And his subtlety nonexistent.

"Maybe you can do me a favor then."

"Anything for you, beautiful."

"Define a word for me?" I ask.

"I'm listening."

"*Rejection.*"

That smile appears as he stops, letting me continue on without him.

My last class for the day releases early, and an irritating new habit surfaces as I leave—my eyes scan for Jordan. Only there's no

Jordan leaning against the tree or jogging over. Still no sighting of him by the time I reach the parking lot. Nothing when I toss my messenger bag in the backseat with my other bag for the weekend.

I start the car and put it in gear. Then I think about him waiting outside the building like a sad little puppy and put it right back in park.

Damn it.

I pick up my phone, intending to text Felicia so that she can take care of him for me, but a random thought pops into my head. Even though I never added the number he gave me, I search my contacts. Always a step ahead of me, *Jordan the Irresistible* shows up. Obnoxious yet amazing.

> *Sorry. I waited as long as I could. Gone until Monday.*

I hit send on the message, officially giving him my number before I pull out of the parking lot.

Every weekend, I drive the same road, and every weekend, I space out almost the entire time. Autopilot kicks on, music plays, the scenery blurs by out the windows, and three hours pass with no conscious effort on my part.

At about six o'clock, I turn off the highway at the sign welcoming me to Waymore, Pennsylvania. The town of thirteen hundred people dwarfs our hometown of Sutterville fifteen miles farther up the road. Even so, the only real differences, other than population, are the paved streets and a lone red light blinking on top of a stop sign they installed after someone hit a cat.

I never know what to expect from my weekends at Lara's house, but when I spot the Mustang GT sitting in the driveway, motor running, I have a decent idea.

My much-less-intimidating black Prius parks next to the blue two-door. I take a deep breath before getting out to grab my bags from the other side. A few pieces of mail fall onto the ground when the bags bump them, and I bend over to pick them up. The second I do, I hear the hum of an electric window rolling down behind me.

"Hey," he says, his eyes glued to my ass, no doubt. "Trying to make me hard? Because fuck, babe, it's working."

I straighten up and ignore him.

One of the joys of a thirty-four-year-old mother rediscovering her freedom after sixteen years in a sham of a marriage? The twenty-two-year-old douche named Tyler she dates, who hits on me anytime she steps out of the room.

The appeal of a guy screwing my mother rates about a negative twelve on the dreamboat scale. Unfortunately, this fact does little to dissuade him from eyeing my chest or watching me walk through the house. Ill-fitted clothes help to an extent, but at the end of the day, he's still a disgusting dude-bro dishing out crude comments.

The door to the house shuts at the same time as my car door. Lara prances down the steps, wearing one of my more revealing tops from high school and skinny jeans. With her dark hair layered and half up, enough of her neck shows to put her fresh hickey on display. Besides her purse, she carries a bag.

"Tyler wants me to stay with him for the weekend. His parents are out of town." She beams at the blond tool whose eyes are still on me. "You'll be fine watching the kids?"

She climbs in without my answer, and Tyler winks, rolling up his window. He revs the engine a few times to verify the size of his dick and throws the car in reverse.

"Sure. No problem. Have a great time," I say to the car disappearing down the road.

I check my phone and see two texts, one from a few hours ago.

No worries. I'll be waiting.

And, *Get there okay?*

The guy trying to hit it and quit it shows more interest in my well-being than my mother. I laugh at the dysfunction and send a, *Yes*, on my way to the house.

I hesitate before going inside. For the next forty-eight hours, I won't be Callie.

I'll be Cal.

165 Days Until 19

Cate sits through one basketball game without issue, but during the second, her fidgeting graduates to full-on acrobatics. She hangs halfway under the bleachers, upside down and about to fall on her ass—or head.

"Catelynn Renee, get up here."

She wiggles her way out of the precarious position and plops onto the seat. Her blue doll eyes pout at me. "Caaaal. I. Am. So. Bored."

From the way Connor's team plays, she'll need to endure another game and a half. For the sake of my sanity, I hand over my phone with its full battery. Her face lights up at the sight. She scoots down the bench, already in her own little world of make-believe. At least for a few minutes.

I flip open the cover to my Psych book about the time Connor scans the crowd for familiar faces. I shout, wave, and let the book fall shut. He acts embarrassed, covering his face with his hands, but a grin gives him away. His attention returns to the game without bothering to further search the stands.

People have packed into the gym, cheering on the different high school basketball teams competing in the weekend tournament. Families, students, teachers, and older locals who continue to support the kids long after their own have moved on and married, cheering on their own children elsewhere.

Two people not in attendance: our parents.

Lara's currently partying with a bunch of college kids while her college-aged daughter cares for her kids with a torn twenty she left hanging on the refrigerator door with a magnet. Not that twenty dollars can even cover groceries for the weekend since behind the fridge door was nothing but condiments and a half-empty container of whipped cream.

As far as Graham goes, who the hell knows his excuse. The short drive from Sutterville never stops him from attending these events. He puts on his Father of the Year facade, talking to everyone, except his children. Connor and I prefer his absence though. The way he acts in front of people makes us hate him even more. Quite the fucking feat.

With neither of them making an appearance, Connor's fan base consists of me and a six-year-old who poses for selfies, making goofy faces. Well, us and my ex-boyfriend Pete's grandparents on the other end of the gym. Small towns are weird places. All the same, rather than study, I watch him play, not wanting to miss any opportunities to remind him that we're here for him.

At halftime, I wrangle my phone from Cate long enough for her to use the restroom. We pick up three sandwiches from the concession stand, and she settles down in a hallway to eat outside the locker room.

I swing the door open. "Connor Henders, delivery."

"A little early, aren't you?" He steps out to retrieve his lunch.

"Sorry. I needed to take advantage of the monster's feeding schedule."

He peeks around the corner at her as she forces half the sandwich into her mouth. "I saw her ass-up on the bleachers earlier. Shocking she made it out of the gym in one piece."

"Yeah, well, she still has time. Now, get back in there. You're playing great. Keep it up. Hustle, hustle, sports stuff." I throw up a few arm gestures like a knockoff cheerleader.

Unimpressed with me, he rolls his eyes as he backs away. "Oh, I forgot it's my turn to host the team's dinner tonight."

"What?" Panic enters my voice. "How many players?"

"Twenty-five." He flashes a grin and secures sanctuary in the depths of the locker room.

Just fucking great.

Putting team dinner on the backburner, I herd Cate back to our seats as the team charges onto the court. They increase their double-digit lead with Connor hitting four three-pointers in a quarter. After he sinks the game-winning shot, he gives me a nod and a quick cheer move on his way out of the gym. He just had to show up my sad attempt.

The gym buzzes as one team's fans swap out for another's. Others stretch their legs in the half-hour break between games before settling back in.

Cate's been uncharacteristically quiet, but she seeks my attention again, brushing the hair away from my face. She holds up my phone to take a picture. "Cal, make a happy face."

I smile at her.

"Now a sad face."

My lip juts out in an exaggerated pout, and my forehead wrinkles.

She giggles. "Do a funny one."

I continue to follow directions from my demanding photographer for a few more shots until her interest fades. She moves three benches higher and pretends to call her boyfriend on the phone. Usually she plays teacher and calls her "students" when bored.

With a brief break from parental duties, I open my textbook and keep it open this time. Between feeding Connor's team—they had all better like spaghetti—and Cate's never-ending requests, I won't find another time to study until Sunday night when I get to campus. Given Lara's track record for showing up on time, the chances of me arriving before midnight are slim.

I finish my reading a few minutes ahead of tip-off and clear one item off my to-do list. Just in time for a few loud clomps on the wooden seat headed my way.

Cate stops next to me and kisses my cheek. "You look beautiful," she says.

My heart melts a little at her sweetness. "Awww. Thank you."

"She says thank you," she says into the phone. "You could? How? … Oh, no. I kissed her cheek." She holds the phone away from her face and kisses my forehead.

Beautiful? Forehead kiss? I disregard her whining when I snatch my phone away, and—unbelievable.

For the last twenty-three minutes, Cate's been on the phone with Jordan freaking Waters.

"Jordan?"

"Callie?" He at least sounds concerned. As he should.

"What the hell are you doing, talking to my sister?"

"Uh … we were tired of texting?"

"What?" I check my texts and find a lengthy conversation between them. It includes several pictures of them making faces and all the ones she took of me. One in particular of him with his cheeks puffed out and his eyes crossed makes me laugh, and I slowly bring the phone back to my ear with a sigh.

"Does this mean you aren't mad?" he asks warily.

"Oh, I want to be furious." I do. I really do. "But you distracted her long enough that I finished my assignment for Monday."

"Sounds like you enjoyed a rather uncomplicated afternoon then."

I smile, knowing he's smug as fuck at a victory. He deserves it though. From three hours away, he actually made my life a little easier.

"Thank you," I say.

"Anytime, beautiful."

I hand the phone back to Cate, who squeals.

"So, Jordan, I think we should talk about what happened on the playground last week."

She scoots down the bleachers, chatting away. A while later, the phone lands in my lap, and she bounds away.

Jordan's still talking when I bring the phone to my ear.

"The best thing you can do is kick him in the shins."

Terrible advice she would have absolutely followed, but I smile anyway. "Bye, Jordan."

He laughs, realizing she abandoned him. "Bye, beautiful."

Supper dishes are drying in the rack, and I flip off the light in the kitchen on my way out.

I check in on Cate. She's sprawled across her bed, the short way, dead asleep. All night, she entertained Connor's friends with dancing and stories, casting her spell on each one.

Physically, the similarities between us are astounding, but she acts so much happier than me at that age. Something Connor and I have worked our asses off to make happen. Neither of us wants her to ever feel like we did growing up.

I close her door, careful not to disturb her unless I want her in my bed all night. Chances are she'll end up there anyway.

A gory horror movie plays on the giant flatscreen in the living room. Connor adjusts his long legs so I can sit with him on the much-too-large wraparound sectional. The only thing on the walls in here is an Eagles banner, and a mini fridge hums next to the end table. If only Lara furnished the house for her children with as much concern as she does her boyfriend. What a ridiculous thought.

I sit next to him, staring at the screen in disgust. A woman impales herself on a metal fence post while trying to get away from the murderer. These types of movies used to give him nightmares, and he would hide under the blankets in my room. At some point, they went from terrifying to fascinating in his mind.

Jordan texts as the murderer slides the dead woman's body off the post. So unnecessarily graphic.

All right, beautiful. I'll see you tomorrow.

Well, him losing interest in me appears to be a bust. Thanks, Cate.

I send, *Goodnight, Jordan. Monday.*

His response pops up right away. *Tomorrow.*

Monday.

He's exhausting.

Connor's knee nudges my arm. "You're smiling. Cate's new boyfriend?"

She told Con all about Jordan after his last game. Everything important to a six-year-old that is.

I drop the smile. "She's rather smitten, isn't she?"

His eyebrow does a quick up-down. "Yeah, *my sister* seems to really like this guy."

"Subtle," I tell him. I knock his foot off the couch as I go to change for bed.

When I come out of the bathroom, he's waiting in the hallway.

"Lover Boy texted." He tosses me my phone, and I glare up at him on my way past. If his feet give any indication of height, he'll surpass the six-foot-three he stands in no time.

Back in my room and away from prying eyes, I drop onto the bed and check Jordan's message.

Tomorrow. Stop arguing.

Letting out a sigh, I scroll through the conversation he and Cate shared. I pause on the closest to normal picture of him in the collection. Even on a screen, his eyes keep their intensity, flecks of darker green standing out.

"Seriously, Cal?" Connor fills up my entire doorway, leaning against the frame with his arms crossed. "Just bang the guy already."

I fling a pillow across the room at him. He catches it and cannons it back, disappearing by the time it hits me.

Younger brothers never outgrow their annoying stage.

164 Days Until 19

I wait until after seven for Lara on Sunday evening. Her last message promised she'd be back no later than six. When Connor opens the fridge and takes out the leftover spaghetti to reheat for a second time today, I give up. Cate sets the table for the three of us, and they tell me about their plans for the upcoming week as we eat. It's our usual family meal, them and me.

After we finish, Connor cleans up while Cate takes her bath. He joins us in her room when he's done, and with my not-so-little brother on one side of the bed and me on the other, she reads us her favorite book. Most of the time, she forgets to turn the page because she recites it from memory. Over the past year, she's heard the story hundreds of times, snuggled between us, never once realizing our little ritual is in place to give her some level of normalcy. A way to distract from her mother's almost-constant absence at bedtime.

We wait until she falls asleep to sneak out.

Connor follows me to the kitchen, my bags and coat in his hand. "Go," he says, shoving them at me. "Three hours puts you on campus at midnight. We'll be fine. I'll text you when she gets here."

A heaviness enters my chest, familiar enough we're besties. I hate to leave him to deal with whatever condition she comes home in, *if* she comes home, but his stubbornness rivals mine.

He pulls me in for a hug, and I wrap my arms around his torso. For the moment, we take solace in the security only we provide for one another.

His chin rests on top of my head. "One hundred sixty-four days, Cal. Don't forget."

A year ago, those numbers meant more than anything. When things were at their worst, Connor saved me with the calendar, counting down until I turned eighteen and was free. He made me promise I'd build a life far away from our parents—be happy and never look back. It's why I chose Easton, my fresh start. My escape.

The second time around, both the calendar and words have lost the magic for me, but he still needs to believe in them, so I nod against his chest. "I won't."

I force a smile as I leave him in the kitchen. The blinds lift after I go outside, and he watches me load up the car. Even from a distance, the two lines between his eyebrows are visible. They form when he worries, more and more often as of late.

On the highway, I roll the windows down, so the freezing air can wash away the hatred, resentment, and doubt that anything will ever get better. Everything that threatens to drag me down if I let it. Except it all stays present this time. My mind never shuts off. Not for a single second of the trip.

I stay in my car for a minute after parking in the lot in front of the dorms, collecting myself before I haul my bags inside. When I turn the light on in the suite, I jump, seeing a body on the couch.

Freaking Connor and his horror movies.

It's not a dead body but a passed-out Jordan. I drop my bags on the floor in my room and grab the extra blanket from my bed. I set his phone on the coffee table and move his arm onto the couch before covering him up. At least someone in my life follows through, albeit it's the guy who wants to bang me all in the name of winning.

I go to my room and check if Connor texted yet. Nothing from him, but I have a missed message from the guy passed out on my couch.

All right, beautiful, in case I miss you, I'll see you tomorrow.

I read the same words as last night and the one before, the consistency oddly comforting. Unfortunately, the phone call I need to make will reverse the effect.

When Lara answers, I jerk the phone away from my ear to save myself from the noise. I can't understand a slurred word she attempts to say as she laughs. She's trashed, and from the sounds of it, she's at a real rager. The most responsible place for a mother of three to be on a Sunday night while her teenage son waits for her, worries about her. I hate her so much.

"Are you going home soon?" I ask.

More incoherent babble.

"Who is it, babe?" Tyler asks in the background.

"My daughter," she mumbles. "The cockblock."

Nothing but class from my mother. So glad I can understand her now.

I take a deep breath and am about to repeat the question when Tyler says, "Tell her to come party with us. I have a plenty of brothers who would love to take a ride on an ass like that."

"No, babe, remember? She acts like a prude now."

"Whatever. She still wants it. Not that it matters. They'll get her so fucked up she wouldn't even know—"

I end the call, not needing the rest of his sentence. I don't know why I even listened that long—other than maybe a small part of me wanted her to stand up for me or at least care that her boyfriend threatened to pass me around his fucking frat house.

A sting hits my eyes, but nothing follows. Even if I could summon the tears, they're not worth them.

I set a reminder to call Connor's school when I wake up. He'll watch a movie or read to stay awake until she stumbles in the door. Then, in the morning, he'll help Cate get ready and walk her to school, but after, he needs to go home and get some sleep.

I text back Jordan, telling him goodnight, and get ready for bed. But I end up just staring at the dark ceiling, not falling asleep. The heaviness from home still clings on, relentless. For the first time in a long time, I can't bury the feelings deep enough to forget. And I really fucking need to.

Five Years Ago

The time it takes for all hell to break loose in The House of Henders: less than one minute.

Around nine, Lara falls through the door. Some random dude scurries in after her. The third one in a month maybe? But why the hell would she bring him home with her?

"Oh, for fuck's sake," I say.

I grab Connor's arm and drag him out of the room. No way will I wait around for Graham's reaction to this disaster in the making.

I push Connor into my room before ducking into Cate's. She sleeps soundly. So, hoping to avoid a screaming baby in addition to the screaming parents, I snag the baby monitor and shut her door. The first crash of an unidentified object being thrown and a slur of insults sound as I return to my room.

I kick off my flip-flops. "You good, Con?"

"Yeah," he says, his voice muffled through the blanket fort.

Given the time, he'll end up sleeping in there. I need to get him ready for bed before they start chasing each other around the house.

"I'll be back with your toothbrush."

"Cal…" His voice shakes.

I drop down on the floor and move a blanket to the side so I can see him. "You're safe, Con."

His eyebrows pull together, concerned.

I engage my fake smile, not wanting him to work himself up. "Promise."

Once he nods, I let the blanket fall. I slide back on my sandals, not wanting to chance a piece of glass in my foot again. The last one took weeks to heal.

Anyone who questions my colorful vocabulary only needs to overhear about five seconds of the argument in the kitchen. Then they would praise me for having such a clean fucking mouth.

I slip down the hall to the bathroom and fill a cup of water and apply toothpaste to his toothbrush. Next stop is his room for his flashlight, a book, and pajamas. When I come through the door, he pops his head out. No prompt needed, he reaches for the cup and toothbrush to brush, sip, and spit. We trade for his pajamas. He tosses out the dirty clothes after he changes, and I throw them in the hamper. I lift the flap and hand him the flashlight and book.

I'm about to crawl in with him when a door creaks open.

Oh shit. It's not my door.

My eyes dart to the baby monitor next to Connor, a bunch of incoherence flooding through the speaker. Jesus Christ, they're in Cate's room.

"Lock the door behind me, Con," I say, running out.

I make a fast right turn and barrel directly into Graham, standing in Cate's doorway. The impact knocks me flat on my ass. He never stops yelling at her, even as I lie at his feet. Upright again, I slide between him and the doorframe. I step around Lara scream-crying on the floor in front of the crib and pick up the baby. Groggy, Cate appears more annoyed than scared—further proof of our fucked-up situation.

"Get the fuck out of here," Graham shouts.

Lara grabs my leg as I pass, blubbering something about her "sweet baby."

Half of me wonders if she's too drunk to remember Cate's name.

"Cal?" Connor asks through the door when I knock.

"It's me."

The lock clicks, and I push it open. He takes Cate from my arms and returns to the fort to put her down. Experience has taught us we can get her back to sleep as long as we lay her down in the dark within a few minutes.

His head appears through an overlap in the blankets. "You leaving?"

My little brother knows me well.

I pull on a sweatshirt. "I won't be far. Just need some air. Diapers and wipes are in the closet if you need them." I listen to determine where in the house they've chosen for their next battle arena. From the echo, it sounds like the bathroom at the end of the hall. "Lock the door."

Connor nods. "See you later."

Another lie of a smile, and I'm gone.

163 Days Until 19

Vibrations next to my head wake me. I slap around until connecting with my phone on the pillow.

Connor: *Home.*

Lovely. It only took her until seven in the morning.

No school until after lunch, I tell him. *Sleep.*

Since I'm already awake, I grab my shower bag. Jess is sitting in her usual study place in front of the couch when I come out, Jordan's sleeping head less than a foot away from hers.

"Think he'd notice if I curled up next to him?" she asks.

"Maybe not at first."

She giggles. "Callie Henders, the woman who tamed Jordan Waters. You'll be a legend."

I ignore her on my way out. He isn't domesticated. We're merely engaged in a battle of wills, waiting for the other to surrender. And I will win.

While I take my shower, all the shit from over the weekend still clutches on for dear life. I turn the water as hot as I can tolerate. The burn on my skin affords a distraction, my mind clearing. But once my body adjusts to the temperature, it all floods back in. I slap off the faucet, cutting the stream of water.

By the time I get back to my room and dress, it's time to call Connor's school. The phone on the other end rings twice before the automated system picks up.

I use my Principal Poole voice—low, harsh, and perfected from two years of practice—and recite the words along with him. "Thank you for calling Norris Central Public Schools. If you know your party's extension, please enter it at any time."

I hit the zero followed by the nine.

A few rings later, a cheerful voice answers, "Mr. Poole's office. This is Gloria."

Now for my Lara imitation—my voice but a tad higher and breathier. Like I'm flirting with everyone in a five-mile radius. "This is Lara Henders. Connor's staying home for the first few periods today."

"Just a second, Ms. Henders." She taps on a keyboard.

Someone knocks on my bedroom door. I swing it open to see Jordan standing there with coffee. Damn, he can pull off the *spent the night on a couch* look—disastrous hair, wrinkled shirt, more aggressive stubble.

"He'll be absent, you said?"

Gloria brings me back to my primary task, and I walk away from the sexy guy, hiding a smile.

"Yes, for the morning classes."

"Everything's okay, I hope," she says, her concern sincere.

"Just feeling a little under the weather."

"Oh, the poor dear. Make sure he stays hydrated and comfortable."

"Right, rest and fluids," I say. "Thank you, Mrs. Rodriguez."

Oh shit. I forgot to call her Gloria.

Luckily, she misses my slipup and says, "You take care, Ms. Henders."

"You too."

I toss my phone on the bed, and when I spin around, Jordan's leaning against the doorframe. His mouth turns up at the corners, eyes on me. Once my focus shifts onto him, the emotions of the weekend finally lose their hold. Apparently, Towel Boy provides the perfect distraction from all the shit.

I relieve him of the coffee in his hand. "Good morning, Jordan."

"Good morning, beautiful."

I hate that my stomach flips when he calls me that since it's probably a pet name he calls every girl. I throw in an eye roll just for good measure.

"Please don't make a habit out of sleeping on our couch." My amusement almost betrays me, remembering how close he came to waking up with Jess on top of him, but I lock it down. I grab my messenger bag and phone and point at the bed on my way out. "The blanket needs to be folded and put back on the bed." Halfway through the common area, I retreat, poking my head in again. "No, I don't need a ride, but thank you for the coffee."

He smiles that damn smile. Since I haven't seen it in a few days, it cuts through me more than ever. So much in fact that it sends me dashing out the door.

Just a smile, Henders.

But my God, it's one hell of a smile.

Determined to enjoy the full college experience, Felicia twists my arm—literally when I try to run away from her—into attending another party. We meet Becca at the house off-campus, and the night proceeds like every other one. Keg in the kitchen. Beer pong set up in the middle of a room. Music blaring from the living room. A pile of coats upstairs where you might retrieve yours from, if no one else takes it home with them first.

"I asked Jordan to come," Felicia says as we wait for the bathroom. "He said no."

A safe choice, considering our last experience at a party together.

Her gaze travels over my shoulder, her expression all I need to know that a man is standing behind me.

"Hey," she says.

I step out of the way, not wanting to come between her and the object of her affection. Average height, average face, average all over nods at her. A friend pops up beside him, just as unmemorable with blond hair and blue eyes, like half the partygoers. His eyes dart between the lovebirds, acknowledging their connection before they land on me.

"A long line for the bathroom at a party," he says. "So passé."

"I heard most places are completely doing away with them."

Felicia and Average Joe stay locked in their stare, neither capable of speech.

"Do you think they can hear us in their current state?" the friend asks me.

Average Joe elbows him. "Shut up, Benson."

He uses the nudge as an opportunity to sidestep toward me, his arm brushing mine. "Now that the mystery's been ruined, I'm Benson."

"Were we going for mysterious?" I ask.

He shrugs, a grin spreading. "Thought it might be fun. But Joe screwed it up."

I laugh at Average Joe's name really being Joe. Benson, of course, thinks it relates to him and inches closer. *So the wrong tree, buddy.*

A group of coeds hurry out of the bathroom. Before he speaks again, I throw my weight at Felicia and force her through the door, pulling it shut behind me.

"Hey," she says, sounding put out. "I was getting somewhere with him."

"I know, but the friend thought he was getting somewhere with me."

"If you honestly have no interest in Jordan, then what does it matter?"

"Not happening." The thought of hooking up with some random guy while Jordan hangs around bothers me. Not to mention, the minimal attraction to said random guy.

She smirks. "You want Jordan. Just admit it."

Maybe the lack of sleep catches up with me or the stress of Lara still lingers or Felicia's more accurate than I want to acknowledge. Hell, it might be something else. I can't pinpoint the why, but my tolerance for her pushing him on me drops to fucking zero, fast and without warning.

"Why, Gibson? Why is this so important to you? Do you want me to admit, if he weren't only trying to fuck me to prove he could, I'd screw him? Fine. I would. Are you happy? Can you drop it?"

Her expression falls. "Callie, I was just kidding."

Still not entirely sure what the hell is wrong with me, I shake my head. "If you want a wingwoman for Average Joe, find Becca." I jerk the bathroom door open and shoulder my way past Benson, not for a second giving him the wrong idea about how little I want to interact with him. The last thing I need is another guy chasing me out of a party.

"Henders?" Becca grips my shoulders, bringing me to a stop in the living room. "What's wrong?"

"Please don't let Felicia follow me."

She nods and moves out of my way without another word.

A few steps out the door, the cold air rushes into my lungs, but my thoughts, emotions, actions all remain muddled. Everything slowly closes in around me. I drag my hands down my face and force myself to pull it together. Of all the potential places to crash and burn, the sidewalk in front of a party house is not an option. The access to alcohol and poor life choices is too easy.

I pull my phone from my back pocket when I get a text.

Jordan: *Band practice starting soon. Need anything?*

The timing is either excellent or terrible. I laugh without humor and tap out a message, asking him for a ride.

Then I delete it and reply, *No, thank you.*

You sure?

Not about anything at the moment.

Yes.

Last chance…

Goodnight, Jordan.

All right, beautiful. I'll see you tomorrow.

I smile at the message even though I shouldn't and wonder if the calm spreading through me is what people experience when they know what happens next. When their life is predictable and not a complete mess all the time.

A breath sucks in as arms snake around my waist, and then hot breath hits my ear. "Wanna get outta here, boo thang?"

I relax and drop my head on the shoulder behind me. "Only if you take me back to your dorm room."

"Hell yeah, I will." Cam drives me forward down the sidewalk. "Just don't expect me to cuddle or anything. My woman's getting off soon, and I don't want to smell like another chick."

"For the best since my roommate will be there. She hates it when I bring people back."

"Correction: she hates when you bring dirty boys back."

We laugh, crossing the street. The lights to Sawyer's car blink, and I climb in. It's only after we've driven away that I realize I forgot my damn coat.

162 Days Until 19

I'm too warm when I wake up.

A faint light from the parking lot streams through the window into my room. I yawn, and in the process of tossing off my comforter, I discover my coat draped over the top. *What the hell?*

I swing my legs out of bed, but rather than carpet, my feet touch a warm body.

One more time, *What the hell?*

The lamp blinds me when I switch it on. My eyes adjust to Felicia in Cam's bed with Jess and Becca asleep on the floor between us. When my room became the site of a sleepover, I have no idea.

"Hey," Felicia whispers, sitting up. She scrunches her face. "Are you still mad at me?"

I rub a hand over mine, still not awake enough to know why I would have been mad at her in the first place. "No?"

"Thank God." She jumps over Jess and Becca and hops in my bed. "I'm so sorry, Callie. I wasn't trying to force you to be with Jordan. I just thought he might be good for you. Someone impulsive and fun, you know?"

Oh right, my minor meltdown in the bathroom at the party. I lean back against the wall next to her and rest my head on her shoulder. "I overreacted. It had nothing to do with you."

"You're sure?"

One hundred percent positive, I nod. "But I would appreciate it if you cooled it with the Team Jordan nonsense."

She kisses the top of my head. "Team Callie all the way, baby."

"I'll be on Team Jordan," Jess says. "I'll be on anything Jordan."

Good Lord, the girl's subtlety needs work.

"How about no teams at all?"

Becca groans and covers her face with a pillow. She mumbles before sitting up. "Why are you all awake right now?"

I lift my head. "Why are you all in my room right now?"

She yawns, creating a domino effect between the four of us until we've all stretched out our lungs.

"I came in to apologize, but you were already asleep," Felicia says.

"I followed her in because I was drunk." Becca drops onto her pillow. "Am drunk."

"And?" I look at Jess.

She shrugs. "I woke up, and everyone else was in here."

I shake my head. "Well, I'm going back to sleep before Gibson gets any bright ideas about pulling out the spirit board or starting a pillow fight."

Felicia bounces off the bed and returns to Cam's. "Goodnight, beautiful."

I flip her off, lying down. "Goodnight, beautiful."

The riffraff has cleared out of my room by the time my alarm goes off. I shower, dress, and cross off another day on the calendar. Whatever the hell crawled up my ass last night seems long gone, and I chalk it up to the stress of the weekend.

When Jordan knocks, I'm loading up my bag. With a notebook clenched in my teeth, I kind of say, "Come in."

The door creaks open, and I glance up at him stepping in.

I drop the notebook in my bag before fetching the cup in his hand. "Good morning, Jordan."

"Do you need a ride to class?" he asks without his usual charm behind it.

I shake my head, studying him. Something's off. "Thanks for the coffee."

His mouth curves up at the corners, and then he slaps the doorframe on his way out without another word. I follow him to the common area, everything about the interaction *wrong*. He gives an unenthusiastic wave to Jess and Felicia and heads out the door.

"Was Jordan weird just now?" I ask.

"Like how?" Jess doesn't look up from her book.

"I don't know … off."

"Everyone has their days," Felicia says. "Maybe he's having one."

I nod and finish getting ready, ignoring the feeling digging its way under my skin.

At least, I try.

A few times during my first lecture, I fully check out while trying to figure out what changed between the texts last night and when he walked in this morning. Bad night's sleep? Family drama? Lost his favorite guitar pick?

Unable to invent a reason, I decide to test the Waters when class dismisses.

He waits on the sidewalk, his expression brightening when I walk straight toward him. "Need a ride, beautiful?"

Satisfied by his response, I deem his behavior from earlier a fluke and only slow down enough to snag the drink. "No, but thank you."

A little farther down the sidewalk, I check back, and he's still watching me.

***

With Jordan around, I never need to check the time. Amazingly accurate, he knocks fifteen minutes before my next class.

"Right on time, Jordan," I say, seeing him in the hall.

He stares at me, no attempt at a response. Now nothing about him seems right. His expression flat, his eyes dull. Even his hair looks the wrong level of disorderly. As if he's been repeatedly dragging his hands through it.

My eyebrows pull in, and I'm worried again. "This is where you say, 'Do you need a ride to class, beautiful?' Then I say, 'No, Jordan, I don't, but thank you.'"

He smiles—not his smug grin or the real one capable of making my heart race, but a familiar one that resembles my own, which I always follow with an, *I'm fine*, that means the opposite. Maybe I dismissed the way he acted earlier too soon.

"Are you okay?" I ask.

He doesn't answer right away, and I'm about to ask again when a switch flips. A spark returns along with his grin. "Of course I am. I just forgot my lines. Thanks for reminding me."

Relieved Jordan's back, I smile, and then I roll my eyes because, well, Jordan's back.

"Whatever," I tell him, shutting the door. "I'll see you later."

I gather up my stuff, and as I walk to my psych lecture, Cam texts that our biology lab later has been canceled. Sometimes, she exhibits a cruel sense of humor, so I check my email to verify. The woman texts the truth.

The promise of an afternoon of freedom makes the next hour-and-a-half drag on for eternity. My torture is prolonged by our professor running over. When she winds down, I jet out so fast that I barely pull on my coat.

I never get a moment to just breathe.

Once I step outside, my eyes complete their habitual scan but no Jordan. Not leaning against the building or a tree. Not standing on the sidewalk or grass. Not walking over from the parking lot. I question the accuracy of the clock in the lecture hall, but my phone confirms. Two-fifty. No missed texts or calls.

For a second, I think about calling him, but then the difference from every other day finally dawns on me. He never once indicated he would see me again, not a single, *See you later, beautiful.*

Holy shit, he gave up. He gave up, and rather than reveling in my victory of no longer being the sexual conquest of Jordan Waters, I'm awkwardly standing here like my prom date never showed up. Abandoned by a one-night stand that never even happened. A damn knot ties inside me, and I actually feel disappointed.

I consider waiting longer, seeing if he's just running late, but then I shake my head at myself and continue down the sidewalk. It was only a matter of time before he gave up or I gave it up and better him than me.

Still sorting out the twist in my gut, I pass a tall guy wearing a flannel winter coat with ash-blond hair in a bun. He holds a sign and watches the people walking by him. On my way by, his gaze stalls out on me. Then I read his sign—*Henders*.

Scratch everything since I walked out of the building, including the knot unraveling faster than it formed.

After I pause and take a better look, I recognize the eighth note tattoo on his neck and two piercings in his bottom lip. The singer from Jordan's band. His eyebrow arches while he ogles my chest through my open coat.

I bend down to meet his eyes. "Are you a Jordan surrogate?"

Caught checking me out, he smirks. "Oh shit. Sorry. Yeah, I'm Benji."

"Callie." I straighten up, his eyes following.

"Jordan had something come up. I'm here to give you a ride." He saunters over and tosses the sign in a trash bin by a bench.

"Thank you, but I can walk."

"Why?" he asks, genuinely confused.

"Because I have yet to accept a ride from Jordan."

"Cool." He gestures up and down his long torso. "I'm not Jordan."

He has me there.

"Look," he says, "the deal states, I haul my ass down here and give you a ride. I already moved my stuff., so my ride's this way." He strolls toward the parking lot like it's decided.

I'm sure more than a few of Connor's horror films start out in a similar fashion, but he must be harmless if Jordan trusts him enough to send him. Wait, that means I trust Jordan. Do I? To not send a serial killer to pick me up, yes.

Benji spins and walks backward, holding his arms out. "Let's go, Calico."

Screw it. I've accepted rides from much worse. So not thinking about *that* right now. Or ever again.

I sigh and follow him. Benji waits for me to catch up beside a silver Jeep with leather seats, probably worth my tuition. Far from what I pictured Benji driving.

"Nice vehicle," I say, crawling in.

His forehead creases as he turns the key. "You really haven't ridden with him, huh?"

I recognize the scent of the interior and huff out a laugh. "This is Jordan's car."

"It sure is." Benji whips out of the parking lot without asking for directions. Before I can give it much thought, he glances over, eyeing me. "You should give him a chance. He's a good guy."

I squint, not sure what to make of this dude yet. "He's doing all this to fuck me."

With a deep chuckle, he nods. "Smart girl. But you have to admit, the man has committed to his cause. All weekend, he stayed glued to his phone. Then last night, he turned down Brooke." He glances over when I don't answer and readjusts in his seat. "Brooke? You must not follow the music scene, so let me give you a description. She's stacked with a fantastic ass, and she does this thing while sucking—"

"I get the picture."

He smirks and shrugs a shoulder. "My point is, this started out one hundred percent to fuck you. But it's more than that now. I've known Jordan a few years, and he's a very in-the-moment guy. He considers ten minutes long-term status."

"And you're a trustworthy source? Don't you have some bandmates' blood oath or something to uphold?"

"Absolutely. All types of woo shit like that. But I'm telling you, he's about five seconds away from admitting this thing between the two of you is a hell of a lot more than he bargained for. He's just not quite there yet." He nods, agreeing with himself as he speeds around a corner.

My stomach sinks—and not from the erratic driving. Jordan developing real feelings seems worse than him winning the game. As long as I drive halfway across the state every weekend and suffer through my parents acting less responsible than their six-year-old, I have neither the time nor patience for anything else—for anyone else.

"So, why have you put up with him for this long?" Benji asks. He tugs on one of his lip rings. "You just yanking his dick or what?"

I take a deep breath and let it out slowly. "Honestly, I thought he'd get bored and give up."

The corner of his mouth hitches up. "You like him, too."

I let my head fall on the headrest and spit out my standard answer, "I can't handle a relationship right now."

Benji brakes hard in front of my building, both of us moving forward with the momentum. He throws the Jeep in park and twists in the seat to face me. "And Jordan barely understands the concept. Yet the two of you have essentially been in a super-intense relationship without any of the good parts for a week now."

I laugh at the truth. Jordan has been my clingy boyfriend and me the bitchy girlfriend who refuses to put out.

"You're pretty insightful," I tell him.

He plays with an air vent. "I just cut through the bullshit. It makes life a hell of a lot simpler."

"Do you really think he wants more," I ask, "or are you his last-ditch effort to manipulate me?"

"Would I lie to you, man?" His mouth hooks up, but his gray eyes stay gentle. "Let me answer that for you. No, I would not."

Why I trust him within a few minutes, I'm not sure. Everyone else in my life jumps through hoops for a long time, sometimes never breaking through. But something with Benji feels different. Maybe it's the fact that he hasn't let his gaze lower from my face since finding out who I am. Or I *want* to believe him.

"Thanks for the ride, Benji," I say, climbing out.

I'm about halfway to the building when he calls after me, "Hey, Calico." I turn around, and he ducks to see me through the rolled-down passenger window. "If you cut the bullshit, I have a feeling we'll be seeing each other soon."

I smile as he drives away, convinced I might have just met one of my favorite people.

When I get upstairs, I crash onto my bed, facedown and not sure what to think anymore. I've always envisioned the situation with Jordan ending one of two ways. Either he nailed and bailed, or he simply bailed. Not once have I considered other options. Especially not any that involve him sticking around for an extended period of time. But when I stop to think about it, over the course of a week, he's cemented himself as one of the most reliable people in my life. A low bar, but still, everything feels a little more tolerable with him around and, as much as I hate to admit it, less complicated.

Damn it.

I roll onto my back, realizing Mission Win Callie Over is a success. An annoying but undeniable success. What makes it worse is, not only do I want Jordan Waters, but I also think I want to be *with* him. A guaranteed disaster, considering I've never even seen a functional relationship, much less been in one. Pete, maybe, but we were just kids, and I tossed him aside without a second thought. All for a dimple attached to an arrogant asshole who brought with him dysfunction equaling Graham and Lara levels.

Despite all of that, Benji's comment about cutting the bullshit cycles through my head, and then slowly I start to give in to the idea.

Three days.

In three days, I leave for the weekend. It gives me more than enough time to stop challenging Jordan's every move and see what the hell happens. If Benji's wrong and Jordan still only wants to fuck me, I'll walk away on Friday. Cleanse him from my life. If Benji's right and Jordan wants more, I'll at least have some indication of what a relationship with him would be like. So long as it avoids a path of complete chaos and ruin, we're golden.

I reach over the side of the bed and dig my phone out of my bag to text him.

I like Benji.

Noncommittal in case I change my mind about the whole thing. Which happens right after hitting send, but then he responds, and my lips turn up.

Jordan: *He check out your rack?*

Immediately.

He sends, *Sorry.*

He drives your Jeep like a madman.

You rode with him?

I text back, *Why wouldn't I?*

He responds as I'm hauling my books out to the common room, and I bite back a smile, setting up to study. Sure, I could enjoy an entire afternoon of lounging around, but not needing to worry about school over the weekend wins out.

As I settle in on the couch, I check the message.

Challenging woman.

I laugh, his frustration evident even through a text.

You like a challenge, remember?

So I can focus on reading, my phone goes between the couch cushions. A chapter later, though, I reach down to fish it out. Before I grab it, someone knocks. Someone almost always being Jordan. My book lands on the table with the rest.

When I answer, relief hits me first. Everything not right about him from earlier has corrected. The sexy smirk, eyes, hair—all has returned to his former self. My pulse kicks, like I've finally given my body permission to react to him, and then I have to lockdown a flurry of nerves because we're not doing that. I'll admit I like the guy, but I refuse to start acting like a tween with a crush.

"Hey," I say, heading for the couch. "My other class for the day was canceled."

Jordan stays in the doorway, unmoved by the time I sit down. His brow lowers, and I can practically see the calculations going through his head. I remind myself to flip the script on him more often. His hesitation only lasts another second, then he strides in, cocky as ever, and shuts the door behind him.

"Good," he says on his way over to me. "You have plenty of time to explain yourself. I bust my ass for you, and Benji reaps the rewards? The world is cruel enough without you adding to it."

He drops down next to me, and I shrug.

"He had a compelling argument."

"What was that?"

"He wasn't you."

"Ouch," he says. "You're breaking my heart, beautiful."

There's that freaking flip. I pile up my books and relax beside him. "So, where were you?"

A half-smile appears, his head shaking a little. "My brother was in town, so we met up for coffee."

"Older brother?" I guess based on a younger-sibling vibe.

"By three years." He glances down between us, his eyes coming right back to mine. "He's in law school at UPenn."

"That's the same age difference as Connor and me."

"Dustin's a complete asshole."

"You two get along then?" I punctuate with a dry smile.

He chuckles and rubs at the stubble on his jaw. "Most of the time, yeah. What about you and Connor?"

I almost spit out a generic yeah, but Benji's bullshit policy pops into my head, so I answer honestly. "He's one of the best parts of my life."

Jordan nods, and a finger starts to tap on his leg. I wonder if he's always so fidgety, and I've never noticed.

"Do you have class this afternoon?" I ask.

His finger stops. "No. Tuesdays, I have a class at ten and one right after lunch."

I drag my leg up on the couch between us, re-situating to face him. "A class at ten?" My knee ends up resting on his leg, but I'm too distracted by what he just said. "If you have a class at ten, why were you at my door earlier, offering to take me to my ten-fifteen class?"

He scrunches up his face. "I mean—"

"Pull up your schedule right now," I tell him, having all the answer I need. Unbelievable. The guy would have missed class if I agreed. Not something I need on my conscience.

His lips twitch as he obliges. He hands me his phone, and I scroll through. At least one of my classes conflicts with his every day, most of his others starting or ending within a few minutes of mine. Then I reach Friday, and my mouth falls open. Our entire day overlaps. One of my classes doesn't even begin until midway through his two-and-a-half-hour philosophy lecture.

"You're not doing this anymore." I rip out a piece of notebook paper and create a schedule. Even if this only lasts a few more days, I'm not letting it screw with his education. I huff and force the paper into his hand. "These are the only times you can *help* from now on."

He makes a face while reading and swipes the pen from my hand. Using my leg as a table, he starts to make changes. Each time he readjusts the paper, his fingers graze over my inner thigh. He rearranges the paper *a lot*, each brush a little higher and seeming to have a direct connection to my clit.

One last, slow drag over my jeans, and he folds up the schedule and gives it back. Stubborn, he's written every class in again, only agreeing to one Thursday morning and his philosophy lecture on Friday, which he marked *Maybe*.

Fine, Waters. Two can play this game.

I lean over and cross out anything with the remote possibility of making him late or requiring him to leave a single minute early. I push back my hair when it falls, and already knowing he won't agree, I hand him the paper.

He no more than glances before he huffs a laugh and tears it up. "Nope. I reject your proposition and end our mediation."

To further his point, he throws the shreds in the air. I try to stay serious despite the paper raining down around us.

"You realize you're picking up all this, right?"

"Yes, ma'am."

He gathers them up from the cushions and reaches for my shoulder, plucking off a piece. Watching him add it to the rest of the paper shoved into his hand, I lose out to the smile and look up at him. Something changes in his eyes, the intensity still there but different. Softer and less challenging maybe. I can't tell exactly, but the way he's looking at me needs to never stop.

"Can I ask you something?" The words more or less tumble out, and Jordan nods, drawing his hand back.

"Go for it."

I hesitate before diving in headfirst. "Are you still doing all this just to prove you can sleep with me?"

We always dance around what we both already know, and no better way to cut the bullshit than just saying it out loud. I expect a joke or for him to say we can add in sex if I want it so badly, but Jordan's jaw clenches, his eyes serious while they stay locked with mine.

"Unknown," he rasps.

In a drastic role reversal from seven days ago, *I* want to see *him* certain. More than I thought I would, which scares the hell out of me.

I swallow and force a deep breath before repeating Benji's words, "Five seconds." Glancing away, I refocus on my goal of not dragging books around this weekend and reach for one. "I really should study."

All the wrong returns to his face as he gets up. "I'll stop distracting you."

Oh no. We're not going backward.

He starts to sulk away, and the thought of reversing direction now twists inside me, so I grab the pen and chuck it across the room. It nails him in the back and lands on the floor by his shoe. He turns around to see what hit him and then looks up at me.

"You forgot something."

I point to my forehead, causing the corners of his mouth to perk up. He stoops down for the pen and comes back to the couch. His knee hits the cushion before he leans down and when his gaze dips to my mouth, my chest rises faster. I won't stand a chance if he kisses me, but he tucks my hair back and kisses my forehead, the warmth of his lips on my skin hard for me to breathe through this time.

Jordan hovers an inch in front of me. "See you later, beautiful."

The exact response I wanted—needed.

I slide the pen from his grasp. "See you later."

He backs toward the door, and once he disappears through it, I let out a pent-up sigh. I smile, and I don't stop for far too long, bordering on giddy. It's incredibly embarrassing. I mean, what's next? Hearts drawn in my notebook?

Absolutely not Henders.

Abso-fucking-lutely not.

The cushion vibrates under my ass, and I dig around for my phone.

Felicia: *Want to go out Friday night?*

I can't. I'm going home.

But it's Valentine's Day.

Shit. I check the date before I groan, remembering the deadline I put on the me and Jordan thing.

Valentine's Day.

How inconveniently poetic.

161 Days Until 19

"Good morning, beautiful." Jordan knocks on his way into my room.

I grab my bag off the bed and stop in front of him, sliding the coffee from his grip. Before he says another word, I ask, "Want to give me a ride to class?"

His head jerks back, his eyebrows pull in, and I take a sip to keep from laughing. I enjoy messing with him far too much.

It takes a second for his usual level of confidence to resurface.

"More than anything," he says.

As we walk through the common area together, a choking sound draws my attention to Jess on the couch. She nearly spits out the "coffee" she's drinking, the sight of us leaving together as shocking to her as me asking for a ride was to Jordan. I wink, just to screw with her, too.

She shakes her head and mouths, *Legend.*

By the time I shut the door of his Jeep, my phone starts vibrating. It continues for the duration of the drive, but I already know what waits for me. A group message from everyone who feels invested in the will-they-won't-they saga of Callie Henders and Jordan Waters. Maybe I should check *their* notebooks for heart doodles.

"You're popular this morning," Jordan says, breaking a comfortable silence.

I shrug, putting my phone away. "I'm popular every morning. You just leave before the other suitors arrive."

He glances at me out of the corner of his eye while turning into the parking lot. "Names and class schedules, and I'll take care of them all."

I smile, climbing out. "Thanks for the ride."

"I'll see you after class, beautiful." Then he adds, "Don't accept any rides from the others until I get here."

On my way into the lecture hall, I check my phone. Sixteen messages pop up. I find a seat and scroll through them, most from a freaked-out Jess. Neither Felicia nor Cam believe her, both demanding I confirm or deny her story. Rather than doing either, I return the phone to my bag.

Even if the whole thing wasn't in a trial period with nothing guaranteed past the next few days, I wouldn't respond. Whatever happens from this point on is none of their damn business.

———

After my afternoon class, I'm lying on the couch and attempting to finish a novel for lit. But the constant tapping has me reading the same sentence for the third time in a row. The book drops to my chest.

"Pen," I demand.

From the floor in front of me, Jordan reaches back with the pen he's been pounding on his textbook, not even looking up. "Sorry, I thought tapping would be less distracting than pacing."

Our fingers brush as I take it away, and the contact of his skin on mine manages to make all his irritating study habits more tolerable. Which happens to be every single one imaginable. Pen-tapping, pacing, reading and thinking out loud. I could pass a pop quiz on metaphysics, thanks to his ten-minute rant while walking in circles around the couch.

Since he insists on maintaining his outrageous schedule, I'm trying to at least minimize the issues. When he drove me back from my last class, I told him to stay until his next one. Otherwise, he would have driven back and forth across campus multiple times in an hour. Benji's at least right about one thing; the guy has committed to his cause.

It only takes a few minutes for his index finger to take up a rhythm on the page he's reading.

My book falls again. "Jordan."

He offers up his hand over his shoulder. "Better take it. It's the only way to stop me."

I smile, and he glances over his shoulder. He snaps his book shut and twists to lean on the couch.

"Now *you're* distracting *me*," he says.

I lose interest in the story in my book, preferring to experience the one playing out in real time. His emerald eyes trace over my face, never stopping anywhere long.

"What are you thinking?" I ask.

He squints, contemplating. "Would you like the smooth answer or the real one?"

"Both," I tell him. "Smooth answer first."

"Very well." He pauses before saying, "You are the most beautiful creature in existence."

My eyes start to roll but stop. I opened myself up for a cheesy pick-up line and need to deal with the consequences. "What's the real one?"

His smirk appears. "You are the most beautiful creature in existence."

I laugh, and he smiles his damn smile. Nothing about this seems complicated. I'm starting to see exactly how he could fit in my life, a much-needed distraction from all the rest.

"Come out with us Friday night." He sweeps his knuckles over my cheek, his intense gaze on mine. "It's my birthday, and the guys are taking me somewhere."

Once all the parts come together, the calm inside me fucking disintegrates. "Your birthday is on Friday? On Valentine's Day?"

His face scrunches up. "Does that make asking you weird?"

Yes. No. I don't know. Valentine's Day, his birthday, and the last chance for this to be anything? A lot of conflicting activities for one day. Well, one half-day, considering I need to leave campus no later than three o'clock.

"I have to leave after my last class to go home. Otherwise, I would. I'm sorry."

His hand stops moving. "You're…" He swallows. "You're leaving Friday afternoon?"

I nod, which evidently triggers a countdown to the end of the world. Panic washes over his face before his head drops forward on the cushion beside me. He lifts it a second later and presses his palms to his forehead, muttering something inaudible. The dramatic reaction confuses me, but it's Jordan, so I also find it sort of entertaining. So my standard response to him.

He's mid-groan when his phone's alarm goes off. He shuts it off and pushes off the floor before staring down at me.

"What are you doing to me, beautiful?" he says, like he wants me to give him the answer, but I can't.

Because I wonder the same thing about him.

He leans down and kisses me like always. "I'll see you later."

Still not sure why he freaked out, I watch him walk out. As soon as he leaves, I curse. I grab my phone before I can overthink.

For the first time in a long time, I voluntarily text Graham.

Something came up. Be there Saturday morning.

I stare at the screen for a long time after I hit send, my throat tight and thumbnail between my teeth. And the longer I wait for his response, the more I worry what it will say when I finally get one.

Jordan wants to drive me to my late study group, but I convince him to go to his band's practice. He promises to be at the dorms when I'm finished, and sure enough, his Jeep is sitting in the parking lot.

I hate how much I like it.

When I walk into my suite, I stop at the sight of him and Felicia on the couch. She's bawling as his face warps in disgust at the TV. He wraps his arms around her and pulls her against him.

Before I can ask what the hell is going on, Jordan says, "Documentary about chicken farms. Worst. Thing. Ever." His eyes stay glued to the screen until he winces, and he looks up at me. "Do you know how they make chicken nuggets?"

Felicia wails out a sob with her face buried in his shirt.

Oh good Lord, not another documentary. She won't sleep for a week.

I race over and push the off button to end their self-inflicted torture. "Why would you keep watching it?"

"Uh," he says, "to learn how the world works, Callie. Duh."

My eyes roll, and his attention diverts to Felicia, pulling away from him. He hands her another tissue, and I shake my head, leaving the pair on the couch to comfort one another.

I climb on my bed and lean back against the wall, checking my phone for the hundredth time. Still nothing from Graham. The rare times I've needed to text him, he's always answered right away. My chest tightens even more, and I start to regret ever sending the message. Silence from him never leads to anything remotely good.

Jordan knocks on his way in, at home a mere twenty-four hours after I've stopped resisting him. Actually, he made himself at home the first night.

"I sent the mess to bed. She cannot handle the harsh realities of our world." He spreads out on my bed and settles his head in my lap. "Do you want me to describe the particulars? The images are etched into my mind for eternity."

"No, I'm good, thanks," I say, distracted while I answer a text from Connor.

"Thank God. Now, soothe me. I'm very upset." He drags my hand from my side to the top of his head.

I start running my fingers through his hair without thinking, but then he relaxes, and I glance down. His eyes are closed, and I watch him, pushing my hand through the dark strands. It's another one of those moments where I almost forget the reason he's here. Except the almost is closing in on entirely.

A massive drawback to my poorly thought-out plan surfaces. I've let my guard down with him. Without knowing how it plays out, I've given Jordan everything he needs to hurt me, whether he realizes it or not. Come Friday, he might end up doing just that.

Ugh. This is Graham's fault. If he had replied, I wouldn't be all doom and gloom. Instead, he's ruined my day without being present, more than likely his intentions all along when he decided not to answer me. He always finds a way to get to me, no matter how long it takes or what methods he needs to resort to.

"You stopped," Jordan says.

Caught up with everything that's supposed to be hours away, I didn't even notice my hand stalling out. I reenter the land of the here and now where a smoldering gaze is staring up at me.

The tension in my muscles eases again, and I smile. "I'm not sitting here all night, stroking your hair."

His mouth hooks up. "Not a problem." He rolls out of bed and onto his feet. "Lie down."

"What? Jordan, I'm not—"

He wraps his hands around my ankles and drags me down the mattress, causing me to squeal.

"Okay," I laugh out. He lets go, and I narrow my eyes at him, moving the rest of the way before he decides to help again.

I lie on my side, and his teeth drag over his bottom lip as he crawls in with me. He shifts his body against mine while he settles in, all the hot skin and hard muscles beneath his shirt a tease. A few inches separate us when he brings his arm up, resting his head on his bicep. Then he sets my hand on the back of his neck.

"See," he rasps, "easy solution."

I resume trailing my fingers through his hair, and Jordan's jaw tightens. He grips my hip and locks me in his intense gaze until my head swims, and then he edges closer, brushing his nose against mine. By the time his eyes lower to my mouth, I no longer care why he's here. I just want him to kiss me. Fuck me. Stay.

Both of us are breathing faster when he looks up. He eases his hand to my cheek like he expects me to stop him, but I don't. I'm almost to a point where I *need* to feel his lips on mine. But then he presses a kiss to my forehead, those lips lingering.

"Goodnight, beautiful," he says against my skin.

He moves his palm to my waist, his eyes already closed when he shifts, head back on his arm.

The way he just stopped catches me off guard, and I stare at his closed lids, black lashes fanning. Jordan Waters from a week ago wouldn't have hesitated. We would be all skin and tongues and moans. In all honesty though, this is the Jordan I want. The one who's five seconds away, maybe even less.

As I lie there, listening to his breathing even out, my mind wanders back to Graham. The resentment creeps through me, spreading the way it always does, poisoning my insides. Each second, it drags me further back to a time I couldn't feel anything else.

I lean over Jordan to shut off the lamp. He's still asleep when he wraps his arms around me. He holds me tight against him, and I relax. All the thoughts threatening me go in a box, which retreats to a dark corner of my mind where none of it reaches me anymore.

I fall asleep with him protecting me.

Whether he knows it or not.

160 Days Until 19

I wake up alone and force myself out of bed.

My shower consists of me trying to stop thoughts of Graham from seeping through my subconscious. Even pulling on my shirt and jeans brings on anxiety about packing to leave tomorrow. The frustrations grow, and the world in which I'm supposed to feel the freest from him feels smaller and more constricting than ever. For once, I want to decide where I spend my weekend. Just. Once.

When I come out of my room, Felicia looks up from where she's painting her toenails on the couch.

"Jordan said the band's going out for his birthday. Did you change your mind about going?"

I shake my head, lowering down next to her. "I leave after my last class."

Cam waltzes in, and her bag drops by the door. "Honeys, I'm home." She leaps over Felicia's legs and lands on the couch on the other side of her.

"Will you be upset if I go?" Felicia asks.

"No, please go celebrate your BFF's birthday."

She sticks her tongue out.

The door opens, Jordan letting himself in. What time he left, I'm not sure, but he looks tired, carrying three coffees rather than one. He smiles on his way over, and I feel a little better. A little more here.

He raises his eyebrows, examining the three of us on the couch. "Good morning, Angels."

Felicia giggles, giving him the response he wants. "Good morning, Charlie."

"Technically," Cam says, "in a *Charlie's Angels* scenario, he'd be Bosley since he's delivering coffee."

He glares at her and squeezes in between me and the arm of the couch. "Guess who's not getting a coffee."

I take the carrier from him, and before he can object, I pass two cups down for Felicia and Cam, keeping the last one for myself. "You?"

His expression softens as he secures an arm around me. "Whatever you say, beautiful."

Flutters, chills—his look delivers them all, and I'm past even trying to deny it.

"Don't you have class this morning?" I say, already knowing the answer.

He grins his cocky grin. "Sure do. But I also have to drive you. Priorities, Callie. You'll understand when you're older."

I narrow my eyes at him. "You can drop me off a few minutes early and make it to your class on time. Compromise, Jordan. Something you should have learned about when you were younger."

He stares at me a few seconds before he steals my cup. "I have a sneaking suspicion you aren't the most familiar with the word either."

I suppose he's right on that one.

On the drive to the dorms from my afternoon class, Jordan turns up the volume on a Nirvana song. All the music he plays when I'm with him matches what I rattled off on the porch the night of the party, even the two-thousands pop. Knowing him, it's not a coincidence.

"May I?" I eye his phone in the cupholder, wanting to snoop through his music.

He nods, not worried about me seeing anything I shouldn't, so I snatch it up. A smile spreads across his face, and I understand why as soon as I read the name of the playlist—*Impress Callie*.

I shake my head, setting it down. "Do you put this much effort into everything you do?"

He stifles a laugh. "Not in the slightest."

"Then why all the effort with me?" I ask, still on the minimal bullshit regime prescribed by Benji. I haven't decided if he's become an angel or devil on my shoulder, but the dude is there.

"Because you, Callie Henders, are my muse."

I sigh at his Jordan-esque reply. "That's the smooth answer. What's the real one?"

A finger taps the wheel, and he shifts in his seat. "I don't have one. Not a solid one anyway. I could make up some bullshit filled with half-truths, but you deserve better."

A better answer but not quite there.

He turns into the dorm parking lot. "I have band practice tonight, but can I come by later?"

Possibly the last night I'll spend with him, depending on what transpires over the next twenty-four hours, so of course, I'll say yes. "Not if you make me stroke your hair."

"Pssh. You loved running your fingers through my luscious locks."

I wrinkle my nose at him even though I can't disagree.

As he pulls up to the building, I relax against the headrest. He shifts into park and gestures for me to come closer. I lean over the center console, and he comes the rest of the way. His gaze touches my lips before he kisses my cheek.

"I'll see you later, beautiful," he says.

All melty on the inside, I pull back. But every bit of good in the moment vanishes when I face forward to get out. My eyes lock straight ahead, and I can't move. Paralyzed as time stops. Everything floats, suspended in the space around me, and nothing feels right or real anymore because my world, this world where I'm supposed to be, doesn't have a blue truck with a rust spot above the rear bumper on the passenger side. Yet I'm staring at one, parked at the curb thirty feet ahead of me. Every muscle in my body tenses, the pulse throbbing in my face. That's the outline of the back of his head in the cab. The cab of the truck that isn't supposed to be at my school.

The voice saying my name warbles, underwater and far away, until warmth touches my cheek. "…where'd you go, beautiful?"

I force myself to look at Jordan.

"Are you okay?' he asks.

I search his face, wishing for the calm to envelop me like last night. When it doesn't, the practiced smile plasters on my face as easy as ever. "Yeah, I'm fine." I can almost convince myself at this point. "I'll see you later," I tell him.

Another part of me takes over from there. I climb out, shut the door, and slowly move toward the building, my head down. Only after Jordan drives away do I turn around and wait, unable to escape what comes next.

The driver door slams, startling me. Graham rounds the bed of the truck. He's wearing his work jeans with a white tank top visible underneath his unbuttoned uniform shirt.

My eyes flash over his face. Once upon a time, my friend Shayna told me she understood how his face distracted people from him being a complete piece of shit. But all I see is fucking red, his features not even registering anymore. I settle my gaze on a button on his shirt, keeping my face expressionless.

"Where the hell have you been?" His gruff voice is louder than necessary, given how close we are.

"I just got out of class."

"Who's the guy? Is that what you do up here?"

"No," I say, hearing the annoyance in my tone. "He's just a guy who gives me rides sometimes."

"Oh, I'm sure he does."

I cringe at his insinuation, but I left myself wide open for it. "What are you doing here?"

A finger points in my face, and I tense even more.

"You *will* be at my house tomorrow at six pm," he says. "Don't fucking test me on this."

"You could have texted or called. You didn't need to drive up here to threaten me."

"And have you say you didn't get them? No fucking way. We're not doing that dance again." He checks the area surrounding us, and I also glance around, hoping no one is witnessing this. "It's not a threat either," he adds. "So, you coming home tomorrow? Or am I taking you with me right now?"

When I don't answer right away, he stomps a step toward me. I withdraw one. He's never hit me, but I would never trust him not to cross the line. I meet his steely stare before casting mine to the ground, unable to look at him longer than a few seconds.

"I'll be there tomorrow," I whisper.

"In the door by six, Callista."

My jaw sets, and all my energy pours into staring at a crack in the sidewalk and steadying my breath. Only a handful of people still call me by my full name, and I hate most of them.

His worn brown boots retreat, and again, the door slams. The truck roars to life, tires squealing as he tears out of the parking lot. I look up and watch the truck disappear down the road. He's gone. Too bad every negative aspect of him has already consumed me.

An abstract box won't do shit to stop it this time.

Felicia and Jess are on the couch when I storm through to my room. My bag lands on the floor along with my coat. I step onto the chair and then onto the desk, my head just meeting the white drop-down ceiling tiles. I shift over the second one from the corner and slap around above me until I hit the plastic bag—my stash of shooters. With two in my hand, I slide the tile back and jump down.

I empty a bottle of vodka and another of spiced rum, one after the other. The warmth spreads but accomplishes little in soothing my nerves. As the walls close in, my eyes dart to the calendar, the day's date not yet crossed out. I dig out a permanent marker, a pen not worthy of my mood. I don't stop until the entire square is blacked out. One hundred sixty days left of him. Of not being in control of my life.

The marker slams against the wall, and I sit back on my heels. The gas filling my lungs feels too heavy for real air. Each breath transfers more weight into my chest, pulling me down. Further and further. I'll suffocate without relief. An escape. I can only think of one place I might be able to breathe again.

The first time an officer pulled me over because Graham had falsely reported my car stolen, I laughed. The second time annoyed me. Then came the canceled health insurance. Lies about Cate being in the emergency room. Withheld mail.

All futile attempts to regain control of me after I turned eighteen and refused to see him. I was no longer the slave of a custody agreement, and he couldn't do a damn thing to change my mind about cutting all ties. I could finally erase him.

Or so I thought.

Since Lara never planned on giving me any of the money, she never mentioned the stipulation in their divorce agreement requiring Graham to pay child support until we turn nineteen. Her lawyer intended for the extra money to help during our first year in college or out on our own, but my mother just heard *more money longer*.

So, when nothing else worked to get me to go see him, Graham twisted it into a manipulation tactic. He told me that unless I adhere to the visitation schedule with him for another year, he'll stop writing his monthly check for all his children. At first, I ignored him as usual, not believing the threat, until Lara threw a fit over her missing money. She wouldn't buy groceries and told Connor and Cate she couldn't afford them because of me being selfish.

As always, the only ones suffering were the three of us. I had already endured six thousand five hundred seventy-four days of misery. What was another three hundred sixty-five?

The answer: hell. A year in this strange limbo between the life I want and the one I want to leave behind is absolute hell. And at the moment, I'm doing a shitty job of balancing them.

I bail on my standing date with Felicia and Jess for movie night, not much for company right now. Instead, I reconstruct the blanket fort from my bedroom at home. Even with everything from my and Cam's beds, it could use a few more pillows but will do for the night. It's warm and safe, and most importantly, I can breathe a little.

A movie plays on my phone, something light and unimposing. Mostly, my mind drifts in and out, barely paying attention to the couple on the screen. One realizes their love for the other a few minutes too late, leading them to rush out the door and across New York City, attempting to win the other back.

The blankets muffle a knock on my bedroom door, and then light travels across the fabric. It grows more localized as someone approaches. Someone almost always being Jordan.

After hitting pause, I crawl to the opening and stick my head out, glancing up at him long enough to tell him, "Shoes off."

Rule two of being under the blankets.

I return to my spot, back against the side of my bed. Jordan's head pops through, and he scans on his way in. Seeing my highly honed skills in architecture, he can't possibly resist me, and if that doesn't do the trick, my ratty shorts and tank top certainly will.

He doesn't say anything, just settles in beside me. I resume the movie, not ready for an actual conversation anyway. It only has a few minutes left, their grand romantic kiss bringing on the credits. I shut it off, my focus still split. Part of me is three hours away under a different set of blankets, and part is here with him, where I want to be.

"May I ask why we're hiding under a pile of blankets?" he says quietly, almost like he's not sure if he should.

"Nothing bad can happen under the blankets."

The first and most important rule.

I sigh, laying my head on his shoulder. His cheek presses into my hair. Then my screen shuts off, leaving us in the dark together, and I close my eyes.

He sits with me in silence until I say, "I'm in a very bad mood."

"Does Very Bad Mood Callie like to talk?" he asks, moving when I lift my head from his shoulder.

"No." I switch my phone to flashlight mode and light our small hideout in a warm glow. As I prop it in the corner, I can already feel his calming magic working wonders on me. "She also doesn't like to be around anyone."

At least I haven't before, but Jordan Waters seems to be an exception to everything lately. He must consider himself exempt as well since he empties the contents from the pockets of his sweatpants. His stuff goes next to my phone.

"My presence is nonnegotiable." He stretches out, filling most of the space with his body.

The look of a challenge enters his eye, but he won't get one from me. I slide his arm over and make room to lie down next to him. Just like last night, his arm wraps around me, pulling me closer. My head rests on his shoulder, and I watch my hand on his chest rise and fall as he breathes. Even breaths that mine sync with, bringing back the real air.

Weightless.

"Do you like your parents?" I don't know why I ask. Right now, I just want … something.

A deep breath presses against my palm. "I think I like them as people, but not as parents."

My brow draws in. "Can you elaborate?"

He runs a hand over my hair. "I come from a family of firstborns. Simply by being the second child I began a lifetime of disappointing my parents. My brother either does everything first or someone else does better. Win a science fair? Dustin already won two. Graduate second in my class? Elsa Parker's kid was valedictorian. I accepted it as a losing battle not worth fighting a long time ago."

"A perfect GPA isn't you trying to prove something to them?" I ask.

"Nah, that's a compulsive need to outshine Dustin at every turn. Our parents think he can do no wrong, so it's my job to keep his ass grounded."

Impossible-to-please parents and a competitive streak with a sibling. No wonder he takes challenges so seriously.

"How do you know about my GPA?" he asks.

Oh, great. Now I sound like a stalker.

"Have you met Felicia?" I say, no issues sending the credit to her. "That girl knows everything about everyone."

Well, not quite everyone. Over the summer, while getting ready to leave everything behind, I deleted my social media accounts. She couldn't just click a button to learn every little detail about me. It took months of evading questions before she stopped digging for info on my life away from school.

"Does she keep a file on me?"

I shrug, not putting it past her. "It's entirely possible. She spent the entire day of that party trying to tell me every detail she could dig up about you."

This piques his interest. "What all did she tell you?"

That we'd be perfect together.

"Not nearly as much as she wanted to. Your major, age, but she didn't know your future plans."

"Hmm, well, unless I can convince my parents to let me do anything else with my life, I'll be attending law school after graduation. Another battle I've probably already lost."

We make quite the pair. One defeated by the future and one by the past. It sounds like the start of a tagline to a superhero movie.

His fingers skim their way up my arm, a chill chasing them the entire way. I cuddle closer, and in the process, my palm slides lower, over the washboard abs beneath his shirt. They tense, and Jordan swallows, his voice turning gravelly.

"So, now you know about my overly competitive rivalry with my douchebag brother and my status as constant disappointment to my parents. What about you? Do you like your parents?"

I tense more than his abs at the question.

"No." Unlike him, I reply without consideration, knowing the answer since before I could ride a bike. Probably even earlier if I really think about it, but I won't. Searching for the first moment I realized Lara and Graham were terrible people isn't a rabbit hole of memories I'll willingly dive down.

Jordan strokes my hair. "Who was your first childhood crush?"

Grateful for the redirect, I try to relax again and focus on him. "Pete Daniels in preschool. You?"

"Maggie Larsen, our babysitter. What about your first kiss?"

"Pete Daniels." I raise my head to gauge his reaction. "Just to save time, he was also my first date and first boyfriend." A couple of other things, too, but we're not going there.

He shakes his head. "Pete needs to die."

Tinge of jealousy noted, I ask him the same.

"Maggie Larsen," he says, not missing a beat.

I smile. "Really?"

"No, Callie." He shoves my head down. "She was fifteen, and I was five. Shockingly she wasn't into me."

I laugh, pressing my cheek to his chest. "A real ladies' man would have sealed that deal."

Jordan scruffs up my hair.

We keep asking questions back and forth. His heartbeat and the rumble of his voice under my ear are so fucking grounding, and not once does he tread near all the things I desperately want to avoid.

For a while, nothing outside of the blankets matters. Nothing else even exists. Just him and me, and I realize how much I like it. How much I like him and his innate ability to make me forget all the heaviness and just be.

It's easy, and I need a little easy right now.

Far too soon, his phone vibrates over and over, probably with birthday messages, which means we're approaching midnight. He shuts it off and tosses it in the corner, but the spell's broken. Everything on the other side of the fabric has infiltrated our tiny space, including the possible reason he's even here with me.

Doubt sinks back in, and I sit up. "You can't possibly want to start your twenty-first year on the planet in a blanket fort with a bitchy girl who won't put out."

Jordan stares up at me. "You're right." He lazily lifts his hand, dragging his thumb over my lower lip. "My birthday wish included a bitchy girl who *will* put out. Do you think Jess knows how to build a decent fort?"

Playing along, I shrug. "You could go ask. If not, you two can use this one."

He makes a face. "Celibacy sounds preferable." Then he tips his head. "Now come back down here."

I lie down on my side, and he slips his arm under me. He turns his head to look at me, my cheek resting on his hard bicep. His eyes trace my features while mine search for the answer to the question hovering around us.

"Is this still just to screw me?"

Jordan rolls over, studying me right back while sweeping his thumb over my jaw. "Ask me on Saturday," he says.

Not sure what that has to do with anything, I whisper, "I won't be here on Saturday," distracted when his heated gaze drops to my lips.

My breath hitches when he leans in, hand running down the side of my neck. The air between us warms and turns fuzzy. He slowly kisses my forehead, his mouth trailing to my cheek for another, and then one more on the tip of my nose. Then he takes a deep breath, his breath hot on my skin when he exhales.

"Just do as you're told, you maddening woman."

Less than an inch separates us, the small space even smaller the longer we stay this close. All it takes is one of us, one move, one moment, and this will all be over. Except I still have no idea what "over" means.

Needing distance before I lose my mind, I flop onto my back and let out a frustrated groan. "This is the longest five seconds in the history of the world."

"Five seconds?" His eyebrows shoot up. "Why do you and Benji both keep mentioning five seconds?"

Damn it, Benji.

In need of a diversion, I fish around over my head until I find my phone. "Less than a minute to midnight. Should we start a countdown?"

He snags away my phone, not falling for it. "Yeah, let's start one at five seconds. Until then, you can explain the relevance."

I quickly sort through responses, but he's already provided me with the perfect one.

"Ask me on Saturday."
His words out of my mouth make him smile that damn smile.
Tomorrow might end up hurting like hell.

159 Days Until 19

"Isn't it customary for the person who doesn't live here to sneak out in the morning?" Felicia asks.

I shut the door to my room, trying not to wake the sleeping Jordan inside. "I'm going for coffee. Not making a run for it."

She gives me a soft smile, relieved to see my mood improved. "Bring me a latte?"

"This I can do," I say on my way out.

The kid behind the counter at Java Quest only needs me to repeat the order twice before he shuffles off. Upon his return, he pushes the carrier toward me.

"You remembered the extra shots?" I ask.

He slides the drinks back and starts over. I wonder if this is what Jordan deals with every day. Finally, he gets the not-so-complicated order right. I wait until I park at the dorms to drink one coffee down far enough to dump in a shooter of whiskey I brought from my stash. I taste-test it before replacing the lid. A little early, but hey, it's his twenty-first birthday.

A knock on my passenger window scares the shit out of me. I shove the bottle in my pocket before glancing over. My panic ceases when I see Benji grinning. Fuck. He needs to not sneak up on minors with an open container in their running vehicle on campus.

"Calico," he says as I climb out. "Just the woman I want to see. I need you to evict your guest."

"Unless you have other plans for him this morning." Rusty appears out of nowhere, giving an up-down with his eyebrows. "In which case, we should probably tell Gavin to stop hiding in the Jeep. How long do you need? An hour?" He pauses but not long enough for me to answer. "Two? Three? Shit, Callie, pace yourself. The dude's more than his dick."

I laugh. "Great to see you, too, Rusty."

He winks.

"You coming out with us tonight?" Benji asks, propping against the side of my car.

"No, I leave this afternoon."

They exchange a look, Rusty's forehead creasing. "What time?"

"Around three. Why?"

Another moment of concern passes between them before Benji grins with less Benji than earlier. "We'll return him to you in one piece before then."

"You're kidnapping him?" I ask.

They both nod.

So once I send him out the door, I won't see him again until after my last class. *Great.* Damn him for having friends who want to celebrate his birthday with him. And damn him for still not giving in over the whole challenge nonsense.

"No later than three, Benji," I say, backing away from them.

"No worries, Calico."

"And at least sober enough to form coherent sentences." I point at Rusty, sensing him for the type to feed someone shots before noon. Even though, technically, I already am with the coffee.

"Yes, ma'am," he says as I turn around.

The door to the suite almost hits Jordan when I rush in. The couch, the floor, the guy could sleep anywhere and look incredible in the morning. He has his hood over his head, dark hair still falls perfectly underneath, and then the gray sweatpants.

I smile, not even voluntary anymore, and walk around him. "Good morning, beautiful."

He shuts the door behind me. "You steal my line and my move on my birthday? Have you no shame?"

And the morning voice. Low and raspy.

Speaking of no shame, my eyes dip to the outline of his cock, and I take a deep breath, looking away before I climb him.

Felicia relieves me of the drink carrier, and I take him his special blend.

"I think you'll find my coffee delivery service adds an extra pep to your step." I wink at him and hang up my coat.

As he sips, he follows me to my room. We tear down the blanket fort, returning everything to its rightful place, in no time at all. Every now and then, he catches my eye and smiles. Each time, I wonder if it's the last time.

He waits on Cam's remade bed while I pack for the weekend. Facing away from him, I text Felicia so that she can help me get him out of the suite. Her gorilla power will come in handy when he ultimately tries to argue. She clears her throat from the other room, signaling she'll act as my muscle.

"Time to go, Jordan." I grab his hand to lead him out.

He drags his thumb back and forth over my skin, the touch traveling all the way through me. Damn, I need him to figure out his shit over the next few hours.

"You can't kick me out on my birthday," he says.

I tug my hand from his when he won't let go and open the door. "I'll see you this afternoon."

"No, you'll see me after—"

He never sees Felicia coming. She drops her shoulder like a football player, drives him through the door, and swings it shut before he recovers. The combination of looks on his face and hers makes me cackle as she returns to the couch like nothing happened. I go into my room and pick up one last pillow lodged under the bed before crossing out another day on my calendar. My last day with Jordan, and I'll barely see him.

Damn it.

The thought sinks in my belly, and then I'm dashing out the door after him, not sure what I'm doing. I spot him about to leave the building and call his name. Just shy of the door, he turns around, smiling when he sees me on the stairs.

It would be so easy to kiss him and end the stalemate. Then he would admit to the stupidity of the challenge and tell me everything I wanted to hear. We'd run up to my room and spend the entire day under the blankets in a different way, the rest of the world be damned. He wouldn't leave with his friends, I wouldn't go to Graham's, and we could just be—the two of us.

Except if I start kissing him, I won't stop even if he says nothing of the sort. He'll still fuck me, but it might end with him getting me out of his system and me stuck with him in mine.

So, rather than risk what I've avoided so far, I stop in front of him. "Say it."

He smiles. "I'll see you later, beautiful."

I pull his face down until his lips touch my forehead, his hand wrapping the back of my neck to keep me there a little longer. Then I let go and step back, swiping the cup from his hand. "You were done with this, right?"

Before he answers, I dash up the stairs, finishing the coffee on my way.

We've reached the end of our game.

***

Why would I ever trust a group of musicians to show up on time? I ask myself this question several times, sitting on the hood of my car in the parking lot outside my last class. The only answer I come up with: I'm an idiot.

A faint roar grows louder, and as the ugliest station wagon in existence rumbles down the block, I imagine "Flight of the Valkyries" is playing somewhere. Benji drives the faded brown clunker—exactly what I pictured him owning— and slows down once close to me. The back-passenger door opens, and someone pushes Jordan out of the still-moving car. The three guys still in the vehicle wave, driving away.

I slide off the hood. "Day drunk?"

"Day buzzed," he says.

My eyes roll in response to the more than buzzed grin on his face. *Thanks for nothing, guys.*

"I need to go," I say, meeting him at the back of the car.

He doesn't answer, just slides his hands over my waist and keeps going until he grabs my ass and jerks me forward. I suck in a breath, hitting his chest, and grip the pocket on his hoodie while he dips to nuzzle against my neck. It takes me by surprise, but I clasp my hands behind his neck and close my eyes, feeling his mouth skim my skin.

I want it to be real, more than I should.

"Tell me it's not about sex." I say it and realize whatever happens next decides it all.

Jordan pulls back, and the way he stares down at me can't mean nothing. Or maybe I see what I want. He presses his lips to my cheek, and I stop breathing when they sweep down to the corner of my mouth.

But then, he says, "Tomorrow."

My mind scrambles, searching for an excuse not to walk away. A reason to wait a little longer. But unless I want to give him the chance to really hurt me, I need to follow through.

Before I convince myself not to, I back away. "Goodbye, Jordan."

"I'll talk to you tomorrow, beautiful."

He won't. I think a part of me has always known that.

I climb into the car and leave him in the parking lot.

Stubbornness along with annoyance completes the first half of the drive. Eventually, the annoyance reigns supreme, and the confines of the car become more than I can bear. I park behind a gas station, needing air. Like a lunatic—or Jordan studying—I walk back and forth by my car, torn. So very torn.

Why couldn't he admit to actual feelings? I, Callie Henders, the chick who avoids emotion at all costs, can manage. What the hell is his excuse?

"Oh, ask me tomorrow, beautiful," I say in my best Jordan voice, which turns out rather spot-on. Bullshit. The whole thing has gone on for too long already. If we can't even come to terms with wanting to be together, a relationship would be an absolute disaster.

"God, he's so *frustrating*," I shout at no one.

Actually, I shout at a truck driver, who eyes me through his rolled-down window. *Fucking great.* Towel Boy has me ranting aloud in front of a stranger behind a seedy gas station in the middle of nowhere due to his ability to perfectly balance infuriating and irresistible.

Oh. My. God. I stop and cover my face with my hands.

It happened. I find him irresistible.

"You all right, darlin'?"

I peek through my fingers at the truck driver, who is clearly worried about my sanity. A concern that I share right now, too.

My arms drop to my sides. "Yeah. Romantic crisis."

He nods and politely returns to staring at me.

After a few deep breaths, a sigh of resignation, and an oh-what-the-hell groan, I jump in the car, no clue what the hell I'm about to do.

A few minutes to six, I grab my bags from the passenger seat and go inside. The bags land on the floor, and I rub my neck to alleviate the tension. A mixture of three hours in the car and everything else has combined into a solid knot.

Connor texts.

He's here. Shut off your phone.

Well, Henders, no turning back now.

As my phone powers down, Felicia bounces into my room with Jess on her heels. "Ready?" she asks, reaching out her hands.

Despite the massive weight of anxiety compressing my chest, I nod. She squeals and pulls me out the door.

In true Felicia fashion, she won't let a single minute of our Friday night go to waste. We meet Cam for dinner. The four of us are rarely together all at once at the dorm, so everyone joining forces for a meal constitutes a damn miracle.

On her way to meet Sawyer for Valentine's Day, Cam drops the other three of us off at the bar. I consider turning my phone on, but it's already nine, and three hours' worth of texts and voicemails from Graham hold zero appeal. Felicia loops her arm through mine, not giving me a chance anyway. We flash our fake IDs at the guy manning the door and walk right in, no problem.

The music and voices create a buzz in the air as we scan the at-capacity crowd. With Jess's eye for Jordan as sharp as ever, she points toward their table. I keep waiting for her strange obsession with him to bother me, but the possibility of her ripping his clothes off every time he comes near amuses me to no end.

We move through the bodies in their direction, but Benji steps in front of me. "Well, look who just won me the award for best damn birthday gift."

A grin delivers my only warning before he scoops me up and throws me over his shoulder. I laugh as he carries me through the sea of people. Now I'm the angel/devil on *his* shoulder.

He deposits me in the chair next to Jordan. "Don't say I never gave you anything."

Jordan's eyes widen, and he smiles for a second before it flips to a frown. "What are you doing here?"

A million miles away from the greeting I expected. "You invited me."

"I just didn't think I was seeing you until Sunday." His eyes dart between me and his beer, which he slides in front of me. "You can have this one."

"Thanks," I say, wondering if Jordan plans on making an appearance or if I'm risking the wrath of Graham for the dude sitting next to me.

Felicia slips into my lap, handing him a shot. "Happy birthday—the right way."

"Thank you, Gibson." He smiles—a fake one—setting the glass down. "I'm pacing myself."

She shrugs and hops up, her sights set on someone across the bar. Jordan stares off, not showing interest in anything. Especially not me. It makes little sense. His hands and mouth were all over me a few hours ago, and I wonder what the hell I'm missing.

"I'm jealous." A guy takes over the chair on the other side of me. "Everyone has these fantastic stories of meeting you, and all I get is walking up to you in the bar and introducing myself."

It takes a second to recognize him because nothing visually connects him to the rest of the band. No tattoos, smaller stature, dark hair buzzed short.

"Gavin, I take it?"

"Bassist extraordinaire. And you're Callie Henders, aka Calico, aka Coconut Chick, aka The Girl."

The numerous aliases I've gained without my knowledge impress me. "So, we need a more exciting first encounter?"

"Exactly what I'm saying. If you're short on ideas, we can recycle one. Like when you met Jordan and made out with him."

"Sure. But you'll want to get mostly naked first. For accuracy and all."

He grins. "I like you, Callie Henders. I approve."

Our conversation ends when Rusty's shirt peels off on the far side of the room. Gavin goes to wrangle him over to the table. When they return, Jess abandons Team Jordan in favor of Team Rusty and sidles up next to him. An interesting development.

But not even losing one of his biggest fans garners a reaction from Jordan. He offers me a halfhearted smile once, and then the water glass in his hand becomes his obsession. He nods and contributes to conversations so long as they don't involve me. To the untrained eye—or any eye for that matter—my presence seems to be single-handedly ruining his birthday.

After about an hour of awkwardness, Benji nails me with a piece of ice from across the table. He looks to Jordan and back, holding up five fingers. I shake my head and flash all ten multiple times, letting him know how wrong he was about the entire situation. He rubs a hand over his chin and switches seats. He hooks his arm around Jordan's neck and leans in. I'm not sure what he says, but Jordan's gaze flies to me. Benji winks at me before forcefully removing Jordan from his seat and dragging him through the crowd.

As they disappear, I notice the decorative centerpieces for the first time. Red foil hearts and flowers in a basket. They take up room on every single table, except for ours.

Then it hits me. I truly am an idiot. A guy and girl being together on Valentine's Day carries specific implications, and every woman in the bar can see him with me. My presence doesn't ruin his birthday but instead a slew of potential hook-ups. Jordan's never wanted more, and again, I let him make me doubt myself.

At least this time, he also makes it easy to walk away.

Felicia catches my arm as I gather up my coat. "Hey, what's wrong?"

"Nothing," I say, forcing a smile. "I need some air and might call a ride to the dorms."

"You want me to come?"

I shake my head. "No. Stay. Find your Valentine, Gibson."

She gives me a quick squeeze before I push through the crowd, my expression fading the second I leave her sight.

A cold wind whips against the side of my face when I get outside. I pull out my phone, stopping short of powering it on. All the messages and threatening calls wait for me. Since the payoff no longer exists, the potential consequences of defying Graham grip me full force. Not ready to deal with them yet, I wander down the sidewalk and around the corner of the building where the wind doesn't bother me.

The black screen continues to taunt me as I lean against the wall. I consider the possibility of staying here all night to avoid turning it on. Other than boredom from standing in the shadows like a creep and the eventual need to pee, I can't think of anything to stop me.

But then, from around the corner, I hear Jordan say, "Hold on. I can't hear you with the—oh shit." He stops short to keep from running me over.

Unbelievable. A girl can't catch a break.

He puts his phone away. "I've been looking for you."

"I don't care." Rethinking my anti-phone stance, I shove past him to the front of the building.

And, in an event that shocks no one, anywhere in the world, he chases after me.

"Callie, ask me the question again."

"No, Jordan. I'm done playing this game with you. At this point, I'll sleep with you just to make you go away."

He blocks my path, forcing me to stop. "Ask me," he demands.

I cross my arms and narrow my eyes at him, unwilling to concede.

"Damn it, you stubborn-ass woman." He steps closer, the look in his eye morphing to one I feel all the way to my toes. "No. This isn't about having sex with you. On some level, it's always been about more. I have wanted to be with you in some way, shape, or form ever since I hit the damn turn signal to go to the coffee shop."

I feel my breath falter, startled by the admission. Even though it's what I've been waiting for, it takes a moment for everything to shift from ideal to real. In the time it takes for my mind to process, the look on Jordan's face morphs to concern. He's standing there, staring, waiting for me to jump into his arms or something.

By now, he should know better, so all I give him is a shrug. "Okay."

He blinks. Once. Twice. "Okay?" His voice shoots up. "After all that, the only thing you have is *okay*?"

"Okay," I say. "Now, was that so hard to admit?"

He lets out a relieved breath, his mouth turning up at the corners. "You have no idea."

I smile, and he yanks me forward, and his mouth collides with mine. On take three, nothing else enters the equation—no countdown or frat partygoers—just us, the way I want it.

His palm wraps the side of my neck, and he tugs my chin down with his thumb in a silent demand. I part my lips for him, and he groans when his tongue pushes between them. I pull at the back of his hair, not getting enough of him yet and wanting him closer. He strokes down my back and then palms my ass while he holds me to him and backs me up into the wall, pinning me there with his body.

When I nibble on his bottom lip, he thrusts forward, grinding the hard ridge in his jeans on my hip.

"You feel so fucking good." He mumbles the words against my lips. Then he grips the backs of my legs and lifts me, my pulse racing. He has all of it from my body right now. Pulse hammering, skin tingling, panties wet.

"I can't stop," he rasps.

"Then don't." I wrap my legs around him and whimper when he rocks his hard cock against my clit. Maybe we *should* stop because I'm pretty sure I'll let him fuck me right here if he wants. Out in the open. Freezing air.

He drags his tongue up my neck before sucking at my pulse point and then licking higher. His fingers start working the buttons on my coat, his mossy eyes locking onto mine. I tug at the back of his head until he kisses me. Hard. Pulling open my coat, he slips under my sweater, and his palm grazes up my bare skin. The cold hardly registers, his touch almost burning.

"Damn, get it, Waters," a guy yells.

Jordan's growl vibrates against my lips. I look over and receive a wave from Rusty and Gavin, smoking by the door. Neither appear the least bit sorry for their interruption. Just us was nice while it lasted.

Jordan sighs, putting me down. I have to breathe, de-lust my brain before I have any chance of moving. He shoves off the wall behind me and readjusts his erection, then he kisses me again and slips his hand into mine like he's done it a million times, tugging me down the sidewalk.

About five feet away from his friends, he glances over with the twinkle in his eye. "Say, 'Goodbye Callie,'" he says to them.

"Goodbye, Callie," they repeat in unison.

He lunges for me, and I yelp, going over someone's shoulder for the second time in one night. His arm tightens around my thighs as he dashes across the parking lot to his Jeep.

He sets me down by the door. "Priorities, Callie."

I laugh, not complaining if he wants to bail on his own birthday celebration. In fact, I encourage the hell out of the behavior.

The drive to the dorms only takes a few minutes, him touching me the entire way like he finally can and doesn't want to stop.

As soon as he parks, he runs around to my side and drags me out. He walks backward up the sidewalk, grasping my hips to make sure I follow. Every now and again, he checks behind him to avoid falling, and I can't help but return his damn smile.

Everything's finally as it should have been from the beginning. Almost too right.

Jordan backs into the wall by the door of my building before pulling me to him. I sink into his chest, staring up at him.

"Still *certain* about me never getting another show?" he asks.

"Well"—I bite my lip and pretend to consider—"it *is* your birthday."

His head nods wildly, but he doesn't let me go, so I tell him, "I'm not stripping for you until we're inside."

The door hits the wall when he flings it open.

He walks backward again and leads me like I might get lost before we make it to my room. His talent on the stairs deserves special mention, not slowing down or unsteady in the least. Our mouths fuse at the top, his hands everywhere and pulling me with him. I might even start pushing him faster, sliding my hands over his hard pecs under his shirt.

After we round the corner to my hallway, I check behind him, not wanting him to trip over anything. An injury is the last thing we need to ruin our night.

No.

The second to last thing.

Everything stops, including my breath when I see them behind him. They're standing in front of my door. Large yellow letters spell out *SHERIFF* across the backs of their dark brown jackets.

Sometimes, the body confuses falling asleep with dying. It jerks and creates a fraction of a second of uncontrollable panic to kick-start your system again. The sensation coursing through me feels exactly like that, except immobilizing and not stopping. The consequences of defying Graham are no longer avoidable. They're here. In the flesh and waiting for me.

Jordan touches my cheek, bringing me back to him before he glances over his shoulder. "Cops?"

Both turn at the sound of his voice. The first has a harsh expression on his square face, cold and hard. The other is a younger version of the man next to him, except for shaggy, dark hair. His mouth turns down, displaying a more regretful look.

As he fucking should.

My dread turns to a burning rage, customarily reserved for Graham himself. But they'll most certainly do. I storm toward them, any chance of maintaining composure long gone.

"You don't have any fucking jurisdiction here, Kevin." My voice bounces through the hall.

"Calm down." Trey reaches out to stop me, touching my arm. He recognizes the mistake too late.

I drive my palms into my cousin's chest. It thrusts him backward despite the fifty pounds he has on me. Before I can get to him again, hands grip my shoulders from behind and drag me away from him.

"Callie, stop." Jordan's voice breaks through as I scowl at Trey, trying to convey, through only my expression, how much I despise him in this moment. How much he fucked up.

With even more remorse on his face than before, he shifts half a step over to place himself between my uncle and me. "Either we came or Graham was coming."

The attempt at justifying his actions sends a new wave of pissed-off surging through me. "Screw you, Trey!"

"Callista—"

"Callie," I hiss at Kevin.

"Whatever." My uncle extends an arm, moving Trey out of his way. "Pack a bag."

"You can't make me go with you."

"I'll say it one more time. Pack. A. Bag."

My nails dig deep into my palms. The aggression demanding an escape. "I have to admit, the sheriff doing Graham's dirty work is a new low. Nothing better to do tonight than help your little brother fuck up my life? The taxpayers must be proud."

His eyes narrow as his shoulders broaden. "Damn it, Callista, enough!"

"Callie," I shout back.

"Cal, please." Trey holds up his hands, reinforcing his plea.

The three names swirl in the hall, each with a different set of expectations. I sense one of those moments—the worst kind—as my worlds collide for the first time. The past in front of me and the present behind me, and I stand in the middle where they'll crush me. Unable to stop them. Unable to move out of their way.

Helpless.

Kevin zeroes in on Jordan long enough to justify my fear before he smirks. "You been drinking tonight, *Callie*?" He spits my name like an insult.

A lump forms in my throat, and my mind races to figure out where he's going with the question.

Before I can, he sticks his chin up, his stare back on Jordan. "You have ID on you, son?"

Trey's wide eyes connect with mine, his father's intentions crystal clear to both of us now.

"Dad, don't." He raises an eyebrow at me, saying what his words can't.

Message received, I spin and touch Jordan's arm, so he looks at me. "Don't show him anything. Don't *say* anything. He can't do anything here."

He nods, returning his unreadable gaze over my shoulder.

"Either you're a minor or you're not," Kevin says. "Judging by *Callie*'s reaction, you're not. So, if she were to blow anything that registers on a Breathalyzer, smart money says you'd be suspect of furnishing alcohol to a minor."

What a fuck. I roll my eyes, rotating around. I'm not a fan of keeping my back to my enemies, and Kevin currently meets all the requirements. "You couldn't possibly prove that."

He's a few feet closer than before. "Hard to say. Local law enforcement would need to investigate such a suspicion."

I stand up taller, not wanting him to see me unnerved. Jordan's hands return to my shoulders. They bring a hint of comfort with them, but part of me wishes he would bolt out the door, sparing himself from whatever my uncle is prepared to unleash.

"But…" Kevin steps toward us, wagging around a finger, ready to reveal his master plan. "Since they're here, I might suggest they search the dorms for contraband. Maybe check Callista's back pocket for her fake ID. You still keep it there?"

No. Fucking. Way.

I actually gasp as he raises the stakes to a whole new level. Even though his threat to Jordan won't amount to anything, Cam and Jess both keep alcohol stashes in the suite, as do several other students on the floor, along with weed. I might not care about him being right about my ID, but he and I both know I won't let him throw innocent bystanders in the line of fire.

All hail King Kevin, the temporary holder of the crown for the most manipulative person in our family. Quite the feat, considering Graham, who will more than likely win back his title sooner rather than later.

Trey's big brown eyes beg for an apology before he lowers his head with no offer of help. He's never been capable of standing up to his father, and with Kevin as his boss, it's even less likely to ever happen. No, I'm on my own, and once again, control over my life goes to the highest bidder. A hell I'm thinking will never end.

With nothing left to do but submit, I take a shaky breath. "I need a few minutes to pack."

Kevin steps aside to let us pass. Trey attempts to follow us in, which would end terribly, so I shoulder the door shut and force him back into the hall. He lets out a sigh, presumably realizing he will spend the rest of our natural lives making up for his betrayal. Maybe longer.

Jordan flips the switch to light the common area, immediately studying me. In the span of a few minutes, with no preparation, he has witnessed a condensed version of the depravity my family offers. I wait, dreading him asking any of the questions hanging in the air, but without a word, he pulls me to him.

I bury my face in his chest and fight off the feelings running rampant inside me. All the disgust toward Kevin and disappointment in Trey. Fear over facing Graham. Heartbreak from losing the only place I could escape them all. Because that's what this place was supposed to be. My sanctuary.

For a second, I think the tears might come, but the sting disappears faster than it should. It leaves me to wonder what it'll take for the pain to fully surface. Honestly, I'm a little terrified to find out.

Jordan's chin rests on top of my head. "Are you going to tell me what's going on?"

"Can we talk about it on Monday?" I ask. My nerves need time to recover from the showdown in the hallway before diving in deep again.

"You're going with them?" He eases back, concern in his eyes while he searches my face. "Is that safe? They were just threatening you—and me."

Great. Now I need to defend their abhorrent behavior to keep him from worrying. "It's fine. My uncle and cousin are harmless."

Mostly anyway.

Kevin sometimes tightens the handcuffs more than necessary to prove a point, and once, when we were eleven and eight, Trey decked me. Although, I'd just broken his nose, so fair play.

"Graham's your dad?" he asks, slowly gathering the pieces left around us.

I nod, hating how his voice sounds saying the name. His eyebrows draw in, and he's still not satisfied. But I need him to be for tonight at least. So, I drag my finger over his bottom lip.

"Rain check on the floor show?"

Jordan's face relaxes, and I bite down on a smile before kissing him. Slow this time. The distraction is as much for my benefit as his. He tightens his arms around me, and what happened in the hallway no longer matters to either of us. I glide my hands up his neck as he kisses over my jaw and down mine.

Only it all comes rushing back when Trey says, "Cal," and knocks.

"I might end up hitting a cop," I mumble.

Jordan's lips keep working while he groans. "That would be incredibly sexy."

"Don't move." I back away from him before I can't and retrieve my bags from my room. "I want you to be right there when I get back Sunday night."

"All right, beautiful," he says. "I'll be waiting."

God, I hope so.

I leave him there in my suite. As soon as the door shuts and Trey enters my field of vision, my expression vanishes. I drop my bags on the floor and step over them. He sighs again, gathering them up. He follows me to the bottom of the stairs where Kevin is waiting. Once we get to the parking lot, I head toward my car, but Kevin snares my arm and redirects me to his sheriff's cruiser.

I slow down, resisting enough that he glances back.

"No car this weekend, Callista," he barks.

The space around me closes in fast. The air heavy and each breath a struggle. I'm already suffocated, and we haven't even left yet.

No car means no escape.

158 Days Until 19

We arrive in Sutterville at one-thirty in the morning.

Connor is sleeping at the kitchen table when I walk in. His head pops up, and he blinks several times, confused by his unusual napping place until he notices me. The chair tips over as he comes rushing over.

"I'm sorry, Cal." He grabs ahold of me and smashes my face against his chest. "I'm so sorry. I tried to keep him from going batshit."

"You have nothing to be sorry for, Con. I should have just come back."

He releases me and flashes to the fridge, retrieving a plate of spaghetti. It goes in the microwave before I can tell him I'm not hungry. Still in hyperdrive, he delivers my bags to my room and sets a place for me at the table. I sit down as he brings the food over. Whether or not I want to eat, he needs to feel like he's taking care of me. And I let him, because if I can't make myself feel better, I can at least help him.

We quietly talk while I more or less push the pasta around. High school gossip is fascinating when you're not the subject. But Connor stops mid-sentence when a door shuts down the dark hallway.

Graham stomps into the kitchen and comes straight for me. I stare straight ahead, my heart pounding as he leans into the side of my face.

"Short-term memory loss?"

I force a swallow, concentrating on each breath—slow, steady—not giving him the satisfaction of knowing his presence causes every muscle in my body to tense.

"Hard of hearing, too?" he shouts, so close I feel his breath on my cheek. "I want your phone."

My eyes lock on Connor, across the table. His mouth forms a hard line, his jaw clenched and grinding beneath the skin. One of us needs a phone, just in case. He gives the slightest hint of a nod, signaling he has his.

Even still, the thought of offering up what feels like the last shred of my freedom gnaws at me. Alternative scenarios cycle through my head. I could run, beg, argue, fake cry, but only one thing will prevent the situation from escalating any further. So, I hold up my phone and let Graham rip it away.

He straightens up, and I close my eyes, attempting a calming breath. They open in time to see terror flood Connor's face. His pupils constrict to pinpoints, and he shoots forward in his chair as Graham's arm swings. I flinch, but his hand narrowly misses me. It connects with the plate in front of me, sending it flying. Metal clangs, and the ceramic shatters on the tiled floor. I see the wide blue eyes watching from the shadows. They disappear, Cate's footsteps running down the hallway.

There's not another movement, sound, or breath until the door to Graham's bedroom slams shut. I suck in air that only adds more weight to my chest, not satisfying the intense need to breathe. Connor's already on his feet for the broom, his energy focused on cleaning up the shards of plate. My hands shake as I wet a washcloth. I sink down and wipe up the tomato sauce splattered over the tiles and cupboards before it stains. It's incredible what the mind deems important when trying to shut out reality. We clean in silence, neither of us acknowledging the closest call we've had in a long time. We never will. Not out loud anyway. At some point, it becomes more exhausting to relive it than just file it away.

After eliminating all evidence of Graham's outburst, Connor follows me down the hall to my room. He toes off his size fifteen sneakers while I slip off my shoes by the bed. I kneel next to him in front of the hanging blanket that slightly moves.

"What's the password?" Cate asks from the other side.

"Catelynn is my favorite," we reply.

"You may enter."

Connor crawls into the blanket fort ahead of me. I built the first one almost ten years ago to give him a distraction from a screaming match with no end in sight. Somewhere he could go to escape the moments that became a little too scary. A place he could feel safe in a world of uncertainty. Of course, the moments never let up, and the damn thing has ended up a permanent staple in my bedroom decor.

A six-year-old version of myself attacks when I enter behind Connor. She squishes my cheeks between her hands and kisses my forehead—her new way of saying hello and goodbye. She flops over to Connor and snuggles in beside him. He puts his arm around her for extra protection and squeezes her tight.

She closes her eyes, not a care in the world. "Now we're all safe."

His chest heaves at her words, and his forehead wrinkles. One of the only sights capable of shattering my heart anymore is him crying. I move over beside him, and he leans over, so I can put my arms around him. It's my turn to protect him and squeeze him tight.

"Nothing bad can happen under the blankets, Connor," I tell him.

He sniffs, blinking away unshed tears. "Promise?"

I rest my chin on his shoulder and respond the same way I always have, the way I always will as long as he needs me to. "Promise."

A majority of the weekends spent in Sutterville, Graham only graces us with his presence in short intervals. He sporadically stops in to yell at us for a variety of things, such as existing. But since I dared to miss a single Friday night at his house, he abandons his normal in and out and refuses to leave at all on Saturday, wanting to keep an eye on me. Seriously, his selfishness and relentless need for control operates on a level unachievable by most humans.

Cut off from the rest of the world outside of the Podunk town and being trapped with him have me crawling out of my skin. He works on hour four of a nap in the recliner when I walk into the living room.

I kick his steel-toed boot. "Graham."

"What?" His eyes stay shut.

"Give me the keys to the truck. I want to go to the gas station."

"Walk."

I flip him off, not that he'll ever know.

Cate has Connor playing with dolls at the kitchen table. He uses a high-pitched voice, talking about going to the mall when I interrupt.

"I'm going to the S-Stop," I say, pulling on my coat.

His concern radiates across the room, the two wrinkles forming between his eyebrows. "Are you sure—"

"If I stay here any longer, I'll claw my eyes out."

I slam the door on my way out for no reason other than to piss off Graham. It does nothing to improve my mood, and the six blocks of walking fails as well.

Rounding the corner of the gas station, I check the cars in the parking lot, not wanting to run into certain people. I only recognize the busted-up Cadillac parked in the employee spot. It belongs to one of our old neighbors, Rhonda. She waves at me as the bell dings, announcing my entrance.

The soda selection holds my attention for a minute, but I deem a mixer unnecessary. I snag a fifth of vodka off the bottom shelf and return to the counter. Rather than ask for my fake ID, Rhonda inquires about school. I politely respond while paying with the cash I stole from Graham's wallet. If he hides my phone, he should know better than to leave his wallet out on the dresser. I consider it a late birthday gift. Or Christmas since he missed that, too.

I walk down the unpaved street on my return trip, gravel crunching under my feet. Out of four-hundred-and-some-odd residents, two use the sidewalks—both mailmen. My two-drink rule goes the fuck out the window, and another long pull out of my bottle in a brown paper bag continues to dull my nerves, still raw from last night.

Almost to Graham's, a black Grand Am, with a crack in the front bumper from slamming into a light pole, speeds past. The tires displace rocks, skidding to a stop behind me.

Seriously, my day can't get any worse.

With nowhere to hide, I stop once the car doors open. Tony appears first, laughing. His fiery-red hair sticks out under his stocking cap. The pinches to my sides come courtesy of Pete on his way around me. Shayna follows them, her mischievous grin engaged.

Three of the worst best friends imaginable. The four of us made up a third of our class from the time Tony popped up in the sixth grade until Sutterville's and Waymore's schools merged our junior year. Even with more students, teachers scrambled to keep no more than two of us in a class at once—out of fear of mutiny. A fair concern. As a group, we drift toward the wild side rather quickly. More often than not, on my orders.

Senior year, I distanced myself, and after graduation, I abandoned them altogether in favor of a clean break and a fresh start. Not something any of them hold against me. Also not something they ever let me forget.

Now, they literally circle me—vultures to prey.

"Henders, where the hell you been?"

"Couldn't stay away any longer?"

"She's back every other weekend, guys. She's just too good for us now, remember?"

Everyone but me laughs.

"We're having a party tonight."

"Look, she's already pre-gaming."

I offer the bottle to Shayna. She throws her blonde head back, taking a swig, and wipes her mouth on the sleeve of her sweatshirt before passing it to Pete. Rather than drink, he hands it off to Tony without ever looking away from me. His soft gaze has stayed unchanged despite the months of me dodging him.

"Well, you coming with us?" Tony holds out the bottle in my direction.

He waves it around, encouraging me with his stoner grin, until I swipe it from his hand. I run through my numerous options that include sitting around, miserable, with Graham for the rest of the weekend or—no, that's the end of the list. Since I would rather stick hot needles in my eyes than be anywhere near my father, I pluck the cigarette from behind Tony's ear and take another drink.

They all smile when I ask, "Where are we going?"

———

Horrific country music blares from the speakers in the living room, volume maxed out. Tony shakes his head, disappearing from the kitchen.

The sound lowers, and he returns to the seat across the table from me. "Please continue."

Attempting to get in my head, Pete hovers over my shoulder. Drinking in moderation for months has wreaked havoc on my alcohol tolerance, but my focus remains unbreakable. My wrist flicks, the quarter bounces off the table, and the coin clatters in the glass.

"Drink," I tell him.

Pete shakes his head, sitting down next to me. "Just remember, hour four is when you usually lose hand-eye coordination."

"Bet it's not the only thing she loses tonight." Tony winks.

I make a face at him for being an ass. "I'll take that bet."

"You sound confident." Pete smirks before taking a sip of whatever random concoction he has in his cup. "Good thing I have plenty of mental images on instant recall." He taps the side of his head with a finger.

"Me too," Tony says, mimicking him.

"Mine are better." Pete effortlessly bounces the quarter into the glass. "Drink."

I roll my eyes, not impressed with either of them, as I drain my cup. "Here I keep trying to purge the memory of us sleeping together from my brain."

"Every time or just a specific instance?" Pete asks.

"Remind me again how it happened more than once?"

He grabs his chest, feigning offense. "So cold."

I give him a cheesy smile and stand up. Even with the unwelcome trip down memory lane, I've missed the hell out of him. And Tony. However, I won't admit to missing Shayna until she stops picking such awful music.

Once the room stops spinning, I leave them to reminisce about me without me. Cold night air rushes my lungs when I step out of Shayna's trailer, but even outside, the air smothers me, compressing my chest. The handrail her grandmother installed a few years before she passed away helps me down the steps. I ease down on the bottom one and rest my head on the frigid metal pipe bracing the rail. Something I've done countless times. It's strange how time can rewind, careening you back with it to a place you thought you'd left behind forever.

At least, you hoped.

A door slams, and my head jerks in the direction of the truck. Under the streetlights, a stupid square face with floppy hair walks toward me. But I only care about what he is wearing—street clothes.

"I wasn't expecting to see you here." Trey smiles, genuinely surprised.

I stand up and mirror his expression until he stops in front of me. His face falls, eyes widening in the split second before my fist connects with his nose. His head snaps back.

"*Jesus-fuck*, Cal!" He staggers backward, covering his face with his hands.

"You came to my school, Trey. Seriously?" I rush him and knock him back farther, no longer able to ignore the hurt from his betrayal. "How could you?" I'm screeching at this point. "You knew how badly I needed this."

He attempts to keep me at arm's length, but drunken fury wins out. I twist around, and my elbow collides with his cheekbone.

"Goddamn it," he shouts, his patience for me gone.

This time when I charge him, he drops his shoulder and scoops me up. I kick and scream, beating on his back with my fists.

Unfazed by my flailing, he carries me across the lawn. My fingers grip the handrail on the way up the steps, but he pries them off one by one before hauling me the rest of the way inside. Not a soul dares to intervene as I continue to thrash around on his shoulder in the kitchen. Tony and Pete even disappear into the living room. Anyone who grew up with us knows we have our own way of handling issues. An unhealthy one but effective nonetheless.

It only takes a few minutes for my legs and arms to tire, and I go limp over his shoulder. He deposits me on the counter without a word and tosses a bloody towel from his nose in the sink. He places one hand on each side of me, and we stare at each other. His nose is still bleeding a little; his cheek is split open and swelling, along with his eye. I huff, still furious with him, but damn it, he looks terrible. And sorry. So very sorry.

My lower lip juts out in apology, but he shakes his head.

"I deserve it, Cal. I deserve it all."

He steps back, and I slide off the counter. I grab him a beer can from the refrigerator. He holds it to his face as he pours us each a shot of whiskey.

"Here's to you forgiving me someday," he says.

I clink mine to his, take the shot, and slam the empty glass down in front of him. "It's a start."

He pours us another.

Then another.

157 Days Until 19

At first, I can't get past Trey, but he miscalculates, and I dart by. Once I hit the grass, nothing can stop me. I run across the lawn and into the street, scooping down to collect rocks. The handful of gravel spatters across the rear window of Kevin's sheriff's cruiser. He slams on the brakes, and in the other direction I go.

"Cal!" Trey shouts. As I run up the steps, he opens the screen door and says, "Hide her."

Tony tugs me through the house to a closet and shuts us both inside. We giggle in the dark, him more so than me. My ankle turns when I step on something, and I stumble into him. He sets me upright, his hold firm on my shoulders.

"Fuck, Henders," he says, his hands falling away. "You smell too damn good, and I'm too damn drunk to be in here with you."

The light blinds me as he opens the accordion door, steps out, and closes it behind him. Kevin's voice bellows through the house, others yelling back at him. He needs to hurry and leave before I pass out. I yawn, lowering myself to the floor—a poor combination, given my lack of coordination. My balance fails, and I fall the rest of the way. My hand flies to my mouth to mute the laughter bubbling out. I haven't been this drunk in a really long time.

Outside the closet, all the voices stop, except for one. It slices through me but not in the satisfying way it once did. No, this is more of an I-never-wanted-to-hear-that-voice-again kind of way. Even so, my pulse skyrockets.

A shadow appears in the strip of light on the floor. The door folds open, and there he is, staring down at me.

"Hey, gorgeous." Brock drags me to my feet and right into his arms.

"No one told me you were back," I mumble against his shirt, fighting the automatic urge to hug him back.

The feel of him, the smell of him—everything about him is so familiar and yet completely foreign to my current life.

"I would have called, but..."

I changed my number over the summer, clean break and all. Other than Trey and the rest of my family, no one from here has the new one.

Brock releases me but stays close, intense brown eyes threatening to melt me. "God, I fucking missed you," he says, pushing hair away from my face.

I'm trying to remember the last time I saw him. Not long after our official breakup since he moved away a few months later. Given our history, I can assume the encounter included a fight. Toward the end, that's all we ever did. Fight and fuck. The former with each other, the latter not always.

Toxic.

He guides me to the living room with his hand on my back. I sit on the couch, still in shock, and stare at him. Longer blond hair and a piercing in his eyebrow are new, but the air of confidence and the dickish grin remain the same. He screams arrogant asshole. He has since the moment we met. At least now, I can clearly identify the traits.

With him being here, the entire scene unfolding comes straight out of the past. The group's dynamic seamlessly shifts back in time, everyone returning to the role they once played. Brock brings me a drink and sinks down on the cushion next to me. Trey hovers around us, acting as my protector. His eye and cheek are both discolored and bruising. Across the room, Tony and Pete smoke a bowl. Both laugh, probably at different things, neither funny. A few people gathered in the doorway part to let

Shayna through. She dances her way into the middle of the room, swaying to a seventies rock ballad.

We've done it all before, more times than I can count. I half-expect to sleep through homeroom alongside Tony in the morning.

"It's after one," Trey says. "We should get you back to Graham's." He takes the drink from my hand, but Brock grabs the cup from him.

"I don't think she's ready to deal with dear ole daddy yet." He secures his arm around me, holding me closer to his side. "What shit did he pull this time?"

I don't answer him, my hazy mind drifting to the *goodnight* text Jordan undoubtedly sent to the phone that's shut off and hidden somewhere in Graham's bedroom. Without even knowing it, the man ripped away the only thing resembling stability in my life. The one thing I can count on despite everything else I can't. He's taken away too much and left me with nothing but an unwavering hatred for him.

I notice the tear rolling down my cheek when Brock wipes it away. I wish he hadn't because it's the only one.

"Uh-oh, guys. My baby needs cheering up. We might need a trip to the farm."

Tony and Pete punch at the air and drunkenly chant, "To the farm."

"Brock, no." Trey crosses his arms over his chest, standing taller, even though he already has everyone beat. "She's going back to school tomorrow. Plus, she's seeing someone."

"Jordan," I say. "His name's Jordan."

Brock shifts next to me with an annoyed click in his jaw. I poke his cheek, and his expression reverses, his dimple forming beneath my finger.

A dangerous gleam enters his eye. "What do you say we make some bad life choices and get rid of some of that pent-up resentment? You know, for old times' sake."

Trey shakes his head. "You're just pissed at Graham."

I jump up and grab his face in my hands, careful with his injured side. "And you, Trey-tor. I'm so unbelievably mad at you right now."

He mirrors my position, grasping my face. "I'm sorry, but this isn't what you want. Please, Cal."

He's absolutely right; I don't want any of this. I want to be at school, far, far away from here. I want to never see the waste of space who is my father again. I want control over my life.

I push his hands away. "No one cares what I want."

"I do." Brock steps between us and sets my cup in my hand. "What do you want to do right now, Callista?"

Over his shoulder, Trey begs me with his eyes not to answer. He knows what I want to do. It's what I always do when it all becomes too much, and I can't breathe.

I want to escape.

To forget.

Five Years Ago

What set off the death match underway in my parents' bedroom, I won't bother investigating. Once again, I want nothing more than to flee the scene of destruction. I need a break from all the shit that is my fucking life before I lose my mind. More specifically, I need to get away from them.

One of the night's broken objects hurled against a wall for dramatic effect is a picture frame—their wedding photo. They replace it at least once a month. I pick it up on my way through the kitchen and shake out the loose glass.

Initially, I only plan to sit outside on the steps, but Jesus, do their voices carry. I keep walking. Maybe I'll wander in the direction of Uncle Kevin's. Misery loves company, but no one else's presence other than Trey's seems manageable at the moment.

Headlights behind me on the gravel street cast my shadow twenty feet ahead of me. It significantly shortens as they drive closer. Any other town in America, someone walking down the middle of an unlit road in a black sweatshirt might move. Not in Sutterville, PA. Everyone knows to just dodge the pedestrians.

Except whoever is following along behind me.

The lights blind me when I glance back. With my less than tolerant mood engaged, I flip them off. The engine revs, and they pull up beside me. I stop to tell the drunken yokel exactly where they can go, but a drunken yokel they are not.

"Need a ride?" he asks through the rolled-down window.

Just like the first time, I feel his voice everywhere at once.

"I'm almost there," I say.

He leans over, and the passenger door swings open. "Want one anyway?"

The glow of the dash lights up the dimple in his cheek when he smiles. God, that dimple. Despite all the reasons to say no, which probably number in the thousands, I climb in.

"Where we headed?"

"Red truck." I point at the driveway less than a block away. "I told you, I was almost there."

His expression never falters as he stares at me. "It's the strangest thing." He shifts the car into drive, eyes still on mine. "The gas pedal doesn't seem to be working anymore."

We creep forward, the car coasting down the street, and I can't help but smile. "I should have walked then."

"Nope," he says, switching his focus to the road. "This just means we have plenty of time to get to know each other."

"What happened to the truck?"

"Taillight needs fixed." His eyes dart to the beer can in the cupholder. "Couldn't chance a conversation with a cop."

"You're safe." His eyebrows draw in, so I further explain, "Mandatory family dinner at the sheriff's house every Thursday night at six. Then, they watch some lame country-western movie."

"Good to know." He motions toward the frame in my hands that, until now, I forgot about. "What's that?"

I trace the last shard of glass still attached in the corner with a finger. "My parents like to throw around their wedding picture, so I figured I'd do them a favor and get rid of it."

He checks out the windshield. "Sweet of you."

"It's the least I could do, considering their level of devotion."

"None?" His eyes return to mine. "Just guessing."

I nod. "What gave it away?"

"The heavy sarcasm."

"Damn, I should work on that then."

We stop moving.

"Shit," he says. "Don't look." His hand shoots over and covers my eyes.

What the fuck?

Some of those reasons for not getting in the car definitely involved abduction, and the concerns return full force. Panicked, I grab on to his arm to pull his hand away, but he holds firm.

"What are you doing?" I ask.

"Just give me a sec."

The grip on him proves useful to secure me in my seat when the car speeds backward without warning. It brakes hard and then jerks us forward again. When his hand lowers, we are in the exact spot as before but once more crawling toward Trey's truck.

I laugh and relax, releasing my hold on him. He smiles, and his fingertips graze over the back of my hand before returning to the steering wheel. It sends a shiver trailing the entire length of my arm. I shift, uneasy at how a simple touch affects me. Just like his voice. And that fucking dimple.

"You really plan on making me work for a name, huh?" he says.

I shrug. "I don't remember you offering yours either."

Watching me again, he licks his lips. "Same guy from the other day?"

"What?"

His head tips toward Trey's truck not very far ahead. "Same guy?"

"Yeah." Then I add, "He's my cousin."

Why I want to clarify the relationship bothers me since mentioning Pete seems far less important.

The car stops in front of Kevin's house, and he puts it in park. "Stay there." He hops out and runs around the car to open my door. "Now you may go."

"You're very demanding," I say, climbing out.

We stand face-to-face for the first time. He's a few inches taller than me, wearing a gray tank top that clings to his body, and his black sweatpants hang low off his hips.

"Only when I know what I want," he says.

A motion light kicks on across the street, revealing golden-brown eyes. The way they draw me in leaves me unable to move until they lower to my mouth.

"Thanks for the ride."

I start walking away, but an arm snakes around my waist and pulls me in the opposite direction. Then he's in front of me, stepping toward me until his warm body pushes me back against the cold metal of the car. I suck in a breath when the heel of his hand presses into my hip to keep me in place.

"Tell me your name," he demands, our faces less than an inch apart.

"I have a Pete. I mean…" I close my eyes to break the stare and try again. "I have a boyfriend."

His cheek brushes against mine as he brings his lips to my ear. "Still not your name."

"Callista," I breathe out.

He pulls back, and the hand on my hip moves to the again forgotten picture frame. He slides it from my fingers. With the glass already broken, he easily rips out the photo and tosses the rest into the street. His body shifts against mine while he reaches in his pocket.

"Here." He shoves a lighter into my hand. "Think of it as cheap therapy for shitty parents."

I look from it to the picture in his hand to his eyes. My thumb flicks the lighter, brightening up the space between us. I hold it to the corner. The flame licks at the print, eating away at the joke of a couple who strive to make one another miserable regardless of those caught in the cross fire.

Nothing in my life has offered even a fraction of the release. I can breathe for the first time, and I never want the relief to end. Desperate not to suffocate anymore.

His eyes are still on me when mine return to him. He lets the burning relic fall to the ground. "Next time I have you alone, I won't give a fuck about the boyfriend."

He pushes off the car behind me and leaves my entire body as on fire as the fucking pile of ashes at my feet. It takes a second for me to remember how to function, but I manage to straighten up and walk across the lawn.

"Callista," he calls after me.

I turn around, not feeling like I could resist if I tried.

The smile. That dimple.

"I'm Brock."

And everything changes.

156 Days Until 19

A rhythmic pounding in my skull accompanies a sense of emptiness inside me. A familiar combination I promised myself to never endure again. I pull the blanket over my head to block the sun streaming in the window. The longer I keep my eyes shut, the longer I put off dealing with what feels like one hell of a hangover.

When I roll over, a sharp pain shoots through my hip. My jaw clenches to absorb the agony radiating down my leg. Whatever the hell is happening needs to fucking stop. The drum in my head intensifies as I ease off the mattress, careful to keep pressure off my right side.

Felicia sits up in Cam's bed just in time to see me tugging down my sweatpants. I don't even remember coming back to the dorms.

She tosses off the blankets and scrambles out of bed. "Oh my God, Callie. What happened?"

A severe bruise covers my tender hip and extends down my thigh, the entire area red and swollen.

What *did* happen?

Memories flood in, fragmented and disjointed. Tony running from a bull. Bacon sizzling. Jordan's mouth on mine. Trey carrying me to his truck. Pete sprinting down the pond dock and me screaming. A barn door hanging off its hinges. Rough stubble scratching my skin. Stars shining through bare tree branches. A lighter falling to the ground. Pete, already shirtless, taking off his jeans. Brock whispering in my ear, his body pressed against mine. My clothes all over the floor. My hands in someone's hair.

"No. No. No." I grab my phone from the nightstand.

Buried between panicked texts from Connor and concerned ones from Jordan are two from an unsaved number, but I recognize it. I brace myself for what waits.

Hey babe.

I miss you already.

What feels like iron-laced air vacates my lungs upon seeing Brock's messages. I swipe at my burning eyes with the baggy sleeve of my sweatshirt—*oh shit. Not my sweatshirt.* I grasp at the fabric, pulling it away from my chest until I see the high school's logo and Pete's old jersey number on the front. A whimper escapes as I peel it off my body, not knowing which memories explain the clothing swap and which prompted Brock's texts.

Either way I feel fucking sick.

Felicia gasps, rushing over. "Your shoulder."

She touches my back, and I reach behind me. I flinch, raw skin stinging beneath my fingertips as they explore. I back to the mirror and crane my neck around to check the reflection. A wide scrape spans the width of my right shoulder blade. Bringing my arm in front of me, a long, thin burn on my left forearm catches my attention, the skin bright red with a sheen.

Felicia asks again what happened, but I just shake my head, unable to answer. It's as if someone else has been living in my body. I don't know what they've done with it. But I can guess.

Thoughts and feelings crash their way through me. I sink to the floor, the physical pain no match. Felicia lowers next to me and wraps a blanket and her arms around me, but awareness of her and everything else fades away. It's just me and the broken memories ripping me apart.

Fucking wrecking me.

Felicia returns from her afternoon class, finding me where she left me. In bed. Once the door shuts, I uncover my head. I swallow the pain relievers and empty the bottle of water she left on the nightstand. I carefully readjust and position the fresh ice pack under my hip. The cold soothes the feverish skin.

Brock texts again.

When can I see you?

It's the seventh one. The splinters of my weekend flash through my mind again, no more detailed than the last several times. Putting in my earbuds, I let the music drown out the noise in my head. I don't think about how I've thrown my life into chaos. I stop worrying about why I woke up in Pete's sweatshirt. What happened with Brock isn't haunting me.

The reprieve only lasts for a moment. But right now, I need as many of them as I can get.

I must fall asleep, because the next time I open my eyes, darkness covers my room, except the light shining through the open door.

Felicia's outline bends down over me. "Jordan's here," she says, sweeping my hair from my face. "He said he's been calling you all day. What do you want me to do?"

I can't imagine why he wants to see me. According to her, he was here when Trey hauled me in the door last night. Jordan volunteered to stay, and I kicked him out in the middle of the night. I vaguely remember ordering him to leave. A total Callista move, which guarantees the reasoning makes little-to-no sense.

"I'm not ready to talk to him yet."

She squeezes my arm and leaves without pushing the subject.

Cautious of how my weight shifts, I crawl out of bed and switch on the lamp. A blackout of this magnitude normally takes a few days to recover from, both mentally and physically. But I hate dodging Jordan and need to know what happened. Ready or not.

A climb to the ceiling tiles is utterly out of the question with my hip, so I take advantage of Cam's stash in her bottom desk drawer. Even though the thought of consuming anything with a higher alcohol content than fruit juice triggers my gag reflex, what I prepare to do requires, at the minimum, a buzz.

One bottle empties, the whiskey still biting when I tip back a second. I retreat to the safety of my bed and wait for the warmth of the alcohol to loan me courage before I send the message.

What happened the other night?

Brock answers right away.

You don't remember? Way to insult a guy.

Cut the crap. Did we have sex?

The words on the screen look surreal. Like they're from someone else's life. I'm watching through an old, dirty window. The image distorted. The sound muffled. The girl on the other side of the glass lost in a mess of her own making. A place she's been countless times.

No vibration or any other warning precedes his response. The pixels just appear, arranged in such a way that they shatter any illusion of being an onlooker, and my window transforms into a mirror.

Of course Callista.

I read it over and over, the heaviness in my chest increasing with each pass. On some level, I already knew. Regardless of how long I maintain control, my anger toward Graham eventually overpowers everything else. Each and every time, I end up back here. Empty. Alone. Miserable.

My phone lights up with another text.

All right, beautiful. I miss you. I'll see you tomorrow.

As I read Jordan's message, a wave of guilt crashes over me. The consequences of my actions stare me in the face, and I know what needs to happen next.

My parents have made a sport out of dragging other people down with them. Friends, family, each other. They don't care who they hurt as long as they aren't alone in their unhappiness. Brock and I tortured each other and those around us the same way, desperate not to suffer alone. Now I'm about to fall back into the toxic cycle with Jordan. Except I promised to never do that to anyone again. Of all the rules I've made for myself, this has to be the one I don't break. Not even for him. *Especially* not for him.

It's clear I can't escape the dysfunction and chaos. So, I need to let Jordan go. Otherwise, I'm afraid I'll light us both on fire, and he'll go up in flames along with me.

154 Days Until 19

Can we talk?

An incredibly cliché line. But if I want to keep my black hole of a life from sucking Jordan in, I need to gather the damn courage to hit send on the three words I've tapped out and deleted eight times already. I pull the blanket over my head, leaving myself alone with the screen to cycle through another attempt.

A bang interrupts me, and I rip the blanket off. There he stands, just inside my doorway in a black band T-shirt and jeans and his hair a perfect disaster.

Absolutely furious.

Equally pissed, Felicia shoulders her way past him. She stares daggers at him while his death glare focuses on me. I remove an earbud as his attention shifts to her, ringing the bell for Gibson versus Waters.

She plants her hands on her hips. "I told him he couldn't come in here, Callie."

"And I told her I didn't care, *Callie*," he mocks.

"Stop acting like a child, Jordan."

"Oh, that's cute, coming from someone who cries during *Bambi*."

Felicia's jaw drops, and she shoves him with zero results. "Shut up!"

"I have a better idea."

Before she can react, he snatches her up and carries her out the door. He quickly shuts and locks it. "She's almost as frustrating as you are," he says, turning around. His eyes narrow at me again.

After I've avoided him for two days, he deserves to barge in and demand an explanation. I set my earbuds and phone on the nightstand and cautiously move to sit against the wall, ready for him to lay into me.

He looks like he will until his eyes grow wide. "What the fuck?" The anger turns to panic as he rushes over. He brushes his thumb over the horrific bruise on my thigh. "Is this from the tree or four-wheeler?"

"What?" I lean back and grimace until I find a position that keeps pressure off my shoulder blade.

"Trey said you fell out of a tree and wrecked a four-wheeler."

Four-wheelers mean we went to Pete's grandparents' farm. A frequent stop on our group's drunk tour of Sutterville and the surrounding areas. I thought we probably had given my memories of the bull and the pond dock. They also have an old tree I would climb to sneak through Pete's bedroom window and a red barn that matches the door I remember.

"I wrecked into a barn door?" I ask to clarify.

He shrugs. "He just said a barn."

"Tree and barn would correlate to hip and shoulder then." I mentally check injuries one and two off the list and set the ice pack on my hip.

Jordan settles in next to me on the bed and pulls the blanket over my bare legs. "What happened here?"

He traces the burn on my forearm, and I shrug. His touch feels better than any ice pack or burn gel. With him here, all the reasons for keeping him away struggle against all the reasons I want him to stay. Maybe it would be different this time.

"What's going on with you?" His hand slides down to mine.

I pull away from him before my resolve crumbles entirely. "I don't think we should see each other anymore." Our eyes meet, and I force out the rest. "I meant what I said about not being able to handle anything else right now. I never wanted anything serious, Jordan."

I've no more than said his name when he pushes off the bed. I think he's storming out, but he circles back and paces from one end of my room to the other.

"Let me get this straight. On Friday, you were adamant I admit to wanting more, which I did. I *do.* Then you didn't answer your phone all weekend and drank so much that you blacked out. You kicked me out because I wouldn't fuck you when you were drunk."

I made him leave for not *taking advantage of me? God, I really am messed up.*

I can't focus on it for long because he continues, "Which, okay, whatever. Sorry I'm not a creep like those other guys…"

There's more, but my mind rushes to Brock and Pete and what else Trey would have told him to make him say something like that. I jump up, not caring about the ache that follows. "Other guys?"

He walks away. "Never mind."

I block his path, so he can't ignore me. "What *other* guys, Jordan?"

He stops a few feet from me, dragging his hand through his hair and shaking his head. "Felicia and I found pictures your friend Shayna posted from high school."

My entire body goes cold, several images popping into mind. All our stupid, drunken escapades, none of which paint me in a flattering light. Not expecting him to know about any of that, I close my eyes to regain my equilibrium.

"Fuck," I whisper. I force myself to open my eyes, to look at him. "You saw those?"

"I more than saw them." His voice is harsh, eyes even harsher. "They're all seared into my mind. You half-naked and passed out with different dudes and their hands all over you."

Even worse, he's talking about the last leg of my downward spiral. Parties, random guys, and a whole lot of blackouts. So many that, if not for Shayna's thorough documentation, I wouldn't even know what happened for the better part of eight months. Unfortunately, they also remind everyone else.

I blink my gaze to the wall. "She said she took them down."

"Well, she didn't. And after seeing what you were like back then, your striptease makes perfect sense."

Jordan's words have stung before, but this time, they rip a fucking hole inside me. He sounds like Graham and Lara and Brock, throwing the past in my face. What tears me open further is he looks at me like they do while saying it, like that is who I will always be to him now.

"Shit," he says in the same breath. "I'm so sorry, Callie. I didn't mean that."

I hold up my hands when he steps toward me. "You see pictures from a few years ago and have it all figured out?"

He tries to apologize again, but my emotional knob has already cranked to pissed off.

"I'm just some slut, right? But ... if I'm so fucking easy and you still haven't screwed me, what does that say about you?"

I cock my head at him, and Jordan angles his the same way, and I have to ignore the regret etched into his face.

"You know I don't think—" he starts, but I never intend to let him finish.

"I think it says you should go back to banging groupies and anyone else stupid enough to fall for your pathetic bullshit."

His eyes shut for a second, a nerve hit. The muscles of his jaw work beneath the skin when he looks at me again. "Is that out of your system now?" he bites back.

I glare and retaliate without a second thought. "I don't know. Are you finished disappointing everyone now?"

The moment it leaves my mouth, I wish for nothing more than to take it back. But I can't. The words cut that time, his eyes showing the hurt.

"How do you want me to respond to that, Callie?" he asks.

I want him to yell. To scream or throw something. Anything that punishes me for using what he told me about his parents against him. Except he doesn't have even a hint of fight to his tone or on his handsome face. Jordan just patiently waits for my answer, only convincing me more of the right one.

I sink my teeth into my bottom lip, needing a physical distraction from what I'm about to do. "Walk away."

"You want me to walk away?"

We stare at each other until I manage to nod.

He puts his hands on the back of his head while he takes a deep breath. "If I walk away, I'm done. I'm not chasing you anymore."

"I never wanted you to," I say, my voice barely carrying the few feet between us. "I told you from the beginning that I wasn't worth wasting your time."

His gaze softens into the one I can melt into. The one I can live in. Breathe in.

"You were worth everything."

I have to look away. If anything, the last few minutes have proven the opposite. That he's much better off away from me and my life. I step around him to open the door. My eyes close as he passes me, taking the last of the real air with him on his way out. By the time the suite door slams, all the heaviness I've been staving off invades my chest, settling in that newly torn open space.

Felicia rushes in, stopping short when she sees me. "Are you okay?"

I frantically wipe away the hot tears streaming down my face, everything more wrong than I thought possible. "I'm fine." Then I smile the smile I can summon even as the world burns around me. And right now … it is.

149 Days Until 19

Despite being a Monday, a party rages on around us. In game one of the beer pong tournament, Felicia loses all hand-eye coordination. She couldn't hit a cup if it meant her soul mate would pop out like a freaking genie. Becca needs a miracle to help them win against Parker and Harrison. Or as the sign-up sheet calls them, "Long Dong and Longer."

Felicia finally sinks a ball, and Becca arches a brow in my direction. Scratch the miracle comment. She needs my tits. Before we left, she made me change, claiming my breasts as her secret weapon for the night. Two hours later, I have yet to determine whether to take offense or accept the flattery. Either way, I tug down the already-low-cut V-neck to expose my black lace bra.

Target acquired, Parker watches me and loses focus on the cup he just lifted off the table. He pauses with it halfway to his mouth, his eyes following the finger tracing down my neckline. Too easy. The distraction grants Becca all the time she needs. Her ball soars through the air and lands in his cup to win the game.

"Boom." She points across the table.

Harrison slaps the beer out of Parker's hand. "Dude, you have got to be kidding me."

Parker scowls at me, but honestly, he should know better than to ogle a woman in the middle of a game. Especially one who hasn't given him the time of day since walking through the door.

He and his bruised ego stroll over as the teams switch, his head shaking. "I knew you would get me in trouble."

"Don't you have some beer to drink?" I ask.

Without breaking his dark eyes away from mine, he reaches for a cup on the table. "I can multitask."

"Clearly you can't, or you'd still be playing."

He chews on his lip. "And the temptress who helped defeat me goes by…"

I give him half a smile. "Callie."

"Actually, she prefers Calico."

My heart trips up when Benji appears beside me. I scan the room, wanting to see Jordan and not wanting to see Jordan—*holy shit, I can't see Jordan yet.* I need more than five days.

"He's not here," Benji says in my ear, taming my inner freak-out.

"And you are?" Parker raises his eyebrows, observing Benji's arm snaking around my waist.

"Good, thanks." With a smirk, he walks away with me in tow. "Get a drink with me."

Not like he gives me a choice, hauling me across the room. He escorts me all the way to the keg before he lets me go. While filling my cup and trying small talk, he casually steps between me and a smiling frat boy, then he ushers me into the living room where he barricades me off from a group of guys. His intentions are obvious—keep Callie away from anyone with a dick.

He would have proven useful over the weekend to keep Tyler at bay. My mother's boy-toy insisted on a foolproof method to help me forget all about my problems. It involved blowing him in the back of his "'stang." Gag. I told him I'd meet him out there. He slapped my ass on the way out the door, and I promptly locked it behind him. Half an hour later, Lara finished her shower, found him, and let him back in.

An XY-chromosome configuration wanders too close, so Benji shuffles to my other side.

"How much do you charge for babysitting?" I ask, amused by his misplaced concern.

"I consider it volunteer work." He bumps my shoulder and looks around. "My buddy's a member here and owes me money."

I search the crowd with him, no clue what the guy looks like.

"He's a mess," he says, eyes back on me.

"Your buddy?"

"Jordan."

Until now, no one has said his name to me, and hearing it out loud hits me in the worst possible way.

I bite my cheek, desperate for an excuse to leave. "I need a refill."

Benji peeks over the rim of my cup. "No, you don't."

Three large swallows rectify the situation.

He shakes his head, disapproving. "Text him, Calico. He's miserable, and from where I'm standing, you're not doing so hot either."

"I'm fine," I say, not bothering with the fake smile. "Take care, Benji."

When I walk away, he starts to follow, but someone stops him to talk. Smiling Frat Boy takes care of me at the keg, and I return to Felicia and Becca, fresh drink in hand. They're only halfway through their game. I secretly will Felicia to keep missing, so we can leave soon. This party no longer provides a distraction from everything Jordan related.

"He your boyfriend?" Parker steps beside me, sipping from his cup.

I shake my head. Although Benji as a boyfriend would be quite the experience. All wisdom all the time, except when he sings in a rock band. What type of girl does he even date?

"Good." He watches me out of the corner of his eye. "So, back to you killing my winning streak."

"Do you want an apology?" I ask, looking over at him.

"No," he says. "You owe me something else."

And all I can think about is when Jordan jumped off the banister on the porch, wearing my pink hat and his cocky grin.

"I think you owe me something else, too."

Parker continues talking, but I can't even feign interest anymore, because no matter how much I pretend it doesn't, missing Jordan really fucking hurts. The hole he ripped inside me, the weight and ache and everything I've been trying to avoid since he walked away, hits me at once.

Finally, I can't stand it anymore. In my head, I politely excuse myself from the conversation. In actuality, I walk away without a word and head up the stairs. Someone steps out of the bathroom at the perfect time. I don't even turn on the light, just lower onto the floor to the cushy bathmat. The chill of the porcelain tub seeps through the back of my shirt. I focus on it and the heels of my hands pressing hard into the floor, but the ache spreads further, tightening and overpowering my senses until I feel it rising in my chest, throat, eyes.

"No," I scramble off the floor. "No. No. No."

A bathroom at a party is the last fucking place I will cry. I brace my hands on each side of the sink and challenge the girl in the mirror to bury it all one more time. To shove every shred of emotion into that stupid, empty space. She stares back at me, resembling my mother more than ever with the dark circles under bloodshot eyes, but she at least appears equally determined not to become a cliché.

Slowly, I regain control, and everything returns below the surface. Not as far as it once stayed, but far enough for now.

I give myself another minute and go downstairs. Neither Becca nor Felicia look anywhere near ready to leave, so I catch up with another group going back to the dorms. On my way out the door, Benji swipes the phone out of my hand.

"Unlock," he says, waving it around. I comply, and he taps away for a few seconds before tossing it back. "Text *me* then, Calico. Anytime. Any reason."

I note my new contact, Benjamin "Badass" Jones and find it in me to give him a small smile. "Thanks, Benji."

He shrugs. "Don't thank me yet."

With that cryptic comment, he spins on his heel and walks away.

When I get to the dorms, I tromp up to the suite and unlock the door on autopilot, but halfway through the common area, I stop. I retreat a few steps, wondering if Smiling Frat Boy messed with my drink because why the fuck am I hallucinating a shirtless Rusty on my couch?

"Hey, sweetheart," a very real Rusty says.

My eyebrows pull in as he kicks back with his black boots on the coffee table.

He notices the look on my face and adds, "Oh, I'm smashing Jess now."

I bite down on a smile at the matter-of-fact delivery of his line and head to my room. No questions asked.

144 Days Until 19

By the time I get to Graham's on Friday night, he seems to have forgotten about my transgressions from two weeks ago. Whatever line of bullshit Trey fed him when he picked up my stuff must have worked. He doesn't speak to me from the moment I walk in, and on Saturday, he returns to his normal, absent self, leaving me with my phone and the keys to my car. Helpful, since I need to throw myself back in the fire and fill in the last of the missing pieces.

The lines form between Connor's eyebrows as I put on my coat. "Cal…"

"I give you permission to hunt me down if I'm not back in two hours." I swipe my hair out of the neck lining.

"How much damage can you do in two hours?"

I purse my lips, seriously contemplating his question. "Better make it an hour." I wink and back out the door.

Typical for a Saturday afternoon, Main Street is empty, except for two cars in front of the grocery store. I circle the block to the parking area behind the bar. Pete's grandparents bought the place when we were little. We spent more time playing in the apartment upstairs than anywhere else. Now he lives up there and splits his time between working here and the farm.

A sheriff's cruiser and extended cab truck are the only two vehicles in sight and the only two I need. I park and grab the cobalt blue sweatshirt from the seat. The heavy door sticks as I pull open the back entrance. After nearly tripping over an empty cardboard box, I maneuver around more on my way down the hall.

I push through the swinging door into the main area and find Pete sprawled out on top of the bar with Trey perched on a stool, drinking a beer.

Pete's head tilts back to see me. "Shit, Cal. Why couldn't you have felt this undeniable attraction to me five years ago?"

Trey plants his hands on Pete's hip and shoves him over the edge where a thump precedes a groan.

He hops up and grabs an empty mug like nothing happened. "Beer?"

I join my cousin, and Pete slides me a draft.

"I figured you'd be in hiding all weekend." Trey smiles, but it stops short of his eyes, the guilt for the part he played in my lost weekend showing through.

All of his calls since then have gone unanswered. Even now, I'm not ready to talk to him, but I need to know the details.

"How does your boyfriend feel about your obsession with me?" Pete's playful grin waits when I look up from my beer.

"Here." I toss his sweatshirt at his face, ignoring his comment. "Do I want to know why I woke up wearing this thing?"

"I might have thrown you in the pond."

Thanks to the prompt, I recall what followed him running toward me on the dock and my scream—a whole lot of wet and cold.

He tucks the sweatshirt under the bar. "We went inside to dry off while Shayna found you clothes to wear in her car. But *someone* literally couldn't keep their shirt on. Or your bra—making Tony the clear winner of your bet, by the way." He busies himself, cutting a lime. "Anyway, I threw my sweatshirt on you."

A tension releases from my shoulders. Nothing happened other than Pete being his usual self—the nicest guy imaginable.

His expression softens as he watches me relax. "All innocent, m'lady," he says. "We were nowhere close to reliving prom night."

"No offense, Pete, but thank God."

He pours us each a shot of tequila to go with the lime wedges. "Good thing I got you covered when I did. Brock came in a second later. Keeping him off you clothed was enough of a chore."

All the tension returns at the mention of his name.

"The key was to keep you talking about Jordan," Trey says. "Brock wanted nothing to do with you then."

"It must not have worked that well." I clink my glass with theirs.

Pete and I take our shots, but Trey sets his down.

He turns toward me on his stool, his brow furrowed. "What the hell does that mean?"

I shrug, lime wedge still in my mouth. "I still had sex with him."

Now Pete's face matches Trey's, both staring at me.

"What?" I ask.

They glance at each other before Trey says, "Cal, we never let you out of our sight. Pete, Tony, or I were with you at all times."

"I even stood outside the door when you took a piss. We weren't going to let anything bad happen to you." Pete's head rocks, weighing his comment. "Except the whole falling-ten-feet-from-a-tree incident."

"Also, her driving the four-wheeler directly into the barn door." Trey throws back his shot. "Tony really dropped the ball on that one."

"But I remember being alone with him…" I skirt around explicitly telling my cousin and ex what part of Brock's body I remember pressed against me and focus on the only other detail. "Outside by a fence somewhere?"

"Oh, fucking fuck." Pete slaps his bar rag down. "You're talking about by the bull's pen?"

"Maybe? I remember Tony running from the bull."

"No," he says, his mouth turning up. "He was running across the pen because you kneed Brock in the balls for getting too close."

"It was great," Trey adds.

"No." I shake my head. They have to be wrong. "Brock texted me the next day and *told* me we had sex."

"Motherfucker," Trey hisses at the same time Pete bites out, "We're kicking his ass next time we see him."

"It never happened," Trey tells me. "I swear."

My head spins, for once the alcohol not to blame as the truth slams into me. Brock lied. Of course he lied. I created the perfect opportunity when I admitted to not remembering. Hell, I delivered the damn thing wrapped with a fucking bow. Then I chose to believe the guy who'd spent two years breaking promises and starting fights with me out of sheer boredom.

Trey nudges my shoulder. "Where'd you go, Cal?"

I keep staring straight ahead, not focused on anything. "I ended things with Jordan. I'd fucked up and lost control and slept with Brock, and I ended things, so next time I fucked up, I wouldn't hurt him."

"Oh shit," he says. "Are you okay?"

I shake my head, and it finally happens then. Not a single tear like in Shayna's trailer or the silent stream from after Jordan left for the last time. A whimper escapes, and then all the pain pours out at once. Real, soul-breaking tears that turn into uncontrollable, ugly sobs, slashing through me and seeming like they'll never stop.

But I don't want them to. Not until every last bit of feeling is out of me. I want to be free of it all.

Numb, so none of it can hurt me anymore.

<hr>

Everything stops eventually.

I lie on top of the bar, staring at the fan as it completes each slow rotation. The shadow spins on the vaulted ceiling above me.

Trey monitors every breath, waiting for me to fall apart again. I won't. My head pounds, and my eyes burn, but the emotions have subsided. Plunged back below the surface. For a while at least.

An assortment of fried snack foods appears next to my head. When Pete reaches to set the basket on the bar, I notice a mark on his forearm. I sit up and grab his hand and push his sleeve farther up.

"We match?" I hold out my arm and compare the burns. Fresh pink skin and the same size.

"Tony has one, too," Trey says, rolling up his sleeve and adding his burned arm to the mix. "I'm jealous if you were able to forget."

"Be jealous then, because I don't remember."

"Tony decided we needed to see who was the toughest out of the three of us," Pete says. "We heated up metal clothes hangers with a lighter and whoever held it against their arm the longest won." He chuckles. "You said we were sexist for not including you and Shayna. Turned out, you were right and beat us all."

An odd relief floods over me as the last piece of the puzzle falls into place with all injuries accounted for. "God, we're idiots." I smile for a moment before it fades. "Some of us more than others."

Trey shakes his head. "From what I could tell, Jordan's a pretty understanding guy. I mean, he should have beaten my ass for bringing you back to school like I did. I'm sure, if you explained—"

"No." I douse a fry in ketchup. "Enough people already deal with my baggage. He's better off."

Pete steals the fry from my hand. "So, you're back on the market?"

Trey launches a fried cheese ball at him. "Dude."

"What? He might be better off, but I've dealt with your family's drama most of my life. Plus, dating Cal provides perks that being friends with your ass just can't match." He makes a kissy face toward Trey and then winks at me.

"Dream on." I flick beer from my glass at him.

The soda sprayer appears from behind the bar, Pete ready to squeeze the trigger. "Think about your next move very carefully, Henders."

"Don't make me shoot, Pete." Trey pops off the lid of the ketchup bottle and aims. "They trained us for these types of situations at the academy."

Pete's grin widens as his other hand rises with another sprayer. "If I'm going down, I'm taking the whole damn bar down with me."

They stay in a standoff until Trey ever so slightly arches his eyebrows at me. I smile at him before I dive off the bar, tackling Pete to the floor.

139 Days Until 19

The meltdown in front of Trey and Pete proved therapeutic, and by the time I finish my last midterm on Thursday, I'm looking forward to spring break. I'll spend the weekend at Lara's—eye roll—but campus will be a ghost town when I return. An entire week to myself sounds like what I need to refocus.

Before I leave for Lara's tomorrow, I agree to go with Felicia to an always-eventful party at the state college an hour and a half away. Her cousin and his friends are throwing some big kickoff at their house. I would have passed on the invite, but Becca has already left for Connecticut, Jess bailed to spend time with Rusty, and Felicia going alone worries me. State parties shoot to the rowdy end of the spectrum sooner rather than later. Sure, the cops usually bust them within a few hours, but a lot can go wrong in that amount of time.

Felicia parks about a block away and glances around as we get out. "Think we can sprint this far when the cops show up?"

"We might want to stretch now, just in case," I deadpan.

Both of us reach for our phones at the same time.

"Mine's Jess," she says. "She's coming after all and bringing Rusty. They're forty minutes out."

Their relationship remains an unsolvable mystery. She won't let him in her room, and neither seems keen on being seen together on campus.

"Who's yours from?" she asks.

I tip the phone, and we read the message from Benji.

My dearest Calico, see you soon. P.S. No, he's not coming.

I shove my phone in my pocket, relieved, disappointed, and a few other conflicting emotions always related to Jordan Waters. Between Jess, Rusty, and Benji, the day will come when he and I wind up in the same place at the same time. As much as I should dread the moment, part of me can't fucking wait.

To say this party is unique would constitute a flat-out lie. Other than different faces and a rougher crowd, everything seems business as usual. Red cups. Loud music. Stale beer and weed.

We walk around the beer pong table set up in the living room and locate the keg in the kitchen. I immediately forget Felicia's cousin's name after he introduces himself. He chats with us in the living room and educates me on all the details of the amazing party.

"The best of the year."

If I hadn't known the relation before, it would be obvious with that comment.

Felicia pushes up to her tiptoes, looking over heads toward the door. "Jess should be here by now."

I check the time, surprised we've been here an hour already. "Maybe they got lost?"

"I'll call them." She heads toward the front door, the bodies swallowing her.

Left alone, Cousin and I share an awkward smile that lasts far too long before I say, "Bathroom?"

He points out the long line spilling into the living room from the hallway. "If you go to the end of the hall and hang a left, there's another one."

I nod a thanks and entrust him to relay my whereabouts to Felicia.

A well-known fact, State kids are sloppy drunks. Several are already leaning against walls, unable to stand, while others stumble around. I have to step over one passed out in the middle of the floor. Once I clear everyone, I follow the long hall far past the bathroom line. At the end, I turn into an abandoned corridor with several closed doors on each side. What even is this house?

After a few wrong attempts, I successfully locate the smallest bathroom in existence. Quite the treasure hunt, but hey, no line.

On my return trip, I consider recommending Cousin offer a tour guide or sell maps at the gift shop. The place is enormous, and a less fortunate soul not adhering to a two-drink rule could become lost in the grid-patterned floor plan.

As I round the corner back to the main hallway, I collide with a large body. A hand plants low on my back after the initial impact.

"I thought I saw you come this way," he says.

My eyes snap up at the voice, and I back up to gain space from the towering, muscular blond in front of me. Some people find the dimple in his chin and the heat in his eyes sexy—my mother for instance—but not me.

"Tyler, what are you doing here?"

He stares at my chest without shame and trails his hand up my arm. "My school, babe. What are you doing here?"

Right.

"My friend's cousin lives here."

"Nice." His gaze rakes up and down my body, so I doubt he's responding to what I said.

I can't remember the last time I wore anything form-fitting around him for this exact reason. The pig can't keep his eyes in their sockets. I wrap my arms around myself, hiding what I can in my cropped sweater.

Behind him, at the end of the hall, people are still waiting in line for the bathroom. Farther still, more walk by where it opens to the living room. A lot of distance separates me from them. It seems like even more with him standing between us, and I want to close it.

"Well, bye."

I try to pass him, but his backward strides match mine, step for step.

"Come on, we never get to hang out, just the two of us."

"Why would we?" I spit back.

"Let's go somewhere." He stops, requiring me to as well since he's again blocking my path. His eyes are glassy, and he reeks of alcohol.

"You're drunk. So, how about I go back to the party, and you sleep it off. Or better yet, call your girlfriend."

I attempt to move around him, but the back of Tyler's hand presses against my bare stomach to keep me in place.

"Come back to my place."

Before I can shove his hand away, it slips around to my ass.

"Back off," I say, prying it away.

He grabs again with the other and pulls me toward him. "No one has to know."

A bit of panic kicks in after another failed attempt to get away. I'm on his turf, without Lara in the next room, and he can be more aggressive. Which he is. He steps into me so that I back up. The distance to the rest of the party grows when we round the corner. Everyone out of sight.

His head dips down, and I put my hands up for a barrier, turning my face away.

"Tyler."

He moans when I say his name, and my back is against a wall by the time his mouth touches my neck. The hot breath crawls over my skin. I shove on his chest with my forearms, but he won't budge.

"Knock it off," I warn him, but my voice trembles on the last word.

The next time I push him, he pins my wrists to the wall by my sides. Then his lips creep all the way up my neck to my ear. "Why are you always such a bitch to me?"

"I'm sorry," I say because I don't know what else to do. "I'm sorry. I'm sorry."

"I've heard all the stories, Callista." He thrusts his hips hard, and a wave of nausea hits me when his erection digs into my stomach. "I know what you really want, even if you won't admit it."

I see the moment barreling toward me now. One of those capable of changing everything. What happens next flashes through my head, the dread of it flooding through me. Desperate to stop it, I try to free my hands, to get away. He tightens the grip on my wrists as his body smothers mine and his mouth works lower. The next time I jerk at his hold, he bites me, his teeth clamping down. I cry out, but it doesn't matter with the music from the party. I can't move. Can't stop him. Can't do anything but be there.

Helpless.

Burning tears spill out when I crush my eyes closed, and a panicked whimper escapes. "Please, Tyler."

"Yeah, babe. Beg for—*fuck*!"

The weight of his body leaves mine, his hold releasing. I gasp for air, my eyes flying open as he stumbles backward, his face warped in pain. It takes a few seconds to process Rusty behind him with a fistful of blond hair.

"I found Callie," he says, quiet but seething.

I wipe away the wet from my cheeks just as Benji comes around the corner. One glance at Rusty and Tyler, and he bolts over, his eyes scanning my face. But I watch behind him. Rusty throws Tyler back into the wall before letting him go. He places himself between us, his stance broad and more intimidating than I imagined him ever capable of being.

"Hey, guy. What are we doin'?"

Tyler straightens up, puffing out his chest in a challenge. "We were just catching up."

"Yeah, I fucking bet." Rusty's fist clenches at his side, and he turns his head enough I can see his profile. "Do I kill him, Callie?"

"I'm telling you, we were just talking."

"I didn't fucking ask you." Rusty stalks toward him.

"We were just talking," I blurt out, desperate to stop them.

Adrenaline shakes through my voice as much as the rest of me, and three sets of shocked expressions zero in on me. I force a deep breath to fend off the genuine possibility of collapsing to the floor.

With Rusty distracted, Tyler sidesteps away from him, a smirk on his face. "See ya later, Cal," he says before disappearing around the corner.

The departing words stab deep, somewhat because he uses my nickname but mostly because he *will* see me later. He might even sit across the dinner table from me tomorrow at Lara's. If pitted against him, I've no doubt she'll choose him in a heartbeat.

Rusty grips my shoulder, all of him softer now. "You okay?"

"I'm fine," I lie, but as soon as I say it, I shiver.

Benji slips his hand into my trembling one. "You and Jess, ride with Felicia," he tells Rusty, never taking his eyes off me. "We're heading back now."

"Yes, sir." Rusty hands off a set of keys.

I don't argue with them deciding for me. I don't even put up a fight when Benji leads me out of the house without either of us saying goodbye to Felicia or Jess. I just follow along like a catatonic puppy.

Within a few blocks, Jordan's Jeep comes into view.

"We wouldn't all fit on Rusty's bike, and my car doesn't do well over forty."

We stop at the passenger side. I stare through the window, not making a move to get in.

"You have to let go, Calico," Benji says.

My eyebrows pull in. "What?"

"Unless you know a very creative solution to how we're both getting in the car…" He lifts his hand, bringing mine with it. "I need my hand for a few seconds."

I release the chokehold on his hand, not realizing I'd still held it this entire time. He waits for me to get in before he rushes around to the other side. While I buckle my seat belt, he digs around in the backseat.

"Here." He lays a sweatshirt in my lap.

Like a lovesick middle schooler, I smell Jordan's hoodie, breathing him in. A move that doesn't go unnoticed by Benji.

"Stubborn-ass people, man," he says, pulling away from the curb.

He doesn't push me to talk. We ride in silence with the music playing in the background. I use the hoodie as a blanket and watch road signs out the window. I thought my mind would be replaying what had happened. Reliving it over and over again. But I just stare, a little number than usual. Like all the years spent burying these awful things has rewired my brain. I've trained myself to not only hide it all from other people, but also from myself. Experience the hurt and then hold it deep inside, pretending it's not there until it becomes too much and threatens to destroy me again.

"My father manipulates me into visiting him." The words rush out, and as soon as they do, I wince and then peek over at Benji.

He stares straight ahead, his expression unchanged. "He sounds like a prick."

I laugh at his response, oddly relieved. "You have no idea."

"Want to talk about it?" he asks.

I don't even need to think it over because, for the first time in my life, I really do.

***

Benji nods along, every now and then interjecting a muttered, "Fuck," at something.

He develops a death grip on the steering wheel when I tell him about Jordan's birthday and the last few weeks. Then he officially loses his chill when I tell him about Tyler.

"You're fucking kidding, right?" His fingers further tighten around the wheel. Even in the dark, I see his knuckles turning white. "You're not telling anyone what that piece of shit did to you?"

I shrug and rub the sore spot below my shoulder where he bit me. "There's no point. My word against Tyler's would mean nothing to Lara. She'd probably call me a liar and accuse me of trying to fuck her boyfriend."

"Rusty should have killed him." Benji glances over and tugs Jordan's hoodie over to cover my arm. "We're listening to some tunes now before I turn our asses around and finish the job."

I sink back in the seat, and he cranks the volume. Music blares from the speakers, the world flashing by out the window. I've mostly zoned out when he turns off the highway and stops for gas.

When he gets back in, he starts the engine, but we go nowhere. He drums a finger on the wheel a few seconds before he hits the knob to shut off the music.

"I call bullshit," he says. He shifts to face me. "Don't get me wrong. I think what you're doing for your little brother and sister is admirable. Most people would just bail. And the second you decide on the route of patricide, I'm here to help, but you're letting your old man—no, he doesn't even get that. You're letting this gutless trash win, and it's bullshit."

I turn toward him, not sure how to respond. Not that he gives me a chance.

"Right now, that small-dicked bastard can tell you to be in a specific place at a specific time, but his control should end there. Instead, you're giving him all this power over you and choosing not to fight for your own happiness."

Benji's intentions are pure, but he doesn't understand. I'm tired of fighting against Graham. Tired of trying to keep him and Lara from tainting everything around me. Tired of the emotional drain. Tired of wanting to escape my own life.

Just so fucking tired.

I stare down at the gearshift between us, not wanting to cry. "The worst part of my life can't destroy the best parts if there aren't any."

He tips my chin up, so I look at him. "For starters, get rid of the absolutes. Life is hard enough without living it all or nothing. You need to blur the lines a little. Seek out those gray areas and let the positive dilute the negative." He shrugs a shoulder. "When it gets too dark, search for some damn stars, you know?"

It makes me think of something Pete's grandmother used to say to him. "Watch for the sun to shine when it rains."

"Exactly," he says. His eyebrows pull in as he tries to come up with another one to further his point. "Find the exquisite twilight ... hidden between..." He makes a face and shakes his head. "Nope. I can't finish that one. I should have quit while I was ahead."

My mouth turns up at the corners. "Exquisite Twilight is a great band name."

He chuckles and spreads Jordan's hoodie over me again. "That it is, my friend. At the very least, a killer song title."

I lean back in my seat, and he stares out at a dark field in front of us, not saying another word. He gives me the same silence I offer Connor when he feels unsteady. I'm left with my thoughts but not alone as I regain my balance. A balance I lost longer ago than I've ever admitted.

My hate for Graham has been growing and evolving all my life. The roots are twisted deep in my core, constantly present. I always thought the drinking and partying were my misguided attempts to prove he couldn't break me, but sitting at an abandoned gas station with my personal sage, I'm finally accepting the truth. I shattered the moment the hate for him consumed me, and I've been drowning in it ever since.

"I think I understand what you meant earlier."

He readjusts in his seat. "Let me hear it, woman."

I pull my knees up to my chest until the makeshift blanket covers me, protects me. "Graham—"

"The spineless waste," he injects.

"He should only get my physical presence every other weekend, but I keep giving him so much more." I tip my head against the headrest. "No matter where I am, the slightest reminder of him shuts me down. I can't see anything else. I can't think about anything else. It ruins my entire day, sometimes more, and I let it happen every single time. I *let* him effect all of it, and you're right. It's complete bullshit I give him that kind of power over me."

Maybe the answer has always been obvious and in my face, but all the rest blinded me to it. The way to take control away from Graham is to not give it to him in the first place. He can only make me miserable if I allow him to, so I refuse to let him anymore. End of story.

Benji still hasn't said anything, so I look up, and he smiles. "Sounds like you've solved the puzzle."

I huff out a laugh, feeling like I have. Or at least, sorted out enough to see it in a different light.

"Should I tell you what you've won?" he asks. I nod, and he's serious again. "A life, Calico. Now you get to live your life."

Even though his words cause actual freaking goose bumps, I roll my eyes. "You couldn't spring for a pony? I mean, this is a pretty significant revelation."

He contemplates for a second. "Would you settle for something a little more the size of Jordan Waters?"

I chew on my lip, remembering what I said to him. "I called him a disappointment for no other reason than to hurt him, Benji. I knew it would, and I did it anyway."

"So, apologize and do better next time."

"Is it really that simple?" I ask. "I apologize, and he forgives me, just like that?"

He digs out his wallet and tosses me a folded piece of notebook paper from inside it. "Our failed songwriting attempt from the other day."

Unfolding it, I recognize Jordan's handwriting. Most of the page, he covered in doodles, and a lot of words are crossed out. But Benji taps at four lines in one corner that I can still make out.

Certain of the unsure in a meaningless void.
Frantic beauty hides beyond her serene blue eyes.
She left as mine but never returned.
A scab not yet a scar in a messy, wounded life.

"The kid's lyrics were straight out of a boy-band-broken-heart ballad," Benji says. "I'm damn near positive I'm in the presence of his muse."

"Messy and wounded sounds like me."

A scribbled-out section toward the bottom steals my attention, the words hidden beneath the blue spirals, barely visible.

What I wouldn't do for five more perfect seconds with you.

I smile at the words. Maybe it can be that simple— uncomplicated. "I apologize, and he'll forgive me."

Benji snatches the paper out of my hand and returns it to his wallet. "Now, can we please go fix his poor, tormented soul, so I can get my lead guitarist back?"

I've hardly nodded when the locks engage—in case I change my mind, I guess. He speeds away from the gas pump, and the tires squeal, pulling onto the highway.

"I thought Jordan was the dramatic one," I mumble.

He shrugs. "The guy rubs off on you. Consider this your warning."

I pull out my phone to text him but stop, thinking of something he once said, and suddenly I'm inspired with a Jordan-worthy plan. "Hey, you wouldn't happen to know anywhere that screen-prints T-shirts, would you?"

"Calico," Benji says, "I'm the lead singer for a fucking band. What do you think?"

He glances over and winks, and Mission Tell Jordan Sorry commences.

138 Days Until 19

In the morning, I meet Beta Void minus their lead guitarist at the T-shirt shop. Since Benji needs to leave for Vermont before Jordan's finished with his last midterm, he volunteers Rusty and Gavin to help. It takes all of two minutes to regret involving them, but it's too late because we're already synchronizing the watches none of us wear.

After the unnecessarily elaborate planning session, I return to an empty dorm suite and pack for the weekend. According to a text from Lara, Tyler called her in the wee hours of the morning with last-minute spring break plans for them. The chances of him making said plans after our little encounter are near a thousand fucking percent. Regardless, anything improving the odds of not seeing him earns my approval.

I change into my new T-shirt and check the mirror one last time. I've never been one for nerves, but they kick in as I realize what I'm about to do.

No backing out now, Henders.

The second I park in front of Jordan's house, Gavin texts.

Upstairs window.

When I look up, he gives me hand signals. Except we never agreed on any, so he very well might be telling me to steal home. While I appreciate the enthusiasm, it's a little much. I wiggle my hands around in response before I flip him off. He grins and disappears behind a curtain.

I grab the box from the backseat and button up my coat on my way to the front door. The thought of abandoning the plan altogether enters my mind at least a thousand times even though I'm the one who came up with the damn thing. I knock, and my throat tightens, and my brain goes to mush when he answers.

Jordan and I stare at each other. Him on one side of the threshold with his sexy hair and confused green eyes, me on the other with my little cardboard box and my heart hammering the hell out of my rib cage. On the floor next to him sits his luggage for the airport. In about an hour, he will be leaving on his brother Dustin's Spring Break Extravaganza—a week of Tijuana, booze, and women. All the more reason to hurry. Well, that and we're approaching the minute mark of neither of us speaking.

"Hey," I say.

His chin lifts. Barely. Nothing else.

I almost smile, witnessing him speechless for the first time. "I didn't think you'd be here. Your Jeep's gone, and Benji said you had a midterm."

He takes a deep breath, and the surprise from seeing me fades. "Sorry to disappoint—*again*," he says, his tone clipped.

Well-deserved but ouch all the same. I thought he would ask why I showed up on his doorstep, but he wants to go in a different direction apparently.

I roll my eyes. "Nothing can ever be easy with you." I shove the box at him and leave him in the doorway.

He hasn't moved by the time I back out of the driveway. The rest of the plan hinges on him opening the box and caring enough to chase after me one more time. Given the unreadable expression on his face, I worry he doesn't, and he won't.

I park out of sight of the house and reluctantly answer a video chat from Gavin. "I thought I said we weren't doing this."

He ignores me, his face flashing in and out of view. "He's on the move."

The camera flips to show him opening his bedroom door. I toss my coat in the back and snag the coffee from the cupholder.

On my trek over to the house, I watch Gavin descend the stairs to their living room, and then Jordan comes into view, pacing, staring at the box.

"What's in the box?" Gavin asks, centering on Jordan picking it up and shaking it around.

I climb the steps to the deck outside their back door as Jordan resumes walking back and forth on the screen. All the while, he stares at the box once again on the coffee table.

Suddenly, he stops and looks straight at the camera. "Are you recording my misery?" he asks.

I tried to warn the guys a video chat would tip him off, but why would a group of self-proclaimed Jordan experts ever listen to me?

"You're acting insane," Gavin says, recovering. "This is documentation in case we need to have you committed."

Jordan's attention snaps back to the box. He drops onto the couch and rips open the flaps like his life depends on it. He digs, his frustration growing until he dumps out the packing peanuts. More sorting before he finally realizes the box holds—

"Nothing?" Furious, he jumps up. "She got in my head over *nothing?*"

Jordan starts across the living room, and I hang up on Gavin. Whatever happens next won't involve anyone else. Just us.

I step out of the way of the door just in time. It narrowly misses me when Jordan bolts out and down the steps, oblivious to me standing a few feet away. He storms toward where they park their vehicles. I'll give the guys this one. So that he couldn't go anywhere, they insisted Rusty conveniently borrow his Jeep. A fact that appears to hit him halfway across the lawn because he stops and breaks into a stream of curses.

I follow him down the steps, reaching the bottom right before he turns around. He freezes when he sees me, and I can't remember a damn thing I planned to say when our gaze meets. His brow dips in confusion while we stare at each other, and I worry my stunt might have broken him.

"Good afternoon, beautiful," I say, my fingers tightening around the cup.

He says nothing, but his eyes lower to the picture of him wearing a towel, an obnoxiously pink hat, and a frilly purple scarf on my T-shirt. I twist around and pull my hair out of the way, so he can read *Mission Tell Jordan Sorry* printed across the back.

When I turn, he stares at me. The most dramatic person I've ever met is not reacting at all. Missions, T-shirts, and coffee might have worked to win me over, but they appear to do little the other way around. Confidence in my plan prepares to swan-dive off a cliff when he starts walking toward the house. I wait, wondering if he'll go right past me and inside, hating me forever, but then he slows down.

"For future reference," he says, stopping in front of me, "everything at once is overkill."

My nerves vanish as his mouth turns up, and I let out a breath before sipping the coffee I brought him. "You know, I was a little worried about that."

"Pro tip—spread it out over a couple of hours."

I check the invisible yet synchronized watch on my wrist. "Sorry, but I'm working under rather restrictive time constraints since someone plans on fleeing the country."

A smile I've missed spreads across his face, and he erases the last few steps. He stares down at me, slides his hands up my neck, lining both sides of my jaw with his thumbs.

"Let's fast-forward then, shall we?"

Then he kisses me. It brings all the missing air rushing back at once, the last of the heaviness gone. I want nothing more than to breathe the real air and feel his lips on mine, but my well-rehearsed apology speech starts pouring out. Most words end up mumbled against his mouth as he continues to kiss me. About halfway through it, he pulls back.

"Your apology is distracting me from forgiving you."

I smile, and he looks at me in a way that rights all the wrongs between us, everything seamlessly shifting back into place. The past two weeks are done, over, and I never want to think about them again.

He grabs the coffee and slides his hand down to mine. "So, the box?" he asks, walking up the steps.

"A decoy. The idea was for you to chase after me. Full circle and all."

He shakes his head and holds open the door. "What if it didn't work?"

"Gavin was going to get you all riled up over it until you did." The only backup plan without the risk of Jordan winding up in need of emergent care. "Your friends are not loyal to you in the least, by the way."

From the entryway, we veer off to a kitchen so Jordan can throw his already-empty cup away. He leads me into the living room. Gavin smirks, finishing the cleanup of green packing peanuts Jordan left behind. He proudly sports his team T-shirt and straightens to guarantee Jordan notices.

Which he most certainly does, his eyes narrowing at me. "Oh, come on."

"What? They were cheaper by the dozen." I wink at him.

Gavin bounds up the stairway, calling back, "Face it, Waters. You've met your match."

I pull out my phone to check the time, knowing I need to get on the road to Lara's house soon. Jordan has disappeared when I glance over my shoulder. His voice drifts in from the kitchen. It sounds like he's canceling his car. If only I could abandon my plans as easily, we could stay locked up together for the entire weekend.

Connor texts, *Taking Cate to a pickup game at school.*

Arms slip around my waist, and Jordan presses his nose against my neck before his lips. Chills, shivers, all the amazing feels he brings with him delivered. I hate leaving without giving him a real explanation and apology. I hate leaving period, but I promised Cate we'd do something fun for break.

"Does this mean you aren't going to Tijuana to bang chicks?" I ask.

He moves my shirt, so he can kiss the space between my neck and shoulder, lips still on my skin when he says, "Not unless you want to come bang chicks with me."

I reach back and run my hand through his hair. "I have another idea."

"Go on."

"How do you feel about road trips?" I turn around to gauge his reaction. "I have to go home for the weekend and want you to come."

He tenses, an uneasiness washing over him. Understandable, since the girl who lost her shit, dipped out for a few weeks, and showed up, still not explaining herself, just asked him to spend an entire weekend with her with no way to escape. He would be out of his mind to even consider it.

"Sorry," I tell him, "I shouldn't have—"

"I'll go," he says.

Oh. Holy shit.

———

I wait at the counter with the gas station's impatient cashier. A bag of beef jerky lands on top of the pile of candy, and Jordan walks away from the counter for a third time. He returns with sour gummy worms.

Before he can head for more, I snag his arm. "Three hours, Jordan. The trip is three hours, not three days."

"Fine," he says, pulling cash from his wallet. "But if we have to stop again, it's on you."

A burden I'll willingly shoulder.

As I pull out of the parking lot, he connects his phone to my car. "Help me pick appropriate background music," he says with a piece of licorice hanging out of his mouth.

"We need a soundtrack for this?"

He looks at me like I questioned whether the Earth is round. "Well, I don't want the music contradicting the tone. I mean, we can't have you talking about a traumatic life event with Bieber playing. What about a happy story with Nine Inch Nails? That would be pure lunacy, Callie."

I roll my eyes but smile anyway. Even a road trip turns into a production with Jordan Waters. Not sure of what type of music will go with our upcoming conversation, I don't answer him. A few more minutes of silence pass as he struggles to decide. Finally, a song comes through the speakers. I smile at his choice. Angsty pop punk fits the situation well. He lowers the volume and shares a piece of his candy with me.

"Are you ready now?" I ask.

He nods and settles in for story time.

I chew on a bite, those nerves reappearing. One would think, after I just talked about this with Benji, I would be ready to go, but I skimmed over a lot with him. Jordan deserves the whole exhaustive account, especially since he is voluntarily wading straight into it.

Lord help me, here we go.

"So, I've never had a stable or healthy relationship with my parents. Graham and Lara were sixteen when they had me and got married. It only took me until five to realize they hated each other, and by seven, Graham made it clear I was to blame for everything wrong in his life. That's also when they started daily screaming matches and throwing things. It escalated until I was sixteen, and she finally filed for divorce after he threatened to lock her in the house and set it on fire."

I don't let myself check over to see his response but notice him shift.

"How do you know he blames you?" he asks after a few seconds.

One of my least favorite memories makes me pause. Other than when I told Trey and Pete over a decade ago, I've never repeated it out loud. "His exact words were, 'I should have just left you in a dumpster to die so I wouldn't have ended up stuck with this cheap whore.'"

"Fuck, Callie. What did your mom say?"

A wry laugh huffs out as I remember her reaction. "Lara slapped him for calling her cheap."

Then they fought over whose life I'd ruined more. In front of me.

"You were seven?" His voice wavers.

"Pretty great parenting, huh?" I glance at Jordan when he doesn't answer. He stares at the dash, his expression unreadable. "Trust me. They've only gotten better with time. Lara's borderline neglectful now, and Graham…" I trail off. "We'll get back to him."

He still doesn't say anything, so I give him a minute. Never before has a mortal attempted eighteen years of the Henders family all at once.

"I'm sorry." He says it and then strokes his fingers down a section of my hair before tucking it back. Such a short sentence and small gesture. It shouldn't hurt.

"Before they split," I continue, "when they had Cate, I couldn't wrap my head around how they could bring another kid into so much toxicity. By that point, I had so much anger and resentment toward them. I was miserable and shut everyone out other than Connor, Trey, and Pete."

"Your first boyfriend Pete?" he asks.

I nod. "His grandparents sent him to camp the summer I turned fourteen. That's when Trey and I met Brock—the second worst thing ever to happen to me."

"What was the first?"

"Graham," I say without hesitation. "Brock was my solution to all of it. He was every red flag imaginable. He taught me to drink and get high to forget the rage eating me alive on the inside. For two years, we were so fucking toxic to each other and everyone around us. We were my parents."

A carbon copy of them, all the way down to the determination to destroy one another. I think we needed to hate each other to distract from other parts of our lives.

"The pictures of you as a blonde we saw were from when you dated Brock?"

Oh, great. He saw me as a blonde. An attempt to no longer look like Lara, which ended up pointless since I started acting like her.

"Most of them, probably. Trey did what he could to keep me relatively safe. All my friends from back then got dragged along for my spiral of self-destruction. Even Pete after I dumped him. I wish they wouldn't have, but..."

It's the most like my parents I've ever been, drowning them all with me. I've always wondered, had they not gotten mixed up in my messes, if their lives would have turned out differently. Not that any of us headed down a path toward employment with NASA or anything, but still.

"Two years," Jordan says. "You broke up when you were sixteen, so when your parents divorced."

"Yeah. Lara took out a restraining order and moved us to the next town over. The towns' high schools were combined, and without a reason to go to Sutterville anymore, Brock and I stopped seeing each other. It seemed to solve a lot of problems at first. But then my parents realized they could use the divorce to control one another. It made a bad situation so much worse. Shayna's pictures tell you more about the next several months than I can even remember."

He slides his hand into mine where it rests on my thigh and intertwines our fingers. I glance over, and his intense eyes are on me.

"I was such a fucking dick for bringing up the pictures the way I did, Callie. It was out of line."

"I blindsided you, and you reacted. I'm the one who used what you'd said about your parents against you. Out of everyone, I should know better, and I'm so, so sorry."

"Forgiven," he says. "So, so forgiven."

I smile at him but lose it a second later, looking at the empty road stretched out in front of us.

"Connor's actually the one who saved me from myself," I tell him, a squeeze in my heart from even thinking about it. "He gave me a calendar counting down to my eighteenth birthday when I wouldn't have to follow the custody agreement anymore. It's silly but crossing out the numbers changed everything. Each day closer to freedom, the less power they held over me. I stopped partying and avoided anyone who might start it back up again, including my friends. I spent the summer working my ass off on Pete's grandparents' farm to save money. The plan was to leave for school and never go back. All the bad memories would be hours away, and Graham would just be someone I survived."

"But now, you have a countdown calendar to nineteen and drive back on the weekends."

"Enter Graham's desperate need for control." I breathe deep to re-center. My first real test of not letting reminders of Graham send me spiraling.

"Thanks to an amendment in their divorce agreement, he pays child support until we're nineteen. In his mind, he owns us until then, but I turned eighteen and refused to see him. That's when the stream of texts and calls started. When those didn't work, he withheld my mail, used Cate and Connor to get to me, canceled my insurance, reported my car as stolen."

"The piece of shit said you stole it?"

"Twice." Another long exhale required. "He tried whatever he could think of until he found what worked."

"What's that?"

"He stopped making support payments. Not just for me, but for Cate and Connor, too. Lara blamed me the first month her money didn't show up. Since I caused the problem, she expected me to fix it."

"So you agreed to visit him."

"Every other weekend until I'm nineteen. If I don't, he resorts to his alternatives."

It might not even end then. He could still threaten not to pay for them. A thought I quickly push away for the sake of my sanity.

I turn onto the highway that takes us straight to Waymore, one where we might meet seven cars over the next fifty miles.

"You were supposed to be there the night of my birthday," Jordan says as we catch up to the now.

"Yeah. I told Graham I'd be home Saturday morning, and he showed up at the dorms to inform me otherwise. It pissed me off, and everything started to domino. Uncle Kev showed up and made me leave my car. Then Graham took away my phone when I got there. I felt isolated and trapped, and I couldn't take it anymore."

Being here with him and explaining what happened takes me right back. All the emotions settling on the surface in a muted form. Fuzzy around the edges. Scabs not yet scars—in Jordan's words.

Not sure if my back-in-commission tear ducts will surprise me, I pull off onto the shoulder. Once I park, he grabs my hand again and turns the music down more. I face him but keep my gaze down, not wanting to chance him looking at me like he did in my room again.

"When I woke up that Monday, I only remembered out-of-order pieces from the weekend," I finally tell him. "Without context, everything was pretty damning, so when Brock texted and lied about something happening between us, I believed him. For the first time in a long time, I felt like Callista, the girl with a less-than-stellar reputation who lets the worst part of her life ruin the rest of it. I didn't want you dealing with the fallout."

He brings my hand to his lips. "You should have just told me."

"I know, and I'm sorry." I look up, needing him to know how much I regret how I handled my blackout. How I regret the way I've been handling *everything*. "I wasn't ready for you to know what a mess my life is. I'm still not entirely sure I am, but I'm sick of missing out on things because of it. And it really is a disaster, Jordan. Seriously, you should run right now." I rush the last part and slap at the button behind me to unlock the doors.

It's only fair to give him an opportunity to run.

Rather than grab the handle to make a grand escape, he moves a hand around to the back of my neck, bringing me closer. He erases the last of the space and rests his forehead on mine.

"I'm not going anywhere, Callie." Jordan locks his intense gaze on mine. "I don't care how messy your life is. Messy, complicated, unpredictable—I want it all if it means I can have you."

I want to warn him I'm not worth the trade, but he seals his mouth over mine.

"I can handle it," he says against my lips. "I'm *certain*."

I search his eyes for anything that says otherwise but find nothing other than his normal assurance.

This is what Jordan Waters looks like when certain.

He kisses me again and again, and I believe him more each time. By the time he pulls away, not much exists outside the car.

I put my hand on the gearshift but stop, remembering something else. "One more thing…" As much as I wish we could skip it, I promised his friends I would tell him about Tyler. "Rusty almost got into a fight with Lara's boyfriend last night."

He relaxes in his seat, a whole new level of confusion on his face. "He was at a State party?"

"Tyler's only twenty-two," I explain. "I try not to talk to him, so I didn't even think about him going there until I saw him."

"So, why exactly was Rusty going to fight him?"

I chew on my lip, not sure how he'll respond. "He got a little aggressive with me in a hallway."

He goes tense, expressionless. "He fucking what?"

The edge in his response catches me off guard, and my eyes flash to his. I switch into damage mode. "Don't worry about it. He was just drunker and more persistent than usual."

"Than usual?" His voice rises right along with my pulse. "Shit like this has happened before?"

"Nothing serious," I say fast. "Until last night, he's always backed off after a few comments or grabbing my ass. For whatever reason, he pushed it further, but Rusty rode in on his white horse and pulled him off."

"Fuck, Callie." Jordan's head drops back on the seat, and his jaw clenches.

I shouldn't have said anything. I pushed him with my screwed-up family and now upset him with Tyler. Once again worried I broke him, I try to reassure him and put my hand on his arm.

The wrong choice.

In the time it takes to blink, he throws off his seat belt and launches out of the car. I unhook, too, thinking I need to chase him down, but he comes around the car and flings open my door, then he pulls me out, his arms enveloping me.

"Fuck, I'm sorry, baby."

I press my face into his chest, tears burning my eyes, but he's close and safe and exactly where I want to be. The only person I've ever wanted to let exist in both of my worlds.

Still 138 Days Until 19

Jordan Waters in Waymore, Pennsylvania, gives a whole new meaning to a fish out of water. His eyes dart all over the place as I drive through the small town. After I park in front of Lara's house, he checks around like he expects a killer clown to pop out.

"Do you feel like I've brought you to the middle of nowhere to kill you?" I ask.

Still on high alert, he says, "The idea has crossed my mind."

"Just stay out of the woodshed out back." I wink and leave him in the car to contemplate his impending doom.

He recovers by the time I've collected our bags from the trunk, and he carries them in. Since we step through the door without being attacked by a six-year-old, I safely assume we have the house to ourselves.

The bags hit the floor the second he walks into my room, and he sets his sights on the photo collage decorating my wall. Of all the pictures taken over the years, the ones hanging in my room represent the better moments—early morning fishing trips Trey used to force me to go on, summer carnivals, water parks, even my prom pictures with Pete. According to the wall, I've lived the life I always wanted.

He scans over them and points at one. "How old are you in this one?"

I glance at the picture of me at the lake and take his coat. "Seven? That's Trey on the left, and Connor's on the right." I kick our bags out of the way and close the door.

"Is that the science building on campus?" He looks at one of Trey and me cheesing it up for the camera a mere twenty feet from where he charged into my life.

"Last October, Trey drove me to Easton for a tour." I finish hanging our jackets on the hooks behind the door and return to his side. "We snuck off on our own and ran into a group of girls. He made up a ridiculous story about being an oil heir named Bradford. They pointed out his name tag said Trey, so he hunted down a marker. After he changed his name, he asked who I wanted to be while we were there."

I pull the pin from the top of the picture and show him the back. The *Hello, My Name Is* sticker is still firmly attached with *Callista* crossed out and Trey's scrawled-out *Callie* in red marker.

"You were Callie," Jordan says.

"I have been ever since."

He flips my wrist over and circles a section of sidewalk on the far-left side with his finger. "Right there, Callie met Jordan."

Another reason to love the old part of campus.

I pin the picture back in place next to another of Trey at an amusement park. The last trip we went on together before I left for school, celebrating him becoming an official sheriff's deputy.

A tug at the hem of my shirt brings my attention to Jordan.

"The shirt has to go, beautiful."

My chest flutters. I missed him calling me that.

As for the shirt, I shrug and stick up my arms. If he no longer wants to look at his face on my chest, he can fix the problem himself. He doesn't hesitate to peel it off, then he skims his hands over my hips until I reach for the bottom of his. He reaches back and drags it off, tossing it on the floor. I lick my lips, shamelessly checking out his carved pecs and rippling abs and the trail of hair disappearing into his jeans. Before I'm finished with the view, he jerks me forward.

"You guys have met, right?"

He places my hand smack dab between the lines of his V. Not that I complain. My fingers happily run over every dip of his torso. Then he's kissing me like he might not stop, down my neck and over my collarbone.

Only he does stop.

He stops and tenses, staring at—fuck.

It physically hurts to know what he sees, but I expected it to happen eventually. The sore spot below my shoulder has turned into a deep bruise. A bite mark. When I checked earlier, the indentation of Tyler's teeth still showed.

Until now, I haven't been around anyone with it visible. If anyone were to see it, I can easily sell running into the side mirror on a parked truck. No one would be close enough to see the details that say otherwise.

Except Jordan.

So much flashes over his face, and I hate it.

I say his name, and his gaze lifts, the muscles of his jaw tight beneath the skin. I brush my fingers over them.

"It's fine," I tell him.

But he looks at me like it's anything but. "The bastard bit you?"

He skims the tips of his fingers over the bruise, and I open my mouth to say … I have no idea.

I search his eyes, desperate to not talk about this. Now. Ever.

His expression softens after a second, and like under the blankets, Jordan gives me what I need. He slides his hand into my hair and kisses me. "I'm sorry, baby."

Sighing against his lips, I kiss him harder and pull him closer. I press my hand to his chest, moving him backward until he hits the bed and sits.

I climb onto his lap, and he tugs me down with him when he lies back. Our eyes lock, my pulse thrumming while his palms feel their way up my thighs. They keep going, smoothing over my hips and up my back. I have no idea how I've gone this long without his hands on me.

He cradles my face in his hand, the other pressed between my shoulder blades. "Pretend I said something funny."

I trail my fingers through his messy hair, my mind not functioning on a conversational level. "What?"

"The blood supply to my brain is lacking, but I want to hear you laugh right now. So pretend I made a hilariously witty comment about pheasants or acorns or anything as long as you find it funny."

"Acorns?" I ask on a laugh.

He smiles. "Fucking acorns, beautiful."

My laugh cuts off when he slams his mouth into mine, his hands framing my face. I forget all about acorns when his tongue pushes into my mouth. I forget about everything.

Running my hands up his chest, I kiss over his jaw. His stubble scrapes against my lips, and the thought of it scraping my thighs causes my pussy to clench.

Jordan doesn't let me have control long. The second my tongue travels over his skin, my hips grinding down on his erection, a husky groan vibrates through his throat. He grabs my ass and thrusts his hips. I whimper, my clit dragging over his cock, and I need more.

Jordan tangles his fingers in my hair, pulling my head to the side and bringing his lips to my ear. "You finally going to let me play with this pussy, Callie?"

I'm already nodding when he drives up again, and I pull his mouth back to mine.

A car door shuts. It sounds faint enough that I convince myself a neighbor slammed theirs down the block, but then the front door creaks open. All those things I forgot flood back in. I straighten up, no longer rocking and touching my lips where the sensation of his remains.

"No," Jordan says. "No. No."

I look down at him, my body also chanting no when I tell them both, "Terrible timing."

Even though he continues to beg me with his eyes, I crawl off and toss him his shirt. "Think about baseball or a car accident or—"

"Nana Waters." He sits up, less than enthused.

I smile at his pouting and retrieve a top from my bag. "Think about Nana Waters then. The monster descends upon us."

As he pulls his shirt on, I peek back for one last glimpse of the gorgeous guy on my bed. If not for the footsteps stampeding down the hall, I would lock the door. Instead, I open it, and in barrels Cate. She bypasses me, sights set on her prey. Before he can react, she climbs onto his lap, squishes his cheeks between her hands, and kisses him on the forehead.

She sits back on her heels. "Hi."

Completely unaware of what he's gotten himself into, Jordan replies, "Hi."

She giggles and grips his shirt to keep from falling when she hangs back to see me. "Can we keep him, Cal?"

I bite my lips together, doing my best not to laugh and encourage her.

Connor leans on the doorframe next to me. He crosses his arms and tries not to crack up as well. His head shakes to clear the hair out of his eyes. "Come on, Monster. You left your coat on the floor."

Cate's dismount deserves top scores. She twirls past me, through the door, and keeps spinning down the hall.

Connor kicks off the doorframe and nods at Jordan. "Nice to finally meet you, Lover Boy."

Unimpressed with the revival of the nickname, I slap at his arm, but he knocks my hand away.

"Pizza for supper?" I ask.

"Whatever," he says, walking away.

He gives me a grin before ducking into his room, and I roll my eyes.

I pick up our bags and haul them over to the bed. Without warning, Jordan's arms shoot out, and then I'm staring up at him from my back. His body covers mine, hips settled between my legs, and his focus on my mouth.

"Lover Boy, huh?" He kisses me, deep and slow, and I should have locked the door. "Small children go to bed at, like, seven, right?"

Following the same route as my mouth a few minutes ago, I sweep my fingertips over his jaw. "She needs fed, bathed, and read to. After that, I'm all yours."

"That's the sexiest thing I've ever heard, if I disregard everything but the last three words." He gets up and yanks me to my feet. "Let's go play house."

Words I never expected Jordan Waters to ever say to me.

Per Cate's command, I pop my head out of the bathroom. On the floor, back against the wall, Jordan waits with the pretty pink princess crown in hand. We both smile, and I shut the door, returning to the bossy girl in the bathtub.

"He's right where you left him—tiara and all."

"On his head?"

I nod, squeezing the shampoo into her hand. "He's beautiful."

She giggles, shutting her eyes and rubbing her head.

After a rinse, towel-dry, and slight disagreement over the pajamas I brought in for her to wear—princesses instead of fairies—I comb out her hair as fast as possible.

"Cal, hurry," she whines.

"Done," I say, laying the brush on the counter.

Out the door she goes, hands planted on her hips. She stops short in the hallway. "Oh. You are wearing it."

I follow, picking her up. "Bedtime, my monster queen."

"Jordan has to read to me." She reaches down in his direction, her lip jutting out.

He stares up with a mixture of exhaustion and uncertainty in his eyes and a glittery tiara on his head. I spin around, searching for a way to spare him from the voices she'll request for each character. The guy can only tolerate so much.

"Jordan doesn't know how to read."

"He doesn't?"

"No, and he's very sad about it. But I bet if you read to him, it would make him feel better."

She appears dubious but agrees, and Jordan shuffles down the hall behind us.

Once they settle in with a book, she dismisses me. He nods when I check with him, so I leave him to fend for himself. I finish cleaning up in the bathroom and grab my phone from my bedroom. A message from Benjamin "Badass" Jones awaits me.

Update me, woman.

I reply, *Beta Void will live to play another show.*

Forever grateful for your service.

Can I thank you now?

Soon.

Connor's spread out on the couch in the living room. I drop onto the cushions and land on his feet. After a few kicks without me budging, he retracts them. Whatever he watches involves screams and buckets of blood. A typical Friday night.

"Where's Lover Boy?" he asks.

"Stop calling him that." I whop him with a pillow and steal the blanket from him. "He's reading to Cate."

"Alone?" His attention returns to the screen. "Rest in peace, man."

Despite Connor's lack of confidence in him, Jordan emerges a while later, unscathed.

I lift the blanket for him to join me and cuddle up beside him. No matter how many horror movies I suffer through for my brother, I can never predict them and want the protection. The first time the killer lunges at someone, I bury my face in his shirt.

Interest in the movie vanishes at that point. Partly because I hate being scared but mostly because, hello, Jordan Waters.

I drag my fingers across the ridges of his abs before sneaking under his shirt. His breathing changes when my hand glides over his muscles and stops at the top of his jeans. He keeps his eyes on the screen but sinks deeper into the couch, shifting his hips down the cushion and straightening out in anticipation of me going lower. I fight off a smile at the clear approval.

Not to be outdone, he slides his hand into my sweatpants. A slow stroke up my thigh distracts me from what I'm doing. He reaches the edge of my panties, and I glance up to see him watching me. I hold his gaze, swallowing when his fingers run down the hem. His touch grows lighter and lighter until he pushes between my legs. I draw in a breath, and now I move, silently asking for him to keep going.

A groan sounds behind me. "Come on, guys. Your room is literally a thirty-second walk away."

I scrunch my face at Jordan, blaming him for my brother noticing us. "Watch your movie, Con."

"Seriously, no one moves that much under a blanket unless they're getting some action."

This gains my full attention.

I shoot up, my head snapping in his direction. "What the hell do you know about getting action?"

He grins and gives his head a shake to move the hair from his eyes. "Dude, I'm almost sixteen. Don't for a second think you're the first girl to be felt up on this couch."

My mouth falls open at the thought of him being sexually active in any way. Teenage pregnancy is the last thing we need— precisely why I went on the pill years ago. Oh God, Graham and Lara as grandparents? Now *that* would be true horror.

On the other side of me, Jordan chuckles as he withdraws his hand from my sweatpants. The two of them bump fists over the top of my head, and my glare flies back to him.

"Do not encourage him."

He stops, but his eyes hover over my head again. Since younger brothers never outgrow their annoying stage, I whirl around. Connor's waiting for another fist bump, and I launch myself at him. He catches me and then laughs, holding his hands up.

"Okay. Okay. No more feeling up girls on the couch." He pauses, cocking a brow. "Full-on sex or nothing. Cal's orders." Before I can react, he tosses me in the opposite direction and runs for his damn life.

I fall back into Jordan's waiting arms and sigh. "He stresses me out."

"Want me to help you relax?"

A split second after I nod, he hops up and carries me to my room. I smile as he sets me down, and I head right back out.

"I'm going to take a quick shower. Be in bed when I get back."

By quick, I mean an everything-rushed, shortest-shower-of-my-life quick, but it's not fast enough.

I come into my room to find Jordan reading his phone on one side of my bed while my angelic sister snores like a demon on the other.

"Sorry," I say, walking over. "I'll move her. Just prepare yourself because she's going to scream."

Before I reach her, he jumps up and snags my hand, pulling me toward him. "I can sleep on the floor."

Great. He's fallen victim to her magic.

"Jordan, you don't have to do that."

He pushes back a wet section of my hair and kisses me, gentle and unhurried. "There's nothing in the world I would rather do."

I smile, falling under quite the spell myself.

137 Days Until 19

Heavy breathing coaxes me into consciousness while about forty-three pounds on my back prevents me from moving.

An upside-down, goggle-wearing Cate leans over my face. "Hi."

I grunt a response. She giggles and dives off the side of the bed. Worried she landed on Jordan, I roll over, only to find the space on the floor empty. The folded blankets and pillow are stacked at the end of my bed. I consider the possibility of him making a run for it in the middle of the night until the sweet aroma of coffee fills my room.

It drags me out of bed. I throw my hair up and head down the hall, passing Connor's closed door. Most weekends, he either attends practice or plays in a game. With break, he doesn't need to go anywhere and must want to sleep in. In light of the little reveal about his couch activities, I decide on a pit stop before the kitchen and retreat to my room.

Supplies in hand, I sneak through his door, careful not to wake him when closing it. I stand by his bed, and once I've dumped the entire box of packets over top of him, I clear my throat.

"Condoms are nearly as effective at preventing pregnancy as the pill when used correctly. They also drastically reduce the chances of contracting a sexually transmitted infection."

Connor's head pops up, a look of horror on his face. "Cal, what are you doing?"

Ignoring him, I continue, "If the condom breaks, emergency contraceptives can prevent pregnancy when taken within seventy-two hours. Keep in mind, though, the sooner after unsafe sex, the more effective."

He picks up one of the condoms scattered across him and his bed. "Oh my God."

"Fact—teenagers can be at high risk for STIs, such as HIV, hepatitis, HPV, herpes—"

Scrambling out of bed, he clamps a hand over my mouth and emphatically shakes his head. I mumble into his hand, rattling off every other one I can remember from health class.

"You win," he says, lowering his hand. "Please fucking stop."

I pick up a condom and slap it against his chest. "Always wear one. We're totally unequipped to handle a baby."

He nods. "The dysfunction quota has been reached in this family. Noted."

"Connor—"

"Trust me," he says, more serious.

It's my only real choice unless I want to chaperone him twenty-four-seven. I squint one last warning at him and retreat. Then, not being a total hypocrite, I double back and snatch a handful of the condoms off his comforter. His laughter follows me out the second time.

With my parental duties complete and contraceptives returned to my bag, I seek the much-needed coffee. I stop in the doorway, the scene unfolding in the kitchen worthy of a pause. At one end of the table, Jordan is wearing a blue bathrobe over his clothes and oversize spectacles. At the other end, Cate is kneeling on a chair in her pink robe and swim goggles.

He shakes out a newspaper, a fake pipe hanging out of his mouth. "Well, my dear, Sport and Kitten should be down for breakfast soon."

She giggles, flipping through a comic book. "They'd better hurry, or they'll be late for school."

"Would you like me to drop them off on my way to the office?"

"That would be nice." She sighs, dropping her chin to her hand. "I need to mop the floors again."

"Very well." He shoves something nonexistent across the table. "Would you like more ham?"

I laugh at their act, and Jordan looks over. Jesus, even in costume as a sitcom dad, he looks incredible.

"What the hell, Cate?" Connor's elbow jabs one of my ribs as he pushes past. "You can't just strip away a guy's dignity as soon as he walks through the door. You have to build up to embarrassing him like this."

Jordan throws down the pipe and refolds the newspaper. "I'm not wearing a pink ballerina tutu, holding a doll and watching *Swan Lake*, so I'm going to say I'm ahead in the dignity department."

Connor's eyes narrow. "Cate showed you the photo album?"

"First thing this morning. Now, sit down and eat, Sport." He puts the glasses down with the newspaper and fetches me coffee.

I slide the mug from him and take a sip, loving the return to our morning ritual—and not just because of the coffee.

"Good morning, beautiful," he says. Cate growls, and his lips twitch. "I mean, good morning, Kitten."

He glances over his shoulder. She nods and returns to her comic. When his focus comes back, he robs me of my cup and sets it on the table.

"Honey, Kitten needs help with her science homework before I drop her off at school."

"That's nice, dear," she says, not paying attention.

He slips his arms around me, and backward I go into the living room. We keep going until I hit the couch. He lowers me down and crawls on top of me. I laugh as he brings the blanket all the way over us, covering our heads.

"Anatomy, right?" His mouth drops onto my jaw, kissing down one side and up the other. "The strongest muscle in the body is in the jaw," he says.

"Is that so?"

"Mmhmm. And this is the longest bone in the human body." His hand runs up my thigh, leaving chills in its wake.

"The smallest is in the ear," I say. A body part he identifies with his teeth on the lobe.

I sigh, trying to keep breathing even. He makes the task even more difficult when he brushes my fingertips over the stubble on his jaw and then grazes his thumb over my bottom lip.

"The lips are hundreds of times more sensitive to touch than the fingertips."

Whether or not anything else he says holds truth, I can vouch for the last one.

"Any other facts I should know?" I ask, distracted by his thumb still tugging at my lip.

He presses my palm flat against his chest and sets his against mine. "Kissing raises the pulse to over one hundred beats per minute."

In excruciating slow motion, he brings his face down. His heart rate stays steady, but mine picks up, the closer his mouth comes to mine. Just short of contact, he stops, staying so close but not close enough. I run my hand to the back of his neck and drag him the rest of the way. He groans, plunging his tongue into my mouth and abandoning my heartbeat to palm my breast through my shirt.

I arch into his touch. "Jordan."

He hums against my lips. "You want one more fact, Callie?"

My eyes fall closed as his hand moves farther down my body and breeches the top hem of my sweatpants. Then he's under my panties, the tips of his fingers stroking my bare skin, and I'm trying desperately to stay quiet. I stare up at him while parting my thighs, needing him not to stop.

"Right here…" Jordan teases lower and swallows, feeling how wet I am for him. His fingers swipe through my pussy, and I whimper when they pause right over my clit. "This is how I make you come."

My body jolts when he presses down and rubs, a desperate sound escaping me. I grab onto his bicep, so close to crying out with each circle of his fingers.

Then it all stops.

I look up and find Jordan watching me with his heated gaze. My brow draws in, not sure if something's wrong until he smirks.

"This concludes our tutoring session for today," he says, "but I am available for…"

Whatever nonsense he planned to say, I'll never know because I slide my hand down to his and then push his fingers back onto my throbbing clit. All the humor vanishes from his face as I rock against them and fight a moan at how fucking good they feel. Jordan curses and picks up the pace. I grab his wrist, needing an anchor when he sinks a finger inside me.

His lips drop to my cheek before he rasps, "Be quiet for me, beautiful."

"Yes," I say on an exhale.

He adds another finger, thrusting faster and grinding his palm on my clit perfectly. The surface of pleasure breaks right as Jordan kisses me, muting the sound when I cry out. He swallows my whimpers and nips at my lip, letting me ride out my orgasm before switching to slow strokes with his fingers. Even the tease of more has my body sinking into the couch. My hold on his wrist falls away, and I shudder when he drags them out of my sensitive pussy.

Jordan slips his glistening fingers into his mouth. "Mmm. Best student I've ever had." Then he tugs at my swollen bottom lip, a smirk forming. "If you enjoyed my tutoring services, please recommend me to a friend."

The exasperating charm of Jordan Waters is alive and well.

"You want me to recruit competition now?" I ask. "Between Felicia and my sister, I don't already have enough?"

Pulling my hand up, his lips press to my inner wrist as he stares down at me in that amazing way. "Competition implies anyone else would stand a chance. We've been beyond that since the first time you increased my heart rate to over one hundred beats per minute."

I swallow. "You should be careful, saying things like that."

"Why?" He has a playful tone, his eyes soft, but my pulse thrums harder again.

"It could make a girl feel things."

"Good." Jordan crushes his lips to mine, kissing me hard, and then he climbs off, the blanket going with him. It lands on me a second later and he says, "My mission is to make you fall in love with me."

His words shock through me like I'm holding on to an electric fence. The thought terrifies me, the word, the whole concept really. But I grabbed this live wire, well aware of the potential consequences. It's too late to let go of it now.

Since Cate won't take off her goggles and Jordan packed his swim trunks, we all go swimming after lunch. The Norris County Fitness Center is a far cry from a beach in Mexico, but at least it's not crowded. The surrounding communities all pitched in to build it between Waymore and Sutterville as an additional revenue source for the county. Unfortunately, not long after the grand opening, a YMCA set up shop a few towns over. Most people choose the higher membership fees and a short drive in favor of a larger pool, weight room, basketball courts, and all-around better facilities.

I pull up next to the only car in the parking lot, a crappy black Grand Am with a crack in the front bumper. Shayna and I started working here together at sixteen. After graduation, I quit, and she went from part-time to full-time.

Cate runs ahead with Connor close behind, carrying our two bags. Jordan's fingers interlace with mine as we climb the steps to the ugly gray building long forgotten by everyone. Shayna's attention diverts from my siblings, descending the staircase to the locker rooms, to us.

She hops on the counter and spins around in our direction. "Thank God it's you, Henders. I thought I might actually have to do some work."

"Anybody come in today?" I ask.

She laughs, pulling at a loose thread on her jeans. "Not a soul. I fell asleep while reading a bit ago."

"A normal Saturday afternoon then." I write my uncle Kevin's name and membership number on the sign-in sheet before Jordan nudges me, wanting an introduction. "Sorry. Jordan, this is Shayna. Shayna, Jordan."

"*The* Jordan?"

Oh shit.

"She's mentioned me?" he asks, his tone smug.

I drop the pen and shoot her a warning glare before she confirms me blabbering about him in my drunken state. We've reached her chance at redemption for not taking down those pictures, an issue Trey promised she took care of.

"She might have said your name once." She can't help a small smile, but at least she changes the subject. "Is Cate taking swim lessons? They start in about a month."

"What are they charging for Saturday classes? You know Lara won't bring her during the week."

And they always charge more for the weekends.

More than aware of my mother's tendency to live at the bar after work, Shayna rolls her eyes. "Regular costs forty-five for six lessons and…" She leans back, checking the papers on the desk behind the counter. "Damn, the bitch charges double for the weekends."

Called it. If we catch Lara on a good day, she might consider paying regular price.

I approximate how much cash Connor has squirreled away from selling my dresses and shrug. "We'll see."

She nods, understanding more than most. "I'll put her name down to keep a spot open."

I thank her and turn my attention to Jordan. "Ready to be assaulted by a six-year-old in swim floats?"

"Absolutely." He follows to the steps but stops. "I forgot my phone in the car. Meet you down there?"

I give up my keys and watch Shayna's head tilt, eyes on his ass as he walks away.

She jumps down once he disappears out the door. "You know I'm checking him out on the security cameras, right?"

Unable to blame her, I shrug and head downstairs.

Connor is waiting outside the women's locker room at one end of the hall. "She stopped singing a few seconds ago, so hopefully, she's still alive in there."

About then, Cate hits a high note our ears were not prepared for.

He shakes his head, walking to the other end of the hall. "Such range she has."

In the locker room, she steps heel to toe, using a bench as a balance beam. I gather her swimsuit and towel off the floor and herd her to the shower stalls. Once we change, she wraps up in her towel, goggles and water wings on. My bag and our clothes go in a locker, and I lead her out to the pool.

Connor lunges from behind the door, lifting her up. He flings her shoes and towel in my direction and dangles her over the pool. Even though she kicks and screams, she laughs, loving every second.

While they terrorize each other, I drop our belongings on the cheap plastic table near the hot tub and toss her shoes underneath one of the four matching chairs. I kick my flip-flops off as Cate lets out a screech sounding like my name. I spin, getting a brief glimpse of Jordan before he snatches me up and plunges us both into the water.

We surface, him grinning.

"Sorry, but to keep it PG, you need to stay submerged from the neck down." He swims circles around me, ready to attack if my two-piece and I challenge him.

I wipe all the wet hair out of my face. "Were you one of those boys who pushed girls they liked in the pool?"

"I wasn't until right now," he says, splashing me.

"Jordan has to race Connor." Cate taps her foot on the side.

Marching orders in hand, he drags me through the water behind him. "I will win this race in your honor."

I laugh as he drops me off at the shallow end, his expression serious when he shakes hands with Connor in a show of good sportsmanship. She counts them down from ten, her excitement causing her to repeat the number four twice. Despite the miscount, they shove off the wall at the same time and glide through the water.

Cate tugs on my arm to sit on the edge with her, so I hop up as they flip around at the opposite wall.

Jordan reaches us ahead of Connor, but rather than starting his second of three laps, he pops up. "Do you want me to lose? Get in the damn water and stop distracting me."

I roll my eyes, pushing off the ledge and into the water. He forfeits the lead to kiss me and launches off the wall a few feet behind Connor. On the final lap, he closes the gap. They slap the wall, both panting, and Cate declares Jordan the winner.

He slumps against the wall. "I won. No thanks to you." He smiles, pulling me to him and tucking me against his side. "Connor, you're no joke."

Connor assists Cate down the steps into the water. "Same, man. You play sports?"

"Lacrosse when I was younger."

"A sport for those who can't keep up in basketball." He sends Cate skimming across the water toward us. "Why did you stop?"

Jordan catches her. "I wasn't playing for the right reasons."

They continue passing her between them, talking about anything and everything. My brother rarely opens up to anyone other than me, and even I need to force him to tell me what goes on in his head at times. But he chatters away like he's known Jordan his entire life.

Once Cate grows bored, we participate in various activities for her entertainment, such as handstand contests and holding our breath. After a while, she chooses Jordan as her favorite and banishes Connor and me to the hot tub.

I switch on the jets while Connor floats on the other side, listing off information about a summer basketball league starting in May. He tells me the leftover money from buying his shoes will cover both the registration fee and the entire cost of swimming lessons, meaning we can cut our parents out of the equation entirely. Always the preferred solution.

His chin rests on the ledge, a protective eye on Cate as Jordan twirls her around in the water. "I vote we keep him."

"He's not a puppy, Con."

"Obviously, but you make decisions based on what's best for us. So, I'm letting you know, we like him. Plus, if you're busy with him, you won't be up my ass about school and girls as much." He cranes his neck around and grins.

The fake expression resembles mine more and more, much less obvious than when he started using it a few years ago. To anyone else, he would appear to be a cocky teenager making a joke, but I recognize the difference in his eyes. The spark is gone. He's worried. Not about Jordan, but about what changes with him added to the mix. If I stop being the one person he can trust to be there for him, no matter what.

I smile, a real one. "I promise, I'll always be up your ass about something. It's one of the few joys of having a little brother."

"Right, because having an older sister is full of them." He flicks water at me, and in a moment of ultimate maturity, I stick my tongue out. He chuckles, at ease again even though his brows draw in slightly a second later.

"What did you do, anyway?" he asks. His gaze dips to my shoulder—to the bite mark marring my skin.

I expected the question eventually and scrunch my nose to play it off. "I was walking between vehicles in a parking lot. It turns out the side mirrors on trucks are sturdier than they look."

He snorts. "Running into parked trucks, and somehow, you're still the more graceful sister."

His gaze travels back to the two in the pool, and a true smile forms when Cate's giddy squeal echoes through the room.

It makes me smile, too. Both the squeal and him.

He'd hate that I'm lying to him—I hate it, too—but he already has a list of worries that keep him awake at night. Things out of his control. I refuse to add to them.

We watch Cate dole out torture for a few more minutes before I climb out of the hot tub. The second I stand up, Jordan's glare lands on me. It follows me as I obstinately walk around without a towel. I wait until I'm out of his sight to retrieve one from the linen closet in the hall and head up the stairs.

Shayna tosses her book to the side and pouts out her lip. "He won't stay out of the water long enough for me to get a good look."

"Want me to parade him around a little?"

"Yes, please." Her chair wheels around as she retrieves a set of keys. She slaps them down on the counter. "I presume you'll be winning our bet today?"

I stare at her, no idea what she's talking about.

"Our bet about who would have sex in the steam room first?"

"You still haven't?" I ask in disbelief.

She shakes her head, raising her eyebrow. "Do I need to reissue the challenge? It's not like you to need encouragement."

I ignore the attempt to provoke me. "I'll drop off the money for swim lessons tomorrow before I leave."

"No need. Jordan already paid."

"What? When did he…" When he said he forgot his phone. God, I adore him. I sigh, snagging the keys off the counter. "Has anyone been in there since you last sanitized?"

She grins. "Nope, and I wiped down everything."

How romantic.

"Well," I say, "I'm sure it's cleaner than the back of what's his name's pickup."

Her eyes bug out, and I dash for the stairs, a box of tissues narrowly missing my head.

"We don't talk about that," she calls after me.

I laugh, and it echoes on my way down.

When I unlock the door, the faint scent of citrus supports her claim of recently cleaning. All the off-white tiles glisten as steam fills the room. I set extra towels on the lower of the two bench seats wrapped around three-quarters of the room and find the Out of Order sign and a broom in the utility closet. I leave them inside the door and head back to the pool.

Everyone remains where I left them. I crouch down by the edge, and Jordan wades over with Cate on his shoulders.

"Rinse off. I'll meet you in the steam room."

Cate clambers onto the side as I stand up. She races to the hot tub to join Connor, which will keep her entertained and him busy for a while. I go out to the hallway and am walking into the locker room when Jordan catches my hand.

"Steam room?"

"No one under the age of sixteen is allowed. It's against policy." I back in, his eyes on me until I step around the corner.

Still 137 Days Until 19

The unfamiliar nerves reemerge as I walk down the hallway past the basketball court to the steam room. Actually, they started during my shower. Now they're amplified, zipping through me. As I reach the end of the hall, I turn off the security camera on the wall above the door, just in case. I swear, Shayna's cackle echoes from upstairs.

Reaching for the handle, I hesitate and take a deep breath before I pull it open. Jordan's already waiting. He's leaning back on the bottom bench, resting his elbows on the one behind him. "Hello, beautiful."

That does the trick, the anxiety no match for him. I smile as I hang the Out of Order sign outside the door. I turn the knob, dimming the lights. A slight improvement in the romance department, right? As an extra precaution, I angle the broom through the door handle and brace it against the wall. He watches me jiggle the already-fogged-over door, proving it won't open.

"What if there's a fire?" he asks.

I motion to the steam surrounding us. "In the case of a fire, I think we'll be safe."

He chuckles and erases the distance between us. His lips reach me first, arms around my waist second. I rake my hands through his still-wet hair. Yet another irresistible look he pulls off with no effort. Although any without a shirt automatically earns a spot on the list.

He parts my lips with his tongue, tasting sweet, like candy.

I break my mouth away from his. "Did you and Cate eat those fruit snacks after I told her no?"

When he grins, I sigh and back him to the bench until he sits down on his towel. The one wrapped around me drops to the floor. No complaints from him this time, he yanks me onto his lap, my knees landing on each side of him.

His eyes melt to the look I've been missing. "What are you doing to me, beautiful?"

I wonder the same of him, not sure I want the answer. I kiss his soft lips and across the stubble of his jaw to his smooth neck. He groans when my teeth graze his earlobe, and he takes over from there. A hand thrusts into my hair and brings my mouth to his while his other hand traces the line of my collarbone in from my shoulder. My fingers trail up his chest as he works lower.

He glances up at me before gently kissing the bite mark. So careful it hurts even more than when he first saw it, and at the same time, it heals something else.

His lips skim over my top, thumb sweeping over my peaked nipple, and then he tugs with his teeth. They might as well have scraped over my clit, and I rock against his erection. He continues to tease me through the fabric, hips meeting mine until we're almost frantic, breathless and needy. I can't remember ever wanting anyone this way.

But then he falls back against the seat, fingers flexing into the tops of my thighs.

"Fuck," he breathes out, "you're one hip thrust away from passing the outer realm of my restraint."

I smile and lean closer. "Yeah?" When his eyes lower to my mouth, I bite his lower lip and slowly circle my hips, challenging him.

He curses and grabs my ass, but he doesn't stop me. His head tips back, eyes closed while I continue trying to break his resolve.

He holds strong—at first. It starts to slip, with a squeeze of his hands. A hard swallow that makes his throat bob in such a sexy way. I lick a line over his Adam's apple, and he groans, gripping me tighter, but then he quits moving altogether.

"Jordan," I say. When he doesn't respond, I try again. "Jordan?"

He lifts his head, keeping his eyes closed.

So damn dramatic.

I fish the condom out from where I tucked it between my hip and swim bottoms and set it in his palm. As soon as he realizes what he's holding, his mouth curves into a smile. He opens his eyes, and in the next second, his lips collide with mine.

All his patience gone, his tongue invades my mouth. I tug at the back of his hair, and his hands run up my sides. He pushes under my swim top, and his lips leave mine, so he can slip it over my head. Tossing it aside, he scans what feels like every inch of me visible, eyes darkening.

"Perfect," he whispers.

He brushes his lips against mine, slow and gentle, unlike a minute ago. They stay unhurried, roaming over my skin. Even though I'm already warm from the steam, everywhere he kisses, touches, licks, and nips burns all the hotter.

Jordan drops his hand between us, rubbing my clit and biting down on my nipple. I moan, and he jerks the fabric to the side and does it again without the barrier. The sound of his groan vibrates through my skin when he strokes through my dripping pussy.

"Tell me we have enough time for you to come on my face."

I almost beg him to do exactly that, but every minute brings us closer to being dragged out of this little bubble.

"No time," I tell him before kissing him, our lips still connected when I mumble, "Fuck me, Jordan. Please, fuck me."

He curses and plunges his tongue deep, every part of him demanding control. Grasping my hips, he stands me up. I strip off my bottoms as he shoves down his trunks, and then I'm staring at his thick cock. Jordan's eyes drink in my bare pussy, hand sliding up and down his shaft.

"Fuck, I need to be inside you," he says, hooking me around the waist.

I straddle him and grab the condom he tossed onto the bench, holding it to his mouth. He snarls and bites down on the corner, so I can rip it open. It makes me laugh, and he pulls my forehead to his, smiling that damn smile.

I kiss him first, but he kisses me harder, my hand stroking him. Wanting him develops into an ache of needing him, and thank God Jordan's already lifting me up onto my knees as I roll the condom down. He lines up the head of his cock and hungrily watches me slide down every inch. My pussy stretches around him, my entire body feeling it once he fills me.

His fingers dig into my skin. "So fucking good," he rasps.

Then he thrusts into me so hard I gasp, my eyes rolling in an entirely different way than usual. Already desperate, I grip his shoulders, rising up and sinking back down with him flexing to meet me.

He moves me faster, his tongue dragging over the water droplets on my breasts. The way it caresses my skin almost feels reverent, and then he slams into me again, his cock hitting deep and causing me to clench. I manage not to cry out at the jolt of pleasure it sends through me, but Jordan groans loud enough that I clamp my hand over his mouth.

"Echoey halls," I say, not stopping.

He growls something into my palm. I eagerly trade it for my mouth, and another groan stays between us. The more he touches me, the more I need his hands, mouth, and breath all over my skin. All of me craves all of him, and I can't get enough.

Jordan tries to slow us down, tensing like his control might be slipping, but I push his hands off my hips.

"Callie," he warns, voice all gravel.

I say his name on the next panted breath, and he takes it as the plea I meant it to be. He drives into me, his hand falling between us, and he rubs circles on my pulsing clit.

"This is what you want, right? This right here?"

A whimper answers him, despite my teeth being buried in my lower lip. But Jordan only goes harder. He takes over, controlling my body and our rhythm.

Then Jordan's lips are at my ear.

"We both know your cunt's been mine since day one, beautiful." Every syllable hums through me, teeth grazing the shell of my ear. "Now I want what's mine to come all over my cock."

"Yes," I tell him, so fucking close. "Fuck, fuck. It's yours, Jordan. I'm yours."

He grunts like he agrees, relentless while he fucks me so far over the edge I can barely breathe. I cry out. I moan. I don't even try to fight it as the pleasure demands every sound I staved off.

My pussy pulses around Jordan's cock, and he hisses out a breath. "Fuck, Callie. Just. Like. That."

He strokes deep, holding me how he wants me, and then groans out his release. When he stills inside me, he slouches back on the seat, bringing me with him. I wouldn't resist if I could.

I close my eyes and melt into his chest. His heart hammers under my cheek, and my fingers trace up and down his bicep. It's a serene moment that can stretch on forever.

At least it is until, out of nowhere, he says, "My birthday was endgame, and I thought you were lacrosse."

Oh no. I wonder if delirium is a symptom of heatstroke.

Once again concerned I broke him, I straighten up.

He smiles. "That's why I didn't want to tell you it was about more than sex."

Still not convinced he doesn't need medical attention, I swing my leg over him and get to my feet. "Care to elaborate?"

He slips off the condom and yanks up his trunks, tucking it in the pocket. "Lacrosse was just a challenge to me. Another way for me to beat my brother. After I met my goal, I stopped caring and quit. I was afraid, if I told you I wanted to be with you before my stupid challenge was over, I wouldn't want you anymore."

I step into my swim bottoms. "What does that have to do with your birthday?"

"The night I followed you home from the party, I had no intentions of ever seeing you again. But then"—he grins, sauntering over—"you roped me back."

I roll my eyes, delivering a mental, *Told ya so*, to my tits. Also, a quick, *Thanks*, before I drag my top over them.

He clasps his hands behind me. "I closed my eyes and pointed to your calendar and gave myself until then to sleep with you. I just so happened to pick my birthday—twice."

"So, you kept trying to put me off until Saturday after the challenge ended." I smile, realizing we might be more alike than I want to admit. "I chose Friday as endgame, too."

His head pulls back. "What?"

"Benji told me he thought you had real feelings for me, so I decided you had until Friday to tell me. Otherwise, I wasn't going to see you when I came back."

His eyebrows shoot up. "Is that why you showed up at the bar instead of going to Graham's?"

I nod, and everything goes in an unexpected, sideways, where-the-fuck-are-we direction.

He steps back as if I slapped him and rubs his face. "Everything that happened that weekend was because I wouldn't tell you how I felt earlier?" He paces the steam-filled room. Bench to bench like a windup toy. "Why would you do something so stupid? Why would I do something so stupid? Damn it, we really are the most stubborn two people."

I agree with the last part, but the rest? "Jordan, stop. Everything's fine. We're fine."

"Fine?" He pauses and tosses his hands in the air. "Callie, you went on a bender. We stopped seeing each other because you were acting like a completely different person. You broke my fucking heart, and all I needed to do to prevent it from happening was tell you I wanted to be with you?"

A lot floods out in one furious rant. He looks lost for a second, fighting with himself over something not his fault—out of his control—and the fact that he would ever blame himself destroys me. *I* fucked up. *I* hurt him. *I'm* the mess.

Without warning, he changes direction and runs straight into me. He clutches my face, and his mouth seeks mine like his life depends on the air I breathe. The kiss is mind-numbing and confounding, and the tighter he holds me against him, the more I need him to never let me go. I have no choice but to accept how incredibly hard I will fall for him. Am falling. Have already fallen.

He pulls away, leaving me breathless, and cups my cheeks, resting his forehead on mine. "We're going to start telling each other what we're thinking. And I'm starting right now."

The intensity in his gaze makes my head swim, and I worry he'll say something he can't take back. "Jordan..."

"Callie, I have to say it." He takes a deep breath, a ghost of a smile forming. "I'm starving."

Frustrating and ... what was the word he used before?

Perfect.

Everything about him is frustrating and perfect.

An empty hallway greets me when I step out of the locker room.

"Thanks for waiting, everybody," I say, coming up behind Jordan and Cate on the stairs.

Jordan looks me up and down. Call it a lingering effect from what just happened in the steam room, but the casual glance alone sends a shiver shooting down my spine.

I dangle my keys at my zombie brother whose phone uses up every last bit of his awareness. "Connor, go start the car."

He grabs blindly for them, and I send Cate out the door with him. Jordan and I need to take care of some business. My fingers lock with his, leading him to the woman knowingly waving a twenty around. The pink in my cheeks offers her all the proof she needs to settle up.

"Pay the man," I say.

As Jordan pockets my winnings, she peruses him with the subtlety of Jess. "I never got a good look," she whines. "What happened to you showing him off for the cameras before he changed?"

With that, I get him out of reach before she dives over the counter. "Bye, Shayna."

"Pete's birthday's coming up," she calls after us. "You should come."

I wave at her, not giving an answer.

A few steps out the door, Jordan pulls me to him. "What's the money for?"

"Consider it the first installment for Cate's lessons."

"First of all, swim lessons are on me." He kisses me without allowing time for my rebuttal. "I have a follow-up question then. What was she paying you for?"

I bite my lips together, heat flooding my cheeks. "We might have won a long-standing bet by having sex in the steam room." Before he responds, I hurry down the sidewalk and join my siblings in the car.

His lips curl up as he climbs in, and then he turns to Cate and Connor in the back. "Who wants to go spend twenty dollars?"

Cate unleashes a death squeal, and even Connor looks up at the chance to spend someone else's money. I twist around in my seat and narrow my eyes at Jordan for being stubborn, but he pretends not to notice.

"Can we have blue slushies, Cal?" Cate asks.

I sense the tension enter Connor's muscles before the lines appear between his eyebrows. The request requires a trip to Sutterville and chances a run-in with Graham. The last thing we want on the weekends we spend with him, let alone our time away. I offer him a hint of a smile and let him decide whether we go. He gives a slight nod, but I wait until the lines fade before confirming with Cate.

When we leave the parking lot in a different direction, I catch sight of a confused Jordan. "Sutterville's convenience store has a blue slushie machine," I tell him.

"Sutterville, as in…" He glances at Cate, not saying anything more, which I appreciate.

I nod. "We usually try to avoid it since *anyone* could be there."

He shifts, seeming to understand. We ride the rest of the way in silence, the air in the car heavy around Connor.

Over the past few months, his tolerance for our father has steadily declined. Then it crashed and burned the night Graham almost hit me.

Basketball provides an outlet, but he's been more on edge as of late. A problem we'll need a solution for sooner rather than later.

His eyes meet mine in the rearview mirror as I pull off the highway. I wrinkle my nose at him, and he gives a half-smile. Not quite genuine but better than nothing. His mood improves further when only Rhonda's Cadillac appears in the parking lot. No sign of Graham anywhere.

Unwilling to wait, Cate speeds in as soon as we come to a stop. Connor rushes after her to prevent a repeat of the slushie fiasco in which we spent twenty minutes cleaning the damn floor to avoid Rhonda's sciatica acting up.

Jordan examines the lack of civilization surrounding him. His hands absentmindedly run through his hair, and God, he's gorgeous. I trail my fingers down his arm, needing to touch him. He opens the door and returns the favor by sliding his hand over my ass when I walk by. Since the bell already announced us, Rhonda watches the whole gratuitous display from behind the counter.

I smile and wave. "Hi, Rhonda."

She smirks and returns to reading a magazine.

Connor's holding Cate up to the slushie machine straight in from the door. I pinch his side before hanging a left to the row of cooler doors in search of water or soda. I stare at the selection, still undecided when the bell dings again. I check down the aisle where Jordan supervises the sacred filling of what appears to be a second cup of blue gunk. Unless I want her in my bed all night again, I need to stop her from starting a third.

I force a decision and bend over for a bottle of water.

"God, I've missed that ass."

The voice hits like a fucking meteor about three seconds before a hand connects with said ass. The slap stings, and the sound cracks through the store. I jerk up, the cooler door slamming shut. Brock's arrogant asshole reflection grins at me until I spin around. Then the actual arrogant asshole grins at me until my knee rams the fuck into his crotch.

He folds in on himself and growls out, "Shit, Callista." He sputters out more bullshit, but I couldn't care less.

Down the aisle, Connor's facing away from me, blocking Jordan, who is holding a scared Cate in his arms. Probably best for everyone if he stays away with the murder in his eyes and blood being harder to clean than blue ice and all.

Brock looks up, his hands on his knees. "What the fuck is wrong with you?"

"Can you seriously be asking me that?"

I head for Cate, but he grabs my wrist to stop me. I rip my arm from his grip and drive my hands into his chest. The force knocks him back. To catch himself, he swings his arm out, and in the process, he clears a shelf of plastic booze bottles and the only bottle of wine the store carries. The glass shatters, and a cheap merlot spills over the floor.

"Don't ever fucking touch me again," I tell him. "Better yet, forget you met me."

My pulse races as I walk away from him. It's a moment almost three years in the making, and I won't forget it this time. Jordan's jaw muscles work overtime, clenched and strained when I reach him.

I pull Cate from his arms, swipe a slushie cup, and smile just for him. "Let's go."

"You okay?" Rhonda asks.

I nod on my way past. "Call Trey if he doesn't clean up his mess."

As I back through the door, Connor and Jordan remain unmoved. I consider dragging them out, and with the adrenaline pumping, I could, but the little girl whimpering against my shoulder deserves top priority. She sniffles as I rub her back.

"You're okay, my monster."

Needing to reroute her attention to keep her from dwelling on what happened, I go around the corner of the building and set her on the picnic table no one ever uses. I wipe my thumb over her cheeks to dry them and offer her the cup. Her head shakes, the tears reforming, so I steal a move from Jordan and drink her slushie in front of her. Well, I pretend to because my body rejects the idea.

The performance—a blue trickle even drips down my chin— gets me a giggle.

"Cal, stop." She pulls the cup away from my mouth and puts college kids everywhere to shame, chugging the hell out of the colored slush. She burps and slaps her forehead. "Brain freeze."

"Oh no," I say, feigning shock. "We have to warm it up!"

I grab her, the slushie cup falling to the ground as we take off toward the street behind the gas station. Once we emerge from the building's shadow, I let her down.

"The sun should help, but you need to spin in circles to be safe."

Not questioning me for a second, she drops her head back and looks up at the sky. Around and around she goes, her arms outstretched and a smile on her face. "It's working." Her hand catches mine as she prances by. "Come on, Cal."

I laugh and twirl with her. Each rotation carries us farther and farther away from the scene inside. Exactly what we both need.

I'm getting dizzy when I feel Jordan watching. Sure enough, a blur develops into him when I stop. He stands next to Connor, witnessing us spinning like lunatics in the middle of the street. Of course, my brother shares in our particular brand of madness and barrels toward us. The heaviness from earlier is gone as he grabs me by the middle and swings me around. He switches to Cate, her squealing until I help her bring him to the ground. We lie in a pile, laughing. All of us feel weightless at the same time, which is becoming more elusive and harder to hold on to.

After a few minutes of trying to keep away from Connor, my little sister drags Jordan over. She demands he protect me before she dashes off again.

He folds his arms around me, his lips pressing into my hair. "Hey, beautiful."

I bury my nose in his shirt and inhale everything Jordan. In his arms, with Connor and Cate happy for the moment, that damn sun finally shines while it rains. Or maybe I've just found someone to help me see it. Either way, things are better than they've been for a long time.

"Are you ready to run yet?" I ask, gazing up at him.

"Only if it's to chase you. But I'm hoping you'll stay caught this time."

Sounds like exactly what I want.

Almost Three Years Ago

The sound created each time I rip up a picture gives me chills. Almost as satisfying as throwing them in the trash can when I finish. Although nowhere near as amazing as it will feel to light them on fire and watch them fucking burn. *Great. He's turned me into some kind of freaking pyromaniac.*

"Pete, I'm out."

No answer.

I check behind me where he's sitting on the concrete, sorting through the pile of photos.

"Pete."

"You got them all, Cal. I'm not finding any."

A coughing fit starts around the side of the house. Once it stops, Tony appears. The red of his eyes competes with his hair. Out of class for twenty minutes and already blazed. He moseys over, a smile plastered on his face for the duration of his high.

I grab the photos from Pete and flip through them, scanning for any hint of the arrogant asshole's face. There aren't as many to go through as there once were since this isn't the first time I've searched and destroyed. But this time is different. I need it to be.

As I reach the end of the stack, his truck roars around the corner and skids to a stop in front of the house.

"Goddamn it, Callista," Brock shouts, slamming the truck door.

Pete hits his feet, and even a slow-moving Tony rushes over to stand in front of me for protection.

Unneeded.

I drop the pictures on the ground and blow past them. "I told you to leave me alone."

"Why?" he hisses, meeting me halfway between the street and house. "Because I was right about you flirting with that jackass?"

"*Jesus*, Brock. He's my lab partner. It requires me to talk to him."

"And touch his fucking arm?"

An exasperated groan answers him because I refuse to explain for the hundredth time that I spilled water and wiped it off. If he'd walked past the door ten seconds earlier or later, he wouldn't have charged in and punched the poor guy.

"You were acting like a fucking slut, Callista."

All my strength goes into shoving him, but he only moves a step back to keep his balance.

"Don't call me that!"

"Then stop acting like one."

Again, my hands hit his chest with little effect.

"I want my shit," he says, storming toward the house.

I cut him off, but he shoulders past me.

"Cal, don't..." Pete's voice fades as I follow Brock inside.

The door slams behind me, and I run through the kitchen and down the hallway to my room where he's picking through the stuff on my dresser.

"Where's the necklace?"

"Get out!" I shout, dragging him back by his arm.

He whips around and stalks toward me. I backpedal at the same speed to the middle of the room. When I stop, he keeps coming until he's flush against me. Wild eyes stare down at me, his chest heaving erratically against mine. My breaths aren't the most rhythmic either as I challenge the glare, equally furious. Then his mouth crashes into mine, all the hostility still present. He pulls me with him, backing up into the dresser. As he turns us around, his arm swings out, knocking everything off the top. I grab at his shirt, pushing at his chest. He lifts me up onto the surface, and once we're face-to-face, we both stop.

"Don't fucking talk to him anymore," he demands, panting.

I reach up to my neck and rip off the necklace he gave me. I go to throw it, but he catches my wrist, his eyes never leaving mine.

Neither of us moves, the air between us as charged as ever. Love. Hate. I can't even tell the difference anymore. I'm starting to think I never could and fear I never will. The person who makes me feel the most also makes me feel the least. Angry and numb, and I want the fuck out.

"We're done," I tell him. "For good."

He smirks and jerks the chain from my grasp. "Remember that's what you wanted when all this shit"—he swings the necklace around, his eyes scanning the room—"closes in on you. Because we both know it will, and we both know what happens when it does."

Brock walks out the door, leaving me on top of the dresser, and I know it's for the last time. I won't let him back in.

As the screen door slams, I promise myself to never fall in love again. It's toxic. But I guess all I needed to do was look at my parents to see that. Love ruins everything, and I'm done with it.

No more love.

No exceptions.

Ever.

133 Days Until 19

In the fourth grade, our class learned how to play those little plastic recorders. Our semester's worth of practice culminated in a recital. Before the performance, the teacher pulled me aside, asking me to only pretend to play so as not to ruin the experience for the other children. If only Jordan knew before he let me near a guitar.

We've been back at his house for a few days, every waking moment spent together. He's lying in his boxers, watching me play at the foot of the bed. The more offensive the sound, the more he cringes, and the more I smile. The sole reason he tolerates me mocking the guitar gods is I'm strumming away in nothing but my thong and bra. I end my noise with a note not meant for human ears and return the poor instrument to the floor.

"When Beta Void finally decides to replace their awful guitarist, I'm auditioning."

His eyes narrow, and the current guitarist attacks the future guitarist in a fit of jealousy. I giggle as he drags me back onto the mattress with him.

I've never had so much fun with someone before. Alone, around other people, freaking grocery shopping—every second with him is incredible, and I hate that we lost so many.

I flip around to straddle him. "Are you bored of me yet?"

"Not yet," he says, his hand gliding up my side. "And when I do tire of you, we just need to have sex, and I'll be good for another few hours."

I roll my eyes and crawl off him to go search through a milk crate full of vinyls. The eclectic collection belongs to Benji as well as the bed and, technically for the next five months, the room.

Turns out, Benji picking me up from class that day cost Jordan his bedroom for six months. The guy went from the primary with an en suite bathroom to a glorified broom closet for me. Since Benji failed to disclose this vital information in his *Jordan wants more* speech, he owes me and can loan me his room for a few days.

I slide an album out of the row. "Polka?"

Jordan swipes it away, turning it over in his hand even though he eyes me. "Come on."

He tosses the vinyl on the crate and leads me downstairs to the living room. I stand out of the way as he scrapes the coffee table legs over the wooden floor, dragging it out of the way. He completes the same ritual with the two couches on either side, clearing a large area in the middle.

"What are we doing?"

He open his laptop next to the sound system and clicks around. "We're going to polka."

An accordion plays through the speakers.

"You know how?" I ask, doubtful.

He nods on his way over. "My grandmother on my mother's side taught me before she died." He throws my hand over his shoulder and holds the other out, his spare hand on my hip. "All right, beautiful. We start with—"

I step back with my right, then left, and my right again, proving his tutorial unnecessary. A smile tugs at his lips as he shakes his head, then we polka our way around his living room. The song ends with a cymbal crash as he swings me onto the couch, dropping down beside me.

"You could have given me an ego boost and at least pretended to let me teach you," he says.

Never, Waters.

"Don't bother trying with the fox-trot, waltz, or square dancing either. Our gym teacher ran out of sports and taught us how to dance."

"I'm with you all the way to square dancing. I draw a line there."

Not a problem. If I need a fix, an intoxicated Tony still calls out steps at random and dosey-does my ass around. In our microscopic class, since no last names fell between Henders and Long, we experienced every group project and partnered activity together, dancing no exception.

Jordan hops up and goes to his computer, grinning when he returns. "Shall we fox-trot?"

"Sex on Fire" by Kings of Leon plays, and he offers me his hands, pulling me to my feet. As taught by a middle-aged woman with no training, I hold up my dancer's frame. Not to be outdone, Jordan matches my form and leads me through the steps. The professionalism dips when his hands slip down to my ass, but we are ballroom dancing in our underwear to a song about sex, so it doesn't surprise me.

What does, however, is Rusty appearing in the doorway halfway through the song. Jordan stops, the two of them engaged in a shocked stare-down, eyes and mouths gaping. Rusty's bag falls off his shoulder at the same time Gavin collapses beside him, both hitting the floor simultaneously.

Gavin lands in a hysterical pile, knees to his chest. "Oh my God."

"Dude. Callie." Rusty holds a hand over his eyes.

I grab a blanket from the couch and cover myself, amused by his reaction. "Hello, boys."

He peeks through his fingers and lets his hand fall to his side.

Jordan dashes to shut off the still-blaring music. When he spins around, he shoos them. "Disappear, hooligans. We have yet to waltz."

Rusty shakes his head, slinging his bag over his shoulder. "Damn, Waters. If this is you with a girlfriend, I'm terrified for our band's image."

He descends to the basement while Gavin climbs the stairs, still squawking after the door to his bedroom shuts. A moment of *fuck me* crosses Jordan's face, no doubt preparing for the ridicule he'll endure. He recovers and returns to the computer. He turns up the volume, drowning out the deranged sounds of Gavin above us, and Edwin McCain sings, "I'll Be."

I smile and drop the blanket. "Are you taking me to prom in the late nineties?"

He walks over and pulls me to him. "Just dance, you impossible woman."

I laugh, and he twirls me across the room. With our steps in time, his hand catches my back after each turn, the rest of the world far away.

By the time the chorus starts a second time, we abandon the waltz. My arms drape over his shoulders, fingers grazing the back of his neck. He holds me close and presses his forehead against mine. He looks at me in his way so intensely that it creates the strangest sensation. Like, if his stare continues much longer, the green in his eyes will mix with the blue in mine. Anyone who's ever painted knows, once two colors combine, they never truly separate again. One permanently stained by the other. A part of him always a part of me.

The feeling becomes overwhelming. I'm about to pull away when the mood shifts along with his hands. He hooks his thumbs in the lace of my panties.

"I'm bored of you," he says.

I jump into his arms and wrap my legs around him. "We can't have that now, can we?"

Dance lessons end as he slams shut the laptop and bounds upstairs. He lands on top of me on the bed and makes quick work of the thong now in his way. The boxers go next and then the bra. I fall back on the pillows and stare up at him hovering over me with his teeth pressed into his bottom lip.

"Perfect," he says.

Jordan kisses me before his mouth works its way down my neck and over my collarbone. A whimper slips out at the shot of pleasure when his tongue swipes over my nipple. His hips flex forward, rubbing his erection against my leg. He keeps going, his hot lips trailing down my stomach. I grasp at his hair and sigh as he reaches my hip bone. He settles between my thighs and then licks up the inside of one. Another sigh from me is quickly followed by a groan from him.

"Jesus, baby." He stops, his mouth leaving my skin. "I'm trying to think of a nice way to say this."

Possibly the fastest way to kill the mood. I push up on my elbows, offended but not sure about what yet. "A nice way to say what?"

He climbs up my body, bracing himself over me with his forearms. "If you don't stop making those fucking noises, I'll finish before we even start."

Frustrating beyond belief and still capable of making me laugh.

"Get your shit together, Waters," I say, snaking my hand between us.

His eyes clamp shut as I grip his hard cock, twisting on the way up, and a deep sound escapes the back of his throat. Muscles still tense, he glares down at me, all heat. "Screw you, Henders."

I bat my eyelashes at him. "That's what I'm waiting for."

He covers the bruise below my shoulder with his mouth, sucking until I squeak in the most embarrassing way. But then he kisses it—*his* mark he left over the one I wanted to forget.

He made it his. Like he made me his.

He pushes between my legs again, spreading them wider with his broad shoulders before he drags the flat of his tongue over my pussy to my clit. His lips seal around it, a soft hum vibrating and driving me out of my mind.

I remember Gavin's upstairs and bury a moan. My hands tangle in his hair as I breathe his name, pushing up against his mouth. He pushes a thick finger inside me. I am so fucking wet for him already, and he thrusts in a second. They drag in and out of my pussy, making me whimper and wonder if I even care if Gavin hears me come.

Jordan's lips travel down my inner thigh, but he keeps rubbing my clit, thrusting harder. A moan escapes, quiet until Jordan's hot tongue slides down to my ass. I cry out, my body jerking but then going back for more.

"That's better, beautiful. Give me that sexy voice."

Officially over it, I moan when he licks a second time before moving back to suck on my clit. Then he starts massaging the tight ring of muscle, rubbing in his saliva. I buck against his mouth and press my ass back, chasing more of both while he fucks me with his fingers. All the sensations weave together, building and heating and intensifying.

"Fuck, Jordan." I end up moaning most of it and pull at his hair, riding his mouth. "I'm so close."

"Allow me, then."

He scrapes his teeth over my clit and adds pressure with his thumb and hits my G-spot all at once. I detonate in the most incredible way. Nothing but lit up nerve endings, moans, and shaking thighs, locked around Jordan's head.

He groans against my sensitive skin, making me shudder. As soon as my thighs release him, he grabs a condom, his cock leaking at the tip. I pull him down the second he rolls the condom on, wrapping my legs around him. He bumps up against my entrance, and I lift my hips.

When he slowly pushes inside me, he hums, but then he retreats, almost pulling all the way out.

"Careful," he says, hovering above me, "or I might think you're needy for my cock."

"I am." I won't even bother denying it with every part of me evidence to back it up. "But not as needy as it is for me."

My heels kick into his firm ass, and his hips thrust forward, filling me all at once. I moan, his lips slamming down onto mine. He kisses me, keeping our rhythm slow. Dragging out and plunging back in.

"*God*, you feel incredible," he says, lips still on mine. "You're wrong. All of me is fucking needy for you."

I pull him closer because it's all of him I need, too.

He rocks into me faster, our mouths still fused. My nails sink into the muscles in his back, and I feel them working beneath my fingers with each of his movements. Everything about him drags me under. His scent and the way he tastes. How he looks when waking up and that just a glance from him can make me smile or laugh or forget about the rest of the world.

Jordan shifts and thrusts deeper, the head of his cock hitting a spot that sends my eyes closed. The pleasure he spiraled through me earlier rebuilds each time he drives into me. I moan out a desperate form of his name, my back arching off the mattress. He pumps harder, each of his ragged breaths intoxicating.

"Let me feel your pussy pulse for me, baby," he says, rubbing my clit.

Then he sucks on my skin, over his mark, and it sets me off. Eternity condenses into a few seconds as I fall to pieces for him.

"Fuck, Callie," he grunts out, hiking my leg higher.

He grinds into me, muscles rippling as he comes. His head drops onto my chest while the rest of him falls onto the bed beside me. Other than my fingers skimming across his shoulder blades and his lips pressing against me, neither of us attempts to move while we recover. The heat of his breath spreads across my overly sensitive skin, and the same sensation from earlier flits up my spine.

Even without him looking at me, those damn colors are determined to mix whether I want them to or not.

125 Days Until 19

A week after Rusty and Gavin catch us prancing in our underwear, I park next to Jordan's Jeep at the house.

The two of them are outside, Gavin balancing on the running board of his van, driver's door open. "Get in there and save him from himself, Henders. He's been working on his hair for the last twenty minutes."

"I'll do what I can but no promises." I return a wave from Rusty, who is climbing in on the other side.

"Just be careful. It's a war zone," Gavin says, ducking into the vehicle. Heavy metal blares out his rolled-down window as they back out of the driveway, thrashing around in their seats.

Since "the incident," both have fully adapted to a girl invading their space on a regular basis. They even put the toilet seat down. Gentlemen, each and every one.

The four of us got pretty cozy the last few days of break before I left for Graham's on Friday. My new perspective might have helped make the trip less miserable than most, but a majority of the credit goes to Jordan and the texts, calls, and other activities that required the lock on my bedroom.

When Jordan answers, I can't tell whether he or his hair claimed victory. Either way, it works. He yanks me inside, his mouth on mine before he swings the door shut behind me. After he has me breathless and wanting more, he breaks his lips away from mine and locks his arms around my waist.

"Sorry, beautiful," he says. "You can't just show up, looking like that, and think I'm not going to kiss you."

"You saw me wearing the exact same thing a few hours ago."

"I kissed you then, too, if you remember."

I remember. The kiss led to him almost missing a lecture. He also ran late to his first one because he'd insisted on resuming his morning coffee delivery service. Not that I can imagine a better way to begin my day than with Jordan and caffeine, but we need to reenter negotiations over his schedule, so the man shows up to his classes on time.

"So, what do you have planned for tonight?"

He brushes the tip of his nose over mine. "A movie, followed by coffee."

"What movie?" I ask, his barely there touch and low, hushed voice about to derail my focus. A job he finishes by pressing his lips against the base of my neck. They skim to the sensitive spot under my ear.

During our week together, he mapped out every inch of me and takes advantage of his newfound knowledge as often as possible—hence the scheduling issues.

Seconds before neither of us leaves the house, his lips pull away. "Something foreign and terrible with subtitles. The perfect movie to not pay attention to." I glare at him, and he grins. "What did you plan?"

"Dinner and open mic night."

His eyebrows draw together, surely because of my far superior plans for the evening.

A large bouquet on the entry table distracts me from his pouting. "Did you buy flowers?" I ask.

"Of course I did. It's Date Night, Callie."

He brings them over, and I smell them because that's what people do with pretty flowers before putting them in a vase and watching them die.

"For future reference, don't buy me flowers."

He tosses them on the table and folds his arms around me. "Coffee and jewelry only, I promise."

Without warning, he dips me almost all the way to the ground. I laugh at the sudden drop, and he kisses me, bringing more blood rushing to my head before he pulls me up.

"Get your hands off my date, man." Benji walks in from the living room, wearing ripped jeans and a flannel—but a nice blue one, clearly reserved for special occasions. "You have a little redhead waiting for you."

He grins as Jordan's eyes narrow.

When Jordan offered to hang out with Felicia, he didn't know what he was setting in motion. She insisted on them going on a proper friend date, and she's been bubbling about it all week. After making fun of him for it, Benji suggested he and I do the same.

Well, technically, he said, *"Hey, since the dude you're banging's busy, let me take you out, Calico."*

No girl can resist such an eloquent request.

Jordan's hands put on a performance, feeling me up before he relinquishes me to his best friend for the night. "See you later, beautiful." He kisses me, his tongue shoving into my mouth just to further bring home his point.

I smile at the dramatics.

His expression hardens, and he gives Benji a pointed look. "Don't get any ideas."

Benji winks in response. Jordan picks up the flowers and hesitantly walks out the door.

As soon as it latches, Benji saunters over with a sly smile. "You ready for the ride of your life, Calico?"

"Wait, you don't mean—"

"Oh, yeah." He jingles his keys around. "We're taking The Beast."

Trey's piece-of-crap starter truck should have prepared me for a ride in Benji's station wagon; however, it did not. The seats' upholstery mostly consists of duct tape, the radio hangs out of the dash—still works though—a strange smell of motor oil and cologne mixes in the interior, and the thing sputters the entire drive. He loves the old gal and claims he'll drive her until she starts on fire on the side of the road. So, another week if his luck holds.

We eat tacos out of a truck parked in a lot of a shopping center. The brave vendor trusted the college kids to make it worth his while to open in mid-March, and given the line, he put his faith in the right demographic.

After Benji throws away our trash, he slides onto the hood next to me and hands me his cup.

I sip and make a face. "Is that plain soda?"

He chuckles at my reaction. "Been a while?"

"Probably the last time I went on a date."

"Wow, a *real* date." He leans back against the windshield. "My last one of those was my senior prom."

"Mine too," I say. "Who'd you go with?"

"Sasha Brown, my last girlfriend. You?"

"My ex-boyfriend, Pete."

He steals the cup, and I settle back next to him as he takes a drink. We stare up at what would be stars if not for the city lights.

One of the only things I miss about Sutterville is, even on Main Street, you can see them shining. Trey, Pete, and I would lie in the middle of the road for hours when we were kids, gazing up and planning all the things we would do. All the places we would go together.

Benji passes the cup. "The first night Jordy came home after chasing you around campus, the guy looked wrecked. I almost told him how in over his head he was with you."

"Why didn't you?" I rest my cheek on the cold glass and look at him.

"You sparked such a fascination in him when no one else could. He needed to figure out what that meant on his own." He rolls his head in my direction, one corner of his mouth curving up. "Plus, if he'd listened and bailed, I would never have met the girl he deemed worthy of a Guns N' Roses song. I mean, that's some serious shit right there."

I laugh, and we go back to watching the sky.

We stay until after the parking lot has cleared out, and the truck's driven away. Then we once again tempt fate with a ride in the station wagon.

Benji cranks the engine, a grin spreading when it roars to life. "Let part two of our date begin."

A little dive bar across town hosts an open mic night every Thursday. Benji holds the creaky red metal door for me, and I step inside to the exact hole-in-the-wall I expected.

I immediately spot the regulars—six annoyed men crowded in at one end of the bar with a pitcher of beer in the middle of the table. Not one of them looks impressed with the college kids and twenty-somethings invading their space.

Drinks in hand, Benji ushers me through the crowd and pulls out a chair for me at the last empty table, dead center of the room. He slides into the seat next to me while nodding at someone near the stage. The guy drops the mess of tangled cords he's fighting with and comes over.

"You made it." He eyes me, surprised by my presence. "And you brought a lady?"

"Jordan's lady. My date." Benji smirks at his vague explanation. "It's a whole thing; don't worry about it."

The guy shakes his head, dismissing his confusion. "Either way, she sounds off-limits."

Benji gestures between us with his beer bottle. "Callie, this is Mike. He sets up most of the open mic nights around town."

Mike and I exchange a polite, introductory smile. At least we do until Benji clears his throat and leans over. His arm settles on the back of my chair as he stares out a warning.

Oh, good Lord.

Mike's hands go up, and he backs toward the stage. "Off-limits. Got it."

With the ceremonial marking of the territory complete and the perimeter around me once again secure, Benji relaxes in his seat. I sigh, and he struggles to keep a straight face, bringing the bottle to his lips.

"What?" he asks, before taking a drink.

"Just wondering if I should worry about you trying to pee on me next."

"Whatever it takes to keep the other dogs away." He loses his battle and chuckles when I glare at him. "Sorry, Calico, but you might as well get used to the overprotective routine. I take my duties as best friend very seriously. If that means I have to stand in as your boyfriend from time to time to scare a guy away, then tattoo your name on my chest with a heart around it."

I laugh at his dedication, not doubting him for a second. "Let's hold off on the ink. But it's nice to know I have a backup in case I break the real boyfriend."

"Speaking of the real one…" Benji tips his head to the side. "You know Jordan's freaking out about the two of you being together, right?"

I sigh as he confirms what I've been worrying about. The first time I noticed something was off was over the weekend. During one of the few PG-rated conversations Jordan and I had, someone on his end of the call asked who he was talking to.

He answered, "It's my girl—it's Callie."

Another was Tuesday night. We were in the living room, and Gavin wanted me to weigh in on a girl he'd brought home.

Jordan kicked him out, telling him, "She's not your Hot or Not meter. She's my … Callie."

On top of his reluctance to call me his girlfriend, he also shoots me a panicked look anytime other people refer to me as such. It bothers me because Jordan has me. No questions. I can't even look at anyone else without mentally checking off all the ways they fall short. But, as Mike's shock demonstrated, anyone who knows the boys of Beta Void is well aware that none of them ever commit to one girl. I thought after our perfectly imperfect week together, that would change … but maybe not.

"Let me guess," I say. "He's not ready for a relationship."

Benji's forehead wrinkles. "Actually, I'm pretty sure it's the exact opposite. He's waiting for you to either confirm or deny whether *you're* ready. I swear, he slips up and almost calls you his girlfriend at least once per conversation. You really haven't noticed?"

I smile at how neurotic and completely Jordan that sounds. "If that's the case, why doesn't he say something?"

His head drops back, and he lets out an exasperated groan. "Because the day you two are honest with each other about your feelings before a bunch of dramatic bullshit goes down is the day the world ends." He sits forward in his chair, gray eyes searching mine. "He's crazy about you, woman. Cut the bullshit, tell him you're together, and put the guy out of his misery already."

"Have I ever told you how insightful you are?" I ask.

"Not today," he says, clinking his beer bottle against mine.

Feedback squeals through the speakers surrounding the room as Mike takes the stage. He welcomes everyone and introduces the first performer. A kid, dressed in all black, climbs the steps with a ukulele in his hand.

Benji's eyes widen as he mouths, *Fuck.*

The first few performances nearly end him, an agonizing look on his face the entire time, but after Mike nudges him on the way past our table, his demeanor changes. He appears lost in thought, not paying attention anymore. When Sunflower-Sundress Savannah takes the stage with her acoustic guitar to let us know all about her being dumped by a guy named Dean, he scoots his chair closer to mine. "So, I might have had an ulterior motive for bringing you here tonight."

"You mean, it's not just for the beautiful decor?" I ask, gesturing to the bare rafters and the walls covered in street signs and Christmas lights. "Why else would anyone come here?"

The guitar cuts off, and Mike jumps up onto the stage. He snags the microphone from the stand. "Thanks, Savannah." He waits until she wanders off, looking a little lost, then he continues, "Anyone familiar with the music scene on campus will know our next performer. He usually has three guys standing behind him. But the lead singer of Beta Void is going solo tonight." My gaze snaps to Benji as Mike announces, "Let's hear it for Benji Jones."

He grins. "This is why."

Surprised, but not really, I cheer as he climbs the steps to the stage. The only time I saw him perform was the night of the frat party. Although my attention was elsewhere, I remember how in his element he appeared in front of an audience.

An electric keyboard waits for him center stage along with a stool. His expression falters while securing the mic in the stand, but his confidence returns once he sits down.

"Hey, everybody," he says. "As Mike pointed out, I'm used to having other people to blame a poor performance on, so bear with me." He winks at me, and my smile grows. "Uh, this song's called 'Exquisite Twilight,' and it's for you, Calico."

Several heads turn in my direction, but I barely notice because Benjamin "Badass" Jones wrote me a song, and the name alone says it all. We stare at each other, sharing a moment no one else will ever understand before he focuses on the keyboard.

"Here we go." He licks his lips and clears his throat.

His eyes fall shut when he plays a slow, almost sad melody. It drifts through the now-hushed room; even those who talked through the other performances are watching, waiting for him to sing. When his eyes open again, he leans toward the microphone.

When our world seemed destined to break us,
She searched through the darkness for the stars,
And in spite of all the chaos and destruction in our lives,
She never once lost sight of who we are.

His deep, raspy voice sends chills through me, and I instantly recognize the lyrics.

Each time she saw the sunshine when it rained,
She knew the lines would soon begin to blur,
And hidden beyond black shadows and all doubts and absolutes,
She'd find what's really beautiful to her.

Benji smiles at me, and I cover my mouth to stifle a laugh, even though I blink away tears. The words settle in my chest as he transforms the memories from a terrible night into something incredible, beautiful, hopeful even.

LIMBO

He closes his eyes again, the song losing some of its heaviness.

> *Frantic beauty lies all around,*
> *And sometimes what we seek should not be found.*
> *All our lives, we strive and struggle for our truth*
> *Because of this, we'll always remain bound.*

He slows again, the darker melody reemerging.

> *True happiness is for her,*
> *Not for you or me or those*
> *Who choose to sit idly by,*
> *Letting the best parts fade away,*
> *Lost forever deep inside.*

The lightness returns to his playing as he sings the chorus twice more before bringing down the tempo. He scans over the crowd, his lips curving into a smile as he holds the last chord.

> *I'll always remain bound,*
> *Bound to you.*

His hands leave the keyboard, and a second of stillness precedes the crowd's applause. He hops up and gives a proud bow while Mike grabs the microphone.

"Who needs a band with that kind of talent?" He pats Benji on the shoulder. "Next up, we have Dan Williams."

On his way to our table, Benji smirks. "Better than a fucking ukulele?"

I'm already on my feet, waiting for him, and he picks me up. I wrap my arms around his neck and hug him harder than I have anyone in my entire life, needing him to understand how much I mean it when I say, "Thank you, Benji. For everything."

"Anytime. Any reason." His grip on me tightens, and I know he means it as much as I do.

Setting me down, he grins at someone behind me. Someone almost always being Jordan. Sure enough, he steps beside me, his hand finding the small of my back.

"Hear that, man?" Benji asks him. "That's what it sounds like when no one holds me back."

"Yeah, just remember my writing credit after you make it big." He tilts my chin to kiss me, showing no reservations about everyone in the bar seeing his lips on mine.

At that moment, I know Benji's right. He's just as much mine as I am his.

I sit down, and he claims the chair closest to me.

"Where's Felicia?" I ask.

"She found a more attractive guy."

Doubtful, but I jut out my lip to give him the pity he deserves anyway.

Suddenly, my seat relocates in the opposite direction.

Benji's foot unhooks from my chair leg, a satisfied grin on his face. "My date."

I laugh and shrug at an even more sullen Jordan. Our attention turns to the stage and Next-Up Dan Williams as he plucks away on his guitar. A few minutes into what sounds like a three-note song, Benji leans over. "Put him out of his misery."

I wrinkle my nose at him and his smug expression.

Once Mike reappears, he announces a short break between singers and turns on music. The room quickly comes to life. I leave the boys at the table to get another beer, but with a crowd already formed around the bar, I stop in the restroom.

A girl reapplies her lipstick in the mirror while I wash my hands. She pulls her long blonde hair off to the side, and I notice she's wearing one of those purposely torn T-shirts with an intricate braid weaving the pieces back together.

"I love your shirt," I tell her.

She snorts and rolls her eyes at me in the mirror as she drops the lipstick in her purse. Not the expected response to a compliment but whatever. Bypassing the acquaintance stage completely, we proceed straight to best friends forever, and she gives me a once-over, followed by some serious side-eye on her way out.

"Nice to meet you, too," I say to the closing door.

Few people have weeded out from the bar, so I shamelessly flash a smile at the bartender to jump up on the priority list. He nods to let me know he'll be with me after he finishes up a group of giggling girls. While waiting, I catch sight of Benji and Jordan deep in conversation at our table. Jordan smiles, not the heart-stopping one he seems to only give me but gorgeous nonetheless. My view is interrupted when my new restroom buddy enters the equation. She glances at me right before she makes herself comfortable on his lap.

Oh, fuck no.

I start in their direction with every intention of dragging her across the room by her chemically damaged, bleach-blonde hair. But when she trails a tacky, fake nail down his neck, Jordan jerks away from her touch, an irritated set to his jaw. His obvious disinterest brings back my logical, not unstable-jealous girlfriend side. A side until, seconds earlier, I didn't even realize existed. Damn, this guy really has a hold on me.

The chances of me causing one hell of a scene have lowered to thirty percent by the time Jordan's terrified gaze lands on me. Since the ideal lap is at maximum capacity, I drop onto Benji's. His arm slips around me without hesitation, and I switch my focus from Jordan to Bathroom Blonde. She points her scowl in my direction, and damn do I find her annoyance with my arrival amusing.

I fight off a smile. "Jordan, who's your friend?"

"Not a friend," he says. "Brooke, you need to—"

"Wait," I interrupt and check with Benji for confirmation. "This is Brooke?"

My look says *the* Brooke, and he smirks before he takes a sip of his beer.

A random girl being rude I can handle, but this one saw me with a guy on her hook-up list, sized me up in the restroom, and then crawled on top of him to stake her claim. No. Even a proper lady has her limits, and given no one in my life has ever described me as a lady, she's pushed far past mine.

She continues to give me a smug look, so I smile back and decide to offer one more compliment. "I've heard wonderful things about your blowjobs."

The superiority drains from her now-bulging eyes along with the color from her face.

Benji laughs so hard he chokes on his beer. "Fuck, Calico," he says, setting the bottle on the table. He tries to hide his growing grin behind a hand, well aware of what's about to happen.

"The problem is, the lap you're sitting on belongs to my boyfriend."

Jordan's eyebrows shoot up, and he appears more shocked by what I just said than the earlier statement.

"*Boyfriend?*" Brooke glances down at him, but his eyes stay locked on me.

"Boyfriend," I repeat. "And I'd really love for you to move."

She checks again to see if Jordan will correct me, but he still stares at me, not acknowledging her in the slightest. I receive one more glare before she scampers off to the first group of guys she finds in need of validation.

I slide off Benji's lap to my seat. "I can't take you anywhere."

Jordan grabs my chair and pulls it over until it bumps his. "You are fucking incredible, you know that?"

I laugh, and he leans in. Before his lips reach mine, my seat jerks back the other way until it knocks into Benji's.

"My date."

"My girlfriend," Jordan says.

Benji tosses me a glance out of the corner of his eye. "Our girlfriend."

Jordan looks ready to continue the tug-of-war but stands up, digging his phone out of his pocket. Felicia's name shows up on the screen when he waves it at Benji. "Whatever. You and your death trap have our girlfriend home in twenty minutes." He kisses my forehead on his way by, his lips lingering longer than normal.

The second my boyfriend walks away, Benji cocks his head to the side, not even trying to hide his grin. "Pissing on him would have been more subtle."

I burst out laughing, unable to disagree.

123 Days Until 19

When Lara texts to inform me she and Tyler are going out of town again, I barely ask before Jordan agrees to go with me to Waymore for the weekend. This time, we bring his Jeep because he claims my car speakers ruin music.

My siblings react more to seeing him walk through the door than me. They rarely take to new people, so I can't say it bothers me that they like him. Plus, it's nice to have someone else to send Cate to when she decides on Saturday morning that she wants to be a golden retriever named Princess.

After her evening walk, she colors at the table, using her teeth because she can't hold the crayons in her paws. With her distracted, Jordan sneaks off for a shower. I'm watching something mindless on TV when Connor walks into the living room.

"Would you keep track of this damn thing?" He drops onto the couch next to me and tosses my phone onto my lap. "Trey keeps texting you about tonight."

I kick at him. "Quit reading my messages."

"Change your password then," he shoots back.

Even though I already know what my cousin wants, I check the messages.

School.

Tonight.

Please.

"You going?" he asks.

I shrug and set the phone on the cushion. I've seen Pete on his birthday every year since he turned five. Even if only for a few minutes, like last year when I stopped by the party and made an excuse to leave right away. It's one of the few things that has never changed over the years.

Jordan's already dressed, his hair dripping from his shower when I step into the bathroom doorway. I take advantage of the mirror and stare at his reflection. Given the reaction he has to the mere mention of Pete, I can't imagine he'll jump at the opportunity to spend time in the guy's physical presence. Not that I blame him. A few days ago, I almost ripped a girl's hair out because she touched him.

He looks up and sees me behind him. I smile, and he reads me right away.

He drops his towel in the hamper and meets my gaze in the mirror. "What do you want from me?" he asks.

I chew on my lip. "Pete's birthday party's tonight."

His eyes leave mine, and he runs his hands through his hair. Of course, it can't be that easy. I slide my arms around him and press up against his back.

"Not happening, beautiful. I'm not going to your ex-boyfriend's birthday party."

I lay my cheek on his back and drag my fingers down to his stomach. "We can just make an appearance and leave as soon as you want to."

His muscles tense under my touch. "I already want to leave, so no point in going."

"Don't you want to know more about who I used to be?" I ask.

It takes a second for him to answer, "Nah."

Not ready to give up yet, I slip around, between him and the mirror. I usually break him down by pouting, but he looks too determined, so I'll need a stronger argument.

My gaze lowers down his body, and I tug at the bottom of his shirt before my hand drifts down to the bulge behind his zipper. "Not even if we fool around in the Jeep on our way?"

When I cast my eyes back up, rubbing his dick, I don't need him to answer out loud. The hard swallow and heat in his eyes as he presses me against the sink says it for him—we're going to Pete's party.

Since Connor already has plans with his friends, I find a neighbor willing to watch Cate for a few hours.

We detour on our way to Sutterville, and in the middle of nowhere on a gravel road, I follow through on the promise from the bathroom. I'm still breathing hard when we crawl back in the front, and his hair's a sexy mess. I love that every time I look at him tonight, I'll think about the reason.

Before we left, Cate asked for the hundredth time about her book. She left it at Graham's last weekend and has missed it every night since. Not wanting her to suffer any longer, I'll bite the bullet and get it for her. So, instead of sending Jordan to Main Street, I direct him to the south side of Sutterville.

He parks behind Graham's truck. I'm surprised to see it there since it rarely is on a Saturday night.

Jordan glances over with a serious expression. "Is this Graham's house?"

I almost ask how he knows but remember he's seen the truck before at the dorms. "Cate's lived without her favorite book all week because she forgot it," I say.

He grabs my hand when I reach for the door handle. "She'll be fine until next weekend."

The concern in his eyes almost stops me. "In and out. Two minutes, tops."

After a few seconds, his grip on my hand loosens. I hurry across the yard, wanting to keep it under a minute if at all possible.

The light in the kitchen is the only one on in the house other than a strip coming from under Graham's door at the end of the hall. With no plans on letting him know I'm here, I duck into Cate's room and grab the book off her pillow. When I turn around, I suck in a breath, startled by him in the doorway.

"Jesus." I press a hand to my chest. "You scared me."

He says nothing at first, just stands there, arm braced on the frame. My eyes adjust enough to see his shirt haphazardly buttoned and his hair sticking up. Then I hear a high-pitched voice call his name.

"What are you doing here?" he asks, ignoring whatever guest he's entertaining.

I hold up the book as an explanation.

He straightens up and glances over his shoulder. "You alone?"

Before I can answer, he heads for the kitchen. I give myself a breath and follow.

The screen door bangs open, and he leers out across the yard at Jordan. "Who's that?"

"A friend," I say from behind him.

"The same friend you ride?"

I ignore the comment, determined not to let him ruin my night. "I have to go."

When he continues to stare, I push past him and out the door.

"I want to meet him," Graham says.

I pause halfway down the steps, grip on the book tightening. "We're late."

"It only takes a minute to introduce me to your boyfriend. Tell him to get in here," he demands.

"Not tonight."

"I'm not asking."

I force myself down the steps, never wanting to bring Jordan anywhere near him.

"Callista," he shouts.

I flinch, worried he'll come after me, but the door slams. It echoes off the neighbors' houses and reminds me of all the times they've called Kevin over the years because of similar outbursts of slamming and yelling.

Jordan has a protective look in his eye when I get in the Jeep, and he drives off right away. "We good?"

"Mission was a success." I throw Cate's book in the backseat while checking Graham stayed in the house.

"And are *you* good?" he asks.

"I'm fine," I say. The answer's automatic, but for once, I mean it. We sit at a stop sign much longer than necessary, and when I look over, he's studying me. "Jordan, I'm okay. I promise."

The worry fades from his face, and he brings my hand to his lips to kiss my fingers. "Then tell me where the hell I'm going."

I smile and tell him to turn right, not thinking about anything but him.

We park in a gravel lot across the street from the abandoned elementary school at the other end of town. The exterior of the building looks ominous, towering three stories high with dead trees out front and more windows boarded up than not. Every few years, growing up, someone would get the bright idea to fix the place up, but it never went beyond the planning stages or someone mowing the weeds.

Jordan shuts his door with another look of dread, similar to the one from the first time he drove through Waymore.

I smile, trying not to laugh, and pull the sleeves of his hoodie I'm wearing down over my hands. "Are you up-to-date on your tetanus shot?"

"Ha," he says, unimpressed with my joke. "If this turns into one of Connor's horror movies, then we're both dead, considering what you let me do to you in the backseat."

He has a point.

"Sutterville and Waymore consolidated schools a few years ago. The school we went to before sits a mile that way off the highway." I wave a hand the other way. "This place hasn't been used for anything but parties since the nineties."

We use the flashlights on our phones to follow the worn path that takes us around to the back. The playground equipment hasn't been used in years. The wooden merry-go-round and seesaw are both weatherworn and no longer working, and the swings have chains hanging down with no seats. Attached to the top floor is an old metal fire escape slide. In an unusual twist, it is functional and used rather frequently by partygoers.

While Jordan cranes his neck, looking up at the side of the bricks, I grab the piece of wood hiding the busted-down door. As easy as it would be to fix, no one seems invested enough to do so.

People care up to the point it puts them out. When helping requires them to go out of their way, it's easier to pretend you never noticed the problem to begin with. The same can be said about most things in life, not just dilapidated buildings in a dying town.

I tug on the board and wrinkle my nose at the smell of rotting wood. Jordan steps beside me, reaching over to move it for me. Once it shifts enough to reveal the opening, we slip through, and he slides it back into place behind us. As ominous as the outside is, the inside reminds you of one of the reality shows where people stay in a haunted insane asylum. Old desks, chairs, and other classroom supplies lie everywhere in the large, open room on the first floor. All of it covered in decades' worth of dust and cobwebs.

Realizing Jordan isn't following, I turn around. "Are you coming?"

He looks up and dashes toward me with no sign of slowing down. I shriek as he crashes into me and makes a ghoulish sound in my ear. His lips brush down to mine, and it doesn't matter where we are. It's perfect because he's kissing me.

Up the staircase, we walk the hall with lockers on one side and the restrooms without fixtures on the other. I stop at the door with the music thumping behind it. The nerves specific to Jordan pop up in my belly, as I'm not sure what to expect when he meets the rowdy and unpredictable group of friends waiting inside.

"Ready to become a part of Callista's world?" I ask.

He runs his fingers along my cheek and moves a loose section of hair back. "It's all Callie's world to me."

I smile, liking not balancing all the balls separately anymore. At least, not every one of them.

Tony's the first to spot us when we walk in. "Henders!" he shouts, running toward us. His shoulder drops, and he pretends to tackle me, reversing me a few steps. When he straightens up, he gives me a wink and drags a hand over his stocking cap. He tucks it in his back pocket and pulls out the cigarette from behind his ear.

"Jordan, this is Tony," I say as he flicks his lighter.

"Well, he's the guy, huh?"

I don't even bother glaring at him. Tony will say and do whatever the hell Tony wants to say and do without a filter.

But my eyes narrow at Jordan when he says, "I'm starting to get the impression she's talked about me quite a bit."

Tony chuckles. "You have no idea, dude. Welcome." He gestures around the room, proud of his setup. "Everything the light touches is our domain. Fire barrel in the middle for warmth and the burning of shit if you feel so inclined. Beer and an assortment of adult beverages in the red coolers." A hand taps the pocket of his heavy flannel when he turns to us. "And right here, the green if you're keen."

From his heavy eyes and easy smile, I doubt there's much *green* left.

"Where's the birthday boy?" I ask, not seeing Pete.

About then, he sneaks between a few people standing by the burn barrel, one of them slapping him on the back on his way past. He heads straight for me with a look of disbelief in his eye and picks me up in a hug. I secure my arms around his neck, my feet dangling off the floor.

"Happy birthday, Pete."

His chest rises in a deep breath. "It's not a birthday until you say that."

He notices Jordan after he sets me down and rubs the back of his neck. "Sorry," he says, his eyes flitting to mine. "I'm Pete. You must be Jordan."

Mr. Manners, Pete extends his hand to Jordan. Tony and I watch them eyeing each other while shaking hands. Their arms quickly fall to their sides.

"Happy birthday," Jordan says.

"Ah, thanks." He relaxes again a little. "But really, we're just using it as an excuse to party."

They use everything as an excuse to party. New job, flat tire, found a missing sock.

We move farther into the room, my hand finding Jordan's. Shayna tracks us down, giggly and well on her way to drunk. But considering Tony has a bottle of moonshine in his hand, I'm not surprised. She hugs me, swaying and cooing about how much she loves me. Then she does the same to Jordan, much to his surprise.

I laugh, dragging her away from him. "Shay, hands off."

Her lip juts out. "You shared better when we were kids."

Tony passes around the moonshine while we stand around the barrel. It only takes a few minutes before my friends start telling the most embarrassing stories they can think of, all starring a very drunk me. I press my face against Jordan's chest, hiding, and he wraps his arms around me. The memories eventually move on to ones not involving alcohol, but I cut those off after a while, too.

The bottle goes around for the third or fourth time, but Jordan and I pass on the offer. I keep waiting for him to catch my eye and ask to leave, but he never does. He laughs along with Tony and Pete and becomes a pro at dodging Shayna. He fits here just as much as everywhere else in my life.

I'm staring up at him, not even paying attention to the conversation, when a siren blares. The classroom door kicks open, and a light shines in our eyes. Everyone else scatters around the room in a panic, but I wait for it.

"Everyone's under arrest," the voice barks through a megaphone. "For being a bunch of assholes."

The light shuts off, and in strides Trey with a smirk. The fear turns to annoyance, the group groaning at him. Tony plows into him, and they almost knock a chalkboard off the wall. They wrestle on the ground before Trey rolls his way over to us. He uses my arm to pull himself up and pops up next to me.

"Hey," he says. "How's everyone doin' tonight?"

I push him away. Rather than going to bother someone else, he doubles down on the unwanted love. He hooks his arm around my neck and shoves my face into his armpit. I pinch at his sides until he lets me go.

He laughs, nodding at Jordan. "Good to see you again."

"You too, man," Jordan says.

They have a bro moment, slapping hands and then the other's back.

Trey goes to say hi to a few people and squeezes my shoulders on the way by. "Welcome back, Cal."

I smile. I am back this time. For good, I think.

After a tour of the school, which turns into a chance for Tony to brag about his numerous hook-ups, someone gets the bright idea to use the moonshine to breathe fire over the barrel. Something I would have been all about at one point, but now, I shake my head.

"Idiots," I say to Tony.

He proves my point thirty seconds later when he lights his sleeve on fire. He hops around, yelping, until Pete calmly dumps the rest of his beer on the flames.

His head tilts, looking at the singed sleeve of his sweatshirt. "Maybe we should move on to the sword-swallowing portion of the evening."

Jordan laughs. "It might be safer."

To avoid arson charges or an ER visit, Trey comes up with a better idea. He grabs a spotlight out of his cruiser, and we all migrate to the gym.

Shayna and I settle in on a relatively clean and stable spot on the wood bleachers and watch the guys play basketball with an underinflated ball they found somewhere. With Pete and Trey drunk, Jordan easily takes the lead despite a giggly Tony being on his team. Every time Tony catches the ball, his mouth drops open, and I laugh.

Jordan sets up to take his last shot when Connor sprints onto the court and knocks the ball out of his hands. Jordan spins around, surprised to see my brother. As am I.

"Stick to lacrosse, Lover Boy."

Connor chases after the ball and effortlessly sinks a three-pointer in the netless hoop. His friends standing at the end of the bleachers cheer, and my friends converge on him, excited to see him.

He would tag along with us on our more tame adventures. They consider him as much a part of their family as they do me, but other than Trey, he hasn't seen them much over the past year.

After a few minutes of catching up, Tony tries to sneak him the moonshine. I grab the bottle before it connects with Connor's lips. "What the hell do you think you're doing?" I ask, handing it to Tony.

Connor glances at his friends with a smirk. "Not drinking?"

A lie, given his red cheeks and unfocused gaze.

Even though I'm not the poster child for those against underage drinking, I glare at him and plant my hands on my hips. "No, Connor."

"Whatever," he says, walking to his friends. "We're leaving anyway. You guys are lame."

The group behind me laughs at the intended insult, and I have to fight like hell not to join them.

"Go home and text me when you get there."

As soon as he and his friends disappear out of the gym, Tony, Pete, and Shayna fall to the floor in hysterics. Trey juts out his hip and purses his lips, imitating me, and I flip him off.

"Don't make me kick your ass."

He drops low to the ground like a wrestler. "I'm ready for you this time."

But he's not ready for Pete, who attacks him from the other side. They battle it out, burning off the never-ending supply of energy they have when drunk. A glimpse of Jordan's sexy hair distracts me from them. I lean into him, and he dips his head down to kiss my temple.

Connor texts around midnight.

I got the monster. No rush. I'm going to bed.

The first part, I believe. The last part, not for a second. One of those girls smiled way too big at him, and his arm went straight around her on their way out. I remind myself of our conversation and the trust I need to have in him, and I tuck the phone in the pocket of the hoodie.

"We good?" Jordan asks, hauling me against his side.

"We're great." I tip my chin up to see him. "How would you like to see the farm?"

122 Days Until 19

All the lights in Pete's grandparents' house are off when Jordan parks next to Trey's cruiser. When I climb out, my cousin hooks an arm around my neck and drags me around to the front of the Jeep.

"Let's get this out of the way right now," he says, pointing at the oak tree by the house. "Don't try to climb that."

He twists us toward the barn on the other side of the lot, but I stop him.

"Let me guess. Don't crash into it?"

He laughs and pushes me over to Jordan, who catches me. We head down the hill to the bonfire pit near the pond where Pete lights a fire. The cool breeze makes me shiver, and Jordan pulls me onto his lap to keep me warm. I rest my head against his and watch his hand pass back and forth over my leg.

Our calm moment only lasts until the sound of four-wheeler engines rip through the quiet air. I look up in time to see Tony jump the dirt mound on one side of the fire and land on the other, with Pete following right behind. They only collide once, on the ground while trying to beat each other to the ramp.

The night progresses slower than most, all of us talking and laughing. It's been a long time since we enjoyed each other's company without injuries or drama or blackouts. Each one of them seems at ease, falling into a new dynamic rather than filling the old roles. Shayna never sheds a single tear, and Tony lets off the moonshine early. Although that doesn't stop him from making baseless claims of how awesome he is. When he starts bragging about being the fastest person in the county, I happily prove him wrong.

We run back and forth between the barn and fire, him lunging at me anytime I steal the lead, which happens a lot. I slap the side of the barn first, and he snatches me up, spinning me around.

He lets me down and rests a hand on his knee, catching his breath. "I concede. I'm the second-fastest person."

He's still recovering when, out of nowhere, Trey tears past me and tackles him to the grass. I laugh and am about to walk away when something hits my foot. I glance down to see Trey's keys on the ground.

Tony grins and mouths, *Go!*

Maybe not *everything* has changed within our group. We still like to dish out payback when appropriate.

I scoop them up and head over to Jordan. He's sitting on a log by the fire, a focused look on his face while the reflection of flames dance in his eyes.

I drop onto his lap. "Oh, hey."

"Hey, beautiful," he says.

I hold up the key ring and shake it around. "Want to go borrow Trey's cruiser?"

With a grin, I hop off his lap and sprint toward the vehicles.

He doesn't follow, but I'm almost there when I hear Trey shout, "Shit! Caaaal, come on! Not agaaaain."

When I glance back, he's chasing after me. Even with his long legs, I make it to the car and have the keys in the ignition before he dives through the rolled-down passenger window.

"Hey," I say casually, mimicking him from earlier. "How's everyone doin' tonight?"

"Yeah, screw you." He flips over in the seat and pulls his feet in the window. I switch on the red and blue lights and throw the car in drive. "Where we going?" he asks.

"Everywhere," I say.

He laughs, and we fly off toward the pasture.

LIMBO

It's just before sunrise when Trey drags me up onto a hay bale on the east side of the barn. Jordan climbs up behind us. I settle back between his legs, head on his shoulder. He holds on to me like he'll never let go, and the three of us stare out at the stars, which are losing their intensity, night fading and day taking over.

I've spent my entire life staring up at the stars and dreaming about all the places I want to go, but this is the first time I've ever watched the sunrise, being exactly where I want to be.

With him.

101 Days Until 19

Of all the things I never thought Jordan Waters would say to me, "I want you to meet my parents," ranks high up there. Yet here I am, in a dress with my hair up, walking a stone pathway and preparing to do just that.

His grip on my hand tightens the closer we come to the large double doorway, and he rubs his forehead, more nervous than I've ever seen him. He glances over, and I smile, trying to put him at ease.

"Why aren't you freaking out?" he asks.

"Because they're just parents."

"You should freak out."

I adjust the collar of his shirt. "I'll get right on that."

But, really, I'm already battling nerves. I just hide them better.

In the few weeks since Pete's birthday, everything between Jordan and me has been incredible. In my experience, nothing stays this good for long, and tonight feels like the perfect setup for something to go wrong.

I gravitate toward people with shitty family situations. Not on purpose, just likeness seeking out the like, I guess. Trey's mother skipped out when he was six, and Kevin is … well, Kevin. Pete never met his father, and his alcoholic mother regularly beat the shit out of him until his grandparents took custody when he was ten. Brock's parents rarely acknowledged his existence. Shayna's parents divorced, and both started new families. Tony's were never around for various reasons, including a lengthy jail sentence.

Jordan describes his parents as overbearing and impossible to please. Far from what I know. As much as he wants me to believe their opinion won't matter, a nagging part of me says it will on some level. His escalating panic doesn't lessen the concern.

"Maybe we should reschedule," he says. "I mean, with the income tax deadline looming and all."

He's fidgeting more than usual, and I put my hand on his arm. "Jordan, breathe."

His gaze drops to where we touch and flits back to mine, a heat in his eyes. He cups my cheeks and kisses me. I think it will be short and sweet, but his tongue slips into my mouth, then he groans and backs me up until I'm pressed between him and a column. By the time he wrenches his mouth away from mine, I'm out of breath, and he's more worked up than before.

"Shit," he mutters, pushing the doorbell.

The door creaks open, a short woman with dark hair pulled into a tight braid on the other side. Her eyes dart between us a few times. A tentative smile slowly spreads.

"Good evening, Mr. Waters," she says, stepping out of the way.

"Hey, Greta," he says, guiding me in.

Jordan and I come from different worlds. That has been clear from the beginning. But it wasn't until we passed the fountain in the circular drive large enough to park eight cars that I started to understand *how* different. The realization continues when we step into an entryway the size of Graham's kitchen and living room combined. Marble floor, a gold-adorned mirror on the wall above a table with fresh flowers, and ceiling so high that I tip my chin up to see the molding.

I am *so* out of my element.

Jordan helps me out of my coat and hands it to Greta along with his.

"Your parents are in the sitting room with Dustin." She drapes the coats over her arm and looks between us again. "Would you and Jess like a glass of wine?"

My eyes widen. Not so much at being called the wrong name, but more at it being my suitemate's, who is borderline obsessed with my boyfriend.

Jordan chokes back a laugh and quickly says, "Greta, this is my girlfriend, Callie. Why my mother would tell you her name was Jess, I have no idea."

She gives a shaky smile. "I'm sure I misheard her. Two glasses of wine?" She hurries down the hall, her steps echoing as she escapes an uncomfortable situation.

I cross my arms, already glaring, and he holds out his hands in defense.

"There's a perfectly reasonable explanation for Greta thinking Jess is my girlfriend."

"Oh jeez, do tell," I say, stare holding firm.

"When my family stopped by the day after my birthday, Jess was still at the house from hooking-up with Rusty. My mother decided she was my girlfriend."

"So, rather than correct her…"

His lips twitch. "I might have said I wanted to marry her and knock her up."

"Why would you do that?"

"Because anytime my mother gets upset, her face does this pinching thing. It's fucking hilarious. I'm sure you'll see it tonight, considering I never told them you were coming." With that bombshell, he braces for my reaction.

My boyfriend used another girl to torture his mother because the idea of him being in a relationship is so terrible, and then he invited me to dinner to meet them without telling them.

"No wonder they don't like you," I say.

He smiles, and I can't help but return it. The ridiculous situation he's created somehow makes me feel better. At this point, I can't make a worst first impression, so no pressure.

His arm slides around me, and we head down the same hallway as Greta. The entire way to the sitting room, his finger taps against my hip. The speed increases, the deeper into the house we travel and hits a peak when we slow down by an open doorway.

He gives me one last panicked look, and right before we walk in, he slaps my ass.

"Guess who I brought to dinner," he says proudly.

Three stunned faces stare at us, Jordan beaming at my side. After a beat, his mother rises from the couch and floats across the room. All of her jewelry coordinates, her blonde hair pulled away from her face and fashioned with a clip to match. "Jordan, honey, please introduce us to your…" Her gaze flashes to me before she finishes, "…friend."

Oh, this will be a disaster.

"Mom, Dad, Dustin, this is my girlfriend, Callie."

His mother's lips purse at the G-word, her eyes narrowing and nose twitching. The pinch. A look that no doubt displays her utter disapproval. He's right. It's rather entertaining.

"How lovely," she forces out. Without another word, she returns to her seat.

Jordan's father squeezes her knee on his way over. A tall man with dark hair and the same strong jaw as his son warmly smiles. "Callie," he says, voice low and smooth, "please, join us for a drink."

He ushers me to a stiff-looking couch situated straight across from the other. On the end closest to the lit fireplace sits a blond who must be Dustin. Eyes the same color as Jordan's scan over me, his fingers steepled in front of his lips. Jordan quickly fills the cushion next to me. He slides his arm around me and sets a glare on his brother.

Mr. Waters settles back in next to his wife. He starts the conversation, right off the bat insisting I call him Ray. In the middle of him asking if I have any siblings, Mrs. Waters abruptly stands and excuses herself.

Jordan sighs next to me, and Ray's gaze follows her out. Once she shuts the door, he returns his attention to me and finishes his question as if nothing happened.

We chat a few minutes before Dustin tells us about his trip to Tijuana. Unless Benji misled me on the planned activities, he gives a very watered-down version of the events. Jordan's eye roll further confirms his brother's full of shit when Dustin claims they went to bed at ten on their last night to be refreshed for their early morning flight.

A glass of wine later, Mrs. Waters slips back in. Greta comes in behind her to announce dinner. I follow Jordan to a dining room farther down the hall, which looks like it should stay roped off to keep tourists from breaking anything.

The conversation stays light through the salad and main course. Mostly, Ray informs his sons of people he's talked to since the last time they saw each other. Both boys nod along, now and then interjecting comments.

Everyone falls silent when Mrs. Waters clears her throat. She pats her maroon cloth napkin against her mouth, tension building in the air. Her attention turns to me then. "Callie, is it?"

I tack on a polite smile. "Mmhmm."

She tilts her head and studies me like she's waiting for any sign of weakness to surface. "We should have your parents over for dinner sometime next week."

"Thank you," I say. "But my parents are divorced and best kept several miles apart."

The rest of the table laughs, but her stare on me hardens.

"Separately then," she insists.

"That won't be necessary. But you and I should get lunch the next time you visit Jordan."

She laughs at my offer. "Well, we aren't planning on visiting for a while, so we'll see where you two are by then."

She either thinks I won't catch her insinuation that my relationship with her son won't last or she doesn't think I'll call her on it. Either way she underestimates me, and my tolerance for being patronized by a woman I just met hits its limit. Hell, we reached it when she said my name like it was beneath her.

"Of course," I say, upping the wattage of my smile. "We'll be sure to let you know when we plan our trip before school starts in the fall. I'd hate for us to miss you."

We never talked about any trip, but she doesn't need to know that. Her face pinches worse than before, and I glance over at Jordan and wink, sipping my wine. He's not the only one who enjoys screwing with people.

With a smile on his lips, his gaze softens to my favorite one. I could get lost in it, forgetting everyone and everything, if not for his father asking me about sailing. A subject I have no knowledge of, but he seems excited to teach me.

The previously chatty Mrs. Waters has nothing more to say from across the table. Jordan stays quiet, too, eyes never leaving me to the point that my cheeks blush. The longer he stares, the more rigid his mother's posture grows.

After Greta brings out dessert, the conversation moves to Dustin's plans after he graduates law school. Jordan's mother perks up at the topic, and she veers the discussion to her younger son. When she mentions the upcoming LSATs and an internship over the summer with one of his father's associates, Jordan's attention returns to the rest of the table.

"Dad, let's go smoke a cigar," he says.

"We've been talking, honey," Mrs. Waters tells him. "We think you should attend a school out of state."

"Think or decided?" Jordan asks, his tone clipped.

A small smile forms, tight at the corners of her mouth. "We strongly suggest."

"What if I strongly suggest I not go to law school at all?"

Dustin sputters out a few coughs while drinking his wine. The commotion steals everyone's attention, but once he stops, the focus returns to Jordan on our side of the table.

Ray finishes chewing a bite of his dessert. "What would you do as an alternative?"

Jordan hesitates, finger tapping my thigh under the table. "I'm working on that."

"No," his mother says, shaking her head.

"Carol," Ray warns, "we can talk about this."

"No." She throws her napkin onto her plate. "Jordan will attend law school, and he will do so at a university of our choosing."

Jordan stops his finger, a determined set to his jaw. "So now you not only dictate what I do but where I do it? What's wrong with UPenn? It's good enough for Dustin."

"Dustin shows good judgment."

He scoffs. "Wool over the eyes much, Mother?"

Dustin interjects then, and Jordan apologizes for dragging him into it.

I readjust in my seat, uncomfortable when Ray's gaze meets mine. He sets his fork on his empty plate and wipes his mouth. "This is a discussion for another time, but I think we would be open to a compromise."

"There will be no discussion," Carol says. "You will choose an out-of-state school or be on your own next year." She stands and casts another harsh look in my direction. "Now, if you'll excuse me, I need to go lie down."

"Perfect." Jordan does as his mother did, tossing his napkin down. "Then I'll be on my own."

The room goes quiet as she storms out, the air thick with unspoken tension. I feel like an intruder. Maybe the catalyst for the entire argument.

She might have been rude to me, but it's clear that Carol has these dreams and goals for her sons and sees them capable of achieving amazing things. I've never known support like that. My parents hate the idea of me living a life better than theirs and want me at their level or lower, so I can't look down on them. They try to drag me back while his parents focus on driving him forward. Only he seems dead set against letting them. All of these opportunities, and he dismisses them, not interested in the least.

I can't for the fucking life of me understand why.

Breaking the silence, Ray asks Dustin about a feature from *The New Yorker*. I feel Jordan watching me, but I won't look at him. After a minute of me avoiding his gaze, he stands. "I'm going to show Callie the rest of the house."

Ray tells us to find them when we're finished. Jordan catches my hand in the hall and leads me through the sitting room and then out a set of French doors and onto a brick patio.

"Where are we going?" I ask on our way across the backyard.

He digs his keys out of his pocket. "My room."

By room, he means a carriage house at the back of the property. He unlocks the door and flips on the lights, walking in. I glance around at a much larger version of his room at the house.

Books, guitars, concert merchandise, and other little pieces of him are scattered about the living area we're standing in. Up an open staircase is a loft with a bed.

His gaze waits for mine, and he takes a slow step closer. "Why are you mad?"

"Really, I don't want to get into it here."

He gestures around the empty space, void of the suitemates and band members we normally deal with. "If you want to yell at me, this is a prime location."

"Don't be cute," I say.

"Impossible," he replies. "So, will you please tell me why you're mad?"

Fine. If he wants to fight, who am I to deny him?

"Why won't you consider going to school out of state?"

"Why should I have to?"

"Jordan, do you realize how many people would kill to have someone pay for them to go to school? Not only that, but to essentially have a guaranteed high-paying job when they finish?"

"Do *you* realize how many people hate their lives because they're miserable in their careers?"

I squint at him. "Is that *your* reason?"

He looks like he has a witty retort all fired up, but after a beat, he says, "My mother only wants me to go out of state to separate me from you. Well, originally, Jess, but the point remains the same. If I didn't have a girlfriend, she wouldn't care where I went to school."

"What if you didn't have a girlfriend? Would you consider it then?"

I need him to tell me that I have nothing to do with him not wanting to leave for school. To assure me he's not making choices because of me. Of us.

But instead, he lets out a sigh. "I don't even want to go to law school, so this entire conversation is irrelevant."

Frustrated he's avoiding a straight answer, I drop my head back. "Fine, ignore the law school aspect. What if your parents offered to pay for grad school for whatever you wanted—music, philosophy, bull riding—the only stipulation being you pick anywhere other than Pennsylvania? What would you say?"

"Would the only reason they want me out of Pennsylvania be to put distance between us?"

"Don't factor me into the decision."

He rubs his forehead. "Callie, this is ridiculous. We're fighting about a made-up scenario."

"I don't want you to base decisions on me and end up trapped with me, Jordan." The words come out in a rush, but I need him to grasp what I now realize is the most glaring difference between us. "Even if you decide not to go to law school, you can go anywhere. Do anything. I can't. I'm here for the duration, and I won't be a reason you stay."

"What are you talking about? In a few months, you turn nineteen and then—"

"Then what? Connor and Cate magically stop needing me? My responsibilities miraculously go away? The day after my birthday brings the same set of shitty circumstances. My reality stays unaltered. Nothing changes just because of some pointless date circled on a calendar."

It's the truth I've been hiding from Connor. The second or fifth time, the countdown to freedom will always be meaningless. Limbo has no expiration date.

"How long will you put your life on hold then, Callie?" he asks, not giving me time to respond. "Do you plan on driving there every weekend for the next twelve years to babysit?"

I laugh and drag my hands down my face. "Babysit?" I need another second, as I'm in utter disbelief of how he sees my life. "I forge permission slips and give safe sex talks to teenagers. I call Connor in sick to school when he stays awake all night, worrying about things out of his control. I miss class to comb lice out of Cate's hair because Lara has bailed so she won't get them. I sell my stuff to buy cleats and book bags and sometimes their food."

"But you shouldn't be doing any of these things. You're their sister, not their parent."

I blow out a breath and cross my arms over my chest. "You don't get it. They don't have parents. They have Lara living out a drunken, sorority-girl fantasy, chained down by the kids she never wanted. And Graham who, on some weekends, refuses to talk to any of us. But others, he screams at Connor for shutting his door too hard. Or at me for looking too much like Lara."

Jordan steps toward me, hand extended. "Callie—"

"No." I back away from him. "You need to understand what happens behind the curtains. Connor hates Graham more than I do. I'm terrified of what it's doing to him. And what will it do to Cate in a few years? I can't let them go through what I did, let them lose themselves. I just can't."

I bite my lip and focus on not crying. I've seen this moment coming for a while now. The one where I accept the only thing keeping Connor and Cate afloat is me and have to admit nothing will change for us, no matter how desperately I want it to.

"This is my life. It will be for a long time. I can't escape it or avoid it, and even if I could, I wouldn't. I'm all they have, and I'll never take that away from them." I force my gaze back to Jordan. "But this isn't your life, Jordan, and I don't want it to be, because if you make stupid decisions for me, then one day…" The tears spill over when I finally figure out what I'm really scared of. What I truly dread. "One day, you'll look at me the way Graham does, and the thought of that ever happening kills me."

It will happen if he stays for me. Maybe not at first but somewhere down the line. He'll wake up, hating his life, and blame me for everything he missed. Eventually, he'll realize I was never worth any of this.

He takes another step, and I put my hands up to stop him. "What are you doing?"

"I'm going to kiss you," he says.

I wipe the tears off my face. "You can't just kiss me to end a fight."

"You can go back to yelling at me right after, I promise."

Sad, mad, whatever I am, I almost smile. "I hate when you do that."

"Do what?" he asks.

"That thing where you frustrate me and then say or do something…" I stop and give myself a breath before he distracts me from my point. "Promise you won't stay for me, Jordan."

"Don't tell me what to do, Callie."

Two strides bring him chest-to-chest with me. I back up, but he catches me and holds me to him.

His thumb brushes over my cheek. "I'm going to kiss you now, but it's not to end our fight. I'm going to kiss you because I…"

He hesitates, swallowing hard and letting the start of whatever he plans to say hang between us. The heart-hammering gaze he gives me grows even more intense, and an overwhelming panic surges through me. Afraid of what might come out of his mouth next, I'm about to stop him when his thumb passes over my cheek again.

"I'm going to kiss you because I'm Jordan, and you're Callie. And that's more than enough reason to kiss you."

I stare up at him, describing him the only way I can. "Frustrating and perfect."

He kisses my forehead, then the tip of my nose before his lips press to mine. He pulls back, and I clasp my hands behind his neck. Searching his eyes, I'm still unable to find a sliver of doubt in those green depths.

"You never have to worry about me, beautiful," he says. "All the stupid decisions I make in my life will be no one's fault but my own."

"How many do you plan on making?"

"Oh, we're talking about a lot of them." He sways me back and forth, dancing without music. "But the last stupid decision I made turned out pretty great actually."

"What was that one?"

"I chased a girl who wanted nothing to do with me. Now she finds me irresistible and wants me to rail her in my high school bedroom."

I smile, not bothering to mention a part of me always wanted him. It would only further inflate the kid's ego. He kisses me again, and maybe I should still be worrying about all the things I was a few minutes ago. But I'm not. I can't be.

Not in his arms and not with his lips on mine.

87 Days Until 19

The weekend before finals, a bang wakes me.

I take a few seconds to remember where I am, used to waking up tangled in Jordan's arms. Since our fight at his parents' house, we've spent every night together other than last weekend when I went to Graham's and these two at Lara's.

I blink at the alarm clock. *Shit.* It's after two in the morning. I only went to bed an hour ago after getting Connor to shut off the slasher flick. Which is why I'm more than a little terrified to see a shadow looming in my doorway. Light streams in from the hallway, and I squint at the outline of my mother tearing across the room.

"Get the fuck up, you stupid slut." She slurs, but that's the gist.

Before I can *get the fuck up* or do anything else, she grabs the front of my tank top and tries to jerk me out of bed.

"What the fuck?" I kick to get her off me, but she snatches hold of my hair.

Keeping one hand on hers and one tight on her wrist to stop her from pulling harder, I get to my feet while she spits out every name she can think of, one mumbled insult after another. Her other arm wraps around me, and like we're tied together, we stumble across the room until she bumps into the dresser. It knocks against the wall, and a jewelry box crashes to the floor. Lara spins us around, so the edge of the dresser digs into my hip. I squeeze on her wrist, twisting at the skin until her grip releases.

As I shove her away, both her hands grasp my shirt, and she drags me to the door.

"Holy shit," Connor says, jumping out of the way as we come through.

My back hits the wall, her forearm across my chest. I'm about to do something I never thought I would—punch my mother in her fucking face—when Cate screams from her doorway. Terrified blue eyes watch, her hands covering her ears as Lara continues to berate me with incoherent nonsense.

Connor's panicked gaze meets mine, pleading with me to tell him what to do, but I can't because I have no idea. Everything went from zero to fucked up so fast, my head is spinning from it all.

The only thing I can think to do is stop fighting her. I let her yank me away from the wall by the shirt and drag me down the hall and through the living room and push me out the door.

Once we're outside, she releases me with one last shove. I straighten up and turn around just in time for her to slap me across the face so hard that my head jerks to the side. I suck in a breath at the sting and bring my hand to my cheek, looking back at her and trying like hell not to retaliate.

She's fucking wrecked. Mascara runs down her face, lipstick smudged, hair more of a disaster than mine after she used it as reins. "He said … it's your fault," she stutters, wobbling on her heels in the grass.

It's the most terrifying vision of my potential future I've ever seen.

Connor witnesses it all from the doorway while Cate clings to him, burying her face in his shoulder. Lara storms to the house and pushes past him. He only makes it a step in my direction before she reappears and tugs on his arm to stop him. Her fingers fumble with something, and she cusses at what I realize is a set of keys. She slips one off and throws the rest at me. The key ring lands on the ground in front of me. I don't need to look to know they're mine.

"Get inside," she barks at Connor.

The lines between his eyebrows form deep, my brother more torn in this moment than he's ever been. I force a smile and nod at him. With tears in his eyes, he disappears into the house, and then it's just Lara and me.

She glares, backing inside. "Never come back, bitch."

Even though I see the door closing, I still jump when it slams.

Then it's just me, standing in the front yard. No phone. No shoes. Nowhere to go.

Trey's house is a bust. All the lights are off, and his truck's gone. Not wanting to break out a window and crawl in, I turn my car around.

On my way back to Main Street, I drive behind the bar. Light shines through the still-propped-open back door, and I jerk the wheel to make the turn into the parking lot. A familiar head pops out the door as I park.

"Pete," I call, climbing out.

He heaves the black trash bag into the dumpster and slaps his hands together. "Six months," he says.

"What?"

"You purposely avoided me for *six months*. Now I can't fucking get rid of you." He grins as I stop in front of him, but it fades when his gaze drops to my feet. "Why the fuck are you barefoot in Sutterville at this hour?"

I sigh. "Because my mother's an unhinged alcoholic."

He gestures to the door. "Join the fucking club."

When we get inside, he sets the jukebox music to something eighties and wanders behind the bar. I pick the stool dead center on the other side. While he finishes cleaning up, I give him my extensive explanation of why Lara threw me out in the middle of the night.

"I have no fucking idea."

Okay, so not so extensive. I really don't know though. She took off Friday to spend the weekend with Tyler, not even waiting until I got to the house to leave. I haven't heard from her since.

Other than her cryptic comment about *him* saying it's my fault, I have little to go on.

Pete loans me his phone to text Trey about what's going on and to see if I can stay with him. He doesn't answer. Thanks to technology, I haven't memorized a number since I was, like, eight, so I can't call Connor's phone to check in on him and Cate. I'll just have to wait on Trey.

"Here." Pete tosses me a pair of thermal socks when I look up.

I allow my face to tell him what I think of the shade of brown. They go up to my knees, but they're warm and preferable to running around the bar without shoes on.

"Thanks," I say.

"Where's Jordan tonight?" he asks. "I thought he's been coming with you to Lara's."

"His band played at a bar over by State tonight." I considered going but couldn't find anyone to take Cate to her first swim lesson. It ended up working in my favor since I tripped my way into a job. "I ran into your grandparents at the gas station earlier."

"They told me. Sounds like I'm your boss again." He runs a rag over the top of the bar. "I've been saving up so much shit work for whoever they suckered into working here this summer. Now I'll have to do it all because I'll feel bad making you do it."

"Because you cared about making me shovel actual shit last year?"

He grins and tosses the rag in a bin. "You're right. That was kind of fun."

I make a face at him.

So that Pete can spend more time helping out at the farm this summer, I'll work at the bar from open to close Monday through Thursday and pick up the lunch shift on Fridays. I won't make quite as much money as I did last year, but it's a willing trade-off for no manure duty.

"Is Jordan cool with a long-distance girlfriend over the summer?" he asks.

I shrug. "I haven't told him about it yet."

With weekends off, I should be able to go see Jordan a few times a month. Not the perfect scenario, but better than not seeing him at all. He'll be studying for the LSATs he has in June, and then he has an internship at a law firm that will keep him busy. As for me, I have no idea what will happen after my birthday in July, but history warns me to brace for Graham to pull something.

After he slides me a beer, Pete fills himself a mug and grabs a bottle of whiskey. Two shot glasses rattle together in his other hand. He sets them down and leans on the bar straight across from me, a severe expression on his face. "I didn't make an ass of myself the first day of preschool when I stole your scissors."

I laugh and raise my mug. "And I didn't cry and scream that I hated you in front of everyone."

He knocks his mug against mine, and we both take a drink.

Our game started a long time ago, the alcohol aspect added later. We pinpoint specific moments in our lives we would do over if we could. Choose a different path based on what we know now. Small changes that could have potentially rippled. Once both of us are satisfied with the change, we drink. We start with beer and save the hard alcohol for later. Otherwise, we would drink ourselves under the table.

By the time Pete pours the first shot, he's absentmindedly rubbing the scar on his chin. He used to do it more often before it faded. Now he only does it when he's thinking about who gave it to him.

There's a reason we switch to the hard stuff when we reach this point. We never talk about it, only alluding to it as the "accident." As far as I know, other than his grandparents, I'm the only one who knows about what really happened when we were ten. The night his mother went too far and couldn't hide what she'd been doing to him anymore. Most of the marks stayed hidden over the years, the others easily explained away by him being a boy with a rough streak. But I knew. I knew, and no one listened until it was too late.

I curl my fingers around my shot glass, staring at his fingers doing the same on his. We both say the same thing every time. For some reason, it never gets easier.

"The night of the accident, I showed up at your window five minutes earlier and helped you get out."

He lifts his glass, agreeing. "Then we walked to Trey's house, and I showed Kevin the bruises and cuts and burns and—"

I raise my glass, not wanting to hear more. He spent three days in the hospital, recovering from what she had done to him that night, and we'll both spend the rest of our lives with the memories.

He taps his glass to mine, and we drink, the whiskey burning away the pain.

Pete grimaces, already pouring. "One more to clear the fucking palate."

We toss back shot two. I shake my head, mouth open and tongue numb while he fills them again.

"How many one-mores are we doing?" I ask when he holds his up.

"Why? Afraid you can't keep up anymore?" When my eyes narrow, he sets his glass down. "All right, when we were twelve, I never ratted you out to Kevin for stealing the baby Jesus from the manger at the church."

My mouth falls open. "I knew it was you!"

"He threatened to tell my grandparents it was me, so I had to give you up."

I hold up my glass and fight a smile. "Since we're being overly honest about it, I never lied to Kevin about it being you who took Jesus in the first place."

"Damn it. I've felt guilty about that for years, and you fucking deserved it?"

I give an innocent shrug, and he shakes his head, raising his glass.

"Well, I guess this one's for baby Jesus then."

We laugh and drink, and I push my glass over for Pete to pour another.

"Next?" he asks, sliding it back.

"Summer before freshman year."

He tilts his head back and forth. "I didn't go to summer camp, and we stayed at the lake all summer long."

I hold up my glass, perfectly happy with the suggestion with one minor change. "But I still ended up dumping you because you hooked up with Gabby Sinclair behind the boat docks."

"Seriously, Cal?" He keeps his drink on the bar and stares me down. "My first time has to be with Gabby? If I were going to cheat on you, I'd have found someone better than that."

"Fine," I say. I purse my lips, considering it more than most people would. Then again, most people aren't close enough with their ex to pick out who they would cheat with in the first place. "Tonya White?"

"Acceptable."

I touch my glass to his, and we throw them back.

Movement out of the corner of my eye brings my attention to someone at the far end of the bar. The last person I expected, but the only one I want to see. I smile and jump off my stool, not able to get to Jordan fast enough.

"What are you doing here?" I ask, wrapping my arms around his middle.

My cheek presses to his chest, and he kisses the top of my head. "Connor called me on your phone."

My phone. It never occurred to me to call it to get ahold of him.

I pull away from Jordan, and my eyebrows dip when I notice his swollen eye. "Oh my God, what happened?"

"Call your brother first, so he stops worrying."

He hands me his phone, and as curious as I am, I hurry off to the other side of the room.

Connor answers right away. "Is she okay?"

"I'm fine."

A gush of air crackles through the phone. "Jesus, Cal. I was so scared. I didn't know what to do. Trey didn't answer, and you don't have Pete or Shayna or Tony in your phone anymore. The only name I recognized was Jordan."

"Are you okay?" I ask. "How's Cate?"

"She's asleep now. I threw together a fort in my room for her, so I could go on Lara watch."

"You find out what the hell set her off?"

After a few seconds of silence, he says, "Oh, uh…"

All the confirmation I need. "Connor Roland, why the fuck did Lara kick me out?"

"Okay, don't be mad," he says, all but guaranteeing I will be. "I guess they were at the same bar as Jordan, and Tyler got in a fight with him and the three guys he was with. After the cops showed up, Tyler told her he's sick of all the drama because of you and your friends, so he broke up with her."

My jaw clenches.

"He said it's your fault."

Fucking great. My boyfriend goes on a kamikaze mission, and I'm the one being blown up.

"I have to go."

"Wait, Cal, what drama was he talking—"

"I'll see you in the morning."

Pete sees me coming as he takes his shot, eyes wide. I slide onto the stool next to Jordan and empty the glass waiting for me. I slam it down and set my glare on Jordan. He returns the look, neither of us saying anything until Pete disappears behind the curtain to hide upstairs.

"So, I met Tyler and Lara tonight." Jordan reaches for a bag of ice Pete left on the bar and holds it over his soon-to-be black eye.

"A bar fight? Are you kidding me?"

"He swung first," Jordan says, pouring himself a shot.

"Unprovoked?"

He shakes his head and grins, clearly finding humor in the situation.

"Damn it, Jordan." I cover my face with my hands. "He broke up with her because my friends are too much drama."

"Technically, he broke up with her because Rusty told him to."

I groan into my palms, losing all patience for him. "Not any better."

"Sorry, I don't understand how this is a bad thing."

My hands drop to the bar. "She dragged me out of my bed and out of the house in the middle of the night. Cate was screaming, Connor didn't know what the hell he should do, and if Pete had finished cleaning up before I got here, I might still be driving around without socks on."

"How was I supposed to know any of that would happen?" He tosses the bag of ice down, not the slightest bit sorry for setting off this chain of events.

The longer I look at him, the angrier I become.

I push my stool back and stand up. "I can't deal with you right now."

When I try to walk away, he jumps up and grabs my arm. "What do you want me to do, Callie? Apologize? Because I won't."

"What I want is for you not to get in a fucking bar fight with Tyler in the first place," I yell.

His hold on me tightens, and he shouts back, "Ship's already sailed on that one, beautiful. What else?"

"Don't for one second think you get to be upset with me for being mad at you." I rip my arm away, more pissed off with him than I've ever been. "How am I supposed to take care of Connor and Cate if she won't let me in the house?"

"That's what you're worried about?" he asks, genuinely shocked like the possibility never entered his mind. "This guy tried to sexually assault you. If not for Rusty, he might have…" He never finishes, walking away and dragging his hands through his hair. He circles back and stops in front of me, expression hard. "He's out of your life, and I couldn't give a fuck about the rest."

Frustrated, tired, and buzzed, I'm close to saying or doing something I'll regret. Holding up my hands, I back away from him. I go behind the bar to the curtain. "I'm too angry for this," I say, pushing my way through.

I leave him downstairs in the bar and head up to Pete's apartment. Not knocking, I let myself in. Pete is on the couch and looks up from his phone. "Given the yelling, I take it he told you about Lara?"

"He starts a fight with Tyler, gets me kicked out, and thinks I should be, what, grateful?" I rant and pace the large room that holds the bedroom, living room, and kitchen. "For what exactly? Not having anywhere to stay or for him making it a million times more difficult to keep an eye on Cate and Con? Can you believe him?"

"You want the truth?" He stands up and tucks his phone in his pocket. "Because it's not the same as what you want to hear."

I stop by the couch. "Are you saying you're on *his* side?"

Pete stares at me with an expression as stony as Jordan's. "Your mom's boyfriend almost raped you, Callista."

I shake my head, unsurprised that Trey ran his mouth about what I'd told him about Tyler but irritated all the same. "Tyler never would have—"

"Don't," he says, cutting me off. "Trey didn't believe your bullshit about it not going that far, and neither do I. He was going to rape you that night, and chances are, he would have finished the job at some point if not for that guy down there."

Not wanting to admit how close he might be to the truth about Tyler, I cross my arms over my chest. "So, it's okay for someone to just bulldoze into my life and fix one problem by creating a fuck-ton more?"

"Even if Jordan made a mess while doing it, he did what was best. If you can't see that, then you really might be a fucking idiot." He tugs at his hair and continues, "You asked whose side I'm on. I'm on yours. I always have been. Trey, Jordan, Connor— everyone's on your fucking side but you apparently."

"Well, since you and Jordan are on the same team, why don't you go downstairs with him and leave me the hell alone?"

"Yeah, whatever," he says on his way past me. He pauses in the doorway. "He's in love with you, by the way, so feel free to freak out about that up here, all by yourself."

"Screw you, Pete," I shout.

"Right back at you, Cal!"

He slams the door behind him, and I rush over to flip the lock. Except locking him out of his apartment does nothing to stop his words from chipping away.

Jordan's in love with me.

Fuck.

Still 87 Days Until 19

I toss and turn under a blanket on Pete's bed, the words replaying. I think I knew it at his parents' house, in his room when I felt the urge to run. It's a logical progression. You date and fall in love. Only, to love someone, you have to be able to hate them. One turns into the other, bleeding into each other until they become the same thing. At least, that's all I've ever known it to be.

My eyes finally stay closed after a border of dim light appears around the edges of the blackout curtains over the windows. It feels like only minutes later when the mattress dips. Warm arms slip around me, and Jordan holds me close. I roll over, and the harshness is gone from his face. Neither of us says anything, waiting for the other to admit fault or wrongdoing.

We stare at each other a long time before I sigh, giving in. "Pete will never get his place back at this rate."

Once I've ended the standoff, Jordan jumps in. "I'm sorry, Callie." He presses his lips to mine before he kisses my cheek and forehead and returns to my lips. I'm more than ready to forgive him for being impulsive until he says, "But I'm not sorry for what we did."

Realizing he still thinks fighting Tyler was the right decision, I sit up. "Then what exactly are you sorry for?"

"I'm sorry Lara threw you out because she's incapable of putting you and your safety first."

And we're back where we started.

"You still don't get it, and I'm tired of explaining it to you. Connor and Cate need to come first, not me."

He sits up beside me and drags a hand through his messy hair. "Maybe to you, but for me, it's you. It will always be you. You'll never convince me otherwise, so you might as well stop trying."

"What happens if—"

"No." He shakes his head, not letting me finish. "No hypotheticals. No asking what if the three of you are dangling off a cliff, and I can only save two of you. Or what if they need all of your organs for some insane reason that will never happen. We both know you want me to say I would choose them, but I wouldn't. I couldn't. And I don't want to lie to you, so just don't ask."

He has that determined look in his eye, certain of his words, and I believe him. He would choose me over everyone, but I can never promise him the same. Organ donations and threatening cliffs or basketball tournaments and swim lessons, for me, it's Connor and Cate. It has to be, because if I don't choose them, no one will. That's just too heartbreaking to think about.

"You have to tell me what you're thinking, beautiful. Because I feel like a heartless person for having just said that."

I look down at the bedspread. "I'm thinking about how, without a doubt, I'd choose them in both scenarios."

He tips my chin up, intense gaze waiting. "I won't make you feel guilty for that choice. Don't make me feel guilty for mine."

He's right. I can't force my priorities onto him. No matter how badly I wish I could.

Not wanting to fight about it anymore, I sigh. "We'll never agree on this."

"Probably not."

"So, what do we do?"

He tugs me over, so I lean back against his chest. "We go see Cate and Connor because you need to see them."

"And they need to see me."

"And the stars align, and everyone gets what they need," he says against my cheek.

Maybe it can work, him watching out for me while I take care of Cate and Connor. I've never trusted anyone enough to try, but as always, Jordan Waters is my exception.

I feel his arms tighten around me, his chest rising faster behind me. It sets off an alarm inside me, Pete's words once again in my head.

"Callie, I—"

"Don't." I turn my upper body to see the same intensity about him as at his parents' house. Even if he loves me, I can't let him say it out loud. Then it'll become real, and everything will change because I'm pretty sure I love him back.

"Not yet," I say, "and especially not in Pete's bed."

He pauses a beat before his roguish grin shifts the mood. "I guess that means other activities are off-limits in Pete's bed."

"What did you have in mind?" I ask, intrigued with where he's going.

He brings his lips to my ear. "Breakfast," he whispers.

For the first time, I notice the smell of bacon and the tray of food on the table. When he brings it over, I grab the two open beer bottles, so they don't topple off. We sit against the headboard to eat Pete's famous beer and eggs.

"Pete doesn't just make this breakfast for anyone," I say, teasing. "He must like you."

Jordan rolls his eyes and steals my last piece of bacon. "The feeling's not mutual, I assure you."

This time, I don't believe him for a second.

Once we finish eating, we carry the dishes downstairs. Pete scowls when I come through the curtain, so I glare at him. He cracks first, his mouth curving up on one side, and I smile back. It's as much of an apology as we'll ever need.

In the parking lot, Jordan kisses me like we won't see each other in fifteen minutes at Lara's house. With everything that happened, I forgot how much I missed him after only a few days.

We park in front of Lara's, and Connor jumps up from the steps. I haven't even shut the door when he locks his arms around me, smashing the air out of my lungs. He lets go when I grunt out a warning that I need oxygen. Dark circles under his red eyes confirm he slept the least of us last night.

The front door flies open, and Cate screeches on her way toward me. Connor and I lunge toward her to make her stop. "Shh," I say, picking her up. "We have to be quiet."

She plants a sloppy kiss on my forehead and throws her arms around my neck.

I rub her back and turn to Connor. "She asleep in the basement?"

"She passed out around five after destroying everything in the house that reminded her of Tyler."

"Everything?" Jordan asks, beating me to it.

"I saved anything of actual value." Connor grins. "Girls dig that couch too much. I couldn't let her take a knife to the cushions." When he checks for a reaction, Jordan holds his hands up and shakes his head, having learned his lesson the last time.

I ignore my younger brother and set my squirming sister on the ground. "Well, let's go pack up my shit."

The first thing I do when we go inside is change and track down my phone. I text Trey to let him know that, whether or not he wants one, he has a roommate for half the summer, but he won't mind.

Jordan begs to take down my photo wall, asking questions about the pictures the entire time Connor and I sort through the rest of my stuff. I bag almost all the clothes up to donate, decimating Lara's outfit options for the future. We hide the garment bags with the last of the formal dresses in the back of Connor's closet. Everything else I want to keep goes in boxes.

As we finish up, Trey finally texts.

Like I'd let you stay anywhere else.

Connor and Jordan move the boxes while I explain to Cate that I won't be staying there anymore. She sniffs at first, but I promise she and Connor can come see me anytime they want. When that doesn't work, I promise we'll make slushie stops a ritual after swim lessons, and all tears vanish. She dashes off and crawls in the back of the Jeep. I leave Jordan and Connor to coax her out and go inside to check for anything left behind.

The Eagles banner is already down from the wall in the living room, the mini fridge missing from next to the couch. All the walls in my room are bare as well. No sheets or pillows on the bed. Dresser drawers open and closet empty. It's strange how, in such a short time, any evidence of two people has been erased from this house.

Jordan leans against his Jeep, talking to Connor, and I smile at him on my way down the steps.

"You ready to go, beautiful?"

I nod, more than ready to drop everything at Trey's and head back to campus. With my quiet Sunday shot, I need to make up for the studying time I lost.

Connor swoops down for a hug when I reach them.

"I'll be back next weekend after finals," I say. "The rest we'll just have to figure out as we go."

He rolls his eyes. "Wow, Cal, you sure we can manage? We've never had to deal with any of their bullshit before."

I blow out a breath, not in the mood for his sarcasm. "Things were going to change anyway. We only have a few weeks until the summer schedule starts."

As soon as I mention the upcoming switch in the custody agreement, his shoulders tense. "Oh, joy. Can't fucking wait." He kicks through a pile of rocks in the driveway hard enough that they batter against the side of the house.

What the hell?

Before I can stop him, he does it again, the gravel nearly breaking the living room window.

"Connor, knock it off!" I grab his arm, but he rips away from me.

"What do you care?" he shouts. "It's not like you live here."

He storms into the house and slams the door. I look up, groaning at the sky. Jordan steps beside me, and I hide my face in his chest. He strokes my hair and gives me the moment of calm I need after yet another blowup.

"He's becoming impossible," I say, straightening up. "They just keep pushing him. And he has all this anger now."

"I can take your stuff to Trey's if you want to stick around for a while."

I bite my lips together, worried confronting him right now will only make things worse. "No, he needs his space."

"Are you sure?" Jordan stares down at me, and I force a smile.

"It's fine," I say, only half-convinced. "Let's go find the monster."

Cate's chasing a squirrel around the neighbor's yard. I catch her as she sprints past, but I only get a short hug because her sights set on Jordan. She scrambles into his arms to kiss him on the forehead. When she accidentally knocks her teeth into his head, he grimaces, and I choke back a laugh. He only has himself to blame.

After I drop off the clothes at the church, we go back to Sutterville. Trey's dog, Zeus, barks from the backyard when our car doors shut. I meet Jordan at the back of the Jeep and load him up with boxes. He doesn't tell me to stop, so I stack four in his arms and follow him up the sidewalk.

"What's the summer schedule?" he asks.

I drag my attention away from his flexing biceps and open the front door for him. "We spend a week at Lara's and then a week at Graham's. Well, they'll spend a week at Lara's. I guess I'll spend a week here."

A few steps in the door, Jordan drops the boxes to the floor. "You could spend a week with me and then a week at Graham's."

"I could if I didn't need to work this summer and save money."

He tilts his head to the side, a concerned look on his face. "What about us?"

"What do you mean?" I ask.

"When do we see each other? Weekends you aren't at Graham's?"

With all the fighting and whatnot, I never told him about my job at the bar. Who am I to pass up an opportunity to screw with him? "It's hard enough to get a summer job around here." I turn around to pick up a box, fighting off a smile. "Finding one that doesn't require working every weekend is almost impossible."

"Then when am I going to see you?"

I shrug and try to pass him, but he stops me. "Callie, when?"

"What do you want me to say, Jordan? That we won't see each other all summer?"

His eyebrows knit together. "I can't go all summer without you, beautiful."

I start to tell him I'm kidding when Trey stomps down the stairs and cuts me off, "Just let yourself in, Cal." He slaps Jordan on the chest on his way by. "Jordan, you look like she told you she's pregnant."

Jordan doesn't respond, gaze locked on me while Trey chuckles and grabs the box out of my hands. His eyes glaze over, his mind working for a solution to the problem as Trey disappears up the stairs.

Before my boyfriend breaks, I sigh. "Are you freaking out?" When he doesn't answer, I come clean. "Pete's grandparents offered me a job at the bar, working during the week with weekends off." I grab another box off the floor, surprised at how heavy it is. "I planned on telling you last night, but for some reason, I never had the chance."

A lot of emotions cross his face. "Screw you, Henders."

He steps forward but stops when Trey cusses upstairs. His feet pound the stairs on his way down, and he pushes Jordan out of his way. He rips the box away from me and throws it on the ground before he grabs my face. I've never seen him so spooked, and it scares the hell out of me.

"Fucking Christ, Cal, tell me you're not pregnant."

At first, I have no idea what he's talking about, and then I remember the joke he made that neither Jordan nor I acknowledged. I laugh and roll my eyes. "With twins, Uncle Trey!"

The relief flooding over him makes me laugh even harder. From behind him, Jordan catches my eye and smiles. Between the two of them, maybe summer in Sutterville won't be the worst thing.

75 Days Until 19

I was wrong.

A summer in Sutterville is the worst thing. Mostly because I miss Jordan. Even though we text and video chat when we can, it's not the same, and not being around him for an entire week makes me moody. Oddly, the regulars tip better when I'm rude, so at least that's a win.

While I'm doing little more than sleeping and tending bar, he's devoting almost all of his time to studying for the LSATs in June. Thanks to the rivalry with Dustin, Jordan's determined to take it and beat his brother's scores, even if he doesn't end up attending law school. Which is a remote possibility now that, in a surprise turn of events, his parents agreed to discuss alternatives. The way it sounds, his father set up the dinner for next Saturday with his mother less than enthused about the entire affair. Either way, it's an opening he plans on taking, and any spare time goes to figuring out what he wants to do after graduation.

By the time Pete walks in Friday afternoon, I groan in relief. "Finally."

"I'm an hour early," he says, picking up an empty mug as he passes. "Having Jordan withdrawals?"

"Not for much longer." I untie my apron and shove it under the counter on my way to the door.

"Tell him hi from me and that I miss him." He grins when I spin around, my eyebrows pulled together. "Seriously, tell him. I love screwing with the guy."

"You realize how messed up our relationship is, right?"

He gives me a half-interested shrug and walks through the curtain. "See you Monday, Cal."

After I shower off the bar smell, I throw my bag in the car. As long as the trip normally takes, this one lasts so much longer. Even when I get there, I can't go to the house to see Jordan. He doesn't focus when I'm there, and Benji has banished me until he finishes his practice test. So, instead, I park in front of the house Felicia and Jess are renting for the summer. Given the number of cars, their small housewarming party appears to have grown from a few people to a few dozen.

A beaming redhead meets me when I walk in the door. "You're here!"

Felicia hugs me before she latches on to my hand and drags me through the house for the fastest and chattiest tour I've ever been on. She doesn't even slow down long enough for me to give Jess more than a quick wave on our way upstairs to see the bedrooms. We end back in the living room where we started, and she flits off to play hostess.

"I warned you to never come back here," a voice says from behind me.

"What can I say? I like to live dangerously." I turn around, and Cam smiles. "I thought you and Sawyer were off on a road trip all summer?"

"We leave in the morning. I'm actually on my way out. I just stopped by for a few minutes before I pick her up from work and we finish packing." She pinches my cheek. "You and your dirty boy have a good summer, yeah?"

"And you and your woman enjoy yours." I pick the drink out of her hand as she walks away.

It's mostly empty, so I finish it and toss it in one of the many trash cans around the room. Clearly, a Felicia idea.

When I turn around, a guy enthusiastically waves on his way over. "Hey, Callie," he says, giving me a quick and awkward hug. "How have you been?"

"Great," I say, not a clue who he is. "How are you?"

He chats with me like we're old buddies, filling me in on what's new in his life. Then he brings up another party he was supposed to go to tonight, and I realize he's Felicia's cousin, whose name I still can't remember.

About half an hour in, I'm nodding along when whatever Cousin's saying stops registering. My insides go fuzzy because Benji walks in the front door with Jordan right behind him. His hair recently tugged on, blue T-shirt with the design faded.

God, I missed him more than I'd thought possible.

Jess stops him a few steps in to talk, but his eyes meet mine across the living room. I suddenly feel like I can't breathe again until he touches me. We start for each other at the same time. Our gazes stay locked, so thankfully, no couches or end tables separate us, or we would walk straight into them. I jump into his arms and grasp hold of his face to kiss him. The house might as well clear out and the music stop playing because nothing else exists right now. Just him and me and six days to make up for.

"Hey," I say, hating that my lips aren't still on his.

"Hey, beautiful." He stares into my eyes in a way that sends everything inside me into a free fall. "I kinda missed you."

My mouth slams back into his, not caring about the audience. I yank at his recently tugged-on hair, and he groans into my mouth. He can do whatever he wants to me right now in the middle of Felicia and Jess's living room. I won't stop him. Benji, however…

"The two of you are making me nauseous." He grips my hips and pulls me off Jordan. Once he sets me on the ground, he gently pushes me toward Felicia behind me. "You take yours, and I'll take mine."

She giggles and leads me away.

I look back at Jordan, his hair even messier now that my hands dragged through it. "Bye," I say.

"Bye, beautiful." He smiles as Benji nudges him in the opposite direction to the kitchen.

She lets me go once we reach the far side of the living room. As far away from Jordan as possible without making me go outside.

"Were we really that bad?" I ask.

"Yes. But in a disgustingly cute kind of way."

"Who's disgustingly cute?" Jess's sister, Vee, steps beside Felicia.

"Callie and her boyfriend," Felicia says. "You missed them practically ripping each other's clothes off."

"Reason to never go to the bathroom. You miss almost nudity." Vee checks over her shoulder, scanning the room. "Which one is he?"

"He's not in here," I say. "They took him away even though I've suffered a week without him."

I pout out a lip, and Sappy Felicia sighs.

"If you promise to keep it PG in front of the other guests, I'll let him come back in."

A shrug answers her, but it must be enough reassurance for her to retrieve him for me. As soon as she leaves, Jess rushes over, her eyes wild and nostrils flaring. "Where's Felicia going?"

"To get Callie's X-rated boyfriend," Vee says.

I laugh, but it cuts off when Jess mutters, "*Fuck*," and walks away.

Before I can sort out what her deal is, Jordan pushes through the swinging door, his sights set on me. He stalks toward me, eyes smoldering more with each step. Already breaking my half-made promise to Felicia, he walks straight into me, not even acknowledging Vee as he slides his arms around my waist and dips his head down, his mouth latching on to my neck. I step back to keep my balance, but he and his hot lips move with me.

The way I giggle is embarrassing. "Jordan, stop."

He listens to my halfhearted protest by dropping his hands to my ass and pulling me closer.

"Sorry, Vee." I angle my head, trying to see around him. "My boyfriend's apparently an untrained animal." I push on his chest. "Jordan, I want you to meet Jess's sister."

He growls into my neck, his breath hot on my skin. After a second, he pulls back and winks. I smile, well aware we'll break the sort-of promise at least one more time tonight.

"Jordan, this is Jess's older sister, Vee."

He moves beside me and tacks on a grin before he spins around. The second he's face-to-face with Vee, his expression vanishes, the color draining from his cheeks. She looks just as shocked, but it's quickly replaced with something else. Her lip quivers, and she blinks several times like she's fighting off tears.

"We've met," she says, not looking at me anymore. "A few times actually. Over winter break."

I probably take longer than I should to figure out that they fucked. A few times actually.

And the realization feels like a slap in the face.

The rest falls into place after that. The guy from winter break who disappeared on her, Jess's odd behavior when Jordan first came around, and the return of it a few minutes ago.

"Oh," I say, surprised I even managed that much.

Jordan stares at the floor to avoid accidental eye contact with either of us while we all stand in uncomfortable silence. Our triangle of awkwardness ends when Vee pushes past him and runs up the stairs.

He looks at me out of the corner of his eye. "I think I need to have a little chat with Jess."

"Yep," I say, walking away from him.

I stop near Cousin and use him for a shield as I watch Jordan head across the room. Jess sees him and backs her way into the kitchen with a *don't kill me* look on her face, and they disappear behind the swinging door. I stare at it, mad about how he handled Vee, not answering her calls and dodging her so he wouldn't have to deal with her. Also, why the hell didn't he chase after me like all the other times, so we could fight about this, and I could go make him deal with her now?

I glare at the door until I can't stand it anymore and march through the living room, ready to bring the fight to him. But when I step into the kitchen, his hands are on Jess's shoulders, head lowered so it's level with hers. Our eyes meet, and the look he gives me is a combination of apology and guilt.

It occurs to me why he never chased after me. He never needed to. Jordan Waters is fast-forwarding and dealing with the problem on his own.

His hands fall away from Jess, and he crosses the room and kisses my forehead. "I'll fix it."

"I know," I say. And I do.

The guy I met a few months ago might not have cared about making things right, but I shouldn't have doubted that the one standing in front of me would want to.

He half-smiles before he pushes out the door.

A panicked Jess enters my line of sight. "I'm so sorry, Callie. I should have told you the first night you brought him to the dorms."

"Why didn't you exactly?" I ask, not sure how mad I want to be yet.

She knots her fingers together and squirms before she blurts out, "Because he's really hot, and I didn't want Vee's weird obsession to keep you from screwing him."

Benji chuckles from his post, leaning against a counter. "Sound logic."

When I shoot him a look, he slides a hand over his mouth to cover his huge grin.

"I'm so, so, so sorry. Like so—"

Before she hits a new record of *sos* in one breath, I stop her. "I get it. You shouldn't have done it, but you're right. If you had told me, I would have done something stupid to get revenge on him."

"More revenge," Benji corrects. My attention snaps back to him, and he laughs. "Your boyfriend has a big mouth."

I roll my eyes, unable to stop a smile when he winks.

Not wanting the drama to put a damper on the night, I grant forgiveness, and a group hug takes place in which Benji inserts himself into the middle.

After Felicia and Jess start talking about rearranging the living room, he bumps his shoulder into mine. "He's completely lost his mind over you, woman. No matter how many times he fucks up, remember that."

I never have a chance to respond.

The kitchen door bangs open, and Jordan charges in. I gasp as he scoops me up, not even slowing down. He carries me through the kitchen and into the laundry room in the far corner of the house. His foot kicks the door shut behind us, and he sets me on top of the washing machine. He cages me in, standing between my legs, hands on either side of me.

"Jordan, what the hell are—"

"Don't talk," he says, out of breath.

The room's dark, except the soft glow of a disturbing clown-face nightlight in the corner, but it's more than enough to see the look that sends a shot of panic racing through me. My mind scrambles for a way to stop him from saying what I think he's going to say when, out of nowhere, his mouth crashes into mine.

That'll work.

I grab his face so he can't pull away. A husky sound escapes his throat as my tongue finds his, and we're done talking. Everything turns desperate, our hands and lips and breaths. I push up his shirt until he finishes pulling it off. His hands run up my sides, dragging the bottom of my top with them. Once it's off, he slides me to the edge of the washer, and I lock my legs around him. Our mouths meld together again as I pull his hips forward, so he rocks against me. With each grind of his hips, mine move, seeking more contact, and he presses his erection into me harder.

When he breaks his mouth away from me and the friction on my clit stops, I almost whimper. He dashes to the stool on one side of the room and wedges it under the door handle, then he's right back between my legs, lips on my neck.

But I plant a palm on his chest and back him up enough I can jump down. I unbutton his jeans and slip my fingers under the waistband, pushing them over his hips, so I can get to his dick.

I hit my knees, casting my gaze up at him. His is almost feral as he stares down at me while I wrap my fingers around him. He thrusts his hand into my hair. I stroke him a few times before I run the flat of my tongue up the underside and over the tip. My thighs are already pressing together from the taste of him when he sinks between my lips.

"Fuck, beautiful," he grits out.

He groans, and my eyes don't leave his while my mouth slides up and down his shaft. It makes my pussy throb, watching him watch me suck his cock like he can barely stay in control. He thrusts forward, pushing into the back of my throat. As he draws back, his hand tightens in my hair, but then—

"Damn it, Callie." Jordan pulls all the way out, no longer touching me. "You're sucking me off to distract me."

Oh, right. I *am* distracting him.

Refocused, I tug on the pockets of his jeans to bring him back to me. My palm encircles his shaft, our eyes locked when I tease my tongue over his balls.

"Does that mean you want me to stop?" I ask, breathier than I intended.

Jordan gazes down at me. "I love you."

I sit upright, my entire body very, very cold as my hand falls away from him. He said it. He actually fucking said it. But the scariest part is, I almost said it back.

Fuck.

Jordan steps back, tucking away his dick, when I scramble to my feet. I flip on the light when I reach the door, and as much as I want to run, I go back the other way. For one, I'm in my bra, and two, I need to fix this. I need to figure out how to undo the last twenty seconds.

He stares at me while I pace the small space between him and the door.

"Take it back," I tell him.

"I'm not taking it back."

"Jordan"—before I run into the wall, I turn around—"I'm serious."

"So am I," he says. "I love you."

"Stop saying that." I head the other direction, grateful not to look at him for a few seconds because now his eyes are telling me, too. Everything about him is screaming it. "Why do you want to ruin everything between us?"

"Ruin? I told you I'm in love with you. Explain how it ruins anything."

This time when I circle back, I stop in front of him and groan because he said it again. "Just because we love each other doesn't mean we won't destroy each other. I mean, my genetics alone almost guarantee mutual destruction."

His eyebrows infinitesimally draw in. "Say that all one more time."

"And now you're not listening?"

Unbelievable.

His lips twitch. "Sorry, just say it again."

Rather than repeat, I try to better explain, so he'll understand. "Graham and Lara loved each other, too. Then they ended up hating each other and made everyone around them miserable. Fuck, they still do," I add.

At first, he says nothing. Then one side of his mouth perks up, and he steps toward me. I back up until I hit the wall next to the door.

"What are you doing?"

He ignores my question and brings a hand to my face. "For starters," he says, pushing my hair back, "we're nothing like your parents. We never will be."

"How can you say that? We fight all the time."

He shakes his head. "We sometimes bicker and discuss our strong differences in opinion. Which will continue because you challenge me more than anyone I've ever met. It frustrates the hell out of me, but it's also the best damn feeling in the world." He presses his lips to mine, his kiss fast and reassuring before he continues, "When we do fight, we never scream or throw things or make death threats. If we get too heated, we walk away and come back calmer. Ergo, we are not Graham and Lara."

"Jordan, you—"

"Exactly," he says. "I am Jordan, and you are Callie. I can promise you, we will never be anyone else."

I try to relax against him and tip my chin up to look at him. "Promise?"

"Promise." He grazes his fingertips over my collarbone, and I sink even further into him. "Also, to bring you up to speed, you've said we love each other twice now. As in I love you, and you love me."

I think through what I said, and a half-laugh, half-sigh slips out as I realize he's technically right. "I did, didn't I."

I cover my face with a hand, but he pulls it away and kisses the backs of my fingers.

"Now you're going to say the words."

The rush of panic returns. "Then what? We take turns hurting the other until we can't stand the sight of each other?" Because that's all I know. The type of love where it consumes and burns in the worst ways, and you have to fight to even survive in it.

"No, baby." He slaps the light switch next to me, darkening the room. "Then I'm going to tell you I love you, too, and we'll make Gibson regret inviting us to the housewarming party by continuing to traumatize her nightlight."

I smile, once again disarmed by his ability to flip everything from one emotion to another with a few words. My hands run up the back of his neck to his hair. He leans in, but he pulls back before our lips meet. "Hey. I've laid out a plan for the rest of our night. There's no way I'm letting you skip any of the steps."

I want to believe we can love each other without the ugliness and pain. I want to believe it more than I've wanted to believe anything in my entire life. To trust that, even when we're not bright and shiny anymore, it won't matter. He'll still look at me in his way, and I'll find him charming, even when he's frustrating. But I'm not there yet. So, for now, I'll just have to believe him. Trust him. Let him be certain enough for the both of us.

"I love you, Jordan." The way he stares down at me wreaks even more havoc on my already-erratic heartbeat, and I force a breath. "Happy now?"

A slow smile spreads. "Oh, I'm fucking ecstatic."

He dips down to kiss me, but I duck out of the way. "I remember someone being extremely concerned about following a specific agenda."

Jordan cups my cheeks in his hands, expression serious. "I love you, too, Callie. So much it's inappropriate."

His words somehow erase the last of my apprehension. I bite my lip and reach behind me to unclasp my bra. Jordan's gaze drops as I toss it over the clown nightlight to stop it from watching. Without any windows, the room turns even darker. He kisses me, slow at first but the urgency returns. His hands stay on my face, bringing me with him as he backs up. Lips still on his, I laugh as he bumps into everything on our way across the room.

When he stops, his hands drop to the button on my jeans. He spins us around and tugs them and my panties off my hips and down my thighs. His fingers glide up, setting off chills, and he lifts me onto the counter behind me. The unexpected cold of the tiles on my bare skin makes me cry out.

"Shit," he says, "what did I do?" He picks me back up, arms around my waist.

"It's cold."

He blows out a breath and laughs. "I'm sorry, beautiful." My feet have barely touched the floor when he flips me around, and I suck in a breath. "We can't let this sweet ass be cold."

I grind back against his crotch, a low growl escaping him. As he steps back to push down his jeans and boxers, I finish stepping out of mine, then his erection brushes over my ass, the heat of his body behind me.

In the next breath, he reaches around, pushing between my thighs. I moan when he cups my pussy.

"Was it my cock in your throat that has your cunt dripping for me?" His rumbling voice in my ear sends a line of heat to my core. He slips his fingers inside me and starts slowly pumping, rubbing the length of his hard cock between my ass cheeks. "Or did hearing me say I love you do it for you?"

I drop my head back onto his shoulder, already breathing heavily. "It's you. All of you."

Jordan hums while running his mouth up the column of my neck. "Better give you all of me then."

"No condom," I tell him as his fingers drag all the way out, leaving me empty and aching.

"Are you sure?" he asks.

I turn my head to see him. His face is barely visible in the bit of light leaking through the fabric of my bra, but I find his eyes waiting for mine. Green and blue. Mixed. A piece of one always a part of the other.

I smile at him. "I'm certain."

"I'm certain you're perfect."

He kisses me, smiling against my mouth, and then his fingers wrap around my hip. I flatten my palms on the cool counter, arching my back when the head of his cock nudges between my legs. Jordan groans before his hips punch forward, and he fills me all at once. The force of it pushes me all the way up onto my toes. I cry out, feeling him all the way in my stomach, but I still greedily press back, the pressure fucking divine.

Nearly every inch of him slides out, only for him to slam in again. Again. Again.

He bars an arm across my chest and jerks me upright. He cups my breast, holding me tight against his chest, fucking me hard but slow. Every unhurried thrust ricochets through me, leaving me desperate for the next. His breath and rasped words dance over my skin while he gives me what I need.

Him.

I need *him*.

All of him. In ways I never thought I would or could, and in ways that scare the hell out of me. But I'm not letting go.

No, I'm holding onto him for dear fucking life.

67 Days Until 19

The Friday after the laundry room tryst, my siblings and I start the summer custody schedule with our first full week at Graham's. Skip ahead twenty-four hours later, and it already feels like it's been a month.

Since Cate tested out of *two* skills tonight at swim lessons, she earned two blue slushies. The first of which she's already slurping on in the backseat. I'm convinced the limit to how many blue slushies she can consume does not exist, but I never plan on testing my theory.

On the drive to Graham's, she calls Jordan to brag about her mastery of swimming in the deep end and the backstroke. Her interest in him fades when we pull up to the house, and she sees the lights on inside. She realizes Connor's home, and before she leaps out of the car, she tosses me the phone. It lands in my lap with Jordan still chatting away.

"My biggest concern with being a merman is, how will you transfer me from one place to another if we need to go somewhere?"

"Mine is, which parts of you stay human and which turn fish?"

He laughs, used to being discarded on a whim. "Hey, beautiful. If you mean my godlike hair and genius mind, they'll stay as they are."

"Nope. Those aren't the parts I'm concerned about."

"Did she really pass the backstroke?"

"Her instructor questioned the legitimacy of her kicking style but gave in to her whining."

"That's my girl." The pride in his voice is undeniable.

Cate opens the front door and waves for me to come inside, but I could really use a longer break. More Jordan time and less … everything else. I sigh when her gestures become more frantic.

"Well, the sea monster beckons me. Good luck with dinner."

Now he sighs, not at all enthused about spending the evening battling his parents over his future. "We'll see how open they actually are to my alternatives. Dustin promised our dear, sweet mother is coming in willing to negotiate. I think the night will more than likely end with, *Hello, real world and crippling student loan debt.*"

"With an optimistic outlook like that, you can't fail." I crawl out of my car and wrinkle my nose. The smell of burned rubber or plastic hangs heavy in the air.

"*Callista!*" Cate screeches from the steps. The shrill sound cuts through the quiet streets, and the neighbors' dogs start barking.

"Oh. My. God. Catelynn Renee, stop it."

She stomps her foot and marches inside, leaving the door wide open.

"Everything all right over there?" Jordan asks.

I groan, any momentary calm he provided vanishing. "I won't survive an entire week here, Jordan. She's being extra Cate-like, so I took her swimming early to let her burn off some energy. Now she's screaming on the steps."

"And Connor?"

I take a deep breath, not even sure how to answer. We walked in the door at six last night, and the first fight between him and Graham started at six-oh-two when he had the audacity to shut the refrigerator too hard. Forget the fact that the piece of shit only stays closed if you slam it.

They screamed back and forth until I grabbed Connor's face in my hands, forcing him to look at me. His jaw worked under my palm as I told him to go help Cate unpack.

After he stalked down the hallway, I confronted the real problem. Graham was drunk, and given the size of his pupils, he was on something. I asked if he was going to act like this all week, and he stormed toward me, not stopping until we were chest-to-chest. When I refused to cower, he told me to fuck off and wobbled away. The three of us stayed in my room the rest of the night to avoid round two. Too bad we couldn't stay locked in there all week.

"Graham started in on him again first thing this morning about absolutely nothing," I say. "He went to basketball this afternoon, so hopefully, he worked off some aggression, but I don't know. I haven't seen him since he left."

I close my eyes and press my lips together, needing a second. A minute. An hour.

"I don't know how much longer I can keep up with all the fires before they blaze out of fucking control," I admit.

"Want me to come and help tomorrow?" he asks.

The idea alone is enough to take the weight away. "Yes. Please save me. I'll love you forever."

"Your sexy ass is already going to love me forever."

I laugh. "You're right. I will."

And I truly believe it.

Cate reappears on the steps, hands on her hips. "Callista," she shouts. "Now!"

After another groan, I start toward the house. "Cate's screaming again. I'll talk to you later."

"Bye, beautiful," he says.

I tuck the phone in my pocket on my way up the steps. "Okay, I'm here."

She drags me inside by the hand. "Something's wrong with him, Cal."

We pass her room, Connor's room, my room, and stop in front of Graham's door. I look down at her, confused. Graham's truck is gone. He's not home. She lets go of me and pushes the door open.

My heart stops. No, my *world*.

The room is torn apart. Graham's stripped mattress is hanging halfway off the bed. His TV is lying face down on the ground, ripped from the mount that is still dangling by one side on the wall. Clothes thrown everywhere. Drawers all open. The shards from the broken mirror cover the top of the dresser.

And in the middle of it all is Connor. On the floor. Cradling his bleeding hand.

"Cal…" he chokes out, tears streaming down his face.

I drop to my knees, facing Cate. "Go to the bathroom and bring me two towels. One wet, one dry."

She dashes out of the room, and my mind launches into overdrive, trying to decide what to confront first. I hurry to Connor's side. He stretches his fingers out. Not broken. Cate returns with the towels, and I carefully dab the blood away with the wet one to get a better visual of his cuts.

"Shit, Con. I think you need stitches."

"Oh-my-God. Oh-my-God. Oh-my-God." He drops his head forward, still repeating but barely audible.

I catch the scent of bourbon on his breath. "Are you drunk?"

When he doesn't answer, I ask Cate to get him a glass of water. I wait for her to run out before I grab him by the hair and lift his head up. "You have until she gets back to tell me what the fuck is going on."

"He showed up at practice and saw me miss a layup. A fucking layup, and all because I was distracted, watching his Father of the Year act with Coach. When I got back, he said he wasn't paying for me to suck. We started yelling at one another, and—" He takes a deep breath and squeezes his eyes shut. "He burned it all. My jerseys. My shoes. Everything. All my stuff, it's just … gone."

The smell outside.

I shake my head, unable to process such an extreme reaction to an argument with a fifteen-year-old.

"He left, and I was so mad," he says. "I went to Derrick's, and we raided his dad's bar. I'm sorry. I just…" Connor's eyes plead with me, desperate for something but I don't know what. "I hate him so much, Cal. It's *killing* me." He throws his arms around me and clings to me as if I'm his lifeline, shaking and crying. "I'm so sorry, Cal. I'm so sorry."

My heart shatters into more microscopic pieces than I thought possible as I hold on to him, only to outdo itself when Cate comes in to see her invincible big brother falling apart in my arms. He catches sight of her and pulls away, wiping his eyes, but she's already whimpering.

"Come here, Monster," he says, voice trembling.

She climbs onto his lap and secures her arms around his neck, still holding the water glass. I grab it before it ends up down his back.

Blood drips off the ends of Connor's fingers onto the carpet, and light catches on pieces of glass embedded in the cuts.

I stand up and set the glass on the nightstand. "We need to go get your hand taken care of."

He braces with the injured hand as he gets up with Cate in his other arm and leaves a smear of blood across the mattress. She watches me over his shoulder while he carries her out. They disappear into the hall, and the panic sets in. I frantically glance around the room. Whether Graham comes home tonight or in the morning, there's no way we can hide this. I can clean up some of the mess maybe, but the TV and wall mount and bloodstains—I have no idea how I'll fix this, but I need to figure something out. Until then, I turn out the light and shut the door. Out of sight, out of mind, right?

Connor holds Cate, waiting for me by the kitchen door. We're about to walk out when the muffled sound of a truck's exhaust cuts through the quiet house. Sheer panic flashes in Connor's eyes, surely mirroring mine. This can't be happening. We need to get the fuck out of this house.

I grab for my keys, and my entire body numbs. "I left my keys in Graham's room." The truck shuts off outside, and my mind races. "Go," I tell him, turning the doorknob. "Do not come back inside, no matter what."

Connor violently shakes his head. "No fucking way."

"If I'm not out in two minutes, call Trey."

He continues to tell me no until the truck door slams outside.

I open the door and almost push him out. "*Go*," I whisper.

Graham stands near the bed of his truck. He watches us to figure out what we're doing, so I smile at Connor.

"I'll get my keys, and then we'll go for a slushie."

I calmly step inside and shut the door before I tear through the house. My keys are on the floor in front of the bed. I swipe them, already on my way back in the other direction, and close the door behind me.

As I get to my bedroom door, Graham turns the corner into the hall. We both stop. His eyes drop to the keys in my hand. I jingle them around to further prove they are the reason I'm standing here.

Pins and needles cover every inch of my skin. The second he starts moving so does my clock. I need to get out of the house and to the car before he has a chance to react to the condition of his room. What happens after, I'm not sure. All I know is none of it matters if I don't get to the car.

My heart pounds hard enough in my chest that I fear he'll hear it. I take a step toward him; his first one stops my breathing. We pass each other, and I fight the urge to run. I hit the mouth of the hallway as his door creaks behind me.

"What the *fuck*!"

I race through the kitchen, knocking over a chair on my way around the table. The screen door bangs open so hard it doesn't swing back, and cool night air hits my lungs. Connor, my anchor to safety, waits by the car.

Both my feet are out the door when my head jerks back. I cry out, more in shock than pain as Graham starts dragging me inside by the hair. Connor drops Cate and rushes toward us, but he won't make it in time. I throw my keys in his direction, needing him to get himself and Cate somewhere safe. Somewhere far away from here.

Graham slams the door, and the hold on me releases, so he can lock it. The second it does, I bolt from the kitchen. I lock myself in my room and run to the window. The heels of my hands press up on the top of the frame, but it doesn't budge, still painted shut after all these years. I shove up harder, the edge of the wood digging into my skin. My breath comes faster with each failed attempt.

Shit.

I search around for something to break the glass but freeze when my doorknob rattles. With nowhere else to go, I crawl into the blanket fort. It muffles Graham's yelling and beating on the door while I dig my phone out of my pocket.

Trey answers on the first ring. "Jesus, Cal. Connor just called. Are you okay?"

"I don't … I'm not…" Words won't travel from my brain to my mouth, and I close my eyes.

Nothing bad can happen under the blankets, I tell myself, desperate to trust in the make-believe I created for a scared little boy.

"Breathe," he says, his voice soothing. "I need you to talk to me."

"I'm scared," I choke out.

"I'm on my way. Dad's on his way, too, but he's in Waymore. Five minutes, Cal. Hang the fuck on for five minutes."

I nod like he can see me.

Five minutes. Trey only needs five minutes. Such a short amount of time if you think about it.

The pounding on the door continues. My lip trembles when the wood cracks. After a few seconds, the door bangs against the wall, and the floorboards just inside my doorway creak. Trey says my name, still talking, but his voice gets farther away as the phone slides out of my hand.

The blankets do nothing, our refuge destroyed without effort. Graham grasps my ankles and drags me out to the hallway while I kick and scream. He loses his hold on one leg, and my foot connects with him, making him let go of the other. I scramble to my feet and run to the kitchen. Before I reach the door, he grabs my arm and yanks me back. He shoves me, and I backpedal into the living room, trying to keep my balance, while he charges in after me, overturning the coffee table on his way.

His face comes within an inch of mine, shouting and cussing. This time when his hand swings, it cracks against the side of my face.

The backhand doesn't hurt as much as I expected. I've spent all these years thinking about how it could be worse. With each threat and insult, I've reminded myself that he could be hitting me.

Maybe it's shock, but now that it's happening, it feels no worse than the years of emotional torment.

The strike knocks me into an end table, crashing a lamp to the floor. He waits until I straighten up for the next blow. It hurts as much as the month he only called me Mistake. The pain when he grips my shoulders and slams my head into the wall compares to seeing Connor's face the first time Graham told him no one would ever love him. And all the times after.

The world dims for a second as he throws me to the floor. The throb in my wrist when I try to catch myself brings on another memory. I attempt to block it out, focused on a shard of the broken lamp within reach. My hand lashes out for it. When he flips me over, it slices his side before I lose my grip. He lets out a growl and holds me down, my ribs aching under the weight of his knee.

I cry and struggle, not sure what pain comes from now and what's from the last eighteen years. Honestly, I don't know how much more of either I can handle. Five minutes. Five seconds.

I gasp in a panicked breath when he leans over me and fight with everything I have to get him off, but it's no use. I'm trapped and helpless, feeling his hands wrap around my throat. I slap at him. His arms, his hands, anything I can reach. I pull and pry at his fingers, scratching and clawing for relief, but his grip only tightens. As the pressure on my throat increases, the memories flash faster. My lungs burn, desperate for air, and the image of him staring down at me while he chokes me blurs out of focus. Shadows bleed in until my eyes fall shut.

Heaviness and the fire in my chest are all that's left.

"Cal."

Trey's close. He tells me to open my eyes, but I'm tired.

When we were younger, he'd always come over way too early in the morning to make me go fishing. He would pry my eyes open with his thumbs and shine a light in them. He does the same now but without a flashlight. All of him is fuzzy, his face and voice.

He lets go of my eyelids, but only one stays open. While he's talking into his radio, I reach up and wipe away the red streaming down the side of his face.

"Christ, Cal," he says. He shakes his head and lies on his side next to me on the floor. "Stop trying to take care of me, you cracked woman. I'm glad you can move, but don't do it anymore."

Trying to swallow sets my throat ablaze. Everything seems to hurt when I try to lift my head, so I stop. Trey pushes wet hair away from my forehead and pulls a stuck strand off my cheek. His thumb passes over my temple, and I let my eye shut.

He insists I stay awake and rambles about our trip to the amusement park last summer. He pauses a lot to ask if I remember. I do, but I don't answer. I want to sleep, but he says my name every other sentence. Each time, my mind refocuses on him and his stupid roller coasters. His voice fades in and out. Then it stays out, everything quiet again so I can sleep.

295 Days Until 18

No one notices his fingers wrap around my wrist. The people around us only half-pay attention to anything as their eyes glaze over. But they all jump when he shouts, "Go!"

Trey drags me behind him, running away from the group like his life depends on it.

I desperately try to keep up with his much longer legs. "Trey, stop."

"I can't," he says, glancing back at me. "They might catch us and continue the torturous death by boredom."

If I had the extra air, I would remind him that *he* signed us up for the tour at a campus *he* chose. I might also mention that because he forced me out of bed way earlier than necessary to go fishing ahead of the three-hour drive, the physical activity itself will kill me if we don't slow down.

Around the corner of an old brick building, he releases me. I double over, panting. It gives me great pleasure to see him do the same.

Once my breathing slows, I straighten up and spin around. "Everything looks so old."

"Quite," Trey says, developing a strange accent. "Most of the buildings in Easton University's 'Old Campus' were built thousands of years ago."

"Wow, is that so?"

"I read it in the catalog." He walks over and slaps a wall. "Jesus attended religion one-oh-one right here."

I laugh. "That's some impressive history."

He grins before charging a random passerby. "Hey, man, can you take a picture of us in front of this historical landmark?"

The guy has little choice but to take the phone being shoved at him. Trey jogs back over and proceeds to smash the side of his face to mine. I smile with as much teeth as I can manage, and judging by the confused look we receive from our unsuspecting photographer, Trey's face rivals mine. Sure enough, when I check, he's holding his eyes as wide open as possible.

Not one but ten pictures later, he dashes over for his phone. He never makes it back to me, distracted by a group of girls who were watching our impromptu photo shoot.

He saunters over to them. "Hell-o, ladies."

They giggle and take in what he refers to as his "carved from marble physique." More like skinny country boy who needs to hit the gym. I join him, interested to see what angle he uses on them because he always has one.

"My name's Bradford King," he says with the same unidentifiable accent. "Maybe you've heard of my father, Alfred? He's an oil tycoon. No big deal."

One of them points to his chest. "Then why does your name tag say Trey?"

He grabs at his shirt, pulling it out to examine the white sticker. "Ah, shit."

Once again, he latches on to my arm, and we haul ass for absolutely no reason. We put plenty of distance between us and his failed pick-up attempt before slowing down.

"Why didn't you warn me, Cal?"

"An oil tycoon?" I ask, out of breath again.

"What? It sounded cool." Trey heads over to a guy studying on a bench. "You have a pen?"

The student hands him a red Sharpie, which he then launches at me. I catch it and meet him halfway to change his name. "You could just take it off."

"Less fun that way." He snags the marker when I finish and crosses out Callista from my tag. "Your turn."

I shrug. "I don't know."

"Pshh. Try again."

"Callista's fine."

He cocks his head to the side. "You're killing me. You can be *anyone* you want here. No one knows you. And you choose her?"

Meant as a joke or not, the truth in his words strikes me. Other than him, no one knows anything about my horrible parents or my bad reputation or how much I hate nearly every single aspect of my life. They have no idea who Callista Henders is and never need to. It's like a clean slate.

"What about Callie?" I expect an argument because it's just a shortened version of my name, but Trey scribbles it in without question.

He tosses the pen to the kid on the bench. "Thank you, sir."

Bradford then takes Callie's arm in his, and they wander down the sidewalk with no particular destination in mind.

The longer we walk, the more I want to never leave. The campus is beautiful and far away from home and the hate. It's peaceful, and I love the quiet, not something I get much of in my life.

Trey lights a cigarette before he offers me one, but I shake my head.

"Callie doesn't smoke."

"How boring." He sticks the extra cigarette behind his ear. "Tell me more about this Callie chick."

I purse my lips, contemplating all the parts of Callista I want to shed. "She always stops drinking after a decent buzz. *Never* loses control. In fact, she's kind of a lightweight. Two drinks are plenty for her. She also has rules for guys. No cocky assholes for starters."

"Hallelujah," he says, holding a hand to the sky.

We turn the corner, and I stop, taking in the giant courtyard between the buildings. A fountain in the middle and flower boxes and students everywhere. Suddenly, I'm more capable of breathing than I've ever been before.

The last three years have been a constant mess with everything spiraling out of control. The past few months have been better with a light at the end of the tunnel. I've learned from my mistakes, and I know that's not the life I want. It's not who I want to *be*, and in two hundred and ninety-five days, when I turn eighteen, I won't have to be. I'll leave it all behind and never look back.

Finally free.

Being here, I get my first taste of what that will feel like.

"Does she go to Easton University?" Trey asks.

I smile and nod, deciding she will. "Do you want to know the best part, Trey?"

"Sure do," he says, hooking his arm around my neck. "What's the best part?"

"She's happy."

He looks down at me and smiles. "You sound like a fucking amazing person, Callie."

66 Days Until 19

Trey starts bothering me again. Lifting my eyelid and blinding me with his flashlight. He switches to the other side. I want to slap his hands away, but my arms are too heavy, so I clamp my eyes shut until he mumbles something and leaves me alone. My head pounds, and I don't think I could wake up right now if I tried.

What feels like seconds later, someone begins tapping their finger against my hand. Someone almost always being Jordan Waters. His rhythmic fidgeting is relaxing, and it almost lulls me back to sleep. But then it stops, and everything moves backward in slow motion. Trey talking and the light shining in my eyes and his thumbs forcing open my eyelids. The pressure in my lungs, ready to burst, and the agonizing weight on my neck. It crushes down, heavier and heavier until I open my eyes.

Graham.

I can't breathe, his hands clamped down around my throat. I frantically grab at them in one last attempt to stop him, but they're not there. *He's* not there. Air sucks into my lungs in hungry gasps, my body unable to get enough. My eyes search for him. The room is dim with white walls and soft pillows.

Where the fuck am I?

"You're safe, Callie," Jordan says, dragging my hand away. "You're okay."

It hurts my neck to turn to see him beside me. He sits in a chair, and I'm in a bed. Our eyes meet, and the rest fills in. The attack and the pain and Trey showing up. The memories and emotions are raw as every second replays in my mind. Jordan wipes away the tears spilling from the corners of my eyes, and I try to calm my breaths.

Graham almost killed me.

"I'll go get someone," he says.

I tighten my hold on his hand and lock eyes with him. He's not fucking leaving me alone. I don't care if I am in the hospital and Graham's not here. Seeming to get the message, he reaches over to hit a button and brings his hand back to my face. His thumb brushes over my cheek. Nothing's ever felt better, even though the rest of me hurts to varying degrees.

I'm vaguely aware of the cast on my left arm and the stabbing in my side if I take too deep of a breath. My left eye feels heavy, not willing to open much. And when I try to swallow, it feels like razor blades are slashing their way down my throat. I have to close my eyes until the pain becomes manageable, but the gaze waiting for me when I open them again helps me block it all out.

Jordan looks away when a nurse rushes in, and the discomfort returns front and center to my mind. She asks him to step into the hall. As much as I want him to stay, I carefully nod and give him permission to go. I watch him until he disappears out the door. The nurse tells me the doctor's on his way and gives me a sip of cold water.

Frozen razor blades.

A smiley man whistles his way in the door. According to the clock, it's not even seven in the morning, so he loses points for being too chipper. "I'm Dr. Gregory," he says. "Welcome back, Miss Henders."

The next few minutes blur together as he asks about my pain and what I remember. I answer, my voice weak and raspy. My vocal cords feel shredded, so any attempt to talk above a whisper proves to be a challenge. He assures me that Graham's been arrested and I'm safe, and then he rattles off my injuries. A fractured wrist, broken ribs, severe concussion, persistent swelling in my throat, and various other cuts and bruises.

Dr. Gregory clicks on a small flashlight. "May I?"

I nod, and he tenderly lifts my lid to shine the light in my swollen eye. It stings, but he swiftly switches sides.

"You weren't a fan of this earlier," he says, turning the light off. "Kept trying to close your eyes."

I force a swallow. "I thought you were my cousin," I whisper. "He did the same thing to wake me up to go fishing."

His mouth quirks up on one side in response.

When he reaches toward my neck, I fight the urge to shy away, anxious about him touching it. He kneads his fingers over the tender skin, not lingering anywhere and only using the tips. "We want to keep an eye on this swelling for at least the next twenty-four hours. You'll also want to avoid talking for a while." He smiles when my eyes flash to his. "Fine, you can whisper as long as it doesn't hurt too much."

I slowly nod, finding that more agreeable.

"Well, that's all I have for you right now. I'll be in and out to check on you throughout the morning, and Sandy is just a button push away."

From next to my IV, she gives a small smile that comes across less warm than she intends.

Dr. Gregory spins around in the doorway. "Visiting hours don't start for an hour. Anyone wanna take bets on who sneaks back here first?"

Sandy snorts, and he chuckles, backing into the hall. She moves to the side of the bed and adjusts the pillow propping up my left arm and then the ones behind me.

"He said something about scratches on my neck?" I ask.

Her mouth forms a thin line, and she nods. "Mmhmm."

"Can I see them?"

She forces another smile. "Later, dear."

I sigh and drop my head back on the pillow. She continues to mill about, bordering on irritating. I'm about to ask her to leave when she mutters, "Of course it's him."

She shakes her head as Jordan walks in. No love lost between them, he pushes past her to sit down in the chair next to me, and she orders him to make sure I keep taking sips from the cup on the bedside table. I scarcely notice her leave, already wrapped up in him.

"Hey," I say, staring at him.

He looks exhausted, his eyes heavy. But, as always, he pulls it off. "Hey, beautiful."

It feels like forever since I heard that rather than twelve hours. "Cate and Connor?"

He groans and lowers his head onto my shoulder. "I knew we forgot something."

I smile when he looks up. "So frustrating."

"You love it," he whispers, giving one back.

When I swallow, I close my eyes and try not to wince. Otherwise, I'll have the doctor *and* him on me about not talking.

"Want me to leave so you can sleep?"

"No," I say fast.

"Good. My presence is nonnegotiable." He relaxes in the chair, almost farther away than I want him.

Still thinking about the marks, I touch my neck. The tips of my fingers move across ridges in the skin that span from one side to the other. I remember his hands and the pressure. The panic of not being able to breathe. The scrape of my nails while I tried to stop him, digging my way under his fingers to find relief, to get air.

Jordan pulls my hands away, concern washing over him. I'm breathing too fast, and I focus on slowing it while he kisses each of my fingers.

"It was getting worse, but I never thought…" I shake my head, not sure how to even describe what happened. "He snapped."

"He'll never fucking touch you again," Jordan says. He kisses my inner wrist. "Don't even think about him."

A soft knock turns my attention to the door, which is creeping open. Trey stops when I look at him. He's still in his uniform, stitches in a cut over his eye.

We stare like we've never seen each other before and like we never thought we'd see the other again, both at the same time. Then he practically sprints across the room. He folds his arms around me, holding my head against his chest. I pull my hand from Jordan's to hug him back the best I can for the awkward angle.

He rests his cheek on top of my head. "Never again, Cal. You are never putting me through anything like this ever again."

I blink away tears and squeeze him tighter. "And you're never talking about roller coasters again."

His laugh vibrates through his chest. "I think I can manage that." He dries his eyes before he releases me and moves to the foot of my bed. "Our waiting room's getting a little crowded. You know three guys and a redhead?"

"Those belong to me," Jordan says. I assume they mean Benji, Rusty, Gavin, and Felicia, so I give him a look, and he corrects himself. "Well, they belong to us." He jumps up and heads to the door. When he comes back, he's not alone.

Connor.

My brother rushes over to my less-injured side and leans over, cautious about how he touches me. I'm not as careful, bringing my casted wrist over to hold on to him even though it pulls at my ribs.

"I'm so sorry." He pulls back enough so that I can see his face. His breathing is erratic, a few tiny scratches on one of his cheeks and his chin, eyes red-rimmed and shiny.

I brush the hair away from his eyes, unable to imagine what he's put himself through since the last time I saw him. "None of this is your fault," I tell him. "Do you hear me?"

I'm prepared for him to argue, but his eyes dart to Jordan. They stay on my boyfriend for a few seconds before returning to me, and then Connor nods. The exchange makes me think I might not be the only person my brother counts on anymore.

And I'm so fucking okay with that.

I'm surprised it takes so long for Pete to waltz in my door. He catches the arm of a chair on his way by and drags it along behind him. He sets it in front of the window and comes to the bed.

"I'll be over there if you need me," he says, squeezing my hand.

In what feels like another life, he was the one lying broken in a hospital. After I found him and ran for help, I stayed in his room twenty-four-seven, scared his mother would show up to finish the job. Looks like he plans to do the same.

Jordan seems to think he's around for the long haul as well. He lets out a loud sigh as Pete plants in the chair, but his annoyance is only half-convincing. Trey laughs. I would, too, if not for the thousand knives lining my throat. Jordan snags the water glass for me. The water feels better going down this time. He sets it back and returns to his chair.

"Where the hell's Cate?" he asks Pete.

"In the waiting room," he says, eyes glued to his phone. "She was playing with the spiky hair on some guy named Rusty."

Jordan laughs, no doubt imagining the tattooed drummer going through the same initiation he did. Trey convinces Connor they should go save the poor soul from her torment and find breakfast. A good idea since nobody probably thought about feeding my brother until now. Cate would have demanded food when hungry but not Connor.

They both give me another hug, and Trey tells me he'll be back later in the afternoon after he finishes up some paperwork from last night. I know it means making a statement and telling my side of the story a few dozen times. Not something I'm looking forward to.

I'm smiling at the death glare Jordan has locked on Pete when Benji appears in the doorway. He grins on his way over, and without hesitation, he crawls into bed with me. The look on Jordan's face is priceless when he slips an arm around me.

"Thanks for taking care of my Calico, man."

"How the hell did you even get back here?" Jordan asks.

"I'm a charming son of a bitch," he says. My nurse walks in, her smile much sincerer as she delivers him a cup of coffee. "Thank you, Sandy." He winks at her, bringing a pink to her cheeks.

With a little convincing, and using Benji as backup, Jordan agrees to catch up to Connor and Trey for breakfast. He leans over Benji to kiss my forehead, and while he's bent over, Benji plants one on his cheek. I chance a quiet laugh, and as irritated as Jordan looks with his best friend, he smiles at me.

Once he leaves, I readjust to better see Benji. "Can I use your phone?"

He slides it out of his pocket, and I open the camera app, flipping it around to look at myself. A condensed ball of anxiety lodges in my throat right beneath the lines streaking down my neck. Bright red and angry. The split lip, gash in my cheek, darkening around my swollen eye, and the pink hue to it and the other one barely registers next to the claw marks.

"Battle wounds," he says. "Don't think of them as anything else."

I hand him back his phone, wishing I'd never looked.

A little later, Jordan returns with Connor and Cate. Benji slips out the door while Cate quizzes me about what happened. I keep my answers short and vague, telling her I was in an accident.

"You need to be more careful, Cal," she tells me, stroking my hair.

"I will be. I promise."

She twists the strands around her fingers. "Was Daddy in an accident, too?"

Jordan's eyes meet mine, his jaw clenched, and I fake a small smile. "Yes."

"Do I have to visit him?"

"No."

"Good," she says.

She never asks about it again, becoming Nurse Cate and needing to take care of everyone. Rusty comes in, and after she tries to rip out my IV and give it to him, we send them both back to the waiting room. He dips down for a quick kiss on my cheek and then scoops her up and heads toward the door.

"If this is what you're like around a kid," Jordan says, "I'm terrified for our band's image."

Rusty stops to flip him off, only for Cate to shake her head and cover up his finger.

"No, Rusty."

He apologizes and carries her out.

The rest of the morning blurs by with visits from Gavin, Tony, Shayna, and a tearful Felicia. Throughout it all, Pete never moves from his chair by the window, and Jordan remains in the one next to my bed. Whenever it's just the three of us, the room grows quiet enough that I fall into a fitful sleep. The same dream torments me. Graham stares down at me. His fingers curl around my throat while I thrash around, unable to stop him. Every time, I wake up terrified, trying to get the pressure off my neck and gasping for the air he deprived me of. Each time, Jordan catches my hand in his own and says my name to remind me it's not real.

It happens quite a few times before I refuse to close my eyes for more than a rapid blink. They send a counselor in to talk about PTSD. The main takeaway is the dreams could be here to stay for a while.

"A going-away present from Graham," I tell Jordan.

We both fake smiles even though neither of us finds humor in it. The truth is, Graham's reign of terror doesn't stop just because he's in a jail cell. Now I have to deal with it every time I fall asleep.

Dr. Gregory returns, as promised. He increases my pain meds to further dull the ache of swallowing and rechecks the swelling in my throat. Since it hasn't changed, he sounds confident I won't need to stay past tomorrow. I'd much rather leave now, but given the glare I get from both him and Jordan, that's not an argument I'll come close to winning.

Another group effort convinces Jordan to go for lunch. He and Benji are still at the cafeteria when Trey returns. He kicks out Pete and settles in next to my bed. Even though he's changed into a T-shirt and jeans, a uniformed officer by the door tells me this isn't a social visit. She must be from somewhere else in the county because I don't recognize her. Apparently, she was the other officer at Graham's, showing up shortly after my cousin.

I tell them both and an audio recorder what happened, offering more details when asked. Most of my morning feels fuzzy and far away, but every single second from when Graham pulled me back in the house to when I started losing consciousness is perfectly clear.

They bring Connor in once I finish. Since Lara's MIA, they need me present to record his statement. Trey's asking him to clarify a few details when the door opens. Connor freezes up at the sight of Kevin in his sheriff's uniform. Everyone does, no one saying anything as he strides across the room.

My uncle has always known how his brother treated us. Whenever anyone called the cops because of Graham and Lara screaming, he would show up to handle it. The times Pete's grandparents voiced their concerns about what was happening, he assured them he would take care of it. No matter what, he always smoothed things over, kept it from escalating. But this time is different from the others. He can't contain it.

He stops at the end of my bed, eyes locked on the blue blanket covering my legs.

"We're almost done," Trey says. "Go on, Con."

He checks with me before he continues to describe hearing me scream and the lamp break. I watch Kevin's face while he listens. Our gaze meets when Connor says all the sound stopped, his voice cracking at the end. Kevin looks at the blanket again.

Trey clicks off the recorder. "That's enough for now. Why don't you go back to the waiting room?"

The other officer stands, and I give Connor a reassuring nod as he reluctantly follows her toward the door. Kevin clears his throat, and they both stop, turning around. He's always been commanding, but something about his uniform is downright terrifying to some people.

"Before you go, I wanted…" He runs a hand over his face, eyes still downcast. "I need you both to know how sorry I am. None of this would have happened if I had stepped in like I should have so many times over the past several years. Somehow, I'll make it up to you. Cate too. I don't know how, but I swear to you, I will."

Connor and I exchange a glance, neither saying a word in response. Maybe the sentiment should mean more, but right now, it feels like we're the broken swings at the school. Words and intentions are nothing without the follow-through. Kevin's yet to prove anything to either of us.

Once the officer leads Connor out, Trey holds up the large envelope he brought in. My chest tightens, knowing what's inside.

"You sure about this, Cal?" he asks, the doubt heavy in his voice.

I nod, even more anxious with Kevin being here. Chances are, Trey isn't supposed to be showing me these pictures. As scared as I am to look at them, I'm even more worried Kevin won't let me. I *need* to see them.

"You look at these?" Trey asks him, sliding out the prints.

Kevin nods and nervously glances at me but doesn't stop my cousin from handing me the stack. Trey stays beside me, his hand on my shoulder as I flip them over. I suck in a breath at the first picture of me lying on the stretcher. The next ones are close-ups of my injuries from several angles, then the blood covering my hands and embedded under my fingernails.

I stretch out my hand and scrutinize both sides, not a trace of it still present. The nurse told me they cleaned me up, but I never thought about what that meant until seeing the pictures with my face smeared with red and hair wet. Maybe that's why looking through the photos, it never really feels like it's me I'm looking at.

Trey's grip on me tightens, and I'm not sure why until I flip to the next photo and jerk back. Graham is staring at me. I've seen the drunken look over and over again, but this time, it makes me shudder. The same marks from my neck streak down his arms where I clawed at him to make him stop. A gash on his side where I remember slashing him with a shard of the broken lamp. But I can't remember landing a punch for his black eye.

"Was this you?" I ask Trey.

"He's lucky I didn't fucking kill him," he says, giving a quick look to Kevin. "After I pulled him off you, he came at me, swinging. Split open my eye, broke two of my ribs before I tackled him. He also spit in Abby's face when she got there to assist."

I shake my head and lay the stack down. "I'm sorry."

"Don't be," he says fast. "The district attorney is planning to charge him for assaulting two officers on top of assaulting you. There's no chance he avoids significant jail time."

"DA changed her mind this morning." Kevin moves to the side of the bed, picking up the pictures and sorting through them. "I talked to her before I left. She plans to charge him with attempted murder and two counts of aggravated assault, and then offer him a plea for three counts of aggravated assault."

I rest my head on the pillow, processing what this means. No more Graham. What I've wanted my entire life. For me and Connor and then for him and Cate. Now, it's real.

Their conversation cuts off when the nurse knocks on her way in. Jordan slips in behind her, ignoring the look from Kevin on his way by. He carefully presses a kiss to my lips, and as he sits in his chair beside the bed, his hand slides into mine. It stays there while Kevin says goodbye and after Pete returns to his seat by the window. They both stay unmoved as our friends come in and out all afternoon.

The door stops opening when everyone goes out for supper. Pete grants us privacy by dragging the pink curtain around the bed to block our view of him. I offer to kick him out, but Jordan declines, not coming across nearly as irritated as he wants to be.

He climbs into the bed with me, and I relax against him. He hasn't been far away all day, but this is the first time it feels right. My head on his shoulder while he strokes my hair. Just him and me.

"I love you, beautiful."

I cuddle into him. "I love you."

Even though my voice is still a little hoarse, it sounds much more like my own. It still feels like I swallowed a shot glass full of rose thorns, but compared to the truckload of nails earlier, I'll take it.

My arm rests on his stomach, and he messes with the cast.

"Should I be offended you haven't asked me about dinner with my parents?"

"How rude am I to make everything about me?" I say dryly.

"Very, but I'll forgive you if we can fool around later."

Entertaining and frustrating.

I tip my face up to see him. "How was dinner?"

He groans and closes his eyes. "Terrible. I don't want to talk about it."

I laugh and snuggle back into him. "So, you still don't know what you're doing next year."

"Oh, I do. The decision's made."

Surprised, I lift my head again. "Well? Philosophy in Pittsburgh? Music at Berklee? Or what was the third?"

"Pot farmer," he says. "I never expected them to let me make it to my third suggestion, so I didn't put much thought into it."

"Clearly. So? Option one or two—or else Tony will never leave you alone."

"Pete, can you provide us with a drumroll, please?"

He tries again when Pete doesn't answer, and the worst attempt at a drumroll I've ever heard comes through the curtain. Jordan insults him, and Pete calls him an asshole, and before they start bickering like an old married couple, I stop them.

"Just tell me."

He stares down at me, dramatically pausing. "I'm going to attend law school at UPenn."

"You're kidding," I say, convinced he's screwing with me. The goal was to convince his parents to let him do *anything* other than law school at UPenn. He isn't answering me, and I realize he's serious. "After everything? You're doing exactly what your parents expected all along?"

"Technically, but I'm not doing it for them. Or the financial support they'll provide. Or the outrageous amount of money I can earn, working for one of my father's connections."

"Then why?" I ask, curious how he spun in a complete one-eighty since last night.

"Because you, Callie Henders, are my muse."

I roll my eyes. "Smooth answer."

"Real answer." He gently kisses me, pulling back too soon. "You helped me discover what I want to do with my life. My passion, if you will."

Not sure how that's possible, I guess what he wants to practice. "Corporate law?" He makes a face, so I try again. "Mergers and acquisitions?"

"Absolutely not," he says, tracing his fingers up my arm. "I'm more interested in child advocacy. Custody agreements, termination of parental rights, neglect and abuse cases. You'd be amazed at the shit people get away with regarding their children. Someone needs to give them a voice. Who knows? I might even pursue a judgeship one day. I'd hate to limit my future options. I mean—"

I kiss him, unable to keep my lips off his for another second.

Call it fate or destiny or whatever, but sometimes, the people we never knew we needed appear at the exact right moment in our lives. In the case of Jordan Waters, that someone crashed his way in whether or not I wanted him to. Luckily, he also refused to leave. He's my reminder of the other side of the coin. The one where the small moments change everything for the better.

He breaks his mouth away from mine. "Seriously, beautiful, you can't just kiss me to end the long-winded and at times overly wordy speech I've…"

That's all he says before he cups my cheek in his hand and lowers his lips back to mine. This time, they stay there. At least, they do until the curtain rips back. We both look at Pete.

"You guys win. I'm leaving. Cal, I'll see you in the morning." He flips off Jordan on his way out. "Sleep tight, cupcake."

I breathe out a laugh, and Jordan narrows his eyes. "You think this is funny? I'm becoming friends with the guy."

"Everyone ends up liking Pete."

He sighs. "I really wanted to be an exception."

"You're my exception if it makes you feel any better."

"Possibly." He gazes down at me. "It depends on what I'm the exception to."

"Everything," I tell him. "You are my exception to everything."

32 Days Until 19

I've been out of the hospital for over a month when Jordan and I pull up to the house in his Jeep. Even though Graham's truck is long gone in a junk pile somewhere, I still expect to see it sitting there. Rusty bumper and all.

A lot has happened since the last time I was here. Graham took a plea deal for three counts of aggravated assault and another for child abuse after the DA talked to Connor. With quite a few years ahead of him in prison, he signed over his assets to Kevin, which includes the house. Since my uncle plans to sell it, he's kept up on the mowing and fixed the screen door, so the outside looks the same as always. But it feels different. Unlike the place I've lived since I was born. Maybe because now it's where I almost died.

"Hey," Jordan says. He pulls my hand away from my neck. I didn't even realize I had been touching the all but faded marks. He brings it across my body and kisses my fingers as he does when I feel for them.

"You don't have to be here. We're just packing boxes and junking stuff."

I take a deep breath and nod. "I know."

He worries that going inside will bring back the nightmares. I haven't woken in a panic for four consecutive days—the longest I've gone.

After he studies me a few seconds, he leans over and presses his lips to mine. "Let's do this then."

His fingers lock with mine on our way up the steps. No one else is here yet, which is what I told him I wanted. A few minutes alone. Now that he's pulling open the screen door, I wonder if it would be easier with bodies everywhere and loud voices swarming around instead of silence and emptiness.

He turns the key in the lock and twists the knob, then he stops. "Callie, are you sure—"

I reach up with my casted hand and give the door a push. Stale air from inside bombards us, surrounding us in years' worth of cigarette smoke and hostility.

Honey, I'm home.

My grip on his hand tightens, and he squeezes back as he leads me inside. We walk past the living room, Jordan not slowing down, but I glance in. You wouldn't guess anything happened unless you knew a lamp was missing. The dent in the wall from my head has been patched and painted, the blood cleaned from the carpet. My bedroom door has been replaced, too. It looks the same as the old one and yet entirely out of place.

Jordan stops there, but I tug him farther down the hall to Graham's room. He beats me to the knob, pushing it open without hesitation this time. Whatever I thought relief felt like was wrong. I've never known it until I see the twelve-by-twelve room with nothing but brand-new carpet and bare, freshly painted walls.

"Kevin must have stayed up all night to finish," Jordan says.

The kitchen door opens and bangs shut a few times, and a bunch of voices bustle in. Loud and playfully arguing about something nonsensical. Jordan starts down the hall toward them, but I step farther into the room. I scan around, searching for anything that reminds me of my father. But there's nothing familiar, no sights or scents or heaviness. The rest of the house is stained, and somehow, it's like he's never touched this place.

When he realizes I'm not following, Jordan comes back for me. He meets me in the center of the room and holds his arms tight around me. "What are you thinking?"

"He's really gone."

His forehead rests against mine. "He is, baby."

I sigh, that newfound relief coursing through me. Jordan kisses me, soft and slow. Just us, his lips on mine while laughter floats down the hallway. Everything's bright and light, and it's the only memory I'll have in here.

The only moment.

A fucking perfect one.

Nineteen

On my eighteenth birthday, I woke up with a smile on my face. For my nineteenth, I wake with a six-year-old on my back. I grunt, pretty sure it's time we have a personal-boundaries talk. Cate giggles and wiggles, and then someone lifts her off me.

Jordan tosses her to the other side of the mattress. "Scat, cat."

She hisses at him and dives off the bed.

He crashes down next to me and pulls me to him. "Happy birthday," he whispers, his lips grazing my ear.

"Uh-huh," I say, still half-asleep. "Why is my baby sister a cat?"

"She's a tabby actually. We'll blame it on Trey for leaving milk in his cereal dish."

I put the rest together on my own, picturing Cate up on the counter, lapping the milk out of the bowl.

Jordan presses his lips to mine. Once. Twice. "Stay," he says, rolling out of bed.

I stretch and do what I can to fully wake up.

I'm nineteen. It seems rather anticlimactic, considering the buildup. All those boxes crossed off on a calendar, not that I kept up with it after the attack. The day represented freedom from Graham, but I've already gotten that. All three of us won that fight when the court terminated his parental rights a few weeks ago.

We took another step forward last week when I filed for guardianship over Connor and Cate.

Some people have profound realizations brought on by tragedies, such as your ex-husband trying to kill your daughter. They strive to be better, examining their own lives to see what changes they can make. Our mother is not one of them. Having her children full-time scared her so much that she begged me to take them. Even offered to pay child support every month. Now we wait for the judge to approve everything.

Jordan's bare feet pad over the wood in the hallway, and he slips into my room, quietly shutting the door behind him. When he turns around, my eyes zero in on the cup he is carrying.

"God, I love you."

"The coffee loves you, too," he says dryly.

He's playing hooky from his internship to spend the day with me. It's incredible how few questions anyone asks when you use the word *pinkeye*.

I greedily take a sip before he steals the mug back and sets it on the nightstand. I would complain, but he peels off his shirt and crawls back into bed.

"Con left for his pickup game, and I parked Cate in front of the TV, so we have at least twenty minutes to ourselves." He hauls me against him, a serious look on his face. "You ready for your present?"

When I nod, I expect his mouth to devour mine and for us to take advantage of the time. Instead, he rolls away from me and dangles off the bed. I hear something slide across the floor. He sits up again with a flat box. It's featherlight, and nothing rattles when I shake it.

"If this is a box full of packing peanuts, I'm not chasing you out of the house."

He grins and props on an elbow to watch me open it. I shimmy my way up to sit against the headboard and untie the blue ribbon. It's from the same spool we used to wrap the papers declaring Graham's parental rights severed. We gave them to Connor for his birthday a few weeks ago. He considered them a better gift than the car.

Trey and Jordan had pitched in and twisted my arm into it. I was hesitant to buy my brother a vehicle after I heard about the little joyride he had taken while I was unconscious in the hospital, which required Jordan tracking him down. No one is brave enough to tell me the entire story yet, but it'd involved Connor stealing Pete's truck, and then Graham's, and ended with the latter being hauled to a scrap yard.

Whatever had happened cemented the relationship between Jordan and Connor. Jordan even convinced him to start counseling to work through his Graham issues. The two of them have an unshakeable bond now. I'm just not sure either of them will survive to enjoy it once I find out all the details.

I tuck the ribbon away to keep because, at some point, I became sentimental about things Jordan gives me. There's an embarrassing shoebox and everything.

His smile widens as I start to open the box, and I pause.

"Seriously, is this a T-shirt?"

"Just open it, you frustrating woman."

Still dubious, I pull the lid off. Then I groan. "You've got to be kidding me. A countdown calendar?"

He's trying not to laugh. "Look through it."

The cover has a collage of famous sites from around the world—the Louvre, pyramids, Easter Island. I flip it open to January, but there is no January. It starts with July, the first number on the countdown today. It's also short, less than a month. I turn to August, the only other page. The countdown ends with a giant circle on the twenty-first.

"What are we counting down to?"

When I look up, Jordan is holding two plane tickets. "I took the liberty of telling my mother that we'd be out of town for the week, just in case she planned to visit while we were on our trip to London."

My eyes snap up to his as I remember our fake trip that made her face pinch.

His mouth curves into a smile, and I squeal, tackling him back on the bed and kissing him over and over. He chuckles and catches my face in his hands, serious when he says, "Don't think every time you make something up to freak her out, I'll make it come true."

I laugh and kiss him again. Then I hop out of bed, bringing the calendar and tickets with me. He follows me to the wall covered in photos from our summer. Fishing with Trey and Pete, Connor's surprise birthday party, Cate's graduation from swim lessons, a random show Beta Void pulled together at the last minute. Even after everything, it's been one of the best summers I can remember. Now I can add best gift to the list, and I have no doubt, by the end of the day, best birthday will join it.

Jordan wraps his arms around me and nuzzles against my neck as I hang up the calendar and pin the tickets next to it. He leans to the side, taking me with him, and snatches a pen off the dresser. He straightens us up and sets it in my hand. "Mark away, beautiful."

I draw a line through the box, corner to corner, and relax back against him. "Twenty-eight days until the twenty-first."

Then, I'm never counting days again.

Epilogue

One Month Later…

Jordan drops down on the couch next to me. "I quit."

"You can't quit. You just started."

Clearly not in the mood to finish carrying my boxes up the stairs, he lets out a dramatic sigh and pulls my legs onto his lap. I can't blame him for wanting to enjoy our first real second of calm since we got back from London last week.

We hadn't even unpacked our suitcases when the courts finalized my guardianship over Cate and Connor. We've been scrambling to relocate them and sign them up for school, which starts tomorrow.

Lara will write a monthly check and see them alternate weekends and holidays—no summer schedule. It's more time than I like, but they'll have Trey and our friends watching out for them. While they might not qualify as ideal candidates to help raise upstanding individuals, they're fiercely loyal and always there in the ways that count. They're our real family. Always will be.

Jordan must decide my legs are not enough because he drags the rest of me over. I straddle him and lean down, brushing my lips over his. He groans when I run my fingers through his hair and slides his hands around to my ass. My hair falls, creating a curtain around us. Too bad it does little on the privacy front.

"Ew, Jordan." Cate stands at the bottom of the stairs in her princess pajamas, hands on her hips. "What are you doing?"

"He's feeling up Cal," Connor says, swooping her up and dashing up the stairs.

"Connor!" I shout after him, but it's no use. The damage has been done. Now I get to explain what *feeling up* means to a six-year-old over breakfast in the morning. *Great.* "Were you like that when you were younger?" I ask.

Jordan shakes his head and smiles. "Absolutely not. I had game."

"Maggie Larsen might not agree," I say, crawling off him.

He narrows his eyes at me for mentioning his old babysitter he crushed on. "I was five, Cal." He brings my legs back to his lap. "Even then, I had Connor beat."

It still makes my belly flip when he calls me Cal, the way he says it more right than I ever thought anything could be.

The basement door shuts, and I crane my neck as Benji waltzes in. Since Rusty and Gavin moved across the street, he moved to the basement to clear out the upstairs rooms for Connor and Cate. When Mrs. Waters finds out about the new living arrangements, her face might pinch itself into oblivion.

As part of the deal for him attending law school, which is back on, Jordan's parents pay rent. The guys were supposed to be paying him to live here, except Jordan never collected. I, however, insist on paying my share, no matter how many arguments we have about it. I have more than enough cash squirreled away from working at the bar. Plus, after Kevin sold Graham's house, he gifted me all the money. It destroyed their relationship, but for the first time, my uncle proved he cared. He hasn't stopped showing us since.

Benji stacks his hands behind his head. "So, what are we doing tonight?"

"*We* are doing nothing," Jordan says. "My girlfriend—"

"*Our* girlfriend," Benji corrects with a wink, and I laugh.

"You know what? No." Jordan shoves my legs off his lap and stands up. "*My* girlfriend."

Then he scoops me up, and Benji waves as he whisks me away.

After jumping a box in front of the stairs, he carries me up, not letting me down until he drops me on our bed. He goes back to the door and double-checks he locked it. A fast learner. You have to be with Cate around or else you wake up with her staring you down.

With the door secure, he flops down next to me and sighs. "Finally." His gaze waits for me when I roll over to face him. He pushes my hair back and looks at me in his perfect way. "I'm done sharing."

"Even with me?" I ask.

"No," he says. "You're the only one I'll share with from now on. Our bed, our room, our life."

I smile at the last one, and Jordan presses a kiss to my forehead.

The life he refers to is messy and complicated and on track to get a whole lot wilder. But none of that matters because the *best* part of our life? All of it.

I love every single part.

Acknowledgments

Callie's story isn't only close to my heart, it's a part of it. Even more so now than when I first wrote Elusion. Thank you so much for going on her journey with me and letting me bleed—first through Jordan's eyes, and then, when I was ready, through hers.

To the five beautiful humans who will find pieces of their reality in this book, you are priceless. I cannot begin to tell you how incredibly proud I am of you.

Thank you to my husband for pushing me to finally let Callie's book out into the world. And for always supporting me, even when you have no idea how to deal with me.

Lauren, you keep me sane. Here's to parallel lives.

Thank you to Nicki and Cassidy for all your help! You're amazing, and I need you forever and always. To all of my early readers, the Cool Kids, and all my author friends, your continued support is incredible. Thanks for being you.

A huge thank you to Jovana and Madison for helping shape my words. You always have the best suggestions and help me grow as a writer.

Murphy Rae, you continue to amaze me with your skill. Thank you for the beautiful cover

All the thanks to the bloggers and reviewers who helped share, promote, and spread the love for this book and all of my books. It means the world to me. And to my readers. You guys are...everything. I can't believe how lucky I am to get to do what I love, and it's all because of you.

And of course, I'd like to thank anyone who's made it all the way here in the book. Whether you loved it or felt *meh*, a review is always appreciated. I would love if you would consider leaving one.

Cheers,
CG

About the Author

CG Blaine writes unapologetically messy and emotional romance novels. She loves her characters complicated, the connections intense, and rip-your-heart-out feels.

She is obsessed with her vicious cat and aggressively cute bunny. Her favorite stories hit with the hurt and then apologize oh-so well.

Never miss a thing!
Join my reader group: CG's Cool Kids
Instagram: @cgblaine
Facebook Author Page: @cgblaineauthor
Website: cgblaine.com

Be sure to stay in the loop and sign up for CG's newsletter. You'll also snag a **FREE** short story.

Sign up at https://www.cgblaine.com